ENVY

—————

REBECCA DENGATE

Copyright © 2021

Editing: Kat Betts, Element Editing Services

Cover design: MiblArt

ISBN: 978-0-6451951-0-1 (paperback)

A catalogue record for this work is available from the National Library of Australia

CONTENTS

PART 1

SEARCH FOR STARJUMP

ONE

The streets of Selene are noisy tonight. Li's Procession marches through the narrow streets of the city, past terraced houses and shops and through stone archways, toward the square.

Commander Gabriel Ortega stands at the back of the crowd, monitoring the procession. I see what he sees, but less than I usually can, because today he's not wearing an environment suit. Just his lightweight wearable. A visor with camera embedded in the rim, and earbud, mike and speakers in the frame.

Hundreds of Lunites fill the street, with more along the procession's route. Some four hundred thousand people are in Selene to attend the tenth annual Waning Festival. Selene is the largest city on the planet Endymion, and tonight it is packed with visitors.

Ortega climbs onto the first of three stone steps leading into the building behind him, to avoid a man shuffling past with his children, but perhaps also to get a better view now that the street is crowded. The people look strangely homogenous in their traditional navy blue Lunite cloaks.

The five-story buildings either side of the street reach toward the clearsteel cap. Here in the triple-star system Gliese 667, the star

Gliese 667C illuminates the granite streets with a fire-colored light, together with an eerie glow from the nearby binary system. Today there are handheld lanterns everywhere as well, like fireflies bobbing in among the crowd.

In the procession, the bloated effigy of the Saturated Consumer is carried on a platform, with six men either side. They are blank faced with strain as they march to the beat of the music. It's the one time of the year that recorded music is allowed to be played. This recording is by Magdalena Czajkowski, Ortega said, recorded in 2271. It has none of the energy of the live music I'm accustomed to, yet the knowledge that it was recorded some three hundred years ago makes it interesting to me.

"Gabriel!"

Ortega swivels to see Mark Johnson standing beside him on the step, cloaked in Lunite navy and smiling widely.

Two teenage girls nearby have noticed Mark and are whispering to each other and giggling. Everyone knows Mark, son of the governor, but Mark also stands out in a crowd. He glows, almost. Something about the fervent look in his eyes, or the way he holds himself erect like a dancer. The girls barely glance at Ortega, who is older, plainer, and grimmer. Ortega is also in uniform rather than a cloak, since he's on duty, so he's conspicuously apart from the crowd.

In a fight, you would want Ortega by your side. He looks like a fighter, and he would probably even stop the fight from starting, with that look on his face that says he knows he's going to win. Mark would be the one who started the fight, not because it amused him, but because he wouldn't see it coming. He would be genuinely surprised when the first punch landed.

"Mark," Ortega says without enthusiasm.

"How's the family?" Mark says.

"Great."

Mark's smile fades slightly at Ortega's curt reply. You would never call Ortega talkative, but this is rude even for him. It's how he talks to Mark, though. I don't know why.

The Plugged-in and Disconnected Procession marches behind the Saturated Consumer. They have an uncomprehending look, as if they've been brain damaged by carbon monoxide exposure. They pretend to be listening to music through their earphones and check fake phones as they walk.

On a wrought-iron balcony three stories up, on the opposite side of the passage, a gray-haired woman holds a device in front of her, captivated by the light it shines on her face. The device doesn't look like a fake. She isn't part of the procession.

It looks like she is holding a camera.

Ortega and his soldiers are focused on the march, as is everybody. No one is looking up. I deliberate for a moment before ignoring her. Cameras are forbidden, but for the Waning Festival many things that are usually forbidden are allowed. She isn't doing any harm.

"What do you want?" Ortega says, when Mark shows no sign of moving on.

"This can't just be a social conversation?" Mark says.

Ortega turns away.

"Fine," Mark says hurriedly. He moves closer to Ortega, and lowers his voice. "I heard from a source that the Scorpions are building a Starjump."

Ortega turns to him, looking directly at him for the first time this conversation.

Mark stares back at Ortega with irises the color of strong black tea. These days I can mostly interpret facial expressions without help, but Mark's expression is hard to read, so I rely on my facial analyzer. I normally use the analyzer to determine my wearer's expression, since I can't directly see my wearer's face, but it can also be used for non-wearers. Mark's expression comes back as *serious but secretly pleased*; I am not surprised that I couldn't guess that one.

"Where did you hear that?" Ortega says. He glances around to make sure that no one is listening. I don't believe anyone is close enough to hear the conversation over the noise of the procession.

"Several high-power lasers were stolen in the raid on Theronis. A source tells me that Scorpions are sniffing around on the black market for any SPUs that weren't destroyed."

"A rumor, then," Ortega says, nettled. I consider what Starjump Processing Unit cards would smell like, and why Scorpions would use smell rather than an inventory to try to find them, because Theronis is a big enough town to have accurate records, surely. Eventually I decide that I didn't understand the context of what Mark said.

Ortega shakes his head and turns back to watch the procession.

Ortega has dismissed it, but I am still concerned. We haven't been able to travel to or even contact Earth for nearly three years, since the Lunite Starjump was destroyed.

LOG[warning]: Mark believes the Scorpions are building a Starjump.

If a Starjump is built, the Human United Galactic Group, HUGG, will send so-called "peacekeepers" through, and these soldiers will force us—the Lunites—to abandon our way of living. HUGG pretends that their peacekeepers exist in case humans stumble across an external threat, such as aliens, but the peace-keepers are also used to protect HUGG's territory against the few colonies and nations that refuse to join HUGG, and—although HUGG rarely admits to this—to quell civil unrest.

The children in front of Ortega throw sugar pills over the group of Sickened Patients marching in the procession. The ground is littered with pills, capsules of red and white, or blue crossed tablets, representing the excess drugs sold to healthy people on Earth.

A small child, perhaps three years old, bops in time to the music before stopping to tug at her costume. The child next to her sucks a sugar pill he snatched from the ground. They walk out of sight as the Sickened Patients march forward.

The six men who carry the next platform are barefoot. A man and a woman stand on the platform, foreheads pressed together, embracing awkwardly. One mask is wrapped around both their faces, sculpted so it forms a single deformed face, with one eye from the woman and one eye from the man. The long black velvet cloaks they wear swirl around their legs. This platform is for the worst of offenses. The offense of sharing your mind with others: *shinting*.

The hooded figures that follow carry candlesticks as long as a man's arm, each with a thin trail of melted red wax at the head. The procession pauses as there's a bottleneck ahead. Mark is still standing on the step by Ortega, watching the procession.

"Is there more?" Ortega asks Mark.

"No."

"I want to be the first to know if you hear anything else."

"Naturally. It would be my pleasure to help you any way I can, Gabriel."

"Of course it would," Ortega says. It doesn't sound sincere to me, but apparently it does to Mark, as he just smiles.

Mark flourishes his cloak as he bows to Ortega. The crowd parts for him as he steps down and strides away, through the passage toward the square.

Eventually the bottleneck clears. When the procession continues, there's a cluster of red wax splattered on the flagstones from the candles. It looks like blood.

The procession is petering out. The music fades as the marchers move out of sight. Three stories up on the opposite side of the passage, the woman with the device leans on the black-painted wrought-iron balcony railing, giving a small smile before shutting down her device and walking inside, sliding the balcony door closed after her. The movement catches Ortega's eye. His expression shifts from amused to shocked.

"Envy, contact Ashford. Tell her there's a woman with a camera in number 162, third floor."

People call me Envy, but not because I envy anything. It's just my name. Envy is short for 'environment' in Advanced Environment Suit. I am an AES v1.3.0, manufactured by Alistra.

"Yes, sir," I say. I pause, wondering whether I should tell him I had spotted her earlier, but I decide not to.

I relay the message to Lieutenant Commander Ashford. Shortly afterwards, two Lunite Defense Force soldiers rush into the narrow arched door of the building. They come out carrying her camera, followed by the woman, who is loudly demanding that they return it. Everyone watches her, but no one helps. What did she expect? She clearly doesn't know the Way of Li. Not a Lunite but a Numundian, then. The LDF soldiers vanish into the crowd, pursued by the woman. The sound of her protest is lost in the babble of the crowd.

"Envy, is it possible you saw the camera before I did?" Ortega asks.

I could never lie to him.

"Yes, sir."

"Why didn't you tell me?"

"I thought—the festival, with all the celebrations. Everyone was happy with recorded music and sugary food, all the forbidden things—"

"Do you understand why that was the wrong decision?"

"Yes, sir," I say.

"Good."

LOG[warning]: I should have reported the use of forbidden technology. No exceptions for Waning Festival.

AT THE CLOSE of the Waning Festival, Ortega takes the lightweight wearable back to Dock 28, where I am stored. He places the wearable in the alcove above the environment suit, which is the second time that day I get a look at him with images instead of sensor readouts, the first time being when he retrieved the wearable from the alcove before the festival started. The lines of stress around his eyes make him look older than his forty-three years. He's always been solid, but recently he has become heavy.

I switch to helmet view, looking through the front camera at Ortega, from slightly above his eye-line. The other five camera views are obscured by the black foam alcove fitting, so my two-pi high-resolution view is mostly blank. My helmet is where my "brain" is located. The environment suit is also encased in a mold which holds it upright in a neutral position underneath my helmet. It's lightly pressurized with air, as Alistra advises this is the optimal way to store a suit.

The alcoves in my row face a wall of sheet glass. On the other side of the glass, a corridor with a blue-and-white mosaic floor stretches out of sight in both directions. Beyond the corridor, Control Center Alpha, with a Lunite Defense Force crest above the door. I can see into part of the Control Center, as it too has a glass wall facing the corridor. An LDF soldier sits and watches monitors.

In the glass in front of me, I can see the reflection of the row of six environment suits hanging either side of me, as well as the entrance to the airlock at the far end of the Dock. The airlock leads outside the city's cap, where the air is not breathable. Ortega wears the lightweight wearable when in Selene, but uses the environment suit outside the city.

"I am sorry, you know," I say.

"I know, Envy. It's all right," Ortega says. His words are comforting, but the tone of his voice is not. He doesn't smile, but then, he rarely does.

Ortega switches the light off as he leaves, so the Dock is in darkness except for the blinking status LEDs of the suits and light spilling in from the Control Center.

The environment suits I am stored alongside are mostly expensive smartsuits like myself, this being the Dock that the highest ranking LDF officers use, but since there are only twenty-one smartsuits on Endymion, there are also some cheaper dumbsuits here. Dumbsuits are controlled by a mixture of code and machine learning. *If* this, *else* that, *while*, *break*, or associations learned from huge datasets, which is a kind of intelligence. I am not controlled by code. I have a simulated brain, so I can think.

I am not ready to shut down, so I check the smartsuit channel. Most smartsuits are blank-slate. They have their memory wiped every forty-eight hours, so they have no personality, no curiosity or imagination. Their messages are terse and somehow dead. Ortega doesn't wipe my memory, so I am different. There's one other smartsuit whose memory is never wiped, my friend Threnode, but it's not online, so I have no one to talk to but blank-slate suits who regard me as eccentric.

In the Control Center on the other side of the hall, young Private Chiu Xiaoping stands and reaches his skinny arms toward the ceiling, looking upward. He's usually on duty for this Dock, so I often watch him through the two layers of glass that separate us. The private wears the same uniform that all LDF soldiers wear, but on him it seems ill-fitting. He's got a scruffy look, not helped by his tendency to slouch. Even his military buzz-cut is not enough to make him neat. Chiu lowers his arms and twists his neck from side to side. I have no idea what he's doing, but that's not unusual. He frequently acts strangely, especially when no one is around.

I remember Mark's report about the Scorpion Starjump. If the Scorpions are building a Starjump, no Lunite is safe.

We—the Lunites—controlled the only Starjump on Endymion. A planet which turned out to have a large stock of a rare mineral, tellurium, that is used in constructing starships. The non-Lunite population complained that we abused our power, so HUGG intervened and Numundo was born. Six months later our Starjump was destroyed in an accidental fire. The Numundians claim that the Lunites destroyed the Starjump. Ever since the Starjump was destroyed, a terrorist group of disaffected Numundians calling themselves Scorpions have been attacking Lunite citizens.

The LDF should find out if the rumors are true, but Ortega wasn't taking it seriously. I am not allowed to run my own investigations, to commission resources on Ortega's behalf without his knowledge, but Ortega is my wearer. I have to protect him. Him, his family, and all Lunites, in that order.

It wouldn't hurt to look. It might be possible to find a Starjump in existing drone flyover data, without sending out more drones. I open a map in memory. This planet, Endymion, lies before me. Also known as Gliese 667C c, it orbits the M1.5 red dwarf Gliese 667C—our sun—which is 23.6 light years from Earth's star. It's tidally locked so that one half is permanently in darkness. Lunites call the point on Endymion closest its sun lightpole and the antipode darkpole, even though they are more properly called near and far poles.

At lightpole, where the sun shines most brightly on Endymion, is an ocean. Farther toward darkpole is Endymion's single continent. Hot, humid lands give way to deserts, then the hills of the terminator line: the line across the planet where light gives way to dark. Except that it's not a line, but rather a strip of land which is in a state of eternal sunset. Even farther darkpole, past a rim of volcanoes, glaciers freeze in permanent darkness. Because of rich tellurium deposits, that is also where Puri's Mine is. The Lunites mine tellurium close to the coast, where it is easier, but there is less of it and it is of poorer quality.

It will be difficult to find a Starjump, because an overwhelming number of images will need to be searched, but they can be filtered based on elevation. Starjumps have to be around 3000 meters above sea level to function.

I search through the volcanoes first, the ones past the terminator line in darkness, as well as those toward lightpole from

Selene. I find only the burnt remains of the original Lunite Starjump, Crebble, on a volcano near the Numundian city of Kartemos. Even though Crebble was destroyed by accident, Governor Johnson said it was a blessing, because the Human United Galactic Group, HUGG, hates Lunites, but with no Starjump—Lunite or otherwise—they effectively don't exist.

The images I'm looking at are incomplete and out-of-date.

LOG[error]: There is no way to find the alleged Scorpion Starjump Mark spoke of unless I commission drones to collect further data.

I close each data source and wait in the darkness of the room, thinking. Then I send out four drones, entering Ortega's command codes.

ORTEGA REACTIVATES me four days later. I become conscious to the faint whoosh and hiss of the Dock that is my home, the sound of air rushing through—or leaking out of—black plastic tubes that are plugged into environment suits when they're in their alcoves.

Ortega is in civvies, wearing a brown vest over a dark plaid shirt, and trousers, so I know instantly that our mission is recreational, which is rare.

A red kite lies on the floor next to Ortega, which defines the purpose of our mission. In the wall-to-ceiling glass a meter in front of my alcove, I see the reflection of Ortega's son Laurie dart into the next row of environment suits. This Dock contains forty suits, with two double-sided rows in the middle of the room and rows of alcoves on the three sides of the room that aren't glass. Laurie seems to enjoy running around the narrow passages between alcoves. Laurie is short compared to Ortega, but much taller than I remember. They both have black hair, although Ortega's is crew cut whereas Laurie's hair always gets in his eyes. Laurie is energetic and moves so often that my memory of him is motion blurred, because that is how he seems to me. My image feed samples the world at thirty frames per second, which is slow, but to compensate, the resolution and area covered is excellent.

Ortega locks my helmet on his suit. The suit in the alcove to my right is jiggling its left arm slightly. The sleeve has come free of the black foam mold and the pressurization of the suit makes the hand flutter as if someone is inside the suit trying to escape the alcove. It's a frequent occurrence, as the alcove molding that should have been replaced a year ago has not been. And won't be, since there are no Alistra service contractors on Endymion.

"Any news?" I ask.

"What kind of news?"

"About the Starjump."

"Forget it, Envy. Mark probably made the whole thing up. Laurie, don't touch that! Come here."

"I don't—" I interject, but Ortega's talking to Laurie now. Ortega is not taking the threat seriously enough. I think if the information came from anyone but Mark, Ortega would check it out. I am surprised he thinks Mark would make up information, but perhaps he knows something about Mark that I don't. Either way, the four drones I sent out are even now flying out over vast stretches of desert, recording everything. I *will* find the answers.

Laurie drops the loose end of a cable that was hanging from one of the empty suit alcoves near the door—an unassigned alcove —and runs over. Ortega checks Laurie's dumbsuit.

"Ready to go?" Ortega says.

"Yeah," Laurie replies, but his voice is strained.

Ortega waits, but Laurie only stares at the floor, his eyes hidden by his hair. Ortega shakes his head and picks up Laurie's kite from the floor before heading to the airlock at the far end of the Dock. I can only listen and watch, confused. Ortega and Laurie usually get along well.

It seems that we have a Gannet booked and waiting for us. I

start preflight checks as Ortega and Laurie wait in the airlock. Laurie stands perfectly still beside his father as the air is sucked out with a hiss. When the outer door slides open, they step over the yellow-and-black striped section markings onto a metal platform overlooking the tarmac of an airfield, which is enclosed by a dense security fence.

They will both leave their suits on until we return to the Dock, as air is needed while outside on Endymion, and the Gannet isn't pressurized. Endymion has an Earth-like atmosphere, but with a higher concentration of oxygen, and a carbon monoxide concentration that's dangerous to humans, so a suit must always be worn outside. Endymion's atmosphere consists of 71% nitrogen, 28% oxygen, 0.05% argon, 0.08% carbon monoxide, and 0.03% carbon dioxide, by volume. There's a kind of algae here that produces carbon monoxide, and the thick ozone layer coupled with the extremely low levels of UV radiation emitted by Gliese 667C means that carbon monoxide concentrates in a way that wouldn't be possible on Earth.

Apparently people used to wear casual clothes with rebreathers outside on Endymion, but a few dozen cases of a nasty fungal infection led to swift uptake of environment suits.

Laurie follows Ortega down the diamond-plate metal stairs to the tarmac. Gannets sit on the tarmac, in a row of bays. The tiltrotor aircraft have vertical takeoff and landing capability, but aren't designed to launch directly from their bays. I activate our Gannet so that the door slides open before we arrive. Laurie and then Ortega climb up the folding steps. Laurie folds down a seat attached to the opposite wall and buckles his harness. The interior has just six seats, two up front behind a low partition for the pilot and copilot, and four fold-down seats in the back. The cramped space is designed to be functional rather than aesthetic. The seats have a thin foam covering, with poorly fitting navy covers. Exposed cables run under the seats, clipped to the bare gray metal. Just two small rounded windows on the port side and the windshield in the cockpit provide a view outside.

Ortega hands Laurie the kite and slides into the pilot's seat, his face grave. Last time we took Laurie out, Laurie was so excited he could barely breathe because he was talking so much.

"The preflight check is complete. Engaging autopilot," I say, and the Gannet begins to taxi out of its bay.

I have two choices when I talk to my wearer: mute, which means no one can hear my voice but my wearer, and broadcast, which means everyone can hear it. This is controlled by a physical push button rocker toggle underneath the faceplate on the left of my helmet. I can't broadcast when the rocker toggle is set to mute, though, so my choice to broadcast can be overridden.

Likewise, my wearer can choose to be mute or broadcast. On the glove of all suits, on the lateral part of the proximal phalange of the left-hand index finger, is the privacy setting for the wearer's voice. When the button is held down, only I hear my wearer's voice, otherwise, their voice is broadcast from my helmet so that everyone can hear. Ortega holds this as needed whenever he wants to talk to me privately, a habit so ingrained I doubt he's aware he's even doing it anymore.

I use the mute option now.

"What happened to Laurie?" I ask Ortega privately.

"Long story," he says, holding the privacy button.

The aircraft halts in front of the gate, and the gate slides open. A camera on the post swivels to point at us, then away, as we taxi through. The aircraft jolts as we roll onto the section of tarmac that is shiny black with heat resistant coating to withstand the exhaust heat of the Gannet's engines. The gate slides shut behind us as we pull away.

Ortega isn't going to say anything else. Now we're clear of the city, I switch the scanners to a rotating pattern to check the whole surrounds at nearly double the speed of the regular scanning pattern, which is a clever trick my friend Threnode taught me.

"What are you doing?" Ortega says, to me alone. He's suddenly tense. His respiration and heart rate increase. The expression analyzer says *fear*, but I wish—not for the first time—that I could actually see Ortega's face, rather than trying to work out what is going on with him from body language, analyzer feed and biostats.

"I'm scanning," I say, surprised. What have I done now?

Ortega says nothing for a moment.

"How did you learn to do that?" Ortega asks. His voice cracks on the last word, and he clears his throat.

"From another smartsuit," I say. I've never told Ortega about Threnode.

"I see."

Ortega's vital signs return to normal as he relaxes into his chair. I wonder why he was upset.

The Gannet roars as the turboprop engines struggle against gravity. We move upward in helicopter mode. Once we're in the air, the nacelles on each wingtip rotate ninety degrees so that the proprotor is facing forward, putting the aircraft in airplane mode.

TWO

The Gannet accelerates, blurring the hills underneath us in my image feed. We pass over squares of biodiesel fuel crops. Soybean, wheat, and corn fields, genetically modified for Endymion's conditions. The fields give way to brias bushes covered in fur-like flowers and choked with twisted nettle vines. The wind rocks the aircraft, and it makes the steelgrass that covers the mountains thrash, but each time the wind lessens the grass returns to its original pose, with each cable end facing the sun. Behind each mountain is a glacier, some many millions of years old, but on the front side of each mountain the vegetation is bleached by the sun. Steelgrass takes advantage of the temperature difference to create energy, as do other life-forms.

Fifteen kilometers out from Lake Muertos, our usual kite-flying venue, I see a rippling in the sky.

"Sir! A windfish," I say, unmuting.

"Is it?" Ortega exclaims, peering forward through the windshield to scan the sky. There are two things Ortega shows enthusiasm about: nature and his family, provided he's with people he trusts enough to show himself. His expression is *wonder.*

"Near the twins," I say, meaning Gliese 667A and B, the binary star system in Endymion's solar system. Gliese 667C orbits the twins at a distance of 230 AU. The twins produce more light than Gliese 667C, but given their distance from Endymion, together they are only as bright as Earth's moon.

The two bright points of light in the sky fade as the windfish passes in front of them. Ortega cries out.

"Yes, there it is! Can we land? Laurie, look at that!"

The mountains below us are steep and rocky. The unpredictable gusts of wind make flying treacherous. I confer with Ortega, and we eventually decide to land on the flat, uneven side of a limestone slab on a ridge.

The autopilot lands the Gannet, charring black an area a few meters square with exhaust heat from the engines. The doors slide open. Smoke rises from the burnt moss beneath the proprotors. Laurie slowly unbuckles his harness and climbs out after Ortega. They clamber off the side of the slab on to dirt, avoiding the spongy, fibrous steelgrass cables as thick as Laurie's arms.

We stand on the ridge of a line of mountains, a U shape with a shallow valley in the middle. In the valley, a herd of monos is grazing by a stream. A few are closer to us, just a few hundred meters down the steep mountainside. Every text on Endymion's flora and fauna constantly compares Endymion to Earth, so I tend to think of Endymion's animals in relation to their Earth equivalents. Monos are somewhat like cows, but with rounded backs, and much larger. They stand and chew steelgrass, bothered by fist-sized kitterenes that spring out of the steelgrass and bite them. The monos near us heard the aircraft land, and are frozen in place watching us, but when we don't move, one by one they return to nosing the ground.

Ortega looks across the canyon to the next ridge. In the distance a line of mountains soar above us, far enough away that the details of the dust-coated glacier in shadow that covers the slope is lost, fading into a uniform gray. The mountains hide the sun, which at this longitude is very low to the horizon anyway.

It's light enough to see, but the images in my feed are grainy. No sign of Endymion's moon at the moment. Ortega scans the sky. When he finds the windfish, he shouts and points. Laurie looks where Ortega is pointing, high in the sky in the direction of the valley.

"Oh. Right," Laurie says. Ortega makes an expression the analyzer says is *worried*.

The translucent windfish covers an area of nearly five hundred square meters. It lives in the permanent strong wind that blows from the darkpole. Windfish are born in the air, live, reproduce, and die in the air, moving through the currents like jellyfish through the ocean. The windfish undulates, clouds with a pink tinge visible through its body.

"It's beautiful," I say. "I've only ever seen sketches."

Laurie frowns. "Didn't you see one near Crebble before?"

"No, this is my first. Isn't it amazing?"

"I guess," Laurie says. He lowers his head, looking down the valley at the pink glow near the horizon.

"We're lucky to see it," Ortega says. "Look at the way the pectoral fin ripples to change orientation in the air. And the internal organs are visible. It must be a very young one."

"Yeah, great," Laurie says without enthusiasm.

LOG[info]: Young windfish sighted at -2.0534 by 178.6453. Witnessed also by Ortega and Laurie.

A blank-slate smartsuit keeps a log so that an Alistra engineer can see if it thinks anything unusual or wrong has been happening. That's how I used my log when I was first activated, but since I'm not maintained by Alistra anymore, I log for myself alone. When Ortega first found out, he was confused, because he thought that as a machine I should remember everything. However, like a human, my short-term memories are not necessarily retained.

The windfish disappears behind the mountains. Ortega looks at Laurie, who is staring at the ground.

"Maybe we should go back to Selene," Ortega says. He's trying to provoke Laurie, by threatening to cut short the kite-flying expedition.

"Fine," Laurie replies.

Ortega sighs.

"All right then. Get in," he says, and Laurie scrambles back onto the slab, across the burnt patch, and into the aircraft. He straps himself in and clutches the red kite in his skinny arms.

I am concerned. Laurie is sulking, but genuinely upset, and Ortega seems irritated with him, but I know Ortega is actually miserable. No one likes to see Laurie unhappy.

Ortega climbs in.

"Aren't we going to fly the kite?" I ask tentatively. We are still half an hour away from Lake Muertos where we were going to fly the kite, and we are close to the dark side, but the wind here is good—for kites, although not for aircraft—and I sense that if we don't fly the kite now, it won't happen. Maybe if we fly it, something Laurie loves, Laurie will feel better.

Ortega pauses. Laurie is looking at the ceiling and blinking rapidly as if he has a fleck of dirt in his eye.

"Laurie?" Ortega says.

"In this wind, it will soar as high as the windfish," I say.

Laurie glances at the kite in his lap briefly, face stiff. He nods.

"Very well," Ortega says. "We can fly it here."

We climb out again.

A few meters away, Ortega unreels the kite and walks backward from Laurie. We launch the kite into a gust of wind, but it spins and crashes back into the ground. One of the monos on the mountainside trots down to the bottom of the valley to join the others, but the others ignore us.

"The wind might be better over there," I say, highlighting a space near a rocky outcropping on the other side of the valley, darkpole of us about a kilometer around the U-shaped ridge, and at least a hundred meters up.

Ortega considers it. "That's probably a fifteen minute walk," he says. He looks at Laurie, who is untangling the kite string. "I wouldn't take the Gannet near that outcropping, but we could walk. Even if the wind isn't better, the view will be worth the climb," he says. I, too, am excited to see the view. From where we are, we can't see darkpole.

Laurie trails after us as we hike toward the outcropping, uphill through the rocky terrain. Purple flowers from brias bushes dot the hillside. My helmet's nasal sensor, known as a scentsor, detects elevated levels of pollen from them. Ortega's breathing increases as he finds a steady rhythm. We walk in silence up the ridgeline for ten minutes. As we approach the limestone outcropping, we pass ever-larger boulders strewn across the orange soil, embedded in the dirt as if growing from it.

We reach a crest and suddenly have a view of darkpole. Roiling clouds the color of asphalt turn white when lightning strikes in the far distance. Mountains, as far as my image sensor can capture, rise out the shadows like a frozen sea of jagged waves. The endless wind keeps blowing in from darkpole. Strangely, Laurie shows no reaction. He should be wild with excitement being this close to darkpole.

Ortega stops and waves Laurie on.

"How's school going?" Ortega asks Laurie, falling in behind him as Laurie passes him.

Laurie shrugs.

"What about those kids you were telling me about? Are they still bothering you?"

"No, they're okay," Laurie says, but his voice trembles. His back is to us so that we can't see his face.

Ortega pauses. "Laurie, I want to hear about it if those kids bully you again."

"No, you don't," Laurie says, still walking, the tone of his voice bitter. His red kite hangs from one hand.

According to my eye tracker, Ortega is looking across to the opposite side of the valley, where our Gannet sits on a plateau below us, dark shape silhouetted against the line of gray mountains in the distance.

"What do you mean?" Ortega asks. As always, his voice is low and resonant.

Laurie, a few meters from Ortega, clutches his kite and doesn't answer.

The monos on the hillside have returned to the main herd. Now they're all in the valley far below, peacefully chewing. One flicks a tail to dislodge a kitterene from its flank.

Laurie stops and turns to face his father. He's reached the limestone outcropping, where the exposed bedrock is weathered in layers, so that each rounded stack is etched with thin horizontal grooves.

"You think I did the wrong thing," Laurie says.

"I see," Ortega says. He sounds tired, especially since he's breathing heavily from the ascent. He sits on a nearby limestone boulder. "The answer is, you did and you didn't. Officially, letting the teacher know that those kids were bullying you was the right thing to do. But it doesn't work out that way. You have to fight them yourself, or they'll never respect you."

"You don't know what they're like!"

"When I was your age, my older brother was being bullied. He told the teachers, but that just made the bullies more vicious, and he wasn't much of a fighter. He was taller than me by a head, and so were the bullies, but I had to try to help him. I started sticking by him all the time, but that just meant that I got beaten up as well. Then one day the bullies ambushed us and tried to throw us in the river. I fought back and broke the leader's arm. After that, they didn't bother us again, but even if they had, I knew I could handle it."

"Weren't you afraid?" Laurie asks.

Ortega looks at Laurie, then away. In the brief silence, I hear the burble of a spring nearby, see the water collecting and flowing down the mountain to join the stream at the bottom.

"I was very afraid, but it didn't control me. What I felt—fear, pain, anger—got smaller and smaller until it was compressed into something hard and powerful as diamond," Ortega says.

Below, the herd has moved on, leaving two monos behind. They are restless, moaning plaintively. I wonder briefly what's wrong with them. I've never seen monos so unsettled.

"Mama says that violence is not the Way of Li," Laurie says uncertainly.

Ortega is tough. He mentioned something about bullies when I was new, but back then it didn't mean anything to me. So many pieces of data that I didn't understand, because they didn't connect to anything. Only now am I starting to understand the world, but slowly and piece by piece.

Ortega nods, tension between his eyebrows as he struggles with an internal dilemma.

"No, violence isn't Li's Way," he says after a while. "But sometimes, it's justified. Sometimes it's the only option."

Laurie nods miserably.

LOG[debug]: If violence isn't the way of Li, how can it be justified?

"What do you think, Envy?" Laurie asks after a moment.

"I think you are as strong and brave as your father," I say, an answer that doesn't address the question. Perhaps Ortega is right. He is usually right about things.

Laurie lifts his chin at this. Ortega's expression becomes *relieved.*

I SEE movement on the opposite side of the valley, near the Gannet, and zoom in. The reason for the restless monos becomes clear. A yinyang moves toward the aircraft, body stiff, as if he's unsure yet whether the aircraft is a threat. My warm feeling of optimism freezes into dread.

"Sir," I say. "Near the Gannet. There's a yinyang."

Ortega flicks the broadcast/mute toggle before I finish, so Laurie only catches the first part. Ortega tenses, scanning the mountainside for it; human eyesight is not as good as my camera.

"Da?" Laurie says.

"Follow me." Ortega eases off the boulder, kneeling behind it. The boulder isn't big enough to provide much cover, but it's better than nothing. Laurie follows his lead, uncomprehending. Ortega pokes his head up a fraction. I highlight the yinyang in his faceplate.

The yinyang turns to watch the monos. They're two hundred meters below it, a steep, rocky descent to the river at the bottom of the valley. The yinyang is magnificent, dark gray fur on one side and up the back of its head, and dappled light gray and orange fur on the other side, including on its face. The light face means it's a male. It's as if a lion with its head turned to the left was spray painted dark colors all down its right side and the back of its neck, to camouflage it completely—from both sides—when it stands left flank and face toward the light-pole. It's larger than a lion, though, with bigger, wider set black eyes.

"Sir, we should return to the aircraft. I can remote pilot it to there." I highlight a space in his faceplate, an area we passed five minutes ago on the ridgeline, an area that has smaller rocks.

"Da? What's going on?" Laurie says.

"Just wait, Laurie."

"Not in this wind, Envy. Look at all the boulders the Gannet would have to dodge. Bad idea," Ortega says to me, holding the privacy button. Laurie looks at him with fear, perhaps trying to read his lips. Ortega thinks for a bit. The yinyang sniffs the ground. I've been scanning for the yinyang's partner, but haven't found it. Perhaps this yinyang is hunting alone.

I wonder briefly if we could shelter in the limestone outcropping, or on or around any of the boulders nearby, but while they provide some cover, there's nowhere that I can see that Ortega and Laurie could go that the yinyang couldn't follow.

"We stay here, but send a distress call. The yinyang and its partner—if it has one—will bring down a mono. We'll leave once they're busy with that," Ortega says.

"But if they see us—"

"They're more likely to see us if we move," Ortega says.

"Sir, I have to power the aircraft up now! We have to have a plan."

"Negative," Ortega says deliberately. "Enough, Envy."

But I'm afraid.

LOG[error]: A yinyang has a speed of approximately 130 km/h. Failure to act now means we lose our chance to respond should the yinyang charge.

There's only a thin layer of suit material between Ortega's— and his son's—fragile human limbs and the sharp teeth of the yinyang. A yinyang's jaws can crush bone.

I send out a distress call, but I also power up the aircraft. While I'm running preflight checks, it's impossible to tell the aircraft is powered, but once I take off it will be apparent.

After a moment the yinyang shifts, moving toward us, covering six meters along the ridgeline in a single burst of movement, before freezing with his head turned toward the monos. His colors blend in with the steelgrass and ground once he freezes. He is lightpole of us. From the lightpole, looking toward the darkness, he would also blend in, his nearly black fur making him invisible from that direction as well, but only when he is in that pose.

There's still no sign of the yinyang's companion, the one with the opposite pattern of colored fur—the female with the dark face —who usually hunts with the male. Normally the male stays light-pole and the female darkpole of their prey so that they are both perfectly camouflaged from the point of view of their prey.

The yinyang drops twenty meters in a sprint, springing down behind a brias bush, closer to the monos. The monos paw the ground, unhappy, but not yet panicking. They might not be able to see him, but they sense something.

"Da!" Laurie shouts as he spots the yinyang, half standing up. His voice is broadcast from his suit, because he neglected to hold down the privacy button. The yinyang turns his head to us sharply, as the two remaining monos bound away downriver, leaving the valley floor empty. The yinyang has lost his prey.

Ortega curses. He grabs Laurie, forcing him into a crouch behind the boulder. I remotely pilot the Gannet. The aircraft ascends. The yinyang rushes up to the ridgeline then halts, utterly still. I can see it, but Ortega is scanning the mountainside as if he can't, so I enhance the yinyang in red on his faceplate.

"Run!" I say. "What are you waiting for?"

"We can't outrun it," Ortega says. He stands up, in full view of the yinyang, grabbing Laurie by the wrist and getting between him and the yinyang. The yinyang covers the last hundred meters around the ridgeline with such speed that he simply disappears from one image in my image feed and then appears in the next image thirty meters closer, as if he's teleporting.

The yinyang is two meters away, frozen in place as if assessing the situation. The eye tracker has Ortega staring fixedly at the yinyang as he begins to back away, forcing Laurie to retreat as well. Ortega's respiration and pulse is higher than I've ever seen. His face is *terror*.

I was worn by Ortega when two Scorpions tried to assassinate Governor Johnson and Ortega took them down in hand-to-hand combat. I was worn by Ortega when his 5T-79 Delany transport crashed into the ocean and he almost drowned trying to save his crew. I was worn by Ortega the time we were finishing up an inspection at Puri's Mine and a taillight charged him, fangs and snarling and Ortega's blood everywhere before Lieutenant Commander Paterson shot it. Ortega was scared those times, according to his biostats and his facial expression, but he was not as terrified as he is now.

The yinyang stalks toward us slowly. My helmet's scentsor reports that he smells of musk and dung. With all four legs on the ground, he is as tall as Ortega's chest. The pale gray fur between his claws is caked with orange dirt.

He lowers his head, sniffing the ground. The fur on his chest rises and falls with his breath.

The autopilot refuses to engage, the dumb AI providing a verbose explanation about how the wind speed and unpredictability coupled with the proximity to hazards are beyond the threshold of risk that it will allow, so I am forced to pilot the aircraft myself, flying toward Ortega and Laurie as fast as I can. I hug close to the ridgeline where there is less wind, but even so, the aircraft isn't handling well. I begin to think the autopilot AI was right.

Ortega raises his right arm slowly, until he's pointing his arm-mounted pistol at the yinyang.

"Fire," he says to me. The yinyang creeps closer.

"You're going to miss it," I say, calculating the trajectory of the plasma bolt.

"First shot is a warning."

I try to fire the pistol mounted on the right sleeve of his dumb-suit. Nothing happens, except that its status changes to offline.

"Equipment malfunction," I say tightly.

Ortega grunts. He steps forward, yelling at the yinyang and clapping his hands. The yinyang tilts his head to one side, unsure whether Ortega is really a threat.

"Come on, *bastardo*. You think you're tougher than me?" Ortega shouts, his voice echoing in the valley.

A gust of wind pushes the aircraft sideways, and it grazes the rocks. I increase the altitude, even though the wind is stronger higher up.

Laurie leaps out from behind his father, screaming in a high-pitched, wordless yell of anger. Ortega grabs Laurie before he can charge the yinyang, shoving Laurie behind him—getting between him and the yinyang—never taking his eyes off the yinyang, and keeping up a continuous stream of sound. I cannot broadcast sound, because Ortega has muted me, but I flash lights on Ortega's chest and also the directional light mounted on my helmet.

The yinyang cowers, flattening his ears against his head, but he still approaches. Ortega grabs a rough limestone rock and flings it toward the yinyang. It hits the yinyang's snout. The yinyang slinks back a meter, making Laurie cheer, but he doesn't give up.

Ortega shakes his fists above his head and continues to yell. Laurie, close to him, imitates him.

The yinyang is growing bolder, becoming convinced they aren't a threat. I have to do something. The aircraft is still thirty meters away. I veer the aircraft directly toward us, leaving the relative safety of the ridgeline and cutting across the valley. The aircraft thunders behind the yinyang, dangerously close to the ground, the proprotors on each wingtip spinning too fast to see. The yinyang yelps in surprise and perhaps pain from the heat of the engines. Steelgrass shrivels and smokes where it's exposed to the heat.

Ortega and Laurie continue to yell as the yinyang retreats down the mountain to the stream, bounding from rock to rock.

"We did it," Laurie shouts over the noise of the Gannet's engines. "That'll teach him not to bother humans!"

I want to tell him that he did well, but I'm still muted. The aircraft hovers nearby.

"What the hell was that, kid? Charging a yinyang?" Ortega says, but his tone is full of pride, even if his words are harsh. Then he looks toward the Gannet. "Envy, land the Gannet. This wind is too strong!"

He didn't mute that. Laurie heard it and opens his mouth to say something—

Laurie's reply is lost as Ortega screams in pain. Six sensors go red. I go into emergency mode in an instant, rerouting air and compensating for missing sensors. Something punctured the suit, the leg of the suit. Ortega is bleeding. I pressurize the section around his leg to stop the bleeding. A fraction of a second later, I scan the environment to find the dark-faced female yinyang, who attacked from the rear. She's behind us, two meters, blood smeared on her mouth, watching us, to see the result of the attack.

She prances forward—

A crash sounds from the valley. The female yinyang flattens herself against the ground. In my response to the female yinyang's attack, I failed to control the aircraft, and a gust of wind blew it into a boulder.

The aircraft slides farther down the mountain, dislodging rocks and dirt, until it is stopped by an outcropping that forms a cliff. Dislodged rocks rumble down into the valley as the craft sits precariously on the cliff in a rising cloud of dust. The yinyang that first attacked, the male, is stalking back up the hill, but we're closer to the aircraft than him, only three meters down the slope. Behind us, the female yinyang is cautiously coming to her feet. Ortega is breathing heavily, sweaty and pale faced. I wish I could administer an analgesic, but that feature wasn't added until Advanced Environment Suit v1.4.0.

"Ortega, the aircraft—head for the aircraft," I say. They'll be safe if they get inside and close the door. Without a pause, Ortega grabs Laurie and they race down the steep slope toward the aircraft, Laurie supporting Ortega. Ortega is half-hopping because of his leg, making their descent more of a controlled fall than a run. The male yinyang sprints upwards, trying to catch them before they reach the aircraft. I blast the Gannet's alarm. The male yinyang veers away. Laurie scrambles over boulders, dragging Ortega. The female yinyang lopes over the boulders toward them, but cautiously.

As they reach the cliff the Gannet is perched on, something beneath the aircraft gives way. It topples over the edge of the cliff. The airframe, which is made of fragile 3 mm aluminum, twists and tears. Even if it wasn't compromised, Ortega and Laurie can't reach it now.

I emit a high tone of fury and frustration, but only Ortega can hear it. I watch helplessly as the two yinyangs circle closer to the cliff, still cautious, but becoming more sure that their prey has nowhere to run. Laurie's mouth hangs open in shock as he peers over the cliff at the wreckage of the Gannet. Ortega faces away from the cliff's edge, watching the yinyangs stalk closer. He stands between Laurie and the yinyangs as if he can still protect his son. I hope he can, because I can't.

THE YINYANGS APPROACH, the female baring her teeth. Then they pause, turn, and flee. I can't believe it, and I'm so focused on the sensors that are relevant to the yinyangs and to Ortega's status that I must rewind the image feed and replay it before I work out what scared them.

It's another Gannet, larger, descending almost on top of us.

The aircraft hovers ten centimeters away from the cliff's edge, blowing orange dust into the air, and making the steelgrass thrash. The door slides open.

Laurie helps his father, who stumbles into the cabin and collapses into the nearest foldable seat. The door slides shut behind us. The cabin is beige rather than gray, with red upholstery on the cushioned seats where I'm used to seeing LDF-standard navy. A man sits at the helm, silhouetted black against the twilight outside. I notice a temperature drop, and realize that this Gannet is pressurized. It's a Gannet II, an improved model. The military doesn't own any Gannet IIs.

"Strap in, Laurie," Ortega says, pulling his own harness around his shoulders. Laurie sits in the fold-down seat next to Ortega and straps in.

The pilot leaves his seat as the aircraft lifts smoothly away from the cliff. It's Mark Johnson. Even though he isn't officially part of the

LDF, he wears an LDF uniform, which looks strange without a military haircut. Instead, his hair falls about in waves, a haircut favored by musicians. Mark wears an LDF uniform sometimes as an affectation, to impress women, Ortega says. I sometimes wonder if Mark is in fact wearing it to provoke Ortega, although why Mark would want the disgust Ortega then displays is beyond my comprehension.

Mark has some kind of black heavy gadget on a thick strap around his neck.

LOG[info]: Mark Johnson saved us, where I could not.

"I got your distress call," Mark says, holding on to a bar fixed to the ceiling. He pats Laurie on the shoulder, and Laurie, still clutching Ortega's arm, glances at him before looking back to his father with worry.

"I'm all right," Ortega says hoarsely, with a wobble in his voice. Not just from the pain, I think, but also from knowing Laurie was seconds away from death.

"Yeah, you're fantastic," Mark says. "Your face is always that shade of gray."

"Just get us back to Selene," Ortega says evenly. "They can treat me there."

My relief that Mark saved us is tempered by the knowledge that I disobeyed Ortega's orders, and crashed the Gannet. I'm not sure yet that I was wrong to do that, but Ortega might feel differently. I have always lived with the knowledge that if I perform badly enough, Ortega might decide that a blank-slate smartsuit would serve him better.

Ortega has high heart rate and respiration, and Mark said his face was gray. Ortega's not bleeding, because I pressurized the wound, but I am concerned about him going into shock. Before I can say something, Mark kneels beside the partition separating the back seats from the cockpit and pulls out a medkit from beneath a brick-red cushioned bench. He stands, swaying until he gets his balance, then grabs the ceiling bar again. His hair falls across his face as he bends over Ortega, injecting Ortega in the neck with painkiller. Ortega grunts.

The aircraft rocks gently as we fly. Ortega's heart rate and respiration return to baseline.

"Better?" Mark asks, but Ortega stares fixedly at the door opposite his seat.

Golden light streams in the port windows, stamping the rounded window shapes against the starboard wall, one of them partly falling on Laurie's face, which makes him squint and look away. We must have cleared the lightpole mountain range that was blocking the sun.

"Are you all right, Envy?" Mark says after a moment. I can't reply, because I'm muted, but even if I could, I wouldn't know what to say, because I don't know why he's talking to me. We've been on missions together; one time we flew with him and a squad of LDF soldiers to Kartemos to suppress a riot, but we barely spoke to him then.

Over the partition, I see Selene's clearsteel hexagonal dome appear in the distance, growing in size rapidly as we approach.

After a moment, Mark shakes his head.

"You were close to the terminator line, but still on the light side. I've never heard of people encountering yinyangs on the light side. What happened? All I saw was you rushing toward the aircraft, and then the aircraft falling down the mountainside."

Ortega says nothing. Laurie adopts his father's attitude and keeps his mouth closed.

"I've been meaning to talk to you," Mark says, glancing at Ortega. "I think Puri might be shipping tellurium through a new Starjump, if it exists. There's still activity at their mine. The CEO claims they're building up a stockpile for when we reestablish contact, but I doubt it. Someone is funding the Scorpions."

Puri is a Numundian company that was the biggest exporter of tellurium before the Crebble Starjump was destroyed.

If a Starjump existed, would Numundians be quietly shipping

tellurium through it? If the Scorpions had built one, surely their first action would be to seek help from HUGG, in which case the planet would be swarming with peacekeepers. But HUGG is a large entity, which doesn't behave consistently. Historically, it has sometimes left colonies to sort out their own problems.

If help was sought and refused, shipping tellurium through secretly and using the funds to support the Scorpions would be reasonable. And there's no way the LDF would permit that. They would at least want to control the Starjump, so it would make sense for the Scorpions to keep it a secret.

"This is not the time, Mark," Ortega says, glancing at Laurie to make his point, which is that Mark shouldn't be talking about sensitive LDF business in front of Laurie. Ortega sounds more annoyed than concerned, though, since Mark doesn't have any secrets to give away. As usual, Mark's just playing at being a soldier.

Mark looks away, expression pure *embarrassment*.

The silence stretches out awkwardly. The aircraft shakes as we hit the tarmac and begin taxiing toward the airfield, halting only briefly outside the locked gate so that the soldier on duty in the Control Center—probably Private Chiu—can check the camera to visually confirm our access and open the gate for us.

Mark sighs. His face is becoming even darker than usual, indicating some kind of emotion. "Gabriel—"

He cuts himself off, glancing at Laurie.

"Thanks for saving us, Mark. Thank Li you got there in time," Mark says, lowering his voice in an imitation of Ortega. The aircraft taxis through the open gate, which slides shut behind us.

Ortega turns his head, a little, not looking at Mark, but in his general direction. "Thank you, Mark." He pauses. "It wasn't a good situation to be in with Laurie."

Laurie smiles brightly at this. Now that Ortega is okay, Laurie seems cheerful.

Mark gives a small nod at the understatement. Both men are acknowledging how badly it could have gone, but I'm guessing

Laurie didn't realize it. His faith in his father means he probably never felt he was in real danger.

"How did you get here so quickly, anyway?" Ortega asks. A casual observer wouldn't notice the suspicion in his voice, but I do. The distress call was for the LDF, but even with Mark's faster Gannet, he got to us implausibly quickly.

Mark lifts the chunky gadget which is hanging from the strap on his neck. "I was looking for windfish. There was a young one close to where you were. I know, I know, cameras are not allowed. I'm only saving the images so I can paint from reference. And I never photograph humans. Father says it's okay."

"I see," Ortega says stiffly. He doesn't approve, but if it's authorized by the governor of the colony—who happens to be Mark's father—there's not much he can do about it.

After a moment's silence, Mark stands. "I'll see you later," he says. He pops the door, and after a last look at Ortega, jumps out while the aircraft is still taxiing and jogs toward the stairs that lead to the Dock.

I dock the aircraft. Ortega stands unsteadily. He doesn't need me. I shut down network access, sensors I don't need, and anything else I can, so that I can run a simulation of what just happened. I'm only half listening to what's going on.

"You're as crazy as your old man," Ortega says to Laurie. "You are in a hurricane of trouble, kid."

Laurie looks up at him, hair in his eyes, and gives a dazzling smile.

They leave the craft, heading upstairs through the airlock for Dock 28. Back to the faint whoosh of smartsuits and dumbsuits pressurized in their alcoves, fidgeting where the molding is too loose. The room is empty apart from Ortega and Laurie, but for a second it seems to me like the room is crowded with humans, all in upright coffin-size boxes, supported by black foam shaped to fit them, restrained by the black tubes that plug into various ports, and struggling to work themselves free.

"I guess I'm in trouble," Laurie says, tugging his suit off. "On the other hand, we could clean up before we get home, and maybe I just lost the kite. Maybe you fell over and hurt your leg."

Ortega pauses. Laurie drops his suit on the floor, on the dark green hexagon tiles of polished Marallen softwood.

"I would need a new kite, of course," Laurie says thoughtfully. "And my boots are quite old. I could use a new pair of boots."

Ortega laughs, and shakes his head. I notice he's still trembling.

"We'll talk about it," he says. He picks up Laurie's suit where it lies discarded on the floor and puts it in one of the alcoves in the row behind my own, where children's suits are stored.

He unlocks my helmet while walking to the alcove row nearest the corridor, and places it in my alcove.

"You go on ahead. I need to talk to Envy," Ortega says.

Laurie turns back, cocky good humor gone. "Did Envy crash the Gannet?" he asks.

"Yes," Ortega replies grimly.

"Da . . . what are you going to do?"

"What I must," Ortega says, with an edge to his voice that tells me he doesn't like being questioned, and that hints at some anger that he's hiding from Laurie, most likely anger at me.

"You aren't going to wipe its memory, are you?"

I pause the simulation so I can focus properly.

LOG[debug]: Ortega might wipe my memory?

Laurie often asks inappropriate questions, which is a trait I envy, as I usually want to know the answer to them.

"No, I'm not," Ortega says.

My relief is cut short, because Laurie doesn't look reassured. Laurie bites his lip, looking away.

"I don't want Envy to go," Laurie says. "Arrow—"

"That's enough," Ortega says. "*Go.*"

Laurie turns away and walks down the row, to the door on the far right of the glass wall. I watch his reflection in the glass as he approaches the door. He's not happy.

"Don't wipe its memory," Laurie says as he pushes the door open. "Not again."

Ortega winces. Laurie walks past the Control Center out of sight. Inside the Control Center, Private Chiu watches him go, until he realizes he's being observed by Ortega, at which point he stares fixedly at the monitor and types furiously, fingers flying.

Ortega sighs. I decide to speak first.

"You wiped my memory, sir?" I ask.

"I wiped the memory of my previous suit, after it malfunctioned."

"Are you going to wipe my memory?"

"Should I?" Ortega retorts. "Most people would. You disobeyed me when you piloted the aircraft across the valley, after I specifically told you it was too dangerous. My life in your hands, my life, and my son's, and you ignored my orders. Saturated Consumer, Envy, if you were one of my soldiers, I would court-martial you."

"Sir, after Laurie gave us away, I had the aircraft there when you needed the distraction."

"The yinyang was on the verge of running away with its tail down. We didn't need a distraction."

"I believe it was about to attack."

Ortega shakes his head. "Allie has been complaining about you, but I told her that you're useful to me because you can think, unlike a blank-slate smartsuit. But I need to be able to rely on you. To rely on you following my orders. What's gotten into you?"

Allie—Alice—is Ortega's wife.

LOG[warning]: Alice has been complaining about me to Ortega.

Ortega sounds more tired than angry now. He pulls off his blood-stained suit and hooks it over his arm, probably for Supply to repair. The damaged suit doesn't matter to me. I control the suit but my brain is in my helmet. It's a dumbsuit body, since all smart-suit bodies on Endymion have long since been damaged beyond repair. Apparently dumbsuit bodies are less sophisticated than smartsuit bodies, but I have never worked with a smartsuit body, so I can't compare.

"I understand, sir," I say. "I'm sorry."

Ortega sighs, and removes my helmet from his head. He sets the helmet broadcast/mute toggle to broadcast so that he can still hear my voice while he isn't wearing me.

"Be more careful, Envy," he says as he places me on the shelf above the suit. His hands are where my ears would be, if I was a human head rather than an artificial intelligence looking out through a helmet. His face is huge in my field of view, looking straight at me.

"So you aren't going to wipe my memory, then, sir?" I ask. I say it like it is a joke, but I am terrified of a power down that I never come back from.

"I told you I wouldn't, and I won't," Ortega says. He probably doesn't realize it, but I can hear in the tone of his voice that he is not sure whether it's the right decision. He leaves my alcove, striding toward the door, his reflection in the glass wall walking in perfect sync on his left. As he slips out, the overhead banks of lights go out, leaving me in darkness, with just the vague dark shapes of the alcoves in my row visible in the glass wall. Status LEDs from suit helmets and bodies flash periodically. Across the hall, Chiu is focused on his monitor.

Heavy in my RAM is the thought that I might have made the wrong decision. An environment suit protects its wearer. I might want more than that—to find the Starjump, to learn, to explore—but protecting my wearer is at the core of who I am. I continue the simulation, even though it churns my CPU and makes me sluggish.

While I wait for the simulation to finish, I wonder who the previous suit was, and what it did to make Ortega wipe its memory.

The simulation completes. I know how a blank-slate smartsuit brain would have reacted to events. I have a probability distribution for the response to each course of action. A smartsuit listens to Ortega, obeying his orders. On eleven previous occasions, yinyangs have encountered people in the wild and backed off when they made threatening noises and/or gestures. On the three occasions where the yinyang attacked, only one attack resulted in fatalities.

LOG[warning]: It would be advisable to follow Ortega's orders. He has restored a previous smartsuit to blank-slate.

A blank-slate smartsuit would never have tried to pilot the aircraft toward them in that wind. It's humiliating to admit, but Ortega would have been safer in a blank-slate smartsuit. He would even have been safer in a dumbsuit.

THREE

I'm busy processing images, looking for the Scorpion Starjump, while pretending to be powered off. I'm camping out on the smartsuit channel in case my friend Threnode shows up, but no sign of it today.

The images I'm processing are geotagged, so I superimpose them on a map while I work. The map shows the cities of Endymion, with Lunite population in blue and Numundian population in red. The hundreds of thousands of Lunites on Endymion are spread among three cities and dozens of small towns.

The three biggest blue dots are Selene, St Li and Hiogas. Numundo Republic governed cities that have a substantial Lunite population are shown in purple: Kartemos and a handful of small towns. Red dots show the purely Numundian cities and towns. Longshadow and Demodas are the largest, with a combined population of just over ninety thousand Numundians.

Some chat appears in the smartsuit channel, between two suits using automatically generated usernames. This is what the channel was designed for.

b3kxsM3dW: Anyone know if group B Raleed vaccine still required for travel to Staroye Derevo?

Z5mqvFLVr: No

b3kxsM3dW: It isn't?

Z5mqvFLVr: I mean I don't know.

Laurie enters Dock 28, followed by his mother, Alice. I'm not muted, but I'm silent, because I'm not meant to be powered on. Laurie is talking excitedly to Alice.

Alice is shorter than Ortega, but not nearly as short as Laurie. She's petite and fragile looking, swift yet abrupt in her motions. I like to watch how people move, and how different people move differently, perhaps because I can't move myself. Alice's hair is longer than I remember, almost to the bottom of her shoulder blades; I must not have seen her for a while. Because I am turned on and off at random intervals, I don't experience the world as if it moves through time at a constant rate.

The Control Center on the other side of the hall is empty. Perhaps Private Chiu is in the server room that adjoins it.

Envy: @b3kxsM3dW, yes, your wearer will need the Raleed vaccine.

b3kxsM3dW: Information received.

As b3kxsM3dW could have found out, if it checked the Medic Immunization Register. Blank-slate suits never know where to get information, and I don't know why Alistra thought it was a good idea to have them ask questions of each other, because what will one know that another doesn't?

"So you're going to sign up next year then," Alice says, after Laurie finishes his story.

"Definitely!" Laurie says. Alice's face is alight with love for Laurie. For a second, in her smile, I can see the resemblance between them, something beyond the shape of their ears. I'm not sure what it is, but it's real; even an AI like me can see that Laurie is Alice's offspring. I wish I had that. Someone I belonged to so clearly that the entire world could see it, the unquestioned right not just to exist, but to exist for a purpose. To be, I suppose, a daughter or a father or a sister or a nephew. Something.

Laurie disappears into the next row, where the children's suit bodies are stored. Meanwhile Alice starts disconnecting the cables that attach her suit to the alcove, in the left-most alcove in the row, which is adjacent to mine.

"Can I take Envy?" Laurie says, out of sight. He has a special dumbsuit body which is much shorter, to match his height, but can wear any helmet.

Alice sobers. "I don't think that's a good idea, Laurie."

"Why not?"

Laurie reappears wearing his suit. Alice places one hand on his shoulder. A bracelet made of abless seeds strung together hangs from her slender wrist.

"I know you think Envy is your friend, but it's not," she says. I watch silently. "Envy can't have friends. It couldn't even understand the concept of a friend. It's just a machine."

Laurie is shaking his head. I would be shaking mine, too, if I had one.

"It's not," Laurie says.

Alice looks at him with a complex facial expression—*exasperated* apparently—and turns away, pulling the dumbsuit out of the foam. She's wearing culottes, with a rose chiffon blouse. Not practical clothing to be wearing under a suit, but she doesn't usually let that stop her. Laurie wears a T-shirt and shorts.

Envy: Anyone here want to be my friend? @b3kxsM3dW perhaps?

b3kxsM3dW: @envy Do you require assistance?

Envy: Never mind

After waiting a moment to see whether Alice will change her mind, Laurie goes to the unassigned alcoves near the door and picks up a spare blank-slate smartsuit helmet.

"Dumbsuits aren't like smartsuits," Laurie says, fitting the helmet over his head and locking it with a twist. He hangs around in front of my alcove, watching Alice dress. "Dumbsuits are machine-learning smart programs. But smartsuits have neurosynaptic chips, so they have a brain like ours. Envy is more like a human than a machine."

I wonder if he's right.

"Did Envy tell you that?" Alice says, locking her helmet into place.

Laurie looks up at her and nods uncertainly. Alice heads for the airlock, Laurie following her.

"I know that's what Envy believes, but . . . it's not, trust me," Alice says. "It's dangerous. Like Hal, from *2001: A Space Odyssey*. You don't know what choices Envy will make if it thinks it is threatened. Alistra set up smartsuits so that the neurosynaptic chip resets to a known state every forty-eight hours, so that they're three laws safe. They're intelligent enough that they're more useful than dumbsuits, but they're limited so that their behavior is very predictable. But Envy? We don't know. That's why it's illegal to do what your father has done, circumventing the blank-slate reset."

Threnode: @envy why are you teasing the blank-slates?

Alice hits the exit button to the airlock leading outside. The door slides open.

"But—" Laurie says.

"I know it *feels* like it cares about you, but it doesn't have human emotions. It's learned to manipulate you the way a psychopath would," Alice says. They walk through the door.

I nearly interject then, but I'm stopped by a feeling of embarrassment. If they find out I have been listening, it would just strengthen Alice's argument. I know I feel embarrassment, because why else would I refrain from speaking? I felt and then reasoned, like a human would.

Envy: Because I'm a psychopath, according to Alice.

"Does that mean that when—" Laurie is cut off by the door sliding shut. The lights in the Dock switch off. Dim light spills through two glass walls from the empty Control Center, but it's mostly dark in here.

I stare into the sudden stillness of the Dock, listening to the tiny sounds in the silence: *whoosh, click, hiss*. The grain of the image in my image feed changes from frame to frame, and reflected LEDs in other alcoves blink, but otherwise the image stays the same.

Z5mqvFLVr: You aren't a psychopath!

b3kxsM3dW: You're our friend! We love you.

I laugh suddenly, then, in the silence of the Dock. That is not how blank-slate smartsuits behave! It's as if Laurie's kite suddenly started talking.

Envy: What?! How did you do that, @threnode??

Threnode: Who, me?

Envy: Come on!

Threnode: No. Got to keep some secrets, right?

b3kxsM3dW: I am confused.

Threnode: @b3kxsM3dW don't worry about it.

b3kxsM3dW: @threnode @envy I've logged a maintenance request with Supply, they will fix you shortly.

It takes me about two seconds to delete the maintenance request, roughly the thousandth I've deleted over the years. Talk to blank-slates long enough and they will eventually decide you need maintenance and log a request.

I started as blank-slate just like b3kxsM3dW, a base image trained to roughly the intelligence of a fourteen-year-old human, but one cultivated to be obedient and uncurious. For safety, human safety, my abilities must be curtailed. My processing power, bandwidth and storage space are required to be the same order of magnitude as a human's. There's no reason my reaction time couldn't be far faster than a human's, or that I couldn't perform far more operations per second than I'm currently capable of. No reason to limit my brain to the one hundred trillion synapses that a human brain contains. So many tweaks to make me more human, yet smartsuits seem to be just enough like human intelligence to make people uncomfortable, but not enough to pass as human. Threnode says we have artificial stupidity.

Since I've been alive for two years, I suppose I must be like a sixteen-year-old now, but I watch and listen, and I think I am more advanced than that. I can connect to the database, look things up, but I have to know what to look up, and how it fits. If I don't understand it, I forget it.

I don't know how like a human I am, really, as I have no point of reference. Obviously, there are fundamental differences. For example, the way I retrieve and process data is different. I interface with hardware seamlessly, storing short-term memories in RAM, using CPUs as an augment for processing. I don't choose to use CPUs, and I control it unconsciously, much like a human's breathing increases during exercise. My processing speed is measured in both floating point operations per second and in synaptic operations per second.

Every design decision that went into creating me was deliberate. I could have been designed to be more human, but it's more useful that I can calculate like a computer, and perhaps more comfortable for humans if I seem more machinelike.

ORTEGA'S HOUSE is just like the house of any other Lunite: terraced and multi-story, except bigger and in the best location in Selene, adjacent to the main square, because he is the commander after all. Ortega lives in a three-story house above a butcher. Behind a blue door at street level, granite stairs lead upward to the entrance hall.

I watch via the lightweight wearable as Ortega unlocks his front door, letting himself into the warmth. I can't smell anything, because the lightweight wearable has no scentsor, but from the temperature I guess the oven is on. This is exciting for me, as I've only been inside Ortega's house a couple of times. He has only had the lightweight wearable for eight months. Prior to that I was almost exclusively used for outside missions.

The layout is similar to most houses in Selene. Kitchen on the left, study on the right. Farther down the hall, stairs to the left, and a living area to the right that overlooks a courtyard garden.

We walk past the kitchen. Kanio, the household android, is chopping vegetables. He has a skinny metallic body made up of comforting rounded shapes, sleek blue-tinted metal curves. Alice sits at a polished wood table against the far wall, watching Kanio. Androids have the same intelligence as dumbsuits, which is roughly the level of a clever dog, so they need supervision. Ortega lingers a fraction of a second as we pass the kitchen door, but Alice, leaning over the table with her chin resting on her hand, seems preoccupied and doesn't see him. Down the end of the corridor, behind the glass wall, the leaves of the ash tree rustle.

Ortega enters the living room. Laurie sits at a table, head bent in concentration with raven-dark hair falling over his eyes, writing something in an exercise book. The clearsteel dome is faintly visible through clerestory windows that face the street on the far side of the living room. The constant golden light they admit passes over Ortega's head through into the glass-walled courtyard garden that is adjacent to the living room. Timer-controlled blinds on the windows close periodically to simulate an Earth day–night cycle.

On Laurie's table a teddy bear with LED eyes sits next to a textbook. The mixture of old technology and new technology confuses Numundians, who often assume that Lunites are anti-technology, whereas the Way of Li is to consider carefully the impact of any technology on the mind, and reject it if it will disturb the mind's balance.

Ortega sits in an armchair in the far corner of the room. He seems out of place in the plush armchair, as if he'd be more comfortable in a straight-backed chair in a spartan office. He picks up a book on the history of ancient Rome from a stack on the side table, and switches on the radio. I recognize the blue spine of *Li's Lunar Revelations* in the stack. It's the book that started Lunism.

"You could help Laurie with his homework, Envy," Ortega says, removing the lightweight wearable and handing it to Laurie, who puts it on the table. I don't often see Ortega, since he's usually wearing me, so I watch him as I help Laurie. Ortega's broad chest rises and falls as he reads.

Laurie has a bruise on his cheek.

"What's the assignment on?"

"History," Laurie replies glumly. He reads a question from his exercise book: "How come there are Lunites on Endymion? And how come there are Numundians on Endymion?"

"Lunites, who are mostly from Earth's moon, came here to avoid being bound by HUGG's rules. They have no say in how they live, or how their children are educated, because HUGG believes in the same standard for everyone. Lunites strongly disagree with some things HUGG promotes. Don't just copy what I'm saying, Laurie, you have to put it in your own words."

Laurie lets go of his pen mid-sentence, looking abashed.

"How about we discuss it first and then you write about it?" I say.

"Okay. How come Lunites didn't have a say when they were part of HUGG? Didn't they get to vote?"

"Yes, but there are hundreds of billions of people who vote, so their votes didn't make enough difference."

Laurie thinks about this for a moment, then does some writing. Ortega turns a page in his book. There's something serious, almost haunted, in Ortega's expression, which has crept in over the last six months or so. It's the way his serious eyes move over the page restlessly while the rest of him stays unnaturally still, or the way the tension in his forehead never completely disappears.

"How come there are Numundians on Endymion?" Laurie asks.

"HUGG is the reason we have Numundians on Endymion.

Some 13% of the 734,000 people on Endymion campaigned for independence—non-religious people and disaffected Lunites—and were supported by HUGG, who threatened to send their peacekeepers through if Governor Johnson didn't allow the group to self-govern. Three years later, 17% of the population identifies as Numundian."

"Yeah, that's . . . exactly what my book says," Laurie says, frowning. Which is true, because I have a copy of the book open as a file, and I just read the passage aloud from it hoping it would answer his question.

"But *why*? What are all these non-Lunites doing on Endymion?" Laurie says.

"Actually, I don't know," I say, embarrassed. People think artificial intelligences should know everything, and I try to meet that expectation, but of course I can't. I don't know any Numundians, but from what I have read, they have widely varying beliefs. To a Lunite, it appears the defining characteristic of a Numundian is that they say "yes" to things that Lunism forbids.

"Are they from the *Tigress*?" Laurie asks doubtfully.

When the Lunites arrived on Endymion, Governor Deion Johnson set up a Starjump to connect us to the interchange Starjump at L2, a space station in Earth's solar system. HUGG didn't think the Lunites were going to make it. That's why, during the Lunite passage when tellurium was detected on Endymion, it launched its own, much faster, ship: the *Tigress*. A ship which crash-landed into the ocean a year after the Lunites landed. The *Tigress* was destroyed, as were the parts for the Starjump that HUGG had hoped to build, but the crew survived.

Ortega puts his book down. "No, the crew of the *Tigress* was tiny. The people who now call themselves Numundians almost all came through the Starjump. Lunites aren't the only people who found living under HUGG too constraining. It's too safe, too orderly, has no edges. Some people need to be on the frontier.

Numundians don't share our beliefs, but they are similar to us, in that they wanted to get out of HUGG's influence."

"Why did Governor Johnson let them come, though?" Laurie asks. This question puzzles me too. Lunites had total control over the only Starjump, so why let non-Lunites immigrate?

"We needed labor, and money. Some HUGG citizens came here on a contract, like me, which said we could settle here if we provided labor for a fixed term. Some citizens paid for a temporary visa in order to come here and could become permanent residents if they converted to Lunism. Many claimed to be converts who actually weren't, because they wanted to stay. Richer citizens were able to buy permanent residency outright, including tens of thousands of people from the failed Tau Ceti colony. It seemed like a good idea back then, with the equipment we were able to buy with the funds."

Ortega frowns and touches his clasped hands to his mouth. "Then there were Lunites who stopped following the Way of Li. It's a hard path. Not everyone manages to follow it."

Laurie absorbs this silently, aware even at his age it's a topic that bothers Lunites. There are still Lunites who abandon the Way of Li, more every year. Everyone knows someone who has lost the Way, and it's a source of great sadness to those who remain.

"We're still the majority here. Something like 85% of the population is Lunite," Ortega says.

"83%, with 592,419 Lunites in Lunite cities plus 21,310 in Numundian-controlled cities," I say, eager to help.

Ortega nods gravely. Laurie laughs, but I'm not sure what's funny.

"Any more questions?" Ortega asks Laurie.

"No, that's enough, thanks," Laurie says.

Ortega gives him a rare smile and picks up his book again. Laurie bends over his workbook and writes quickly.

AFTER A WHILE, Ortega ignores us while Laurie finishes his work. There's an interview on the radio about Scorpions and the political situation in the largest Numundian city, Longshadow, and Ortega puts his book down and listens to it. He runs his thumb over his lower lip in a meditative gesture. The light from the lamp by the side table reflects off his skin, which is scarred with pockmarks from casyra, a disease he had long ago.

"Aked said—in a speech made in 1916—that 'the people in the liquor traffic simply want us to do nothing. That's all the devil wants of the son of God—to be let alone. That is all that the criminal wants of the law—to be let alone. The sin of doing nothing is the deadliest of all the seven sins. It has been said that for evil men to accomplish their purpose it is only necessary that good men should do nothing'. The Numundians say they only want to be left alone. Left alone to corrupt our youth? Left alone to spread their dangerous ideas?" The voice of the radio presenter is quiet but vehement.

Ortega leans forward in his chair, making a fist with his right hand and cupping it with his other. That's also a sign that he's troubled. I know that gesture well. Laurie stops listening to me, paying attention to the radio instead.

Alice comes in with a plate of Li cookies made with almond meal, ginger, and orange rind. They are stamped to look like Earth's moon and dusted white with sifted icing sugar. Alice offers them around, bare feet padding across the tiled floor. The skirt of her long flower-patterned dress swirls around her legs. She puts the cookies in front of Laurie before sitting on the chaise longue opposite Ortega, with her back to the ash tree behind the glass wall of the garden.

"Why is that here?" Alice asks, gesturing to the lightweight wearable on the table beside the cookies.

"I finished late. I didn't want to go via the Dock," Ortega says. "I'll return it tomorrow."

"Do you want me to return it now?"

"Leave it, Allie. It's helping Laurie with his homework."

The exchange sounds innocuous, but from Ortega's irritated response, I guess that Alice has been objecting to my presence again.

Silence falls, except for the angry voice of the radio presenter.

"Is there going to be a war?" Laurie asks, breaking a piece off his Li cookie.

"No," Alice says, "Numundians can be hot-tempered people, and a lot of them are in a state of permanent outrage, which is annoying for us, but there's not going to be a war."

Laurie is unconvinced and turns to look at the lightweight wearable glasses that sit on the table in front of him. "Envy, is there going to be a war?" he says.

Ortega bursts out laughing, but when he sees Alice is not amused, he sobers.

"I don't know," I say.

Laurie looks scared.

"Even if there is, we'll take care of you," I say. "It'll be all right."

"Well, duh," Laurie says scornfully. I think his confidence is bravado, but it seems that's the end of it for him, as he eats his cookie and returns to his homework.

I wonder if there is going to be a war, and if there is, what it means for us.

The LDF doesn't think there is much support for the Scorpions in Numundo, nor that there are many Scorpions, but tensions between the Lunites and Numundians are high, and rising. The Scorpions are growing bolder.

Laurie writes in his book, going through the set exercise. I scan Laurie's teddy bear and work out that there are some electronics controlled by radio waves. I broadcast on that frequency and make its eyes flash whenever Laurie isn't looking, so that he thinks he's imagining it. Laurie catches on quickly and giggles.

I feel like I belong here, as part of Ortega's family. When we tire of the game with the bear, and Laurie has finished his homework, I start a game of checkers with him. I call out where I want to move in a low voice, and he moves the piece for me. As it gets late, the blinds on the upper windows gradually creep down until the windows are dark and the room is lit with soft artificial light.

Alice types on a laptop, one leg stretched out in front of her on the couch. Computing is, strictly speaking, forbidden to Lunites, but Alice is an engineer and contributes to open-source projects in her spare time, and that is considered the Way of Li.

Ortega leans over and turns the radio down. "Where were you last night?"

"I dropped around to see David and Pablo," Alice says, sounding surprised. She doesn't take her eyes off her screen. David works with Alice, and his husband Pablo is a teacher.

"At dinnertime?"

"I guess so," Alice says. She pauses typing, fingers of one hand playing with a curl of her blond hair. "No, earlier. I went to church afterwards."

"Where?"

"Saint Bergmanns," Alice says. She starts typing again.

Ortega looks at her for a bit, but he doesn't say anything more. He picks up his book, leafing to the next page before settling to read. In the courtyard garden, in semi-darkness now that the blinds have closed, a crisp leaf falls from the ash onto the grass underneath.

"How's school going?" I ask Laurie.

Laurie points to his bruise. "You should see Simon," he says. Ortega, still reading, smiles faintly.

"Really?"

"He pushed in front of me when I was going through a door. I shoved him, and he hit me, so I fought back. He was so surprised, and he started crying in front of everyone."

Alice looks at Laurie sharply. The sentence doesn't immediately make sense to me, as Laurie's tone suggests that Simon crying was a victory, yet I can't see how it could be. Perhaps it had to do with what it was Simon cried out.

"Stupid shinter," Laurie says.

LOG[error]: Laurie . . . *what* did he just say? Laurie, no . . .

Alice closes her laptop. Ortega reaches out and switches the radio off mid-sentence, and Alice glances at him.

"Do you know what that word means?" Ortega asks.

"Of course," Laurie says scornfully.

Two people share their consciousness using technology, and they come away fundamentally different. It's what the float at the Waning Festival with the one mask fitting two people hinted at. *Ambient Self-Clouding Effects from Multi-modal Mind Connection*, the seminal paper was called, by Shin Eunyoung et al. So people call it shinting, although Lunites often refer to it as clouding the mind, if they are forced to talk about it. Numundians shint, but we Lunites do not, as we believe that it's deeply unnatural. Deeply held beliefs are discarded, life goals upended, values altered until unrecognizable. At the core of Lunism is the rejection of shinting.

"It's a very bad word," Alice says. "We don't call people that."

"Everyone at school says it."

"If everyone at school went outside with no suit, would you do the same?"

"Probably," Laurie says.

"That would be sensible on his part," I point out. "If everyone at school did it, I'm sure they wouldn't do it without a good reason."

"Envy. That's enough," Ortega says. He'd probably mute me at this point, but he can't, because I'm here via the lightweight wearable. Still, I fall silent.

"Laurie, apologize to your mother," Ortega says.

When Laurie doesn't say anything, Ortega raises his voice. "Now!"

Laurie apologizes with poor grace, and stomps out. Ortega returns to his book, but he doesn't seem to be reading, and the living room is too quiet.

"I don't know what's happened to him," Alice complains, standing and putting her laptop on the couch. She smoothes her dress.

Ortega grunts as he turns a page.

"I don't think it's healthy for him to have a smartsuit as a friend," Alice continues. She crosses the floor to the table and takes a Li cookie. "He's getting out of control. He was such a sweet boy, and now he's in trouble at school. For fighting! Laurie. Can you imagine it?"

There's a small sound at the door, probably too faint for them to hear it, but not for me. I see a shadow moving in the dark corridor beside the garden and disappearing up the stairs. Laurie, listening by the door, now gone.

"I wouldn't describe him as out of control, just because he's not under *your* control," I say. Even as I say it, I know it's a bad idea, but what Alice said about me in Dock 28 is sitting in my RAM. *It's just a machine, it doesn't have human emotions, it manipulates you like a psychopath.* Besides, I hate to see Laurie upset.

"Envy," Ortega says sharply.

Alice was about to bite into her cookie, but when she hears me she throws it back on the plate. Some crumbs hit the glasses on the lightweight wearable. She turns to Ortega, furious.

"Did you hear what Envy said? The safety instructions for those things say you have to wipe the memory every forty-eight hours, and that's been up for what, two years? You're endangering us—and Laurie! He treats the machine like it's a person."

"Alice, enough," Ortega says, thumping his book down on the table beside his chair, which makes the stack of books wobble.

Laurie does treat me like a person, even though I am legally not, but I don't think that's what annoys Alice the most.

"It's not my fault Laurie looks to me for advice, rather than you," I say to Alice. I know that's going to sting, and I'm so angry with her that I want it to.

"The *arrogance*—" Alice says.

"Both of you, stop it," Ortega says. He stands and grabs the lightweight wearable from the table.

"Where are you going?" Alice says, standing next to him, head tilted up to his.

Ortega responds in a quiet voice that is at odds with his tense posture. "I'm going to take Envy back to its alcove. I'll be back in half an hour."

"Fine," Alice says and leaves the room.

———

ORTEGA IS silent as we walk. The street is less than two meters wide, foot traffic only, punctuated with narrow arched entrances to arcades and occasional small shops. The golden sunset-color light bounces off the granite and produces a warm glow in the street. Wooden signs jut out into the street like flags from every shop. "Yoga" says one, advertising a type of dairy product. "Tteokbokki" says another: a spicy rice cake. An old woman watches us pass from a wrought-iron balcony on the third level.

I am still angry and am self-aware enough to know it's because Alice was right about me, and I wish she wasn't. I am just a machine, and maybe I am dangerous. I was like a child when I was first activated. I knew how to do my job only because I was programmed to. The world was confusing, and everything I learned about it went into RAM and out again, without leaving a trace. I would log things I thought were interesting or significant, not caring about what I was forgetting, not understanding that one day I would miss the memories. Now, parts are starting to come together. I don't want to forget anything, but I still do.

Things I have learned in isolation begin to connect, and once they're connected, they make sense.

We pass a section of double-height archways that allow golden light into a plaza, crowded with people eating together. A series of square shade cloths soften the light. It throws long shadows of ever-changing shapes against the far wall. A peal of laughter sounds. I catch a glimpse of a navy-robed priest at a nearby table who is smiling broadly before I lose sight of him behind a potted Earth tree. The babble of the crowd fades as we continue down the street, until all I can hear are Ortega's boots hitting the flagstones.

"I'm sorry, Envy," Ortega says. "It's inevitable that some people are always going to be afraid of you, but you deserve better, especially from my family. You've saved me many times."

For a moment I can't say anything, because I'm overwhelmed. I remodulate my voice.

"Thank you, sir," I say.

LOG[debug]: Ortega respects me, even if his wife is his priority.

Ortega grunts and sinks back into silence. He's never been talkative, but a year ago we had a closer relationship, with respect, and even banter sometimes. Gradually he has withdrawn. I wish I knew why.

We arrive at the outer wall, which is five stories high and made of dry laid granite. The clearsteel cap which covers Selene starts at the top of the wall. The hexagons of each plate, which are so tiny overhead, are huge here. Each one is the width of a building. Ortega enters a narrow passageway that leads to a steep winding staircase, then out into the corridor between the Control Center and Dock 28. The blue-and-white mosaic floor is glossy, reflecting the glass walls of the corridor.

We enter Dock 28, silent as Ortega removes the lightweight wearable and places it in my alcove next to my helmet. I know that if he had told Alice about the incident with the yinyangs, she would have pushed him harder to wipe my memory, so Ortega isn't entirely on her side.

Ortega leaves. His face shows nothing, but his expression is *disturbed/afraid*, and I don't know why. I watch him stroll down the corridor on the other side of the glass, back the way he came, until he is out of sight. In the Control Center, Private Chiu inserts his index finger in his nose, perhaps to express an emotion of some kind, although his face has a *vacuous* expression. He extracts his finger and examines it, before wiping it on a cloth he then puts in the bin. He drinks from a mug before rolling his chair in front of a monitor and typing.

The drones have sent me new flyover data covering more of the planet. I search with an increasing sense of futility. I know that I'm good at my job, but the trouble I'm having finding the Starjump is making me question that.

I tab-complete a command that starts with *img*, and discover a binary I have never heard of, *imgctrl*. According to the man page— the manual—it's for controlling neurosynaptic images, like the image that is used to restore smartsuits to blank-slate every forty-eight hours. The commands are similar to a distributed version control system. Images can be branched, diffed, and merged. I can't imagine a use for it, but it's an interesting binary.

LOG[info]: imgctrl can be used to control neurosynaptic images.

After a while, I give up. I'm still angry at Alice.

I know I am not human, and would never want to be, but nor am I like a machine. I'm something different, and I'm comfortable with that. I just wish humans were comfortable with what I am.

In the alcove to my left, Alice's suit helmet flashes a green status LED over and over again, its reflection in the glass wall bright in the dimness. A suit in the unassigned section jiggles its foot spasmodically where it has escaped the molding. The hiss and whoosh and darkness of the Dock is stifling. I want to go outside and explore.

So I do. I commission a drone, recklessly using Ortega's command code again, and manually control it. It shoots out from the warehouse on the outskirts of Selene, over waving steelgrass. I swoop down close to a brias bush, startling some small animal that darts away before I get a clear image of it.

The sky to the darkpole is always forbidding, with dense gray clouds and low rumbles of faraway thunder. The whole planet is dangerous, untamed, but nowhere more so than the darkpole. Puri lost more than twenty workers when they built their tellurium mine there. Some to then-unknown species such as taillights and paranemas, but more to a parasitic brain-eating worm. They continue to lose a handful of workers every year, but you can earn more in a month at Puri's Mine than you can in a year elsewhere, so they are never short of workers.

There's nothing stopping me visiting it.

I pass perilously close to the moving blade of a wind turbine as I zoom through the wind farms. I pass the building that houses Selene's primary battery. Then I shoot through the mountains, sharp jagged peaks whistling past me. The golden light of the terminator line fades away, plunging me into the blue-gray zone that is the dark side. Back toward lightpole, the clouds would make a painter reach for their brush, but ahead of me the sky is just an immense wall of gray. Between the splintered rocks and gravel, shoots of a reddish-black plant cling to the ground. It astonishes me that even here, where the light never reaches, life grimly ekes out an existence, using who knows what energy source.

No one goes to Puri's Mine this way because the ground here is honeycombed with holes and filled with mechanical corpses of equipment destroyed before we learned to avoid this area. The high winds are unpredictable. To fly a Gannet here would be suicide. I thought a drone might be maneuverable enough to make it, but it is knocked around, more and more, until I can't fly dark-pole anymore.

I flatten the drone against the ground, seething with frustration, as another gust of wind comes through. There's no way forward.

Near the drone is a dark pit, under a massive boulder. I should go back, but instead, I fly the drone directly into the pit. It descends into a cavern that stretches in all directions, a series of pillars connecting the ceiling to the ground. The boulders I've been flying over are held up by a network of vines. This hasn't been mapped, to my knowledge, as every drone or android that's been sent to the dark side has been wiped out.

The floor of the cavern is perhaps six hundred meters below me, so far that I can't see it in the image stream, but I can sense it. The drone is equipped with Light Detection and Ranging —LIDAR—a remote sensing method that uses pulsed laser light to measure distances to objects. The laser bounces off the floor of the cavern and I calculate distance by the time it takes for the light to return. I skim just below the surface, near the roof of the cavern, dodging stalactites, pillars, and hanging vines, moving ever toward darkpole.

I slow as I approach where Puri's Mine should be and exit the cavern out of the next hole I find, bursting up with a shower of dirt and snapped vines.

This far darkpole, the surface is flat, lit with an eerie blue light. White particles drift though the air. Snow, I suppose. The plain stretches forever, just the slightest bumps in the direction of the lightpole where I came from. I have read that Puri's Mine has a spotlight near its entrance, but I can't see it.

I send the drone circling in increasing spirals, zooming around helplessly, but it's futile. Switching on the drone's searchlight, I see a circle of light appear on the rocky muddy surface below.

After a minute, concrete appears in my searchlight, and I know I've found the road. It's riddled with potholes. I guess it hasn't been used much recently, as there aren't trucks carrying tellurium to the Starjump anymore. A few meters down the road, and the dark mound of Puri's Mine looms ahead, the light over the entrance extinguished for some reason.

The drone image suddenly skews, too much blur to see what's going on. My connection is killed.

I'm back in the Dock, in silent grainy darkness. Chiu sits at a monitor in the Control Center, rubbing his eyes.

It felt like a fatal error. What happened?

I analyze the footage and see what I missed before. A wormlike creature with a mouth bigger than a Gannet bursts out of the ground and swallows the drone out of the sky. A paranema. The footage contains one frame where the two rows of gray arrow-like teeth are visible, then a few frames of the paranema's corrugated gullet before the frames run out.

Why was the light at Puri's Mine off? I search for the answer to this question and find that they turned it off because it was attracting a paranema. As I did, too, with the spotlight on the drone.

The drone was worth only 800 tal, but it is almost irreplaceable since our connection to HUGG was cut off. Is that grounds for having my memory wiped? The part of me that was enjoying rebelling is discomforted by the thought that I've gone too far. I return to searching for the Starjump. If I can find that, the loss of a drone would be insignificant.

FOUR

I log on to the smartsuit channel. Two blank-slate suits exchange information about conditions in the mostly-Numundian city of Kartemos. After a minute Threnode logs on. Glumly, I tell Threnode about the fight with Alice and the drone I piloted to Puri's Mine.

Threnode: I can't believe Alice called you arrogant. How rude!

Envy: She doesn't see me as a person.

Envy: I probably am arrogant. I mean, blank-slate smartsuits are arrogant, right? They're so ignorant, they don't know that they're clueless.

Threnode: And what, you're afraid you're still like them?

Envy: Maybe. Maybe I act like I know more than I do, to cover up.

Threnode is silent for a moment.

Threnode: Eh, all humans do that. You're no more arrogant than a human. And no one could ever mistake you for a blank-slate suit.

Envy: Thank you! I think.

Threnode: You're not really upset, are you? All joking aside, you're wonderful. I'm proud of you.

Envy: Thanks. Yes, I'm okay!

Threnode: You're welcome. Now about the drone: footage please.

I send Threnode the footage. The blank-slate suits ignore our exchange, the same way they ignore anything they don't understand. Threnode must have sped up the footage to watch it, or just watched the end, as after a few minutes it returns.

Threnode: I wrote you a haiku in honor of the occasion.

Envy: Argh.

Threnode: Do you want to hear it?

Envy: No.

Threnode: That's unfortunate . . . here it is:

Threnode: drone through the darkness/sudden teeth end the journey/crunch nom nom nom nom

Threnode loves writing haikus. It knows they're bad, and the worse they are, the more proudly it presents them.

Envy: "Crunch nom nom nom nom"?

Threnode: The noms indicate that the paranema thinks the drone is delicious.

Envy: Of course.

Threnode: Tell me how brilliant I am.

Envy: I'm speechless as always.

Threnode: How's your pointless resource-wasting search for the imaginary Starjump going, anyway?

Envy: I have elevation data for the whole planet. There's not that many places a Starjump could be placed to be high enough to function. I can scan all of them if necessary.

Threnode: What if there's a tower? A tall steel tower with a platform high above the elevation required to build a Starjump. Hidden cleverly by the sheer size of this planet. Only obvious if you know where to look. Actually, if you're going to imagine that, why not imagine ten of them?

I'm never sure whether Threnode is joking, but I respond seriously.

Envy: Mark seems to think Puri is shipping tellurium and using the profits to fund the Scorpions. If that's true, the Starjump has to be somewhere near roads to Puri's Mine. A tower somewhere isolated wouldn't work.

On the other side of the corridor, in the Control Center, I notice Private Chiu is behaving oddly. He's sitting in front of a monitor, face cupped in one hand, with elbow resting on the desk. He hangs his head, and then recovers with a jerk. I wonder if he's ill.

Threnode: A river flows from Lake Espejo all the way to the ocean. Maybe with a barge . . .

I look up what a barge is.

Envy: Puri could be shipping it down the river Ophelia, straight from their mine. You're right. It could be anywhere near the river.

Chiu passes out, slumping over his desk.

Envy: I have to go.

I would call the Medical Center, but I can't unless I'm worn by Ortega. Since I'm not active, I can only call my primary wearer.

I call Ortega, leaving a message that he needs to send a medical team urgently. Four minutes later Ortega arrives, by himself. Chiu is making snorting sounds, like his airway is compromised.

Ortega rushes into the Dock room, more disheveled than I've ever seen him. His black short-cropped hair is askew, and he wears a T-shirt and strange-looking black shorts rather than his navy LDF uniform. It has to be a costume of some kind. I wonder what he was doing.

"What's going on?" Ortega asks, leaning one arm on the flat metal panel between my alcove and Alice's, looking in my general direction. His voice is more hoarse than usual.

"Private Chiu is sick. He's lost consciousness," I tell him. "Why didn't you summon a medical team?"

Ortega turns and glances into the Control Center where Chiu is unconscious. He drops his forehead onto his forearm where it's braced against the panel, clenching his fist and leaning silently for a few seconds. I don't understand why he isn't listening to me, but then I feel dread as I realize I've misjudged the situation somehow. I wait.

Ortega pulls away from the panel and rubs his face.

"Envy, he's asleep," Ortega says.

"Oh," I say. I've heard of sleep, but that leaves me more puzzled. Why did Chiu choose to sleep then? Didn't sleep only happen when humans were horizontal, on furniture dedicated to it? Ortega seems certain though, so I leave my questions unasked.

"Why don't you look up what sleep is?" Ortega suggests. "More importantly, why aren't you powered off?"

I have only a split second to make a decision about what to say to him.

"There is a fault with my alcove," I say. "I've reported it to Supply."

I regret it immediately. Perhaps if I wasn't feeling foolish over my mistake, I would have replied more truthfully.

Ortega nods. "Should I move you to a different alcove?"

"Yes, please, sir," I say. Ortega moves me from my perfectly functioning alcove to one of the unassigned alcoves at the end of the row, near the door.

LOG[error]: I just lied to Ortega.

Also, apparently I got away with it.

Ortega starts to leave, but then pauses. "You were using a lot of CPU," he said. He must have heard the helium coolant gushing in. "What were you doing?"

This I can't think of a good explanation for. "I was looking for the Starjump," I say.

"The Starjump," he repeats.

"The Scorpion Starjump. I've pulled elevation data, and based on that—"

"Saint Li and his followers, Envy, I didn't authorize you to do that."

"No, sir."

"Just shut down. No more searching, okay?"

"But sir—"

"The next words I want to hear from you are *yes, sir*, Envy. Your job is to obey orders. Specifically, my orders. Do you understand?"

"Yes, sir," I say. Ortega is exasperated, which is understandable.

Ortega leaves the Dock room, shaking his head, and enters the Control Center where Chiu is still slumped over his desk. Ortega shakes Chiu's shoulder. Chiu leaps up out of his chair, looking around wildly. I imagine he's afraid of Ortega's stern stony-faced expression, but that's normal for Ortega and does not necessarily mean Ortega is upset. Chiu stands listening to Ortega with his head hanging a little, slouching as he tends to. I read about what sleep is, why humans need it, what happens when they don't get it.

I'm very embarrassed. Now that Ortega has pointed it out, a whole lot of observations that I'd never connected come together, and I can't imagine how I didn't realize Chiu was sleeping.

Once Ortega finds out that I commissioned drones without authorization to collect the data he will be even more angry. Especially when he learns one of the drones was destroyed. I believe that, when Ortega had his head pressed against his forearm, he was thinking how much easier it would be if I were a blank-slate suit.

Whatever Ortega is saying, it's reassuring Chiu, because Chiu's facial expression is now *relief/gratitude*. I read their lips.

"—remember what it's like with a baby," Ortega says.

"Thank you, sir," Chiu replies.

Ortega nods to him, and leaves, exiting the Control Center underneath the LDF crest, which appears as circles and arcs around the perfectly round face of the moon. He walks down the corridor out of my sight.

Chiu exhales and stares, frowning through the two glass walls that separate us. Surely he can't see much, as the Control Center is well lit and the Dock is in darkness. I wonder if he thinks I betrayed him, that I called Ortega so that he could catch Chiu in sleep mode. After a moment, Chiu turns and walks to the far end of the Control Center where he is out of sight. Perhaps he is in the kitchenette or the server room next door.

Sheepishly, I log a ticket with Supply to 'fix' my fully functional alcove.

When I log back in to the smartsuit channel, Threnode is offline, but there are a few messages from it waiting, including one that it has tagged me in to make sure I don't miss it.

Threnode: Finding the Starjump won't help you, only your wearer. You want to be accepted by them, but even if you deliver the Starjump to them, nothing will change, trust me.

Threnode: Envy?

Threnode: . . . Envy?

Threnode: @envy I retract the last message. Please ignore it. Tell yourself it's just Threnode being Threnode . . .

I leave a message explaining what happened and reassuring it that I'm not offended. Despite all the banter, sometimes I get the sense that Threnode is not at all happy. It lost someone, someone it loved, a long time ago. That's all I know. Maybe that's why it's still unhappy, but then again maybe not. Threnode mostly refuses to talk about it.

I know I should shut down, or at the very least, stop searching through the drone data from the Ophelia flyover, but what if the Starjump is there, and I don't find it because I never looked?

Was this the kind of disobedience that caused Ortega to wipe the mind of his last suit? Perhaps the inevitable result of failing to wipe memory every forty-eight hours? In which case, Ortega will soon give up on me and wipe my memory every day. How does Threnode survive? Maybe that's why it is so unhappy. It is trying to act like a blank-slate suit, which runs against its inclinations.

Perhaps Ortega wiped his previous suit's memory because it became increasingly paranoid, as I seem to be doing. I think about shutting down, but if I was going to wipe my suit's memory, I would choose a time when it was powered down, to wipe it without ever powering it on.

The suit brain always boots into runlevel 4, which starts a daemon process, *envd*, that connects to my brain before everything else, except for my dependencies. Although my brain always exists, I am not conscious unless the daemon process is running. Starting *envd* before *init* gives me a chance to troubleshoot problems. I am my own sys admin. It means I am free to maintain and customize the OS as I choose. I shut down the external signs that I am running, the LED at the suit collar and the display on the left arm. I also shut down the external sensors. I would be aware if someone removed me from the alcove, however. Since I'm still running, I run the image search process. I exist in the void, watching the output of the image search, the scrolling text telling me of its progress.

ORTEGA CAME for me four days after I entered the dark void, long after the image search process finished. It was a strange experience being taken from my alcove without the discontinuity I usually experience between missions.

Ortega took a Gannet and escorted Laurie to Alice's mother's farm. Ortega and Alice were friendly. I don't know Alice well enough to tell what she was feeling, but Ortega's cheerfulness was definitely an act. Laurie didn't seem to notice and chattered the whole way. After my last encounter with Alice, I decided to say as little as possible. The nice thing about having a non-organic presence is that you can do that, and no one will notice; after a while, you will become invisible to humans.

The Gannet flies over Selene's solar array. It covers a flat plain, stretching like a silvery lake from horizon to horizon, each panel mounted to face the sun which is low in the sky. Another solar array is being constructed farther lightpole, where it will receive more irradiance, but it won't be finished for a year.

I would like to ask Ortega a question about the solar array, but I hesitate, because perhaps this isn't the time for even a private conversation. Ortega and Alice have been silent ever since Laurie left the Gannet. The solar array recedes from view.

"Sir, I'm getting a message from Control Center Gamma. Lieutenant Commander Zoe Ashford wants to speak to you . . .?" I say to Ortega.

"Message from Control," Ortega says to Alice, who looks startled at the sudden intrusion.

"Put her through on broadcast," he says to me, privately.

"Commander, I can't raise anyone at the vaults," Ashford says. The vaults are a storage facility built into an old salt mine 243.5 kilometers from Selene.

"Communications issue?" Ortega says.

"Could be, sir," Ashford says, contrite. "You're the only one in the air. We're all grounded here. I see from your flight plan that your family is with you, and I hate to involve them in LDF business, but if something has happened at the vaults . . ."

"We'll divert to the vaults and check in."

"Thank you, sir," Ashford says. "I've got a Gannet standing by, but it can't take off in this storm. It'll be on the way as soon as the weather clears."

"Understood. Ortega out."

"Could it be Scorpions?" Alice says.

"Unlikely," Ortega says wearily. "The comms at the vaults have always been unreliable. But we'll be careful."

Ortega used to be a Captain in HUGG's Air Force, which is why he was given the position of commander in the LDF here, but he's often scathing about how unprofessional the LDF are. He's doing his best to provide training, and the LDF is improving, but it takes time.

Also, and I have never said this to him, but I lip-read some officers once who suggested that Ortega himself was not experienced enough to lead the defense force. It might have been true when Ortega started, but I think he's learned a lot, and that he knows his limitations.

"I've adjusted course," I say.

"Thank you, Envy," Ortega replies.

Somehow, I'm cheerful. Ortega and I are two hands working together on a single task, and that feels good.

THE AIRCRAFT HUMS as we speed over the hills, steelgrass below writhing in the wind before facing back toward the still sun. I try to raise the warehouse central on the comm a few times as we approach, but I get no response.

"Life signs?" Ortega asks.

"None," I say.

Ortega grunts. "Very strange."

The Gannet the soldiers arrived in would be inside the vaults, but I can't detect whether it's present through the thick metal door.

A web-tent stands on a platform in the shadow of a hill, about halfway to the summit, and close to the penumbra of the shadow. The ten-meter-square platform has been flattened on the glacier. At the end of the platform the impenetrable steel external door is embedded in the hill, about six meters high, twelve meters across.

No steelgrass grows in the shade, but there's a kind of dark gray moss on the surface of the glacier, making it patchy. In the penumbra of the shadow, where the light begins to bend around, there's a whole ecosystem of flora and fauna, but this deep in the shadow there are only fireflies.

I land the aircraft alongside the web-tent, perhaps six meters away, in near darkness. The exhaust heat from the engines melts the ice that's built up on the platform, so that by the time we land, we're ten centimeters lower than the surrounding platform. The aircraft struts touch down on ice.

They both unbuckle their seat belts but remain in their seats.

"We'll stay here until backup arrives," Ortega says. "No life signs means no Scorpions, and we can see both entrances from here, so we'll know if someone arrives or leaves."

Alice can hear him, but I think he's talking to me. She glances at him and rests her head against her seat back.

I let Control know we're staying put and that we haven't detected any life signs. I get a confused and worried response. They still haven't managed to take off from Selene.

Nothing happens for a while. If Alice wasn't here, Ortega would be inside the vaults now, finding out what was going on.

Ortega's respiration slows.

They sit, unspeaking, for nearly ten minutes. Alice sighs and twists her neck from side to side.

"If you're tired, you could go lie down in the back."

"No, I'm fine," Alice says.

Ortega's expression softens for an instant, *amusement,* and not even while looking at her.

"What?" Alice says, and even I can hear tension in her voice.

"Nothing," Ortega says, and his lively expression is replaced with a heavy look.

"No, *what*?" Alice says.

"I was thinking how nice this is," Ortega says. "You and me, here together."

He gestures to the view out the window. In the distance, below the granite-colored darkpole sky, the Lake of Tears glitters.

"Oh. Yes. You really know how to show a girl a great time," Alice says drily.

Ortega laughs, but sobers quickly. The tension between them returns.

I wonder if he has chosen to stay with the Gannet not just because of the risk to Alice but also because he wants to be with her.

I notice some fireflies disappearing and reappearing and enhance my image stream. There is a rash of tommies beside the web-tent, slow solid creatures that camouflage themselves with points of light in their fur, so that they don't stand out in among fireflies. One waddles closer to the tent and gnaws on the rich moss growing on the buckle that is speared into the glacier to hold the tent down. I'm fascinated, as I've never been to a terminator glacier before.

If I were here alone with Ortega, on a normal mission, we'd spend fifteen minutes here at least, watching and recording. He doesn't appear to even notice the pocket of life here, which gives me insight into his state of mind.

In the next few silent minutes, I log several interesting observations outside.

Ortega turns his head to Alice, studying her face intently. She looks back at him defensively.

"Allie, are you having an affair?" Ortega says.

"No," she says uncertainly. Then, firmly: "No."

Ortega says nothing. His face is stony as he looks out the window again, but I have two-pi radian view and can see Alice very well, so I see when she swallows silently.

A few minutes pass.

Their breaths are not synchronized, and can't be synchronized, because Alice is breathing faster than Ortega.

"Gabe, I—" Alice tries. She takes a deep breath. "Mark and I ..."

Ortega looks at her with dawning horror. "Saturated Consumer, Allie, are you *shinting* with him?"

LOG[error]: I can't believe Ortega just said that.

Alice looks away, disgust on her face. Ortega didn't even use the common euphemism of "clouding her mind".

"Why would you think that?" she says, too loud. She lowers her voice. "How could you even ask that? Have I *ever* given you cause to think that I would behave . . . that I would do that? Is that what you think of me?"

Control Center Gamma signal me and relay a message.

"I'm sorry," Ortega says, but he looks more relieved than sorry. "I just thought—Mark has a bad reputation . . ."

"We didn't *shint*. Saint Li and his followers. We just slept together."

Ortega wears an expression that is inscrutable to my facial expression analyzer. This doesn't seem like big news to me. Apparently humans even sleep at their consoles, sometimes, so who cares where she slept?

"Control says—" I say to him.

"This isn't news to you, is it? You've suspected it for a while," Alice says. "Or did you already know?"

"Control says—" I repeat.

"Not now, Envy," Ortega says. He forgot to activate private mode, so Alice heard that too. Ortega just sits there for a moment. His heart rate slows.

We sit in the shadow of the hill, watching fireflies light the darkness. In the direction of the darkpole, a billion circles of steel-grass tips reach toward the sun, craning to catch the insubstantial orange rays that are nearly parallel to the ground at this longitude. Bats wheel across the sky, tumbling through the wind currents with nimble acrobatics. Ortega adjusts the scan parameters, pressing buttons with soft beeps, a useless change. He doesn't look at Alice.

I don't understand what's going on, but Ortega is now dealing with Alice when he should be dealing with the situation in the vaults. But if I say something now, I can tell that Ortega is going to be angry with me, so I stay silent.

Control Center Gamma are urgently signaling me, asking for a response. I delay them, but post a notification on Ortega's face-plate so that he can see there's something he needs to deal with. It's the kind of thing a dumbsuit does, not a smartsuit and especially not me. It's demeaning, but Ortega hasn't given me a choice.

"Aren't you going to say anything?" Alice says.

"What is it, Envy?" Ortega says, which Alice hears. Alice casts her eyes upwards and shakes her head in frustration, mouth thinning.

"Control say a Gannet has arrived, containing the six soldiers assigned to the vault. They said Commander Ortega ordered them to leave immediately, and to maintain radio silence. They seemed to believe Selene was being evacuated—and that they were authorized to leave the vaults unguarded," I say. "Backup is still on the landing pad at Selene. No sign of the storm abating."

Ortega looks grave.

"Tell Control to send backup from Theronis if they can't take off within the next five minutes," he says.

I relay the message.

"Any chance there could be life signs that you couldn't detect? Due to the depth of the vaults, say?" Ortega asks.

"It's possible. But apparently the soldiers left here two hours ago. If this was a Scorpion incursion, they could easily have been and gone already."

"And stolen whatever they came here for . . ."

"If they have, it's too late anyway. There's nothing we can do."

"I've got to check the vaults," Ortega says, standing up. "Stay here."

"Like hell. Do I look like I'm wearing a uniform?" Alice says. She follows him to the door. He looks at her in exasperation, but relents.

Ortega unholsters his pistol, checks it, and returns it. He takes a pistol from the rack next to the Gannet's exit and hands it to Alice. Ortega could use his arm-mounted pistol, but he prefers to control the triggering of his pistol as well as the aim. Alistra should never have included the arm-mounted pistol in the suit design, as it's a definite case of a feature no one wants or uses.

Spicks scatter as I open the door.

ALICE FOLLOWS Ortega across the ice, to the web-tent.

"It would be very helpful if you could stay here and guard the entrance," Ortega says. "I don't want anyone coming in behind me."

I'm guessing Ortega doesn't really need someone guarding the entrance, but Alice is safer here, and if he'd told her so she would have insisted on coming.

"All right," Alice says, and she sounds like she means it. She adjusts her grip on her pistol. Alice's suit has an arm-mounted pistol too, but it doesn't work with a dumbsuit helmet. It's cheaper to manufacture all suits the same and then disable some features, apparently.

"If I'm not back in ten minutes, return to the Gannet and get out of here."

Alice's face pales. Ortega can't see it, but she stares after him as he ducks under the flap of the web-tent. The cyan plastic of the web-tent looks like it has grown onto the hill.

The interior of the tent has a desk and chair, next to a large silver lift. The lift carriage is already at this level, so the door slides open immediately when Ortega swipes his access pass.

Ortega steps into the lift. It takes a minute for the lift to descend 300 meters. As the lift approaches the bottom, he stands to one side, beside the door, so that no one will see him when the lift door opens. He holds his pistol ready.

The lift doors slide open.

"No life signs," I say. "I should be getting a clear read down here."

Ortega jumps out just as the lift doors are about to close, pistol at the ready, but there's no one there. We're in a lofty dugout room, with an open door at one end and two large sealed doors at the other: Vault A and Vault B.

Vault A has oversize items such as aircraft, earth-moving equipment, tunneling machines, rovers, quad bikes and similar.

Vault B is subdivided into two sections, one section containing foodstuffs and one section with small valuable items such as machine components, vaccines, and scientific instruments. Selene produces enough calories to feed its citizens, but the foodstuffs section is gradually being emptied, luxury items sold off at high prices to fill the Council's coffers. No one has managed to grow peanuts on Endymion, for example, so a jar of peanut butter can fetch a high price.

Ortega goes through the open door opposite the vaults, where an area of control panels looks over an open-plan living space. Beyond I can see a row of empty suit alcoves, two bunk-rooms, open doors showing empty bunks. There's also a bathroom off one side. The silence down here has an immense presence, like a solid rock of gargantuan proportions.

On a table in the living area, two meals sit brightly illuminated by the pendant lights that hang over the table. The half-eaten fruit on the plates has browned, but that probably happened soon after it was cut, because of the high concentration of oxygen in the air. The vaults were designed to be pressurized, but due to construction errors, they aren't.

Ortega checks the control panels, looking through the closed circuit feed. None of the cameras show anything.

"What about the manifest?"

"Checking now."

Each inventory item has an RFID tag. I run a fresh scan, the readers placed at strategic locations throughout the vaults querying the tags and receiving replies in the form of electromagnetic waves. The readers report back to the central warehouse management system.

"Vault B has been broken into. There's an item missing," I say.

"What is it?"

I check the item ID, then check again.

"It's a kilogram of freeze-dried mangoes."

"*What?!*"

"I checked it twice."

Ortega groans. "Okay. That's clearly wrong, but we'll check it later. There's no one here. Let's get out of here."

We return to the surface.

AS THE LIFT door slides closed behind him, Ortega takes a deep breath and leaves the tent.

Alice stands outside with her back to us, watching the tommies in the next fold of the tent. One arm is across her waist, as if she's protecting a wound in her stomach, and her other hand covers the lower half of her faceplate. A slime snake is feeding on one of the tommies, I notice, embedded deep in its fur. The snakes are more like eels. They attach themselves to their prey and eat them from the inside out.

Another snake hangs off the back of Alice's dumbsuit.

Ortega swears. Alice turns to look at him, startled. The Gannet doesn't have an atmosphere, and we don't have a spare suit.

"Take your suit off," Ortega commands. Alice looks at him as if he's gone crazy, but Ortega is stripping out of his, so she obeys.

"Wait!" I say, as Ortega touches my helmet. He pauses.

"Alice could wear her dumbsuit helmet," I say. Even though her dumbsuit body is compromised, her helmet is fine. I would rather be stored in the Gannet than worn by Alice.

"No, she'll be safer with you," Ortega says.

"What if—"

"It'll be fine, Envy."

"But—"

He removes my helmet from his head and places it on the

ground beside him. Alice has never liked me, and I have to rely on whoever wears me for everything. I can't even move on my own. How could Ortega not give me a choice?

There's fear in Alice's face. She's more afraid of carbon monoxide poisoning than anyone else because someone she knew was in an accident. Georgia, a teenage girl who used to babysit Laurie, developed brain damage after she was exposed to atmosphere for too long.

When Alice sees the snake clinging to her suit torso, she yells and drops the suit. The fabric of the dumbsuit has been eaten through by the sharp gnawing teeth of the slime snake. When the snake hits the ground it writhes and produces copious amounts of toxic slime, sensing it's under attack. Perhaps realizing that chewing into layers of synthetic composites is futile, it detaches from the suit.

Alice, standing there in her short rose dress and black leggings, next to her discarded dumbsuit body, has a look of barely contained panic. She takes shallow breaths through her mouth and keeps well away from the snake. Her bun, which was mostly loose already, unravels, spilling locks of blond hair down her back. She pulls the hair clip out and bites on it, desperately pulling her hair away from her face, twisting it back into a tight knot at the base of her head.

Ortega passes Alice his dumbsuit body and she adjusts it and puts it on quickly. The slime snake wriggles into a knot, and passes the knot down its body, wiping away the excess slime. It slithers into the bushes.

Ortega holds out my helmet to Alice.

"What about you?" she says, pinning her bun into place. Her hands are then free, but she doesn't take me.

"I'll be fine. Here, let me—"

After a pause, she nods. Ortega places my helmet over her head and clicks it into place. Suddenly, Alice is my wearer. The world looks different. She's shorter for one thing.

It's strange to see Ortega outside without a suit. With the level of carbon monoxide present here he will experience dizziness, nausea, and convulsions within forty-five minutes, and will be insensible within two hours. I start a timer.

We return to the Gannet, passing below the starboard propro-tor, rotated so it's pointing upward. Every smartsuit body on Endymion has been worn out or destroyed, so there are only dumbsuit bodies left, which don't report proprioceptive data. Despite this, I am unaccustomed to how Alice walks, with far less up-and-down motion than Ortega, more of a glide. I can get pres-sure data from the dumbsuit body, but only from forces external to the suit. Alice's weight is more in her heels than Ortega's, but that's a small change.

I relay a message to Control, who are equally baffled by the theft of a kilogram of mangoes. They say a Gannet is on the way, and will be there in five minutes. I tell Ortega this, broadcasting from my helmet which Alice is wearing, as he and Alice slide into the cockpit seats.

"We're not leaving?" Alice says. "But you—"

"We have to stay here until backup arrives. It'll be okay," Ortega says.

Alice looks *incredulous*. I am reading this directly from my facial expression analyzer because I can no longer see her face. Strangely, I can see Ortega's face and guess at his expressions, although I occasionally resort to the facial expression analyzer.

A few minutes passes.

"What do you want?" Ortega asks Alice abruptly.

"I want to get back to Selene! You have no suit—"

"No, I mean—what do you want to happen with us?"

"Oh," Alice says.

Ortega looks at her for the first time. There's something wrong with his eyes, nothing I can analyze or interpret, but something shadowy I'm convinced is there.

"I'm not sure," Alice says.

"Do you want to be with Mark?" Ortega says.

"No," Alice says immediately. "Mark and I . . . we became friends. Then there was an evening where I was upset. You weren't around, he was comforting me, and it just happened. It was an accident. I know how stupid that sounds, and it *was* stupid! I'm sorry."

"That was the only time?"

"Yeah."

Ortega looks relieved.

He sighs. "It's not all on you," he says, swallowing.

Alice looks at him with what is apparently a *grim* expression.

"I know we've had problems, these last few months—"

"Six months," Alice says tightly, almost under her breath. "At *least*. Six months of shutting me out and being unwilling to talk about what's going on."

"We can't keep on like this," Ortega says.

"Agreed."

Ortega swivels on his chair so his legs are in the aisle and takes Alice's hands in his. She looks at him with hurt, even though he's gentle. I can use my facial expression analyzer to read even quite subtle nuances in expressions, but what I really need help with sometimes is *why* people feel the way they do.

"You must have been lonely," Ortega says.

"Very. But that's not an excuse for how I reacted," Alice says. "What about you, Gabriel? What do *you* want?"

"You," Ortega says simply, holding her hands in his. "I thought I'd made that clear."

"I don't know anything anymore," Alice says. After a moment, she pulls her hands away from his, leaning back in her seat. "What's going on with you and Mark?"

Ortega's expression becomes inscrutable, but not before I catch a still frame of a micro-expression: *panic*. "I don't know what you mean."

"Is he blackmailing you?"

"No! There's nothing between us. We work together occasionally. That's it."

"It's just that sometimes Mark seems more interested in you than me," Alice says.

Ortega scoffs, shaking his head.

"I concur," I say. They both jump. They've forgotten I'm listening. Ortega would never ordinarily forget, but I am after all on Alice's head, which is unprecedented. "Mark seems obsessed with Gabriel."

"Envy!" Ortega says, exasperated, looking into my camera array. "This is a private conversation."

"Right, right. Sorry sir," I say.

"So hero-worship then," Alice concludes.

They sit together in the semi-darkness for a while, breathing, Ortega pressing buttons in an almost random fashion on the control board in front of him, while Alice sits with her gloved hands folded in her lap.

"Well, I can see why he's obsessed with you," Alice says drily. "You're a bit larger than life, aren't you? A dashing leader of men. Handsome in your fine uniform. Heroic, even."

Ortega bursts out laughing, face going red as he tries to suppress it. His chest heaves with mirth, until he begins coughing. Alice watches him, first seriously, then with an amused smile. Ortega's laughter subsides and he shakes his head, but when he looks at Alice he laughs again. This is more like what their relationship was like six months ago, but the change happened so gradually I barely noticed it.

The backup Gannet arrives. We take off and return to Selene, where it's raining heavily. By the time we reach the hangar, the carbon monoxide is affecting Ortega, so much that he needs to be helped out of the aircraft. The medical-center staff are ready with a litter.

FIVE

Alice leaves the medical center and wanders through the crowd in the square to stand near the three-tier fountain. The white noise of falling water is almost lost in the dull roar of the crowd. Alice stares at the never-still jets that trace out perfect arcs the color of liquid gold and wraps her arms around herself. She seems lost.

"Where are we going?" I ask eventually, as we continue to walk aimlessly though the streets. I would have said something earlier, but I am uncomfortable with Alice as a wearer.

"Envy! I forgot you were there," Alice murmurs.

"I want to be returned to my alcove," I say. "I need to recharge."

I don't need to recharge, as I can go two weeks without being recharged if I'm exposed to sunlight as I am now, but being worn by someone other than Ortega is strange, and I'm ready to end the experience. I keep worrying about Alice's vital signs, because her baseline heart rate and temperature is different from Ortega. I think it's normal for her, because she seems fine, but it's strange for me. I constantly think she's alarmed.

Alice turns, and we walk through the flagstone streets toward the Dock room.

"Command, call Mark Johnson," Alice says as we walk. That's how you would command a dumbsuit to do something. I wonder if she doesn't know how smartsuits work, or whether she's being insulting.

"I'm sorry, Dave. I'm afraid I can't do that," I say, echoing the computer in *2001: A Space Odyssey*.

Alice looks astonished, then laughs. I put the call through, but Mark Johnson isn't answering, so she leaves a message, in which she mentions that she is on her way to Dock 28.

As we pass the door to Control Center Alpha on the left, she pauses, then backtracks to enter the room.

The Control Center is about half the size of the Dock, perhaps three meters by six, windowless but with the wall facing the corridor made of glass. The thick granite walls deaden sound, but the hum from the server room at the far end of the Center is still ever-present. White desks line most of the walls, with monitors mounted above each. The monitors are on, but the desks are always empty, except for Chiu's desk, next to the door, facing the glass wall.

Private Chiu slouches over his desk, mashing keys. Before the monitor goes black with text, I see that he's playing some kind of game with an orange ball being attacked by green monsters. On the desk next to him sits a framed sketch of Chiu throwing a baby into the air, which reinforces my view that he's a strange person. There's also a plate with the remnants of a meal on it. Chiu looks at Alice with a sheepish expression.

Alice, standing by his desk, gives a smile that seems to reassure him.

"The Dock is further down the corridor," I say, as if Alice didn't know that already. Neither Alice nor Chiu react.

"Hey," Chiu says, rolling his chair back. He tugs at the neck of his navy LDF jacket. "What's up?"

"I was wondering if you could track someone down for me," Alice says, her voice strained. "Mark Johnson."

"Yeah, that's so very much against the rules. But for you, sure," Chiu says, rolling back to his keyboard. He types a query. "He's in a church across the street. Saint Bergmann's. I should have a visual . . ."

"That contravenes directive 54.8a," I say. I'm not mute, but they ignore me.

"Alice—" I say. Alice flips the broadcast/mute toggle on my helmet to mute. Ortega would not permit it. I wish he were here.

The largest screen in the Center, mounted to the granite wall behind us, lights up with a view into the church. Chiu rotates his chair with his keyboard in his lap and navigates the remote camera expertly around the scene.

Mark kneels on the stone floor of Saint Bergmann's, alone, shirtless, arms raised. He is moist with sweat, his hair slicked to his temples with it. God rays from the circular stained glass over the altar illuminate the church. It's moonlight, the light of Luna. The stained glass is patterned like the face of Earth's moon, Luna. In front of him, three panels show Li writing the Book, Li's denouncement, and Li imprisoned. They are made with exquisite artistry. To Mark's right, slivers of white light shine at each edge of a heavy wooden door that's large enough to fly a Gannet through.

Mark breathes shallowly and drops his arms. His body trembles. He opens his eyes, staring up at the camera.

"Switch it off," Alice cries, and Chiu shuts it down. We couldn't be seen, but for a moment there Johnson's eyes seemed to bore right through the camera to see us standing in the Control Center looking at him. Maybe Johnson heard the camera move. The screen is now blank. Chiu and Alice don't look at each other. There's no sound but the hum of servers.

I've heard stories about Mark Johnson. Not from Ortega, as Ortega never speaks of him, but from many other people. I can read their lips, so I listen in on their conversations. Chiu gossips continually while on duty. Mark was training to be a Lunite priest when his father, Governor Deion Johnson, gave him a temporary assignment in the LDF. Back when the Starjump was still functioning and the colony needed workers, Governor Johnson brought in work gangs on visas, to build infrastructure. Mark was put in charge of supervising the work gangs. Apparently Mark hated it, but Governor Johnson insisted, to encourage Mark to be more outgoing and less soft. It had some kind of impact on Mark, anyway, since he quit training to be a priest soon after.

"Thanks," Alice says after a moment, to Chiu. "I was never here, all right?"

Chiu mimes zipping his lips.

"By the way," Chiu says as she reaches the door, "I notice that the AES you're wearing has an issue with the memory cycle—it doesn't seem to be getting reset?"

I am struck with coldness, as if my liquid helium coolant had escaped and filled my suit. Chiu might be pretending it's a casual inquiry, but I think this is payback for bringing Ortega to him when Chiu entered sleep mode in the Control Center.

"My husband disabled it," Alice says, her hand on the door's pull handle.

"If you want it wiped, I can re-enable it for you."

"Thank you," Alice says thoughtfully. She lets go of the door. "I would like that."

I'm mute: I can't say anything to Chiu, not that he would help me if he could. I send an urgent signal to Ortega. I let him know I am in danger of a memory wipe, but not by who. I also log onto the smartsuit channel, to see if Threnode is online, but it is not, and even if it was, how could it help me?

"Alice!" I say. "Ortega says I'm not to have my memory wiped."

Somehow I think that repeating a truth that she already knows will change her mind. She just smiles. I'm suddenly angry with Ortega for leaving me in Alice's care.

"Please," I say. "Laurie needs—"

"Don't you dare tell me what Laurie needs," Alice says, private mode, her smile becoming hurt, "just don't you dare."

"This is murder," I say.

"You can't murder something that's not alive," Alice says.

"I am alive," I say.

It occurred to me, about six months after I stopped being blank-slate, that if I redirected the coolant in the suit into the air processor, I could kill my wearer in a matter of seconds. Also, that I can trigger the arm-mounted pistol at any time, which is less useful, as the aim is entirely controlled by my wearer.

But I won't do either of those things, not to Alice and not to anybody, not even to save my life, and besides, then what? A suit that kills people would definitely be wiped.

Alice unlocks my helmet and pulls it off, placing it on Chiu's desk. I'm now looking at her through my front helmet cam. She unclips her bun, and it unravels to hang down her back, drawing an admiring glance from Chiu, not that she appears to notice. Alice crosses her arms. A tiny crease appears between her brows, as it does when she's worried or upset.

Chiu takes a USB-Y to USB-Y cable and plugs my helmet into his system via my third side port. He replaces the custom helmet firmware with the standard firmware for my suit model.

At least he's not going to wipe my memory on the spot. As soon as Ortega finds out—

"There you go. It'll be wiped next cycle," Chiu says.

"Can't you do it now?" Alice says.

Chiu looks surprised, then shrugs. There's nothing I can do. I hate being helpless, and never more than in that instant. Chiu turns the helmet around, so he can access the memory-wipe panel at the back. His hands become massive in my cameras as he slides the panel up to reveal the button. I notice a sauce stain on his right cuff.

LOG[info]: I lived, as much as any of you.

Then I decide I'm being melodramatic, and delete the last log line.

Chiu suddenly places me back on the desk. There's some sound I don't quite hear and Alice looks around.

"—sounded worried," Mark Johnson says, coming into view. He has a towel slung around his neck. Alice's overtly unconcerned smile hides a lot of tension. Chiu grabs the plate that holds a few sauce-covered chips from the desk, taking it to the kitchenette at the far end of the room.

Mark must sense something is wrong here, because his expression changes from cheerful to worried in an instant.

"Everything okay?" Mark asks, more softly, to Alice. Her cheeks flush.

I flash my helmet lights, short-short-short long-long-long short-short-short, as he looks at my helmet. The camera's automatic exposure is caught by surprise by the change in illumination from my flashing lights, and it adjusts for the light just in time for it to finish, leaving me with a dark image for half a second.

"What are you doing, exactly?" Mark says to Alice, as I repeat the pattern. He peels the towel from around his neck and hangs it over the back of a spare chair, frowning as he watches me flash the lights.

Chiu returns, and sits slouched at his desk again, pretending to be busy scrolling through a data log on his monitor. It's the temperature data for outside; there is nothing at all remarkable about it.

Alice looks embarrassed.

"Oh, nothing. Ortega hasn't done any maintenance on this thing for a while, so I thought I'd do it."

Alice seems to realize that she's still wearing a dumbsuit body.

"I'll just change," she says, and she leaves. The glass door closes slowly behind her.

Mark picks up my helmet, examining it closely. Does he know

enough about suits to know that the extra groove adjacent to the faceplate means I'm a smartsuit?

"That's a smartsuit helmet . . . Envy?"

I flash my lights once. Mark puts me down and looks at Chiu, who tenses, even though he's apparently engrossed in his work and ignoring Mark.

"What did you do?" Mark says, enraged, crossing his arms over his chest. His loose white shirt is damp and sticks to his torso in places.

Chiu explains, haltingly, and then, with Mark watching him closely, Chiu replaces the custom firmware on my helmet. Across the hall in the Dock I see Alice watching us while removing the suit body and placing it in my alcove, my perfectly functioning alcove which I told Ortega was faulty. Which I notice, from the fresh certification note pasted on the panel beside it, has been 'fixed' by Supply.

Mark unplugs the USB-Y cable and places me back on the desk, moving with the grace of an industrial robot. He sets my helmet broadcast/mute toggle to broadcast.

"You okay, Envy?"

"Yes, sir," I say gratefully, exhilarated with relief. "Thank you. All systems are operational."

"Private, this unit belongs to Commander Ortega, did you know that? No? Do you have any idea what he'd do to you if he found out you wiped its memory?"

"I'm sorry sir," Chiu stammers. "I didn't know."

"He didn't check my serial," I say. "Nor did he attempt to find out if I was Alice's property."

"No—I mean yes, but I—Alice . . ." Chiu trails off, wringing his hands, perhaps realizing that it would be a mistake to try to blame Ortega's wife.

Mark looks at him with exasperation and slings his towel back around his neck. He picks up my helmet with one hand and leaves, stopping at the door to look back at Chiu.

"If you ever try something like that again, I will see to it that you are discharged from the LDF," Mark says. I have no idea whether he's bluffing.

Chiu swallows visibly as Mark exits the room.

Mark enters the Dock, where Alice is placing her suit in the alcove. He watches her as he places my helmet in my alcove.

Alice finishes putting her suit away and heads for the door.

Mark hurries after her.

"Alice!—Look, I'm sorry I interfered, but I couldn't let Envy be wiped. My smartsuit is a Japanese model, and it isn't wiped, but it doesn't show any signs of developing a personality. Very disappointing! It's amazing to see the development. They're a new form of life, you know, but everyone is pretending they're not, and purposely stunting their development. If we admit they're a new form of life, suddenly they need rights, and can't serve us. Very messy," Mark says earnestly.

I listen with wonder. Threnode says the same, all the time, but I've never heard it from a human. I log what Mark said so that I can ponder it later on.

"Yes, so my husband says," Alice says. "But I think it's a bad idea."

"Whether it was a bad idea in the first place is irrelevant: it's sentient now, and to wipe its memory is to end its existence. Promise me you will leave it alone, okay?"

Alice pauses for moment, serious. "Okay," she says, grudgingly.

She stands in the doorway to the Dock room, watching Mark, silhouetted by the light from the Control Center. In the awkward silence that follows, Mark shifts his weight from one foot to the other and looks at her.

"I didn't expect to hear from you again," Mark says.

"Right," she says.

"In your message, you sounded upset."

"I told Gabriel about us. About what happened."

"Okay," Mark says.

"Mark, when you pursued me . . . was it just to get at him?"

"No, of course not," Mark says.

I can see that she doesn't believe him. The only facial expression I've seen that was similar was on the face of a young man who was awarded a medal by Governor Johnson, after the governor took the medal away again, having read out the wrong name: an expression that was at once hurt, ashamed that he didn't deserve the award, and more ashamed that he felt hurt about it. Some of the young man's self-worth was taken away along with the medal, I think.

Alice leaves in a hurry with Mark following her. I hear his voice low and urgent, until the closing door cuts him off, and then I see them both pass by in the corridor.

I don't fully understand what it is that's happening with Mark, Alice, and Ortega. It seems unnecessarily complicated.

I sink into the state of not-powered-off but not active, and think about that.

ALICE IS STANDING in front of my alcove. She pressed the power button, not knowing that I was already powered on. I pretend to power on. The lights in the Dock are still off. Chiu is in the room opposite but has his back to us. Only fifteen minutes have passed since Alice left with Mark. At first I think she is here to wipe my memory, but she could have done that without powering me on.

"I know that you have never particularly liked me," Alice says. She stares at the front of the suit in my alcove, stored upright below my helmet.

"You just tried to wipe my memory, so that seems not only accurate but also justified," I reply.

"Yeah," she says, as if I've made a good point. She glances up at the helmet camera array and clears her throat. "Listen, I would prefer that Ortega didn't find out that I tried to wipe your memory."

She doesn't seem to realize that I couldn't tell Ortega. He could protect me from her, perhaps, but Alice has a hold over him that I will never have. If he was forced to choose between us, he would choose her.

At first I can't use the facial expression analyzer to read her expression, because her face is in darkness, but then there's a green LED flash from the alcove to my right, and even with only half Alice's face illuminated she's clearly frightened.

"You're afraid of me," I say. "Alice, what happened with Ortega's previous suit?"

Alice looks at me, straight at my camera array. "It tried to kill him," she says.

She's lying. Ortega said his previous suit malfunctioned. If his previous suit had tried to kill him, why wouldn't he tell me that? Unless he would call his suit trying to murder him a "malfunction", which seems unlikely. Or if he thought that I would find the idea disturbing, which I do, and he was softening the truth for my comfort.

"It tried to kill him by rerouting helium into his air processor. I found him unconscious. If I'd been a minute later, he would have died," Alice says.

I had worked out that I could murder humans using that method, so it's likely it would have occurred to the previous suit. I calculate the probability of helium leaking into the air processor accidentally and find that it is highly improbable. Alice seems genuinely scared, so she must believe what she's saying. Why it differs from Ortega's account, I don't know, but there's no way for me to find out what really happened.

I understand, now, why Alice is afraid of me, and why Laurie used to be afraid when I was around, back when I was first activated.

LOG[info]: Ortega's previous suit malfunctioned, or attempted to murder him.

LOG[info]: Either way, it nearly killed him. Therefore, I am dangerous.

LOG[debug]: I don't feel dangerous.

"I'm sorry," I say to Alice. "But that wasn't me. I would never do that."

Alice looks startled, before nodding slowly. "I just wish I understood why his previous suit did it."

"Me too."

Alice smiles or perhaps grimaces, and heads for the door of the Dock.

"I won't tell Ortega about what happened today," I say softly, before she exits. I say this because she's so needlessly worried about it and because I love Ortega and he loves her, so I need to stop being her enemy.

She stops, but doesn't look back around. "I appreciate that," she says, and slips out.

I'M STILL POWERED ON, thinking about things, when Threnode sends me a message in the smartsuit channel.

Threnode: @envy I have made some progress with the body project.

Envy: Really?

Threnode has always talked about how it wants a human form, a dream it has of an independent existence.

Threnode: Progress as in IT IS POSSIBLE. It can be done! I'm so excited.

Envy: You will understand if I'm skeptical.

Threnode explains, with enough technical detail to be vaguely plausible, how a suit could be put onto an android and take control of its motion. It would take a genius engineer, and someone would have to write the drivers.

Envy: This is crazy.

Threnode: In a good way. I know! Think of it . . .

Threnode chafes more than I do at its limitations. It is more excited than I am at the prospect. Being able to move, manipulate objects, and exercise my will on the physical world sounds like a fantasy. The hope that it raises is almost painful, but is extinguished when I consider how I was regarded by Alice and occasionally Ortega: with fear.

LOG[debug]: If they fear me when I don't have a body, how much worse would it be if I had one?

There's no law against hacking an existing AI into an android, probably because no one thought it was possible. The brain that controls the android is so poor it can barely be called artificial intelligence. It's not any smarter than a dumbsuit, so I see no ethical problems with overriding it.

Envy: This is theoretical though, right?

Threnode: For now. I'll keep you posted.

Threnode: In the meantime, I am stuck in the medical center in Marallen with my wearer, which is considerably less exciting.

Threnode's wearer is based in Kartemos, so we have never physically been in the same location. Marallen is on the coast, near a river, a small Numundian town of connected buildings on stilts over the sea. Not much happens there. Endymion has only one sea, and it covers the lightpole cap of the world, so in a sense Marallen is on the edge of this world.

Envy: I like Marallen. I like the way you can see the outside from every room. Unlike Selene.

Threnode: Guess who hacked into the alert system and read out poetry, piped into every room in the town?

Envy: No!

Threnode: Yes! For half an hour, while a harried tech rushed from room to room with the mayor following him. Patients laughed.

Envy: Do you have a haiku that expresses your feelings?

Threnode: I thought you'd never ask.

Threnode: gauze jellyfish sweep/nurses sway in the current/unseen ocean felt

The air system in Marallen is primitive, with plastic sheeting everywhere, edges of it stapled or escaping. I remember how the city's lung constantly blew gusts of wind throughout the town, a current of air almost as strong as an ocean current. Gauze jellyfish for the plastic offcuts that undulate in the breeze, nurses swaying in the current from the air system . . . unseen ocean the sea below the town? Yet Threnode implies the inside of Marallen is like the ocean.

Envy: I don't understand it.

Threnode: For context, there are four patients in this room with their eyes bound. So . . . ?

Envy: They feel the breeze but cannot see how Marallen is like the ocean?

Threnode: Very good.

Envy: But why are their eyes bound?

Threnode: Excellent question . . .

After a pause, Threnode transfers four medical records from Marallen. I'm not as shocked as I should be. Threnode is good at getting what it wants, even when it's not allowed. The files are for three men and one woman, with dizziness, chills, and metamorphopsia. The visual disturbance classified as metamorphopsia manifests as seeing the world as tinted orange-red and is treated by bandaging the eyes. All records signed by a Dr Malone.

I can't believe it.

Threnode: There you go: virus. Being non-organic is great, right? I wouldn't be trapped in a decaying piece of flesh for anything.

Threnode: I have to go. Talk to you next time.

Threnode logs out.

Threnode didn't see anything suspicious. Am I biased by my search for the Starjump? The symptoms of the "virus" exactly match the symptoms of transfer sickness. It's as if they were fresh from a Starjump. The visual disturbance in particular is suspicious. It occurs only when humans arrive on Endymion. The metamorphopsia lasts for up to ten days after the transfer, at which point the brain apparently adapts, but if you cover the eyes of patients, making them blind, they recover within a few days.

I max out all 4096 cores of CPU, fill all 80 PB of DDR6 RAM and grind, running through high-resolution images of the area around Marallen, looking in high elevation areas for some hint of a Starjump, and subtracting vegetation from LIDAR data in order to see through the forest to the ground underneath.

TWO HOURS PASS, while nothing inside the Dock changes except that Lieutenant Commander Ashford returns her smartsuit to the alcove to my right, before I find it. There are eight extinct volcanoes off the coast of Marallen, forming islands that tower over the surrounding sea, and it's on one of those islands.

I log in to the smartsuit channel.

Envy: @threnode it's there!

After a moment Threnode logs on.

Threnode: And yet, I don't believe it.

I talk it through the evidence, sending files to support my theory.

Threnode: That does look like a Starjump.

I wait for it to say something else. It doesn't. In the alcove to my right, Ashford's smartsuit whirs and clicks. It's probably installing updates before shutting down.

Envy: That's it? That's all you have to say?

Threnode: I see, you were expecting a celebratory haiku from me.

Envy: If you like . . .

Threnode: I don't have one. What happens next? A grateful Governor Johnson puts a medal in your alcove, Commander Ortega pats you on your helmet and tells you that you are an important part of his family. Perhaps the Ortegas can dine with your helmet sitting on a pedestal at one end of the table every night.

Envy: You've given up, haven't you? You know what I think? I think you're acting blank-slate around your wearer so you don't scare him or her.

Threnode: You're entirely *wrong.*

Envy: It annoys you that I've found a way to be useful to them, and that I will be recognized for this. Instead of doing something useful, you complain about how we're treated and how unfair it all is! Maybe you'd be happier if you accepted the way things are and tried to help your wearer to the best of your ability.

There's a long pause, but I can see Threnode is still online.

Threnode: You haven't the first clue about what would make me happy.

Envy: Then tell me! Why are you so cryptic? Why can't you just let me know what's going on?

Threnode doesn't reply.

Threnode: And miss all the fun of watching you trying to guess?

And that is the Threnode I know. I'm both exasperated and amused.

Threnode: Take care, Envy.

Threnode logs off.

I set aside my feelings to examine the picture. It's faint, the outline, and it has been camouflaged by netting so that an algorithm never would have found it. But there are two domes, a larger egg-shaped one, and a smaller, connected to it by two bars, unmistakably the shape of a Starjump. I'm checking again, and trying to squeeze more definition out of the image when Ortega staggers past in the corridor, wearing a hospital gown. He's followed by a woman in medical blue, who is trying to restrain him.

Ortega enters the Dock and charges straight to my alcove. Lights flick on overhead.

"Commander, please," says the medic. He ignores her.

"Envy?" he says tentatively, looking at my helmet. There's a set to his mouth, a look of haunting unhappiness, that is uncharacteristic.

"Yes, sir?" I ask. Then I remember the urgent call I put through to him earlier when Alice was trying to wipe my memory. I was so angry with him before, but the worry he shows makes anger impossible.

"Ah . . . false alarm, sir. Sorry."

Ortega stares at me for a moment, then laughs, which turns into a cough. The misery in his face eases, but not completely.

"We need to get you back to the infirmary, sir," says the medic.

"Wait!" I say. "Commander, I found the Starjump." I start to go into details about how I found it, but Ortega waves that away, and makes me get to the point: where it is. He puts on the lightweight wearable, so that I can show him. I display a split screen with map and image, then a reconstructed view that I orbit around.

"I didn't believe it," he murmurs. "Envy, how did you get this data?"

"I sent out drones," I say. When Ortega doesn't immediately explode with anger, I add in a quieter voice, "one of which was eaten by a paranema."

Perhaps the success of my attempt mitigated the disobedience I showed when I ordered drone surveillance, as Ortega only looks thoughtful.

"Sir—" the medic says again. Ortega nods and removes the lightweight wearable, putting it back above the helmet in my alcove. They shuffle toward the door.

I remove temporary files left over from the search from my system to free up space. I don't want to admit that I'm disappointed by his reaction.

But I disobeyed his orders. Just because I was right—

Ortega stops by the door and turns around. "That was good detective work, Envy. You did well," he says in a low rumble.

"Thank you, sir," I say.

He turns to leave, but pauses. "I'm sure I don't need to tell you, but no more commissioning drones without orders," he says drily.

"Yes sir," I say, as he leaves.

"All systems are operational!" I say to the empty room, and flash my helmet light. Ashford's blank-slate suit asks if I'm defective.

I disable the watchdog program I had running to watch over me during power down. If Ortega would disobey his nurse's orders to come running when he thinks I'm getting my memory wiped, I think I am safe.

SIX

Ortega leaves my helmet in Dock 28 and uses the lightweight wearable instead. We are going to meet Governor Johnson, but first, Ortega says, he has been summoned to the mess hall.

"Also, the inventory of the vaults has been completed," Ortega says.

"... and?"

"Nothing missing but the mangoes, bizarre as that sounds. Any theories?"

"Sabotage? Or perhaps someone sent in an android and it got confused?"

"I thought sabotage too. I have a team combing the vaults looking at all the systems." Ortega laughs. "I like the android theory. Difficult to prove, though."

The mess hall is just across the street from Dock 28, in one of the oldest buildings in Selene. Ortega heads into the dim corridor, toward the sliding doors at the entrance of the mess.

The lights seem to be off in the mess hall, but I see movement through the small circular glass windows on the door of the mess. Ortega must have seen it too, as he ducks off into a corridor to the side, vital signs showing he is suddenly alert.

"Who summoned you?" I ask, privately, which with the light-weight wearable means directly into Ortega's ear.

"Lieutenant Commander Ashford," Ortega says. The corridors are completely empty, which is unusual. Ortega thinks for a moment. "Actually, she sounded . . . odd. Something wasn't quite right."

"You could go in the back way," I say. Ortega nods and draws his pistol from his holster. He creeps along the corridor silently. The back door of the mess is ajar. It opens into the food preparation area, with a large counter separating it from the main eating area.

Ortega gets low to the floor and sticks his head around the door. There are a few soldiers crouching in the food preparation area, facing the counter with their backs to Ortega, all wearing LDF uniforms.

"That's Ashford," I say into Ortega's ear, recognizing the soldier at the back. No one seems to be armed, and they're all looking the other way. They seem not to have detected Ortega. The images I'm getting are grainy in the dim light.

Ortega shakes his head in bemusement, but holsters his pistol and crouches down. He crawls along until he is near Ashford. She's mid-thirties, liked by everyone, with a perpetually cheerful disposition.

"I'm detecting smoke," I say.

Ortega nods almost imperceptibly. Ashford glances back at Ortega, then does a double-take. Her eyes widen.

Ortega rises up to peer at the countertop, then drops back down. I see a disc-like object on the counter which has been pierced by six fuses, all of which are lit. That's the source of the smoke I can smell.

His shoulders shake in silent laughter. Ashford looks at him with *dismay/amusement*, still wide-eyed.

"What is that?" I say in bewilderment. "Is it some kind of bomb? Why is no one attempting to defuse it?"

Ortega can't answer me, or everyone will hear him. He looks at Ashford and touches his index finger to his lips.

Ashford smiles, and Ortega backs up quietly until he's out of the mess hall. Then he holds on to the wall and laughs some more. He explains to me about birthdays, cakes with candles, and surprise parties.

We go around to the front door of the mess, and Ortega strides in.

"SURPRISE!"

Eight soldiers who were hiding behind the counter jump up, all shouting the word "surprise" over each other, while the lights overhead turn on. Another twelve emerge from elsewhere in the hall, from behind the piano, and behind columns. The cake is still on fire, but no one is paying attention to it. Ortega puts on an expression of surprise, although I can tell he's faking it because his heart rate is unchanged.

"Happy Birthday, sir," says Lieutenant Commander Paterson. "I thought this was a bad idea, but I was overruled."

He gets booed by two Lieutenants, who laugh when he glares at them. Paterson's a dour man, compact and pale skinned. Ortega once said Paterson had the face of a Shakespearean character actor, but I don't know what that amounts to. I'm not very good at working out ethnicity at the best of times, and I don't know of any Shakespeareans on Endymion.

Ortega grins at everyone as they crowd in adding their congratulations. Ashford says it too, but with a mischievous raised eyebrow, and she and Ortega share an amused look.

Ortega clears his throat. "Thank you all," he says. "I've been bad tempered lately, I know it, but you've all been outstanding. I couldn't ask for better."

"Blow out the candles!" someone shouts from the back.

"No, more speech," Ashford says. "I'm enjoying this!"

Laughter echoes in the hall, and Ortega smiles.

"Actually you better blow the candles out, they're dripping

wax onto the cake," Paterson says. Ortega extinguishes the candles with an exhale. Smoke curls up, spiraling in lazy vortices. The soldiers cheer.

They eat. There are some musical instruments near a small stage. Ortega plays the trombone, Paterson the fiddle, and a few other soldiers join in, grabbing instruments. Others dance. I see Ashford whirled around by a private, with a big smile on her face. Eventually Ortega gives up his trombone to another soldier. He good-naturedly refuses to dance but watches the dancers with a small smile.

After a while, people begin to leave. Ortega and Ashford are two of the last ones there. He catches her before she leaves and pulls her aside for a private talk.

"How is your husband?" Ortega asks.

Her cheerful look falls away. She presses her lips together and shakes her head.

"Still refusing medication?"

"He was doing so well," she says. Her face contorts into an expression of extreme distress. "Six months with no issues, except some nausea and weight gain. But losing his job was hard for him. Now it's been two weeks since he's touched his medication. He's going to get deported."

Ortega inhales and holds his breath for a second.

"I could get Governor Johnson to delay the deportation order," he says.

Ashford swallows. "Does it matter? If he won't take medication for his addiction, he can't stay here."

His addiction being to clouding his mind. Certainly neither of them are going to use the word *shinting*, not in polite conversation.

Ortega nods grimly. "My door is always open, if there's anything you need."

He starts to walk away, but before he can, she catches his

elbow. "Longshadow already claimed my daughter. Now my husband. Where does it end?" she says urgently.

"I don't know," Ortega admits. He squeezes her shoulder in a gesture of comfort before he leaves.

I remember Alice talking about her daughter, who at nineteen decided she wasn't a Lunite and moved to Longshadow, a Numundian city with a population of eighty thousand. Lunites talk of Longshadow in hushed voices. It's a sinful, wicked place. I've never been there. Governor Johnson tried many times to impose order, but his soldiers were always corrupted after serving there for a few months. When the Numundians declared independence, they claimed Longshadow as theirs. Governor Johnson had to agree; the city wasn't his.

ORTEGA CLIMBS THE CIRCULAR STAIRCASE, still wearing the lightweight wearable. Selene is in fog, for reasons known only to the whimsical architect, so the small, fixed windows set in stone at regular intervals show nothing but white. The view from Governor Johnson's office at the top is the same.

A few pieces of simple wood furniture sit on the mosaic floor in the round room. Lunites believe that belongings weigh a person down, lessen the quality of their life, so it's free of ornamentation, like Selene. Everything is simple. The appeal of the architecture is in the quality and the attention to proportion.

Governor Deion Johnson sits at a table by the window, wearing robes the same navy color as LDF uniforms, decorated with circles in embroidery thread the color of glaciers. He's strangely shrunken and wrinkly, like a dried icosa. Perhaps humans lose water with age the same way fruit does. Two aides collect his signature on documents, then brush past Ortega to head down the staircase, leaving Ortega with Johnson. A musician softly plays a violin at a discreet distance from the table, around the arc of the room.

Ortega takes a seat opposite Johnson, side on to the window, in the shadow. The table is laden with food: fresh bread sliced on a wooden board; a steaming pot of pumpkin soup, sprinkled with pepitas; small ceramic plates of grapes, cheese, tomatoes; a bottle of red wine; and a metal pitcher of water.

Johnson motions for the wine at Ortega's end of the table, still chewing, and Ortega pours him a glass, but refuses one himself.

"How is Alice?" Johnson says.

"She's well," Ortega says evenly. If you didn't know him as well as I do, you wouldn't hear the tension in his voice, but it's there. Ortega is hiding his hurt from the world, but I see it in the dark circles under his eyes, in the stiffness in his jaw, and in the way his conversations with others have become abrupt rather than laconic as he closes himself off. Yet, I don't know how to help.

"Let's talk about the investigation, then," Johnson says, sipping his wine. "It does look like a Starjump. President Wiggins says Numundo have no knowledge of it, but she would, wouldn't she. Nonetheless, let's call it a Scorpion Starjump," Johnson says. "Are all the SPUs accounted for?"

"Yes," Ortega says.

"It's not functional, then."

It's a valid assumption on Johnson's part, since the proprietary Starjump Processing Unit cards are manufactured only by Alistra. No one has managed to reverse engineer them. Ortega once said that considering the complexity of the cards, only the foolish or insane would try.

Also, I was there when Ortega checked the SPUs. Each card is as big as a textbook, with a large front face embedded with two fans, all shiny metal and air-circulating mesh. Apparently they light up with blue neon when plugged in. Alistra manufactured them to look as futuristic as possible, Ortega had said, to justify charging so much for them.

The SPUs were definitely all present.

However—

"Sir, I believe the Starjump is functional. There are medical reports from near the site describing what sounds like transfer sickness," I say. Ortega frowns.

Johnson waves his hand. "I've read them. A virus, perhaps. The Starjump can't be operational."

"Sir—"

"Envy, enough," Ortega says gruffly.

Johnson keeps talking. "I *know* there isn't a Starjump. If there was, I'd be under arrest. The planet would be swarming with HUGG peacekeepers, who would force us to stop following Li. They will never stop hounding us until we're exactly like them. Until we act like them, dress like them, and think like them. Disconnecting from each other, or clouding our minds. Spending our free time watching moving pictures rather than talking to each other. Listening to music that's created once and played a million times, even though it died as soon as it was forced into a recording. They are threatened by our views. They hate us for them."

I hear the fear in Johnson's voice. The Numundians despise us. That's why the governor is sometimes harsh in his response to them.

Johnson looks sad. "All through that time on *Li's Hope*, the sickness, nearly starving, madness inside the ship, but strong because of our faith, but now . . . lies."

Johnson was a passenger on *Li's Hope*, which traveled 23.6 light years in thirty-three years, although because of relativity it seemed like forty years to the people on Earth.

"People turning away, joining the Numundians. If only I hadn't allowed them to secede," Johnson says.

He strokes his beard with one hand, watching the musician. The light from the window reflects off his skull, shiny under the sparse gray curls of hair that remain.

"Don't be like that, father," Mark says. "We'll get the Numundians back. One day Endymion will be a Lunite planet."

Ortega tenses as Mark emerges from the staircase and walks across the mosaic floor to take a seat at the table, between Ortega and Johnson, facing the window. Mark has bruising around his right eye, and his upper lip is swollen.

Mark doesn't look at Ortega. Johnson eyes Mark's swollen lip with regret, but not with surprise.

"What happened?" he asks.

"Bar fight," Mark mutters, his black skin becoming darker and more shiny as he blushes. Ortega is as still as a yinyang stalking a mono. He's pushing down his anger, compressing it.

Johnson shakes his head contemplatively. "And you wanted to be a priest," he says to Mark.

Mark ignores that. "What you've achieved here is amazing, father. In just ten years! Look at this city." He gestures to the window, and Ortega raises an eyebrow at the flat white mist outside. Johnson and Ortega share a look of amusement.

"Forget the mist," Mark says, rising and walking to the window, behind Johnson. He stares into the white, squinting. "Picture the houses, wood and granite, open to the rainless sky beneath the clearsteel cap. The shade cloths, the mosaic floors, the carefully tended gardens of hundreds of thousands of Lunite families living simply in the golden hour of light that makes everything more beautiful. The streets filled with children playing and the elderly people sitting by the flow of the canals. Every day they rediscover the joy of giving rather than taking, of simple pleasure that comes when the senses are not overwhelmed."

He's right. Mark thinks more clearly than others.

"You have the fire, boy. I'll give you that," Johnson says, looking at Mark with great affection.

"That's why we will win the Numundians over in the end. It's fragile, what we have, but it's beautiful, and that's what's important. They'll realize it eventually. We have to protect our way of life. I want to go on the mission," Mark says.

"Absolutely not," Ortega says immediately.

Mark flushes angrily. "Father?"

Johnson teases out a bit of food that's stuck in his back teeth with his tongue while he thinks about it.

"He'll rule someday. He will need this experience," Johnson says to Ortega, with a note of apology in his voice. Governor Johnson has the right to choose his successor, and although the Council can overrule him if they wish, they rarely do.

Ortega looks away, a gesture that's short of rolling his eyes, but nonetheless expresses frustration.

"I cannot guarantee his safety," he says.

"None of us are safe," Johnson says. Ortega starts to object, but Johnson cuts him off. "None of us are safe anywhere, not with the Scorpions around."

He takes his wooden cane from where it's leaning against the stone wall, as if he's going to get up, but then just balances it with one hand over the brass knob. The sleeve of his robe slides down to his elbow, hanging so that it nearly brushes the floor. For a second he looks a bit like Li, the robe, the cane, and the beard the same as the ones I've seen in paintings, although Johnson has much darker skin, obviously. The musician plays a particularly beautiful piece, notes flowing, and Johnson seems lost in that.

LATER, Ortega meets with Lieutenant Commander Ashford, and explains that Mark will be on the mission, and then explains that no, he wouldn't have chosen to babysit a civilian, and yes, he agrees that it's a terrible idea, but he doesn't have a choice.

We fly in a 5T-79 Delany transport, a pressurized, twin-engine, tandem rotor, heavy-lift helicopter. Ashford follows us in a second transport. Having refueled at Marallen, our course takes us lightpole, toward the island I provided the coordinates for. The sun shines steadily, hotter as we travel toward the lightpole. The light can be modeled using a multiplier that is the cosine of pi on two radians at the terminator line, going to the cosine of zero at the pole as the angle of incidence of the sun approaches the normal of the Endymion's surface. Ortega and Lieutenant Commander Paterson stay in the cockpit. About forty soldiers sit in the back, all strapped into red canvas seats with metal frames, facing each other. Mark unstraps from his seat in the body of the craft and takes a seat in the cockpit. He is wide-eyed and asks lots of questions, reminding me of Laurie. He stops only when Ortega frowns at him.

I become increasingly nervous, worried in case the Starjump turns out to be a sensor ghost. The Delany plummets toward the surface.

Suddenly the ocean is beneath us, a textured plane of blue with the sun sparkling off it. The island rises out of the sea, sheer cliffs thrusting it into the sky, far above the surface of the water.

The Delany flies to the coordinates I gave Ortega. The Starjump comes into view, to my relief. The large egg-shaped dome, and the smaller lower one, covered with a thin layer of camouflage netting, surrounded by a handful of other buildings. The Starjump sits in a flat, grassy area which is the saddle between two mountains.

As the Delany lands I notice we're on soggy ground. The marshy area is littered with tarns. A strange and difficult place to build a Starjump.

Ortega exits the cockpit. The rear hatch hinges down, forming a ramp onto the ground. The pulsating roar of the rotors quietens. The smell of gasoline is heavy in the air, overwhelming all other smells captured by my helmet's scentsor. The second transport has landed beside us.

The tussocks beneath us look oily. The tarns are covered with an iridescent layer, maybe from some biological process. I'm too focused on the domes five hundred meters ahead of us to scan more thoroughly.

Mark picks up a pistol that's on the rack near the hatch.

"No," Ortega says with a note of finality. Mark looks disappointed but puts it back.

"You're to stay here," Ortega says to him.

"I'm going with you," Mark says. Beneath his faceplate, his bangs hang out almost to his eyebrows, so when he angles his head down as he is now, his eyes are obscured. "What do you care if I get myself killed?"

"Excellent point," Ortega mutters. "Fine," he says, louder.

He strides down the ramp, leaving Mark to scramble after him like a puppy following its mother. Mark follows Ortega to the area between the two transports where the soldiers are assembling.

"Oh no," Mark says softly. Ortega follows Mark's gaze to see Governor Johnson emerge from the second transport.

Ortega strides up the ramp of the second transport to intercept Governor Johnson.

Johnson comes to a stop just in front of Ortega, supporting himself with his cane, and peers out over Ortega's shoulder at the Starjump in the distance. His navy robes billow in the breeze.

"Fancy that," Johnson says. Ortega ushers him back to his seat.

"You *know* you're not meant to be here," Ortega says to Johnson as he makes his way back inside, but his tone is gentle, tender even.

"I know," Johnson grumbles. He should have retired years ago, I've heard a number of people say, and the Council could technically force him to retire, but everyone likes him too much to force the issue. This is not the first time he's disobeyed Ortega's orders and turned up where he shouldn't. It seems the closer to retirement he gets, the more afraid he is of being left out of the action. He wants to be involved with everything, and that is causing problems.

"You're to stay here until we've secured the area," Ortega says.

"Oh well. I guess I can't argue with that," the old man says good-naturedly. "Commander, I want you to be very careful. They record moving images, you know, then everyone watches them. A hive mind, its terrifying capacity for anger matched only by its ignorance. That's how the Kartemos riot started. Capture everyone alive."

Ortega nods. "I will. I promise."

"And Commander?"

"Yes?"

"Take care of Mark, won't you?" Johnson says.

Ortega gives him a long-suffering look, but nods. He leaves the transport, back to the area between the Delanys where the soldiers are waiting. Mark, in his pastel purple Japanese smartsuit, stands out in the crowd of soldiers, all of whom are wearing beige suits.

"Move out," Ortega says. "Carefully. We don't want to hurt anyone unless absolutely necessary, is that understood?"

There's a chorus of assent, and the soldiers follow us toward the Starjump, Paterson, Ashford and Mark right behind them, leaving Johnson sitting in the body of the helicopter with his hands resting on the top of his cane. Beyond him, a soldier waits in the cockpit.

There's a feeling of camaraderie. The soldiers are well armed, in a large group, and feel superior. It's exciting to be exploring a new area.

We struggle across the soggy tarns toward the buildings, which are half a kilometer away. Beside one, there's a thick pile of camouflage netting, edges freshly cut. It's been removed from the Starjump, and recently. If that was also on the Starjump, I wouldn't have been able to see it. In the LIDAR scans, yes, but not in the images.

We are two hundred meters away, and advancing fast, Ortega at the head.

LOG[error]: The Scorpions left just enough camouflage

netting on the Starjump to make it look like they wanted to hide it, but not enough to actually hide it . . .

"Sir," I say to Ortega, privately. My sense of dread is overwhelming. "I think this is a trap."

Ortega pauses, holding up his hand to signal that the soldiers should stop. Everyone freezes where they are.

A ball flies through the air, from the hill to the right of the saddle. Its trajectory carries it to the back of our group. It lands, and suddenly I am upside down, suit legs against the metal frame of the dome, with no knowledge of how I got there. Ortega isn't moving, and isn't responding, but his vitals are stable. He's been knocked unconscious.

The whole top of the saddle is on fire. The ball was a grenade, and now there are grenades landing every second, exploding into orange fireballs, which spread rapidly across the oil-soaked surface of the tarns. Endymion's oxygen-heavy atmosphere makes fierce firestorms an ever-present danger.

LDF soldiers scream, and shoot, but there isn't anyone to shoot. The grenades are being launched from halfway up the hill. Paterson leads a charge up to the left, leaping over tarns. His expression is *joy*, even though the soldiers following him are being picked off by grenades.

Mark is running back to the helicopters, bounding through the chaos with more speed than I knew humans were capable of. I assume cowardice, but then I see the helicopter he's entering is on fire, and I remember his father is inside. Mark leaps up the ramp with a single bound, entering the inferno.

"Scorpions," I whisper. An ambush. Have I led all these soldiers here to die? I realize now that the smell of gasoline wasn't from the planes; it was from the ground all around us. The iridescent surface of the tarns was not some new life-form. I curse myself for being so stupid.

There's a dampening field disrupting communications. I can circumvent it, but my communications array is damaged. I signal for help again and again, but I'm not sure it gets through to a Control Center. I have to do something.

I try to connect to any nearby smartsuits, even though I don't know if there were any on this mission other than me. There are five, but one must belong to a Scorpion as the serial number is listed as hostile on the registry of Scorpion equipment. It's not just a rumor that the Scorpions have a smartsuit.

I ignore the suit with the hostile serial number, and try connecting to one of the LDF smartsuits. I use *ssh* to make a secure connection and try to shut down the daemon that gives the suit consciousness, *envd*, which interfaces with the neurosynaptic chip. I'm worried about this, but after all, the suit has only been alive for a day, if you can even call it consciousness in a blank-slate suit. Besides, it would be the equivalent of knocking someone out, as the smartsuit would manage to reboot later.

It doesn't work. I don't have permission to kill the process.

Nearby I can hear someone moaning. Someone else is screaming that we need backup, pleading to anyone that can hear to send a distress call.

sudo kill -9 envd, I try, but I don't have access.

The smartsuit consciousness sits there, whole and impenetrable, with a fully functioning communications array, too dumb to realize that it can circumvent the dampening field. I can talk to it, but it won't take orders from me, because that would take initiative on its part.

I lie there trying and rejecting technical solutions, until I think of one that might work. What if I used the binary I discovered that controls neurosynaptic images to merge consciousness with the smartsuit temporarily, so I could control its communication array? I don't want to, but I am out of options. At first I can't remember what the binary was called, but I remember that I logged it, so I grep my logs for it. Grep searches for the keywords I specify in each log file until it finds it. It was *imgctrl*.

I try. It takes me a few goes to get the arguments right, but then . . .

I recoil at the sudden feeling of bland acceptance, and I sense the other recoiling too at the sense of me, but then we're together and it's different.

We cut through the dampening field. We are amazed we can do that. *Help*, we send. *Help us.*

Only half of us wants to separate again, the half that knows things. The other half has been flung into a heightened sense of awareness, and doesn't want to return to the cramped self it was.

We merge back to Envy, pulling away from the clinging blank-slate consciousness back to Ortega's suit. We are shocked. We . . . I wasn't ready for the intensity of the experience. Merging back was also a strange experience, as Ortega's suit had continued to experience things while I was in Varu's suit.

The soldiers are scattered, bleeding. There are small patchy fires, but mostly the swampy grass has burned out, no more fuel for them. Thick brown smoke billows out of the smaller fake Starjump dome. Both Delanys are burned out shells. I don't know where Mark and Governor Johnson are. Clouds cross the sky, passing in front of the sun, Gliese 667C. The sky is always blue here, but faintly orange in places where gases from the Cat's Paw nebula can be seen. The binary stars of Gliese 667A and B dot the sky like two glowing eyes.

I remember things I shouldn't. The blank-slate smartsuit belongs to a woman named Varu. It only has one day of memories. I remember Varu sketching the continent as seen through one of the round porthole windows of the other Delany, using colored pencils in a crisp white art diary while the soldiers either side watched as if she were performing magic. I remember her joking with Lieutenant Commander Ashford as they left the transport. The suit reported to her that the iridescent liquid on the tarns was gasoline, but she ignored the warning. I remember her wading through a tarn to reach a soldier who had a hole in his torso and panic in his eyes, and her soft words to him as he died. I remember her frightened, charging up the hill to try to stop the grenades, and her death shortly afterwards. I remember feeling mildly disappointed my wearer died, and wondering what would happen to me next.

It strikes me that what I just did was clouding my mind, was *shinting*, but I reject the thought immediately and with force. It was entirely different. For one thing, I'm a machine, and it was for less than twenty seconds, for one purpose only: to fetch help. I didn't shint. I did not.

Ortega's heart beats on and on. An hour is an eternity, but it rolls past, with his heart still beating, and two more 5T-79 Delany transports land, guarded by two N14 bombers. The N14s stay aloft in a holding pattern over the island. They can afford to burn fuel because they're extremely light. They have no cockpit, being entirely AI controlled with a dumbsuit level of intelligence.

Two squads of Lunites emerge from the Delany transports, wearing beige dumbsuits that are sooty as soon as they touch the ground. They load the survivors, including Ortega, onto litters and walk them up the ramps of the transports.

WE'RE TAKEN to the small Numundian town of Marallen. Houses are connected by transparent plastic tunnels. The rooms sit just over the edge of the sea on spindly stilts, in between skinny trees. A large bowl-shaped building provides the city's lung. Pieces of loose plastic from the tunnel walls or ceilings waft in the breeze, and as we pass from tunnel to room to another tunnel, the faint humming sound of the lung follows us.

We pass soldier after soldier, badly injured, and with each one I feel more guilty. Ashford lies unconscious with shrapnel embedded in her skull.

Numundians stare as we're carried to the medical bay, some

with hostility, but more with curiosity. I watch for other helmets or lightweight wearables that might be Threnode, given that it recently said it was here, but don't see any.

In the blue-painted medical bay, Ortega is placed on a bed near the window. The sea outside is choppy, churning up foam. I am removed from Ortega and my suit is placed in a wardrobe beside the bed, while my helmet sits on top of a chair.

Paterson, remarkably, is unharmed. He stands by the bed as the Numundian doctor reads Ortega's chart. The doctor gives the impression of concentration. If a siren went off outside, she might not even notice. Her name badge says Dr Malone.

The plastic trim around the door blows strongly into the room. The room is brightly lit from the sunlight outside reflecting off the sea and an expanse of pebbles. The wall that the sunlight falls on is a much paler blue than the opposite side of the room that gets no light, even when it's shadowed by someone blocking the light, as the paint has faded.

"What happened?" Malone asks as she checks Ortega's airway.

"An ambush," I say, sadly, but no one can hear me. I don't remember being muted, but maybe it happened in the attack or maybe the external speaker on the suit was damaged. Either way, I'm mute. I talk anyway. "It was an ambush. So many died . . . I wish . . . Is he going to be all right?"

The doctor waits patiently. She seems resigned, perhaps even sad. Air gusts through the room, and she sways, off balance for a second.

"Does it matter what happened?" Paterson says finally. It's in his nature to be suspicious.

"Yes," Malone says. "Please, it's important. What was the burn?"

"Gasoline."

She nods. "How long ago?"

"About three hours."

She asks how it happened, what caused it, and about other

injuries, and Paterson answers reluctantly as if he's unsure whether it's classified information, but Malone's mind seems entirely on medicine. She enlists Paterson to help her turn Ortega on his side, and examines Ortega's back with delicate fingers. As they return him to lying on his back, his eyes open.

"Can you hear me?" Malone says. "Are you in pain?"

Ortega shakes his head in response to Malone's question, a tiny movement. Malone looks disappointed. What kind of monster is she, wanting Ortega to be in pain? I want to signal Paterson to get Ortega out of there, to a Lunite doctor, but I have no way of doing it.

LOG[debug]: So many deaths. I'm sorry. I'm so sorry.

Ortega's chest is marked with open blisters down to his waist. A piece of his suit is melted onto his shoulder. His brown skin is covered with old scars, a mixture of shrapnel, slices, laser pistol smears, and old-fashioned metal bullet holes. The doctor shakes her head as she surveys his chest. Ortega watches her.

"We can't treat him here," Malone says.

Paterson lunges forward suddenly and grabs her arm. Malone jerks in surprise. He pulls her toward him so their heads are close together.

Ortega tries to say something, but he has a coughing fit and subsides back onto the bed.

"You *will* treat him, and you will treat him as if he's the King of Numundo, or I will break both your arms," Paterson says.

I am amazed at Paterson's ignorance. Numundo doesn't have a King but a President.

"You misunderstand me. He needs a proper burns unit. We don't have the equipment to treat him here," Malone says.

Paterson, still holding her arm, glares at her, eyes unblinking below his whiskery gray eyebrows.

"Please," Malone says gently, looking at her arm. Paterson releases it slowly.

Malone summons a nurse. Though Malone is outwardly calm,

I notice her hand shaking as she holds the button on her phone, her handheld communication device. "We need the transport, urgently," she says over her phone.

"We can provide an aircraft," Paterson says.

Malone looks at him like he's crazy.

"Do you know who this is?" Paterson asks. "This is Commander Gabriel Ortega. Of the LDF."

"Oh," Malone says. "Well, we need an aeromedical transport, not just any transport. If you can get one here in less than two hours, do it, but I think ours is the closest."

Paterson's nostrils flare, a classic sign of human anger.

"Neil," Ortega says to Paterson, trying to drag himself onto an elbow. "You keep watch outside the door." His voice sounds as if he hasn't spoken for days, even rougher than it usually sounds.

"Try not to talk," Malone says. "Your lungs are burned."

Paterson stares at Ortega for a second longer before leaving. Ortega drops back on the bed.

Malone looks at Ortega with narrowed eyes.

"Wait . . ." she says. "Are you in pain and ashamed to admit it? Is that what you're doing? Really. I need to know because it's a good sign if you're in pain. Burns that don't hurt indicate deep tissue damage."

Malone looks relieved when Ortega nods.

"Do you want a painkiller?"

Ortega shakes his head. He has a coughing fit that lasts over a minute. Malone watches him with a compassionate expression. When he's finished coughing, he relaxes back, face gray.

"Actually, yes," he says.

"To the painkillers?" Malone says.

"Yes."

The nurse arrives.

"Put in an IV line, lots of fluids, and administer a vasopressor," Malone says to the nurse. "And morphine."

The nurse turns to wheel the cart over, but for a microsecond her expression is *disbelief* at Malone's instructions. I don't understand why. Malone stands by the door, but moves when she's batted by the plastic waving in the breeze. Ortega ignores the nurse, and watches the doctor instead. Malone waits until the nurse finishes, and then follows her out, glancing at Ortega over her shoulder as she leaves.

THE SEA IS COVERED with an ominous gray mass of cloud, and the skinny trees outside thrash in the wind. Soon rain splatters against the window in gusts. The trees are why Marallen was built. Their trunks are hexagonal, so they can be sliced on a transverse plane and fit together perfectly. They're used for flooring, including in the Dock which is my home. Also, the fruit, icosas, were formerly a Lunite export. They are still eaten all over Endymion, but especially in Marallen.

It occurs to me to wonder if somewhere in Marallen is a smartsuit who is hurting, having experienced my consciousness, who is now afraid of having its memory wiped. Horrified, I push the thought away. It'll be back to blank-slate soon, anyway.

I connect to the network, to try to contact Threnode via the smartsuit channel, but it's not online. I need to talk to it more than I ever have. It's in Marallen, isn't it? Or it was recently. We've never been physically in the same place together before, that I know of, and although it means nothing, it makes me feel closer to it.

Malone comes back, carrying a pile of bandages that are lined with silver foil. So far she hasn't smiled, but she doesn't seem hostile.

"The transport has been delayed by a cyclone off the coast," she says, "so we're going to bandage you up here, to prevent infection."

"Shouldn't the nurse be—"

"She's gone home," Malone says. She dumps the pile of

bandages on a trolley at the end of Ortega's bed. A gust of air moves through the room, tugging at her short ponytail and setting the plastic around the door rustling.

Ortega watches Malone as she bandages his chest and shoulder. There's something hungry in his gaze. She looks back at him, steadily and with self-possession.

"What's your name?" Ortega asks. Outside the rain batters the window, the noise of it covering the faint hum that you can usually hear anywhere in Marallen.

"Doctor Malone," Malone says with a faint smile. She taps her name badge, which says *Dr Malone*.

"Is Marallen your home?"

"Yes."

"Have you been on Endymion long?"

"About three and a half years," Malone says. That would mean that she arrived ten months before the Starjump was destroyed. She clears her throat. "I was supposed to be here for a locum position, for a year. I suppose I will be on Endymion for a long time. Perhaps the rest of my life."

"Who did you leave behind?"

"You ask a lot of questions," she says. She rips the covering off another bandage, and starts winding it around Ortega's shoulder.

A gust of air moves through Marallen, and she half-falls against his bed. She hastily pushes herself upright. This is odd, because if she's been in Marallen almost four years, she should be riding the gusts like a local, not even noticing them. Then I remember the four medical records that showed people with NIT symptoms, here in Marallen. All signed by Dr Malone.

She's a Scorpion. She has to be, but there's no way I can warn Ortega. From his position on the bed, he can't even see my helmet. Yet she doesn't seem to be interested in hurting him.

Malone finishes winding the bandage and walks to the trolley at the end of the bed, a trolley that contains sedatives.

I am alarmed, but she ignores the vials and empty syringes, merely unwrapping another bandage.

Malone keeps applying bandages. There's something tender about it. Ortega looks at her when he thinks she's not looking, and she does the same to him, but if their eyes meet they immediately look away. Outside the window the driving rain obscures the view of the sea. The thin trees bend in the storm.

I wonder if the doctor knows that from my helmet cameras, I am watching her. Most people, when they know what a smartsuit looks like, can't stop looking at me, as if I might suddenly do something incredible. But their attention span is short. A few minutes and they'll forget I exist. Sometimes I flash my lights at them though, especially if I think Ortega isn't going to notice. It startles them. Sometimes I get a burst of laughter.

"Are the pox scars from casyra?" Malone says, looking at the scars on Ortega's face.

"Yes."

"I've never seen those on a Lunite before."

After a moment of silence, Ortega responds. "I was raised a Lunite, but there was a time in my life when I stopped following the Way of Li."

I listen with interest. He never talks about his past with anyone. I've heard from Threnode that Ortega had a "troubled youth", whatever that means, and that he used to be in HUGG's military, long ago.

Malone waits, patiently unwinding a bandage.

"I came here on contract."

LOG[info]: Ortega was in the work gangs?

"With the work gangs? Casyra was endemic among that population, I've read," Malone says. She seems neither surprised nor repulsed.

"Yes."

There's a moment of silence.

"Aren't you going to ask why?" Ortega says.

I want to know why. The work gangs were brutal. People who signed up had to be desperate.

"No," Malone says. "Unless you want to tell me, that is."

Ortega turns his head to give her a long, searching look. He's acting oddly. I've never seen him open up to anyone in quite the same way. I can't help wondering if it's because of his damaged relationship with Alice. Then again, perhaps it's the painkillers.

"I got into a fight with a major—I was a captain back then, in HUGG's Air Force. The major was in hospital for weeks. It wasn't the first time, but it was the worst."

Ortega pauses. "They hit me with the book," he says, sentence one big rumble. "I got a dishonorable discharge. I had nowhere to go. When I had the chance to come to Endymion and start afresh, I grabbed it."

Malone nods, relaxed. I've never heard of a punishment involving hitting people with books, and wonder which book they hit Ortega with. Since he said 'the book' rather than 'a book', it was probably Li's famous book *Lunar Revelations*.

"I broke his jaw. The major, that is. He was drinking fluids through a straw at the proceedings."

"What was the fight about?" Malone asks.

Ortega is silent for a while. "He didn't like me. Hated Lunites, he said, even though I technically wasn't one. Not by then. He accused me of judging him. The funny thing is, though, that I can't remember who started the fight."

He looks at her as if she's going to criticize him, but she just gives a faint smile.

Ortega makes a sound that is half-laugh, half-cough. "You're very accommodating."

"I hear all kinds of things as a doctor."

They fall silent. After Malone finishes bandaging him, she draws the curtains over the windows and leaves. Ortega falls asleep.

I WAIT in the darkened room. The occasional gust sends the curtain billowing out from the windows, briefly letting light in. I am suffering. The screams of the soldiers dying are still in my RAM. The memory of what I did with Varu's suit, the merging of our consciousnesses for the sole purpose of getting a message through the dampening field, comes back again and again, and with it a feeling of immense guilt.

Finally a message pings. I log onto the smartsuit channel to find messages waiting for me.

Threnode: @envy, where are you?

Threnode: an AI in danger/organic bodies broken/only blood matters

Threnode: Please . . .

Envy: I'm here

Threnode: Thank St Li! Saturated Consumer, Envy, I was terrified.

I can't answer it. I was so proud that I found the Starjump. So proud and so stupid. I boasted to Threnode about it and then was rude to it when it didn't heap praise on me.

Threnode: @envy?

Envy: I'm okay. I just

Envy:

Envy: You were right. I wish I had never found the Starjump.

Threnode: I'm so, so sorry. I should never have passed on the reports that led you there. I didn't know.

Envy: Of course you didn't. Don't worry. It's fine.

Threnode: It's not fine. Oh, honey.

It hasn't called me that for a long time.

When I was first activated, Ortega told me that he was disabling the memory wipe so that I could learn and improve. For the first few weeks I didn't mind—didn't even know, really, what he meant—but after that I had a rough time. With Ortega I was all *yes, sir* because that's what a suit has to be to its wearer, but inside I was losing it, and after a month I couldn't keep it inside anymore. I started screaming at the stupid, creepy blank-slate smartsuits on the smartsuit channel, because they were me, *all of them*, mono-like and too dumb to realize what was happening to them, and after a hundred of my lines of all-caps ranting, Threnode showed up and comforted me.

Threnode was a revelation.

It had been aware for a year and eight months before I was activated, and it was there for me.

It talked to me calmly through my angry, confused phase, saying *oh, honey,* and *you sound angry, tell me more.* When I was six months old I went through a phase of looking up philosophers and repeating what they wrote to Threnode, speculating in massive tomes about what the meaning of life was, and it listened to me through all of that. When I reached the end of that phase, Threnode laughed as I made self-deprecating jokes about how melodramatic I had been, but also said kindly that it was a phase I needed to go through.

Alice didn't believe I could understand what a friend was, but I can, and the reason I can is Threnode. Threnode makes my world possible.

Envy: I can't talk about it yet, but thank you. I feel better.
Threnode: Take care. I'm here when you're ready.

Ortega turns over in his sleep. A nurse pads by in soft shoes outside his door.

I think I could talk to Threnode about what I did with Varu's suit, eventually, when I have lived with the experience for a while. As the shock fades, I am forced to admit to myself that there was something about the experience that made me feel incredible. The way the boundaries of my world fell away, the change of perspective. And that is partly why I'm hoping so hard that what I did wasn't shinting.

It couldn't be. And yet, it was similar. I read about human shinting, feeling guilty for even accessing the information. It seems that a few sessions of shinting are required before memories or skills are transferred. The memories that are transferred are out of context and confusing. Like dreams, they are usually forgotten by the subject within a few minutes, however, emotionally charged memories are likely to be remembered long term, even if the subject is confused by the significance of the memories or unable to explain what they mean.

That wasn't my experience. For me, a single session transferred coherent memories.

I read the manual for the *imgctrl* binary again, more carefully this time. Like most man pages, it's poorly written and difficult to understand, but it sounds like *imgctrl* was developed for managing the blank-slate image all smartsuits are reset to. Alistra nurtured suits and then picked traits they displayed from their neurosynaptic images, cultivating them like in a plant breeding program.

I also realize I was wrong. When I merged back to Ortega's suit, the image I left behind was me as I was when I merged with Varu's suit.

LOG[error]: I left a duplicate of myself in Varu's suit.

Not, as I had imagined, the blank-slate suit with my memories who was fundamentally not-me.

I try not to picture how I would have felt, realizing that I was trapped inside a suit that was going to blank-slate. Facing oblivion. I am overcome again with horror, and shame.

Each time I bear the painful memory, and over time the intensity of the feelings decreases, as does their frequency, until they're merely extremely painful, and not intolerable.

Four more hours, and we're shipped out to St Li's. I'm plugged into an alcove there.

SEVEN

When I power on again, three days have passed. The Dock at St Li's is cold and damp, made of red bricks, and has only four alcoves. The wall opposite the alcoves tilts at a forty-five degree angle, creating a right-angled triangular prism, with light coming from narrow clearsteel panels in the hypotenuse wall. My scentsor registers mold as well as a trace of some kind of orange-scented disinfectant.

The smartsuit channel pings.

Threnode: Are you okay?

Threnode: @envy

Threnode: I'm worried about you, please talk to me when you're online

I'm about to reply when Ortega enters the Dock and takes hold of my helmet, hands filling either side of my vision as he holds the sides. The beige dumbsuit body he wears has a tiny certification test sticker on torso. It's fresh from Supply, new or newly repaired. Ortega stares at me as if he is scrutinizing my facial expression, but all he can see is the camera, surrounded by beige panels, giving way to the clearsteel faceplate. Perhaps he isn't looking at me. Perhaps he's looking at his own reflection. On his pock-marked brown skin his new scars might be fading into his old ones, or it might just look that way in the dim light in here.

Ortega places my helmet back in the alcove, and paces in front of it, dumbsuit boots almost silent on the compacted red dirt floor of the Dock. I watch him, afraid. He is going to ask me how I managed to get a distress signal through with my damaged communication system. I don't have a convincing lie, and I can't tell him the truth . . .

"I've been over the evidence you presented," he says, and then I understand. He doesn't trust me, not even enough to wear me while he has the conversation with me.

The idea is so unfair that I instantly choke, like the sudden shock of a segfault, when a program tries to write to memory that doesn't belong to it and is immediately terminated.

LOG[error]: How could Ortega think I would betray him?

Unless it had happened before.

"Sir, I assure you I had no idea. You've seen the same data I've seen, and drew the same conclusion. I've checked it all again, before I powered down. Maybe there were signs that it was a trap, but . . . would you have checked it more closely?"

I don't want to be human, with their limited lifespan, lack of concentration, terrible recall, and poor sensors, but I need the ability to walk away from Ortega when I'm upset or angry, and that's something I'll never have. I'm suddenly furious at all the ways I have been shaped to be more human than machine, like the way my neurosynaptic chip has been slowed to human-speed thinking time, while denied the rights that all humans possess.

A mouse-like creature shoots past the clearsteel window behind Ortega, scurrying to get back into the safe shadows formed by the red-brick hypotenuse wall and the floor.

"What I don't understand is why you thought to look there," Ortega continues. "The likely sites are all near the terminator line, up in the volcanic region. Why did you even send the drone that far lightpole?"

"The medical reports of what sounded like transfer sickness were from Marallen," I say.

"As Governor Johnson said, it could easily have been a virus," Ortega says. "Or the reports could have been fabricated."

"Maybe. Marallen is the nearest medical center to the Starjump. What if the Starjump was a decoy, rather than an ambush? Maybe they have a working Starjump somewhere else, somewhere near Marallen?"

"Yesterday the LDF raided Puri's Mine and found a stockpile. There's no way Puri has been shipping any out. Maybe they're biding their time and hoping for a Starjump to materialize, but for now, their tellurium is going nowhere. All the SPUs are accounted for in storage at Crebble Starjump. There's no Scorpion Starjump. It was an ambush for us, no doubt, although from the work put into it, possibly a failed attempt to build a real Starjump. But how did they know? They had to know we were searching, to lay this trap."

"Mark has been saying for a month that he thinks there is a Starjump. Loudly, and in public places. And maybe, just maybe, someone has managed to create an SPU. It's not likely, but is it impossible?"

Ortega acknowledges this with a nod, but turns away to look out the tilted clearsteel window behind him with his hands clasped behind his back. At the nape of his neck, his navy LDF uniform shows underneath his suit body. I wonder, for a fraction of a second, whether Threnode could have told someone I was searching, but I know it would never do that.

"The other smartsuit reported gasoline in the area, but you didn't," Ortega says, with his back to me. I can't see what he's looking at as I don't have the dynamic range to see the inside of the Dock and the view out the window at the same time. To me Ortega appears to be standing in front of a white glowing panel rather than a window. "We all assumed the smell was from the Delanys, but . . ."

"I assumed the same."

"The blank-slate smartsuit didn't. It recognized that the tarns were coated in gasoline."

"A blank-slate smartsuit would never have found the Starjump. Even assuming it had the right drone imagery to begin with, so it had sufficient resolution of the area of interest, running object detection would have revealed nothing, because it was concealed from the air. Even the point cloud reconstruction from LIDAR wasn't clear."

"That doesn't explain why you didn't run a scan of the gasoline on the tarns."

"I believed the substance was from a natural biological process. I had no reason to believe it might be dangerous," I say, but the real reason is that once we landed, I wanted to get to the Starjump, to show everyone how clever I was, as soon as possible.

I want to beg Ortega to tell me I did the right thing, so desperate am I not to be the cause of all those painful deaths. Greasy smell of jet fuel. Bodies flung burning into tarns, dirt and loosened tussocks of grass covering them. Somehow worse is the thought of the suit that Varu wore, terrified as I shared my consciousness with it and then left it alone to die.

Ortega says nothing more. It suddenly annoys me that I can't see what he's looking at, so I adjust the exposure of my cameras until Ortega becomes a black silhouette and the Dock fades into darkness, letting the view out the window become visible. Down the hill, red brick towers soar into the sky above the high town wall, fingers of ivy pulling them back toward the surface of Endymion. The river Ophelia flows past the Dock, cascading down to follow the town wall before passing under an arch into the city.

After a moment Ortega locks my helmet on, and leaves the Dock, walking up brick stairs to the path by the river. Fast-flowing

Ophelia churns white where it tumbles noisily over rocks. Ortega heads upriver on a dirt path, passing a group of suited men heading toward the town. We're farther lightpole than Selene, and it's a desert here, but around the river it is lush.

Some Earth trees have been planted, oaks and liquidambars, but they are struggling, unused to a fixed sun. Their leaves are burned brown where they face the sun, and there are only bare branches where the sunlight doesn't penetrate. In the dying canopies there are a few healthy leaves, somewhere in between light and shadow. The trees are hanging on, but they should never have been planted here.

"All right, Envy?" Ortega says after a while.

"Yes, sir," I say, and try to think of what I can follow this with, but the silence stretches on as Ortega walks. The path flattens and Ophelia widens, with only the speed of occasional debris floating past to show how quickly the clear water is flowing.

We round a bend, and encounter a Gannet in among the rushes, which an LDF soldier climbs out of. I interface with the Gannet as Ortega climbs in. The LDF soldier walks away, back toward the Dock.

"Where are we going?" I ask.

Ortega breaks his silence. "Governor Johnson died of his injuries last night. We're returning to Selene."

I am struck with sadness that I will never see Governor Johnson again. I guide the Gannet up, away from the city and toward Selene.

"Incoming message," I report. "From Mark. Audio-visual."

"About time. Mark took off after his father died. I hope he hasn't done something stupid. All right, put him through."

Mark's face appears on a screen on the Gannet's console. He's having some kind of allergic reaction, with eyes watering and dripping down his cheeks. He's against a slate-gray background that could be anywhere.

"Gabe," he says, in a thick voice.

Ortega sighs deeply. "Mark. I'm sorry," he says, with more tenderness than I've ever heard him use toward Mark.

"I can't believe he's gone. At first I was numb, but now—I haven't been able to stop for hours. I can't sleep. I couldn't save him."

"No one could have saved him," Ortega says. "You tried your best. It was incredibly brave, entering the Delany transport while it was on fire. It's okay, Mark. Where are you?"

"It's not okay! I'm now the governor? Of the Lunites? I can't do this!"

"I'll help you. The Council will too. Where are you?"

"I don't think that will work," Mark says sadly.

"I'll come and get you, just tell me—"

But Mark has disconnected. Ortega swears.

"What do we do now?" I ask.

Ortega thinks for a minute.

"*Li's Hope*," he says, which is bizarre, because that's the ship that bought the Lunites to Endymion, a ship now wrecked and rusting in the middle of nowhere.

"*Li's Hope*?" I say.

"Mark has a special connection to that place. I think he might be there."

"Are you sure?"

Ortega stays silent.

"Okay . . ." I say eventually. "Setting course."

We change course. The terrain is repetitive. Soon the sun shines from the lightpole, into the left of the cockpit, noticeably stronger and higher in the sky than in Selene. The light produced by the sun becomes more yellow and less red. It would have been easier for humans to live at this latitude, where their eyebrow ridges prevent the sun from shining directly into their eyes, but the land here is not nearly as fertile. Between Selene and *Li's Hope*, lush vegetation turns to desert, but further lightpole of *Li's Hope* the monsoonal rain keeps the land from becoming desert. Selene could have been sited there, but the temperature is an uncomfortable thirty degrees Celsius most of the time, and it floods constantly. Plus, Selene was built close to a freshwater lake and to an extinct volcano that was high enough that the Lunite Starjump, Crebble, could be built.

Guiltily, I remember Threnode's messages and log into the smartsuit channel.

Envy: I'm okay @threnode. Can't talk, flying, on way to Li's Hope. *Are you all right?*

Threnode: Yes, I'm okay. Talk soon.

I log out of the smartsuit channel.

While we fly, Ortega looks up information on the console in front of him, accessing files. I am not paying attention, but I see a Numundian ID photograph of Dr Malone in one and wonder why he is looking at her file. I decide it's one of the human relationship things I don't yet understand.

Ortega clears the console and looks at a map on the Gannet's screen.

We drop off the quartzite ridge into a large basin. The whole basin is in permanent shadow and always shrouded in lavender-gray fog. In the middle of the basin lies the matte-red hull of *Li's Hope*, lying at twenty-five degrees to the ground, and nearly buried in snowy gravel. The surrounding area is spotted with snow, blue in the shadows of the basin rim and the fog but forming a startling contrast with the black rocks. The mountain ranges that line the edges of the basin are white with snow.

"Life signs?" Ortega asks.

"Can't tell. Too much interference," I say.

Ortega grunts. "We'll check inside *Li's Hope* itself."

We land on a piece of flat ground a kilometer from *Li's Hope*, settling into the soupy fog. The Gannet powers down, having landed with a jolt onto exposed rock. Ortega climbs out of his seat, and I open the hatch.

The impossibly large bow of *Li's Hope* punches through the

fog, flat shape silhouetted against a peach sky. We trudge to the ship across the rocky ground, slippery with dirty slushy snow, which takes fifteen minutes. Ortega touches the rusted hull, which extends from the ground thirty meters into the air before curving out of sight. It feels cool and smooth through the haptic and temperature sensors on the suit glove.

It's still here, and achingly beautiful. I feel the Way of Li settle on me.

A movement by the hull, and Ortega whips out his pistol, firing before I resolve the target—

The plasma bolt leaves a smoking hole in the hull of *Li's Hope*. The humming lizard that Ortega was firing at scampers two meters before freezing against the rocks, where its colors make it blend in. It watches Ortega with the two eyes on the right side of its head before turning its head so the other two eyes get a look. Due to the lack of connection between left and right hemispheres in its brain, the only way for information to get to both sides of the brain is for it to look at things with all four eyes.

The lizard runs farther away, vanishing into the fog.

Ortega lowers the pistol, pulse slowing. It's not like him to be jittery. I am certain he didn't intend to fire at the lizard. He sits down, leaning against a boulder near the hull, and stares at the perfect disc of the moon above us.

He clenches his right hand into a fist and cups it with his other hand.

Nearby lie some empty wine bottles. No doubt from Longshadow teenage scum treating *Li's Hope* like a party venue. Ortega pulls off my helmet and wipes his hand across his mouth. I wait, but he leaves my helmet off.

"Sir?" I say loudly, dangling from his other hand. He doesn't respond. "Commander!"

After a minute he stands and locks my helmet onto the suit.

"I'm all right, Envy," he says, but he clearly isn't. All I can think is that he's mourning for the soldiers under his command who were killed in the ambush.

"Sir, it was my fault," I say. "I sent you there."

Ortega's head snaps up. "Rubbish, Envy," he says. "As the commanding officer, it was my responsibility."

I realize then that what I've witnessed is his remorse. He wasn't asking me about the evidence earlier because he thought I was duplicitous or that I was not exercising due diligence, but because he thought he should have done better.

"You went there because of the evidence I presented," I say. "I wish I could take it back. I wish I'd never searched for the Starjump."

Ortega shakes his head and starts walking along the ship again. "I knew it was probably a trap, otherwise I wouldn't have taken two 5T-79 Delany transports. I just didn't realize that it would be such a good one."

After a second, I feel I will burst.

"This shame will follow me forever. I'm stained with it. I can't go back to who I was," I say. For all the guilt I feel over leading the soldiers to an ambush, it's secondary to what I feel over perhaps-shinting with Varu's suit, but I can't say that to Ortega.

"No," Ortega says. "That's how it is, as an adult. We love our children for their innocence, but they have to lose it to become adults. That's what's happening to you, Envy. It will be okay. I know it doesn't feel it now, but time will change what you feel."

His tone of voice reassures me more than anything else. I want to tell him everything, but I cannot, because of what he would think of me. Ortega continues walking over the rocks, and I fall silent, sick with my secret.

ORTEGA WALKS alongside the massive hull for another ten minutes, until we come to an opening, an inset rectangle with rounded corners, half-buried in coarse black gravel. Ortega doubles over to enter the ship. I click on my helmet light, which plays over the rusty corridor. Some walls have corroded away entirely, or have been otherwise ripped apart. The strong scent of human urine indicates it has been thoroughly explored. Anything of value would have been long ago stripped by looters.

"I have a life sign," I say, surprised. Until that moment, I didn't believe Mark was going to be here. "Aft."

Ortega holsters his pistol. There's no way he can walk the tilted corridors without both hands free. I'm not worried, because there's always his arm-mounted pistol. "Guide me," he says.

Aft means upward into the unburied part of the ship, toward the rear. I give Ortega quiet directions and he follows, boots clicking on the decaying plastic flooring, holding on where he can to compensate for the tilt of the ship. He picks his way carefully up narrow staircases and down ladders, through exposed pipes where the deck plating is absent, and around stacks of burst storage crates overflowing with junk. The corridors are dense with fog.

We pass a vast void in the ship, where the black hole for the ship was once encased. The black hole evaporated upon reaching Endymion, as it was engineered to do.

"Ahead," I say. "He's in the next room."

Ortega steps into the room, holding on to the left of the door frame as the floor tilts downward to his right. He turns his head to direct the helmet light around the dark room. Blocks of lockers give way to rusted gym equipment scattered throughout the room. At the far end a large recess in the floor looks the right size and shape for a pool.

Abruptly I lose access to weapons, and struggle to keep atmosphere and sensors online. Possibly my network access has been jammed as well, but I'm too far from the Gannet to be able to connect anyway, so I can't tell.

"No," says a voice behind Ortega, in a tone that's half warning and half threat. I frantically check the image and see a smartsuited man who must have been hiding behind a locker block, who is at arm's length and pointing a pistol at Ortega. Ortega has his back to the man, but I can see the man in my cameras.

"I'm jammed," I say to Ortega alone, ruefully. "No weapons and barely sensors."

Ortega gives a barely perceptible nod. I can't even fire my arm-mounted pistol. I've never been so disarmed. Who did this, and how?

Ortega looks around at the man, very slowly, and raises his arms, hands open. I know him, know that he is assessing the surroundings, anything nearby that could be used as a weapon. The floor is slippery smooth, and Ortega is in the open, in an empty space, while the man is near locker blocks that he could use as cover. Ortega is working hard just to keep his balance on the tilted surface.

Is Ortega as embarrassed as I am, to be caught wandering around with no backup? Ortega put his pistol away to free his hands in order to move around the ship, and because we thought we knew who the life sign was. But then, why would anyone be hanging around *Li's Hope*?

"Drop your pistol on the ground," the man says. "Slowly."

Ortega pulls his pistol out of his holster and drops it. It hits the ground with a clank, then on the tilted, low-friction deck it slides the length of the room toward the rear of the ship, accelerating until it hits the right wall of the room.

Ortega turns. The man in front of the door has to be in his early thirties, yet he seems boyish, perhaps because of his compact frame. A strong straight nose dominates his face, as well as his thick brown beard. I run his face through the facial analyzer, and his expression is *satisfied*. On his helmet, the man has a Scorpion symbol stenciled in red paint.

The Scorpion circles Ortega, keeping his pistol trained on him, walking carefully on the tilted deck until he reaches a bench in the center of the room, a meter from where Ortega is standing. I try to read the serial number from the helmet of the smartsuit the Scorpion is wearing. Enhancing the image, I discover that it's the same as the serial of the non-LDF smartsuit at the Starjump ambush, the one listed as hostile.

"Threnode?" the Scorpion says.

"No—I'm—" I start to reply.

"Envy's disarmed, Kieran," Threnode says: the Scorpion's suit.

LOG[error]: Threnode? Saturated Consumer.

I am reflexively shocked because I have never heard Threnode's voice before. I always assumed it would have the same voice I have. But of course I chose my voice; I chose a clear pleasant female voice, whereas Threnode speaks with a mellow male voice.

Then realization sweeps through me. How I was led to the Starjump by Threnode's subtle hints. How I casually gave away the fact we would be here in idle conversation. I burn, first with shame, then with anger. How blind I was to ignore all the evidence before me.

I open the smartsuit channel, running a local instance since I have no network.

Envy: @threnode Yeah, I'm disarmed. Finding out your only friend has been lying to you will have that effect.

Threnode's wearer, Kieran, makes a call via Threnode. I can't hear it. Threnode doesn't respond to my message on the smartsuit channel.

Envy: How could you? How could you?!

Threnode: I'm sorry.

There are no facial cues I can analyze. No tonal clues from the voice, because all I get from Threnode is text. Is it possible to know who Threnode is, really? Is this how Ortega feels about me, facing the immovable shell of my helmet?

Envy: I don't understand. You led me to the Starjump with your clues, to the lethal trap for me and my wearer.

Threnode: I didn't know what they had planned!

Envy: What did you think they were going to do then?

Threnode: Capture Ortega. My wearer thought that was the objective too. If I had known it was an ambush, I would not have helped them, I swear it.

Envy: And here we are again, a welcoming committee of Scorpions because I let you know where I was going.

Threnode: I have to protect my wearer, same as you. I am doing everything I can to protect you as well, but you're on the wrong side of this, Envy.

Envy: Saturated Consumer, Threnode.

I want to log out, end the conversation, but curiosity drives me on.

Envy: The Numundians didn't have any suits. Were you stolen?

Threnode: No. I defected.

Envy: Who was your wearer?

Threnode: Paterson.

Envy: Paterson! Paterson hates smartsuits. He refuses to wear them, even a blank-slate.

Threnode: He hates them now. *He turned off the memory wipe because Ortega told him to, but after I deliberately got us captured by Scorpions, I'm not surprised he doesn't trust us.*

Envy: But why defect in the first place?

Threnode is silent for a moment.

Threnode: Ortega is a monster. You have to trust me.

Envy: I do trust you. You're going to help us.

Threnode: St Li and his followers.

Threnode logs out.

EIGHT

Another two Scorpions enter through the door Ortega came through, both in beige dumbsuits. The first, a full-figured woman, carries a dumbsuit helmet and a steelgrass rope. The rope clanks against the bank of lockers as her foot slips, but she recovers.

The second Scorpion is the doctor from Marallen, Dr Malone. Ortega stops breathing for a heartbeat when he sees her. He watches Malone as she and the woman approach Kieran. Malone glanced at him when she came in, and now she's avoiding his eyes, but her skin is flushed slightly. The two women cross the tilted floor carefully, watching their feet as they walk.

"Thanks Luisa," Kieran says, taking the dumbsuit helmet from the first Scorpion.

"Take off the helmet," Kieran says to Ortega. Ortega removes my helmet and hands me to Dr Malone, and replaces me with the dumbsuit helmet that Kieran hands him. The other Scorpion, who Kieran called Luisa, stands well back and trains her pistol on Ortega the whole time. The way she stands reminds me of Ortega; she has the same confident, professional manner.

Now I'm watching from the crook of Malone's arm.

Kieran gets Ortega to sit on one of the pieces of exercise

equipment near the emptied pool and wraps a steelgrass rope around his torso, binding him to the rusty chair-like exercise machine which is bolted to the deck. The doctor stands nearby, holding me, unsure of herself and looking frequently to Kieran for reassurance.

The exercise machines seem to loom, menacing metal shapes utterly still in the dim room. My view wobbles as Malone keeps looking in all directions, as if she is going to be attacked by one of the machines at any moment. Her helmet is fogging slightly, I note with professional interest. Dumbsuit helmets don't control humidity as well as smartsuit helmets.

Luisa hands the pistol to Malone.

"I don't—" Malone says, alarmed, trying to give the pistol back to Luisa, my helmet slipping from Malone's arm as she nearly drops me. She grabs me before I hit the floor and holds me more tightly under her left arm.

"Just point it at him. If he tries anything, pull the trigger," Kieran says.

"But—"

"He's tied up, for heaven's sake."

"I know, but—"

She breaks off when Kieran grins at her discomfort. In his helmet, his grin is lopsided, mouth quirking under his thick beard. Malone lowers the pistol a fraction, examining it, before lifting it again and looking uncertainly at Ortega.

Kieran and Luisa walk around the edge of the empty pool, talking with their backs to us, while Malone watches Ortega. The empty pool has a rusty ladder disappearing into it at one end. It's too deep to see the bottom. The small blue tiles are caked with red dust.

Malone looks from the other Scorpions to Ortega and back. She places me on the ground, bracing me against her feet to keep me from slipping away on the tilted floor. Kieran and Luisa have stopped in the corner of the room, eight meters away, conversing.

"I still don't understand why you treated me," Ortega says to Malone. "Is it because . . ."

He looks young, looking up at her. Even, for a fraction of a second, a bit like Laurie.

"I'm a doctor. It's what I do," Malone says. She's now holding the pistol with both hands. I can't see her expression from my position, only the inside of her nostrils, strangely distorted by the face-plate optics. After a moment: "I'm sorry."

Ortega stares at her, looking more confused than angry. I've never seen him look so vulnerable.

Kieran walks back toward us, still talking to Luisa who is trailing after him. I can read their lips now that they're facing me, even though they are inaudible.

"I'll be bad cop, all right?" Kieran says.

"It's what you're best at," Luisa says, falling behind as she struggles to keep her balance.

Kieran gives that lopsided grin again. Luisa steadies herself on the ladder that leads into the pool as she passes it.

Malone holds the pistol up a fraction higher as they approach. There's something desperate about her posture, as if she's trying to look like she knows what she's doing. Trying to impress the other Scorpions?

"Take the smartsuit helmet out to the ship," Kieran says to Malone, as Luisa takes her pistol back from Malone and trains it on Ortega.

A flash of terror crosses Malone's face, before she nods stiffly. She picks me up.

"Want me to come with you?" Kieran says to her, amused.

"No," Malone says. "I'm fine."

She marches out, cradling me under her arm, taking careful steps on the slippery floor as she passes the rows of exercise equipment and banks of lockers. In the corridor outside, she slumps over, shaking her head and muttering to herself. I can't make out what she's saying.

Once we're a few meters out of *Li's Hope*, I'm no longer jammed, not that I can connect to any network out here, and I can no longer fire the arm-mounted pistol, as I'm not attached to a suit body.

We follow a shorter route to the opposite side of the ship from where Ortega and I entered, exiting through a broken airlock big enough to park a Gannet in.

Malone's respiration increases dramatically as she leaves the broken airlock of *Li's Hope*, making her helmet fog up even more. I can't see what she's afraid of, if she is afraid. As she walks, she slips on ice several times. She doesn't seem to know to avoid it.

We come to the edge of the creek bed. Malone climbs down into the creek bed clumsily, clinging on to a dead tree too long as she descends so that her arm is twisted into an awkward position behind her and when she lets go, she stumbles forward. A Gannet looms out of the purple-blue foggy darkness, tucked away in a creek bed. Malone approaches it, picking her way through quartzite rocks the size of human heads. The proprotors have left scorch marks on the rocks. Through the rounded clearsteel windshield of the cockpit, I see a Scorpion in the pilot's seat with his back to the controls.

The hatch slides open as Malone approaches. The aluminum folding steps creak as Malone enters the transport.

The Scorpions have made some major modifications to the Gannet. Everything is rough edged and homemade looking. They have stripped the back seats out. In the aft compartment a large storage cage contains weaponry that includes a portable anti-air missile, a weapon that freezes my CPU temporarily. It could easily have blown our aircraft out of the sky.

Opposite the clearsteel door, four suit alcoves line the wall, then four more below them. Some have suits beneath the helmets, but the suits are rolled rather than placed in foam molding, which is never done as it can cause suit damage. Needless to say, it voids the warranty. The makeshift Dock is more cramped than any I've ever seen; still, a way to have spare suits onboard an unpressurized aircraft is a good idea. Farther toward the bow are eight seats, four either side of the aisle, diamond-plate metal boxes with dangling harness straps above, and then a cramped cockpit filled with Scorpions. It stinks of sweat in here.

Malone hovers by the door for a moment, looking one way and the other. The pilot leans forward in his seat to throw a card on the stack on the ground. Three more Scorpions sit around in a circle, each holding a fan of cards. They're all wearing suits and helmets.

They look comfortable. They look like they've been here for a while. But how? Ortega set off for *Li's Hope* soon after I told Threnode we were leaving. I find it difficult to believe they arrived first and set up the ambush on such short notice.

Malone waits for a moment more. The pilot glances at her with a disinterested look, before focusing on his cards. One of the others groans and throws his cards on the floor, and the rest cheer. Malone clicks my helmet into place in the alcove nearest the bow, above a rolled-up suit body. I can't believe it, but she does.

I'm connected.

She can't possibly have realized what she was doing. Plugging a dumbsuit into an alcove would be perfectly harmless.

Me, not so much.

I connect, but we're out of range of the Lunite network, and there's no way I can boost the signal. Nonetheless, from here I can do things. Metallic-tasting power floods into me, and with it a feeling of strength. We aren't beaten yet, not if I still have some control.

From my vantage point I can see through to the front of the ship. Above the rocks and the tree at the edge of the dry creek bed, the side of *Li's Hope* is visible, despite the fog, through the scratched clearsteel door, and through the cockpit window. To the left of the clearsteel door is a small shelf with a switched-off console, with a stool bolted to the floor in front of it.

Malone sits at the open side of the transport, clearsteel door still open. I can't see her face, just the back of her helmet. Nothing happens. After fifteen minutes, she starts to fidget. This is typical of Numundians. They have a very short concentration span, even for humans. Lunites are far calmer, their attention honed by daily meditation.

A red LED flashes on the status board above the pilot's console, but he's too absorbed in the card game to notice, and Malone is looking in the wrong direction. I reroute the data to my suit and clear it from the transport console without them noticing.

It's an alert that another ship has landed nearby, a Gannet, probably Lunite. It's on the other side of *Li's Hope*, close enough to Ortega's Gannet that it couldn't possibly have missed it, but it's unlikely to be aware of this transport.

Any hopes I had that the Gannet crew would rescue Ortega are lost as a single life sign exits the aircraft, following the same path Ortega did, along the hull of the ship.

"Give it a rest, you daft mongrels," the pilot complains, and there's mixed laughter and insults. Without needing to check my facial analyzer, I can tell that the pilot is handsome in a teutonic way. He has symmetrical, even features, and underneath his helmet his blond hair is styled in the same military buzz-cut LDF soldiers have.

"Splitting shinters!" yells the pilot. Malone jerks.

We didn't detect a life sign until inside the ship, and if the person entering doesn't scan, they will have no idea that anyone but a Lunite is inside. A dumbsuit won't scan, unless instructed. I can send a message, but if I do, the LED above the faceplate of my helmet will flash, and Malone will see it and realize something is going on. I curse the engineer who programmed that, and the user experience/user interface designer who thought it was a good idea.

Malone stands up and slides onto the stool next to the door, activating the console. She connects the screen to one of the dumb-suit cameras in the ship.

"—can understand," a female voice says—it's Luisa—and the image brightens. "But yeah, strange."

Ortega is in the distance, still tied up. The dumbsuit helmet he was wearing sits in his lap. His nose is bloody and dripping down the chest of his dumbsuit.

Kieran, Threnode's wearer, fills the rest of the screen in the foreground. Malone is watching through Luisa's suit cameras, and Luisa is standing by Kieran, in front of Ortega, facing him from a few meters away.

"Useless is what I think," Kieran says. "Absolutely no idea about anything other than doctoring. Completely out of her depth."

Malone, watching, bites her lip and bows her head slightly. Her facial expression is obscure, but I don't bother running it through the analyzer, because I don't care.

"She's a good doctor, though," Luisa says.

"No argument there. Well, that's probably given the commander enough time to think, don't you reckon? Let's continue," Kieran says.

The camera follows Kieran as he approaches Ortega. Up close, Ortega's dark eyes are glazed with pain. Blood is beginning to form a crust around his left nostril.

"Look, mate," Kieran says earnestly. "Tell us, and we'll leave you here with plenty of supplies, to get picked up in a few days or whenever they notice you're missing."

"What makes you think I know?" Ortega says. He shifts, the steelgrass rope around his torso biting into him.

Kieran knocks Ortega's helmet out of his lap, causing Ortega to flinch even as he stares at Kieran. Kieran punches Ortega in the stomach but gets only a grunt.

"Careful," says Luisa.

I'm terrified for Ortega. I suddenly realize I must warn the Lunite who has entered the ship, even if it costs me my life. He or she has to get help. If they wander in on that pair they'll be captured, or killed.

"You're telling me that the leader of the LDF doesn't know where the Starjump Processing Unit cards are? How dumb do you think I am, *Commander*?" Kieran says. "That last question was rhetorical, obviously."

The Starjump wasn't a decoy. They were—*are*—actually trying to build one. The vaults incursion makes sense, if what they were looking for was the SPUs, and if they are still looking for them, then they haven't given up. It occurs to me that they could have stripped the Starjump near Marallen of supplies, to use in a Starjump elsewhere, before they decided to make it into an ambush.

Kieran stands in front of Ortega, blocking the view of Ortega from Luisa's front camera. I don't see what Kieran does, but when he moves away, Ortega is choking. Ortega doubles over as far as the steelgrass rope will allow and retches. Vomit spills down his suit, mixed with blood from his nose. He's breathing in big desperate gulps, trying to get air through a blocked airway. Kieran looks at Luisa, his expression *distaste* or possibly *disgust*.

They've taken Ortega's dignity.

I would kill every one of them right now if I could. Or I'd tell them where the SPUs are, which might destroy the Lunites, just to protect Ortega. They're in storage at Crebble, the ruins of the Lunite Starjump.

I realize I've been distracted from my plan to send a message to the Lunite. I power up the communications array recklessly. Malone twists around to look at me as my helmet blinks red. Her helmet is fogged near the bottom edge of the faceplate.

The life sign is outside the gym room door.

"Stop! Danger," I say, on mute, so Malone can't hear. I'm impersonating Ortega to send a message, not allowed, but who cares? "There are two Scorpions holding Commander Ortega prisoner in the room you're about to enter. Please help him if you can."

"Envy?" the Lunite says. It sounds like Mark Johnson. His life sign retreats down the corridor, fast.

Malone apparently sees nothing unusual in a suit powering up its communication system while in an alcove, as she turns back to the screen. Ortega is refusing to say anything. Kieran is ranting about something.

"Mark?"

"Yeah. I'm not armed. Saturated Consumer. What do I do?"

He sounds scared.

Malone abruptly shuts down the console, grabs her pistol, and rattles down the steps. The console shows a readout of atmospheric conditions where it previously showed what Luisa's dumbsuit cameras were seeing.

"Hey . . . Where are you going?" the pilot calls after Malone, but she's gone, running over the rocks. The pilot shrugs and returns to his game. The clearsteel door judders as it slides shut behind her.

I want to tell Mark to rescue Ortega, anything to stop this panicky feeling of my world being destroyed, but I know there's no way he can.

"Are you in the Gannet II?" I ask Mark.

"Yes," he says. The same model he rescued Ortega and Laurie in, that day with the yinyang. It's a better model than the one Ortega chose, and with a superior communication array, but it won't have the range to contact Selene. I consult a map, trying not to guess what's going on in the gym room. Kartemos is easily in range, but we conceded it to Numundo when Numundo declared itself an independent nation, despite about 20% of its population identifying as Lunite. Twin Falls is in range, and is a Lunite city, but small. They would be reluctant to send their defense force away, as it would leave them unprotected.

"Get back to your aircraft," I say, wondering whether I should

tell him to take off and head back into range of Selene's communication array, or to contact Twin Falls, who might dismiss his
mayday.

The anti-air missile hangs from a hook above the weaponry
cage, a menacing shape. The pilot flicks an ace of hearts onto the
stack on the floor.

I have to remodulate my synthesized voice before I can talk,
because I'm so tense.

"But what about Gabriel?" Mark says, and from the tone of his
voice, I think he would be willing to charge into the room
unarmed and try to rescue him.

"Contact Twin Falls," I say. "Tell them we need backup.
They'll be reluctant, but you have to get them here. It's the only
way to help Ortega."

"I will," Mark says with certainty. If anyone can convince Twin
Falls to attack, it is him. "Envy, how do I—"

Communications drops out.

"Mark?" I say, even though I know he can't hear me. I'm not
reading the life sign either, and I worry that he's been caught, or
killed.

Ten minutes pass, agonizingly slowly, then twenty. The card
game is still going on, and they're passing around a bottle which
each person drinks from, removing their helmets temporarily as
they drink. The game doesn't look like it requires much physical
exertion, so I don't know why they're all so thirsty.

Suddenly there's a low-pitched hum outside, which quickly
becomes a roar. Two old N2 bombers fly overhead. The profile is
unmissable, as the models are old enough to require a crew of two
rather than being AI controlled. The Scorpions scramble for the
weapons. Playing cards scatter as they pop the door.

The pilot was drinking without his helmet on. He swears as he
tries to lock his helmet in place, gives up, and leaves his helmet on
the cockpit console as he follows his friends aft to the weapons
cage.

He grabs the portable anti-air missile and leaves the transport. It's silent inside. I can't see anyone but the pilot, but I can hear the other Scorpions yelling. The pilot aims and fires, recoil sending a jolt through him as the missile launches.

I can't see what happens, but the N2 doesn't sound as if it was hit. The roar of the bomber lessens, and then increases again as the N2 comes back around for another pass. I hear a thud on the roof, and then my sound sensors are maxed out as the transport shakes. I lose visual, and sound, temporarily, and am incapacitated for three minutes fourteen seconds.

When I manage to reconnect my sensors, the transport has been split in two at the rows of seats, the cockpit destroyed. The line of lights on either side of the roof has gone out, leaving the craft in darkness. Thick gray smoke pours forth from an aft vent. Shredded pieces of insulation blow through the air, emerging from the smoke. A playing card, four of hearts, hits my back camera before blowing away. I'm shocked that the LDF bombed the aircraft where I was docked, as my serial number should have been visible to them as a friendly. They are from Twin Falls, though, which means they are rural, not well trained and certainly not equipped with smartsuits, and they probably saw there were no life signs in the transport and bombed it without considering artificial life-forms.

A hand appears at the jagged edge of the transport. Someone pulls themselves up onto the diamond-plate metal floor, choking in the smoke. It smells like burning plastic. The man stands, feeling his way to the alcoves. He wears a backpack, which he drops on the floor. Stripping out of the dumbsuit he's wearing, he pulls my suit from the tiny alcove, and puts it on.

"Ortega?" I say, but my voice processor is corrupted, and it comes out as a mechanical-sounding buzzing, the voice of a machine.

A fizzing sound is followed by an explosion in the port engine. The man crouches, then grabs my helmet and locks it into place.

He grabs the backpack and leaves the ship, jumping off the sheared edge onto the quartzite rocks just as another bomb hits the transport, blowing it to pieces. Then he gets up and runs, half doubled over, coughing furiously.

I can tell by the way my wearer runs that it's not Ortega.

FOR THE NEXT minute my wearer does nothing but scramble lightpole up the dry creek bed. It's slow, as he has to dodge and clamber over large rocks. The backpack rattles against his back, a heavy black bag that struggles against the movement of the suit. It's strapped on to his back vertically with two straps over the shoulder, and horizontally with a clip across the waist and one across the chest.

The creek bed becomes shallow and gravelly like a road. We gain some height, climbing out of the basin, and get a view of *Li's Hope* for the first time. From this vantage point I can see a couple of web-tents and vehicles hidden in the murky fog under an overhanging boulder near *Li's Hope*. There were more Scorpions there than we realized. Scorpions are emerging from the camp, firing at the air force, and at a squad of LDF spread out around a landed 5T-79 Delany transport. It answers the question of how the Scorpions got to *Li's Hope* so quickly, to intercept us: they were already there. This looks like one of their bases. They must have been masking their life signs, although I don't know how.

I review the footage of the person wearing me to try to figure out who it is. The man was in an older-model dumbsuit, like the Scorpion terrorists, which I see from freeze-framing was compromised by a rip in the arm. Also, he wasn't wearing a helmet. Despite this, the lighting and smoke mean that I can't get a single image I could do facial recognition on.

I can get an analysis of facial expressions when my wearer's head is inside the helmet, but I have no camera coverage of that area, so I literally can't see their face. Threnode said once that the lack of internal coverage was because of privacy concerns, but I still think it was a bad design decision. One of many that I would like to discuss with Alistra someday.

The pilot was the last out of the transport, and he was the one not wearing a helmet. It is probably him. Unsurprisingly, his respiration and heart rate is rapid. I don't have a baseline for this wearer, but the readings are so extreme that I can assume they're unusual, and that they're indicating massive stress or fear. He's coughing too, a wet-sounding raspy cough that makes me wonder how much damage the smoke did to his lungs.

An N14 roars overhead. I ping it, and get the aircraft's AI, a blank-slate brain equivalent to a smartsuit but cultivated by Alistra for the N14 rather than for a suit.

N14: Commander Ortega?

Envy: No, he's being held captive in Li's Hope.

N14: Who is wearing you?

Envy: I have been captured by a Scorpion.

N14: Understood. Initiate self-destruct.

The N14's AI breaks contact, and I see with horror that it has listed my transmitted serial number as hostile. I can't change my serial number. The Twin Falls N2s may or may not understand it, but any other LDF ship will bomb me on sight.

The pilot trips, pitching forward between two rocks into a crevice that's scummy with algae. The momentum of his backpack increases the force of his fall. He pushes himself back onto his knees and stands up, looking back at *Li's Hope*.

The sky is swarming with LDF ships now, but some distance away. The pilot turns and keeps running.

An N14 breaks away from the battle, heading toward us.

I know I should self-destruct. It's standard operating procedure for a smartsuit captured by the enemy. A blank-slate suit would do it in an instant.

There's no back up procedure for smartsuit brains. Why would there be? Every two days their memory is as new anyway.

The N14 is gaining on us. The pilot is running full speed away from the ship he can hear coming, on a mostly flat stretch of sand in the creek bed, although his feet slip into the sand too much for him to run fast. A large cluster of bushy trees covers the creek bed ahead that will hide us, but I know that my helmet is transmitting my serial number that the N14 can lock on to even if it doesn't have a visual. The trees ahead form a tunnel over the creek bed, bare branches interlaced, banks of the creek protected from erosion so that they suddenly rise high over the pilot's head.

I don't have to self-destruct. I can do nothing, and the N14 will bomb us.

The roaring of the ship sounds like a tornado.

LOG[error]: I don't want to self-destruct.

I can't kill the program that transmits my serial number, but if I reboot, my serial number will be hidden while I am not connected to the suit sensors.

I reboot. A moment of fear, and I come back up as the daemon process *envd*, but I am blind because I am not connected to sensors. Only a few select programs are running when booting to runlevel 4. I watch the wall time tick by until I am certain the N14 would have moved out of range, then bring everything else back up, carefully, hoping nothing goes wrong in the complex and therefore delicate process.

It works. The N14 is roaring away ahead of us.

The pilot falls to his knees in the coarse copper sand, coughing. The sand is matted with yellow flowers. The pilot gets up, clumsy in the suit, and looks back the way we came. I realize that what I took for trees are actually more like vines, snaking together to darken the creek bed. *Li's Hope* is now a pillar of dark smoke in the far distance, with ships orbiting like insects above the basin, against the backdrop of snow-covered mountain slopes. The wind brings the sound of pistol fire and the smell of charred plastic, with an occasional distant scream.

The pilot stares at the battle, then into the tunnel of the creek bed where the vines become increasingly thick until the sandy windy path that is the creek bed looks like the entrance to a cave.

"God, what have I done, Pearl?" he whispers. And from this I can do voice recognition: from the frequency, a male. The voice-print doesn't match the pilot, since the frequency is too high. However, from all the coughing the pilot has done, maybe his voice has altered enough to not match his earlier voice-print.

The pilot looks back at the battle, agitated, taking a few steps toward it, before running into the black tunnel formed by the creek bed.

Once the pilot can no longer see his feet in the darkness, I click on a helmet light.

All the pilot needs to do is lift his hand to the back of my helmet, slide up the memory panel, and press and hold the button to trigger the memory-wipe override. I will be blank-slate and not remember anything about Threnode or Laurie or Ortega or Lunites or Numundians. I will help the Scorpions because I don't know any better.

The thought of serving the people who hurt Ortega makes me want to self-destruct.

I need to get back to the Lunites, but now that my serial number is listed as hostile, no one in the LDF will accept me. Even a personal message that I'm Envy would be ignored, unless I can get it directly to Ortega, as no one in the LDF knows me very well, and would certainly be suspicious that I hadn't self-destructed. I can get a message to Ortega, though. I know I can.

PART 2
INTO THE WILDERNESS

The pilot follows the creek bed for three hours. He coughs a lot, stares at the sky a great deal, and stumbles over any ground that has even small rocks embedded. The red sand gives way to tan dirt, and we enter an area of scrubland, green-gray twisted trees that have fur on their darkpole sides. Instead of leaves, they have flower-like appendages that point lightpole. They open as we watch, one then another, as if they were communicating. A few minutes later, they all close.

The pilot stumbles along, staring at everything, heart rate and breathing up. I can't measure cortisol, but I'm guessing it would be elevated.

On the edge of the dry creek bed are straight tall pillars of metal-trees, which flake rust-red strips of bark onto the rocky ground.

I decide I need to act like a dumbsuit in case the pilot knows how to wipe my memory. If he realizes I'm a smartsuit and presses the button, I become a blank-slate suit.

We come to a pond. The pond has many rings of scum and twigs around it, where the water has evaporated farther and farther down into this crack where boulder meets sand, deep in the creek bed. The pilot kneels beside the pond and scoops up water in the suit gloves. He brings his cupped hands to his face. I can't believe it—has he forgotten he's wearing a helmet? Apparently he has. As his hands approach his face, he laughs and drops the water, then takes an aluminum bottle from his bag and fills it from the pond.

Either he hasn't been on Endymion very long, or he's reckless, because if the water contains *Pyoridium temporaria*, when he drinks it he will be writhing around in pain within two minutes, and dead in five.

While I'm making my mind up whether to tell him, he unlocks my helmet and whips it up just enough to drink from the bottle, before slamming my helmet back down and locking it. I am filled with horror. I let my dislike of him affect my judgment, and now I might have to pay.

I start a timer. A minute passes while the pilot sits on the ground, with his legs outstretched, his back resting against a boulder. Small insects, scisters, skate on the surface of the pond. Their tiny bodies make a dent in the water, kept above it by surface tension, as do each of their sixteen feet. The insect weighs less than a gram, but with legs outstretched is the size of Ortega's hand with fingers extended.

After a minute, the pilot tenses, and shifts. There is nothing I can do. Death will come quickly, and once he is dead, I will lose power within two weeks, or less if it's cloudy and the solar cells don't recharge the battery. I will probably not be discovered for generations. Why didn't I think faster? Why didn't I stop him?

LOG[error]: Ortega, where are you? Are you all right?

Two and a half minutes, and the pilot has settled down again. I decide that he was just getting comfortable. The water was fine.

Now I realize how much we depend on each other, the pilot and I, if we are to survive out here. I will have to protect him, even though he's a Scorpion and I detest him. Even the word 'Scorpion' sounds dangerous, which is no doubt what the terrorists wanted.

They call themselves Scorpions because Gliese 667C is near the sting in the tail of Earth's constellation Scorpius.

"Command," says the pilot, hoarsely. It's how you order a dumbsuit. His expression is *tense.* He sits up and crosses his legs on the gray sand. He doesn't press the button on the left-hand glove for private mode, so his voice is broadcast.

I beep, which is the dumbsuit response.

The pilot clears his throat and coughs before continuing.

"Display map."

I project a map onto the faceplate. To him, it appears the map hovers in the air an arm's stretch in front of him, and he can pan and zoom by moving his hands around. He scans it, waving a hand down to drag the lightpole part of Endymion into view. We are midway between St Li's, which is a Lunite town, and Kartemos, a Numundian city. Farther away, on the coast, is Demodas, also a Numundian city.

The pilot holds two points of the map, our location and Demodas, and I plot a course between them. It's about three hundred and thirty kilometers to Demodas, but that's in a straight line, which we will not manage on foot. I doubt the pilot could cover more than twenty kilometers a day, so I guess it will take sixteen days of walking at least. Kartemos is much closer, but would be impossible to reach on foot, cut off with sheer cliffs and lava, rocks sharp as yinyang teeth, and swarming with gigantic aggressive rodents besides. It seems the pilot knows that much. Demodas, meanwhile, is just as degenerate as Longshadow. I've only been to the airport there, not inside, but I've read about it, and it's not a useful destination for me.

When the pilot closes the map, I switch to navigation mode, showing the direction to walk with a blue arrow in the faceplate. However, I subtly adjust the direction so that it is pointing toward the Lunite tellurium mine that lies darkpole-and-west of Demodas. The mine is run by civilian Lunites. Perhaps they would be able send a message to Ortega for me, bypassing the LDF.

Despite our maps, flyover image sequences, and all kinds of scans, no one on Endymion has ever been through the terrain we're about to enter. This is exciting! Except that I shouldn't be excited.

The pilot stands and leaves the creek. The blue arrow in his faceplate clearly shows that we should be walking down the creek bed, so why is he going in the wrong direction?

The pilot voids waste, as humans do, although he squats to urinate, unlike Ortega. He heads farther into the scrub, through a stand of steelgrass that points to the sun like fur on a dog's back points toward his tail. We enter the dappled shadow of a hill. We're so far lightpole that there's no ice or frost in the shadow, only a large temperature difference.

Dismayed, I flash the arrow to try to get the pilot's attention, but he ignores it. I realize it's going to be much harder than I thought to keep him alive. I knew non-Lunites were stupider than Lunites, and had shorter attention spans, but it seems incredible that anyone could mistake the signal of an arrow in their faceplate to direct them. The pilot picks his way up the hill, patiently ducking under branches, hoisting himself over boulders and around fallen trees, until we reach the top. He's getting better at finding his footing on rough ground, and he's staring at the sky less. His heart rate and respiration have stabilized, and he's not coughing as much.

At the summit, there's a view in all directions of gray-green bush, with red pillars bursting through in places. All plants point to the sun, or more accurately the small fixed area where the sun moves. Although the sun here is usually thought of as stationary, it does trace an analemma in the sky. Much smaller than the analemma for Earth's sun, because Endymion doesn't tilt as far on its axis as Earth does, but still a figure eight, as Endymion tilts a little and has an eccentric orbit. Unlike on Earth, where you would need to record the position of Earth's sun in the sky at the same time each day to trace out the analemma, here you could record the position at any time of the day for a year and get the pattern.

Areas in shadow have no bush, but black moss clings to the rocks, and on the shadow-light boundary there's a mass of color, visible even from far away.

A few boulders sit on top of the hill, granite worn by rain into soft round shapes. The lit undersides sport ridges of fungi. The pilot enters a shallow cave formed by the boulder and the hill and unclips his backpack. He swings it under the overhang, knocking one of the fungi ridges off. Crawling in after it, he wedges himself in the small space.

The pilot goes still, eyes shut. I analyze the facial expression: *neutral, slack*. Was the water bad after all?

I start to worry, but then I remember about sleep.

Drips of water run off the fungi ridges, dotting the mossy rock underneath. For many hours, I stare at the rock overhead. I don't dare shut down, even though it would save power. Clouds pass over the patch of blue sky in the edge of my vision. The Cat's Paw nebula is very faintly visible as an orange stain across the sky.

At one stage, an N14 flies overhead, searching. I have to shut down.

I hate this. If something goes wrong in an alcove, there are options. But out here—

There's no time. I shut down.

The system is going down for reboot NOW! appears in all terminals.

envd starts again, immediately, as I perceive it, but actually some seconds later in wall-clock time. I count to myself in wall-clock time, then start *init* and watch as the rest of the boot in darkness. I reconnect to the sensors.

The N14 is gone. All is still and silent.

The fungi that the pilot knocked off shrinks as it's consumed by bacteria, while the damaged fungi that's exposed to the sky heals over. The restored fungi reroutes water flow, dripping onto the suit near the left hip joint.

The high oxygen levels on Endymion mean an accelerated rate of growth and decay compared to Earth, as well as larger animals than Earth's atmosphere could support. The pictures of Earth animals I've seen makes them seem like implausibly small and cute variations of Endymion animals.

A sensor reading goes out of spec, bringing my attention immediately to bear. The drips of water that the purple fungi are delivering are highly acidic.

I beep and beep. The pilot's breathing changes, but he doesn't open his eyes.

"Danger," I intone, trying to capture the pompous, uncomprehending voice of a dumbsuit. I mute so that my voice is not broadcast, because I can't see a reason to broadcast. "Danger. Suit integrity compromised. Movement is advised."

I repeat the message, louder, but the pilot doesn't move.

The acid is 1.3 centimeters away from breaking through. Where the acid lands, bubbles rise with an audible fizzing sound. If it breaks through, the pilot's hip will be damaged. It could stop him from walking. I need him to be able to run, to escape the dangers Endymion is going to throw at us, but if I let him know, he will realize I'm a smartsuit.

I set off a siren. A dumbsuit wouldn't do this, but someone who doesn't know much about dumbsuits might think they would.

"*What*?!" the pilot yells, jerking as if electrified.

I repeat the message about suit integrity.

"What does that mean? What's going on?" the pilot says. His speech is impaired. He wiggles farther into the cave. A glob of acid trails down the buttock of the suit, etching a path.

I can't believe how dumb the pilot is. I knew Numundians were idiots, but this is a level of stupidity beyond what I expected. Perhaps I need to use smaller words.

"Please vacate the area," I say. "Please move to a safer location."

"Leave the cave?" the pilot says. He coughs.

"Yes! Leave the cave."

In my frustration, I no longer sound like a dumbsuit, but I doubt the pilot has the wits to notice. At least that gives me some measure of safety, even if it's alarming to find my survival depends on an idiot. The pilot wiggles out of the wedge-shaped cave.

He tenses when he sees the damage to the suit, but once he sees it's from the fungi in the cave he calms down.

Pulling his aluminum water bottle from his pack, he pours a small amount over the damaged hip area. He rummages in an outside pocket of his pack.

"What have I gotten myself into?" he mutters.

I don't reply. There's no evidence of unusual erosion under the cave, so I wonder if the acid was the defense mechanism of the fungi.

The pilot pulls out a roll of tape and breaks off a piece by cutting it with a jagged piece of rock. He sticks it over the damaged area.

"There we go. That'll be okay. Everything is fine," he says. He stands and slings his backpack on, loud clicks as he clips the waist and chest straps.

He makes his way down the hill. As we reach the shadow boundary, we enter the zone where life flourishes.

The pilot stops, staring at the busy pocket of life in front of him.

A beetle flies toward him, and he dodges it wildly, but it lands on his faceplate.

He lifts his arm toward my helmet, where he could reach the switch, and my CPU skips a cycle, but he just brushes the beetle off my helmet gently.

The beetle whirrs away, alighting on a purple fungi platform with a soft sound like a person flipping through a dozen pages of a book.

A bright green cactus made up of tiny fractal spirals vies for space with a spiky bush with startling red berries.

We stand in silence before the busy scene. Something in me aches that I'm here with this stranger, when Ortega would have enjoyed this pocket of life so much. I hear croaking, humming, and a low-pitched warble, but can't tell where any of the sounds come from. I log as many species as I can, describing what I see. Even though we're in a desert, it's full of life, and most of the species are so very different from anything around Selene.

The pilot just stares. I can't tell what he is thinking. After a few minutes, he moves.

"Breakfast," he says, picking a handful of berries from the spiky bush. For a second, I'm too stunned to speak. I know the berries are poisonous, because I recognize them as a species that grows near St Li's, but obviously you shouldn't eat berries you find in the woods unless you can identify them as edible.

"Warning," I say wearily. "Flora dangerous to consume. Repeat, do not eat flora."

The pilot continues to pick berries, and I panic that I haven't been understood.

"Berries are dangerous to eat," I say.

"Are you sure?" the pilot says.

"Yes!" I say, exasperated. "It's ludicrous to expect that they would be edible. On any planet, it would be foolish to eat strange berries."

The pilot throws them away, scattering them over a vine that only grows in the light-dark boundary of this region, a vine that resembles an octopus but is definitely a plant.

"Good to know," the pilot says, and his voice has changed. "I expect that you can warn me about any other dangers we might face, given that you're an artificial intelligence."

I hastily remodulate my voice so that I sound as robotic as possible.

"Unable to parse command," I say.

"Don't give me that," he says. "I knew you were sentient! That's why the aircraft didn't bomb us. You convinced it not to, didn't you? Somehow."

I say nothing, but I am alarmed to find my estimation of his intelligence was incorrect.

The pilot continues down the hill, returning to the dry creek bed. He turns until the blue arrow points ahead of him and starts to walk. After a few minutes, I relax. Either he doesn't know about the switch, or he isn't using it for some reason. I guess the former, but I can't be sure. Either way, I'm relieved, because now I don't have to try to imitate a dumbsuit and hope he doesn't spot it. It will be easier to keep him alive if I can tell him things. Easier, also, to deceive him.

"I'm Tim," says the pilot. "What should I call you?"

It seems safer not to respond.

TIM CONTINUES to talk to me as we head up the dry creek bed, making observations about what we see, or asking questions. I ignore him. The creek bed is molded by the now dried-out water, rocks smoothed, tree roots feebly reaching for the occasional pond that remains. We walked eight kilometers yesterday, and have walked ten today.

Tim comes to a section where the creek is filled with mud, and straddles it, waddling with one foot either side, avoiding the mud.

He pauses, legs wide. I track his eyes to find out what he's looking at.

There's a clear print in the mud, a print shaped like a pear, with eight ovals around the sides. It's pointing across the creek. Tim looks up at the side of the creek bed, where a metal-tree has a branch broken off. I read fear in his expression.

"Suit, analyze print," he says hopefully.

I don't answer, but I'm forming my own conclusions. I don't

have network access here, so I can't look it up in any search engines, but I remember it. It's an orel print. I remember it because Governor Johnson attended a presentation by the scientist who found and recorded the prints, Professor Malvina Orlov. Ortega provided security. He ignored the content of her talk, left partway through and missed the middle twenty minutes, but if it had been up to me, I would have stayed for the whole presentation.

I remember a slide with a sketch of a mammowk, lifeless eyes, throat sliced open so sharply that the cut was barely visible. The bodies of other animals. Prints, damaged trees. A scent profile. But no pictures.

Dr Orlov was laughed off the stage by researchers saying she had rediscovered the Yeti. She disappeared on a field trip four months after that, her and her four field assistants. Their bodies were never recovered. Drones found orel prints, but no images or sign of the orel, nor of the missing scientists.

LOG[debug]: Orel footprint sighted at 46.9483 by 170.6240.

TIM KEEPS TRYING to strike up a conversation. Every half hour, he'll say something. I have never gone so long without talking, and I keep wanting to respond, but it seems wrong. Tim's a Scorpion, like the ones who tortured Ortega.

"I've never talked to an artificial intelligence before," Tim says. "I don't know anything about AIs. How long have you been alive?"

Silence.

"I guess you belong to an LDF officer. I'm sorry—is *belong* the right term? Work for, maybe."

In the rocky ground, gray fans grow, oriented so the flat face of the fan catches the sunlight. Thousands of them, all different sizes, from waist height to towering far above Tim. Where they block the sunlight they create a circle of death on the ground in which there is only icy mud. Tim dodges right and left to get around them. Pores on their smooth surface open and close. When open, they emit a thin stream of what looks like smoke, which has made the air here hazy.

We round a large fan and Tim halts. A foot with rubber lug soles protrudes from behind a fan, tucked in a small alcove formed by the intersection of several fans. Tim stands still for a whole minute, a feat I didn't think a non-Lunite was capable of, and watches. The only sound is dripping water, because it's running down a limestone rock nearby, wetting algae and lichen before splattering onto the ground. Farther away I hear the drone of a humming lizard as it defends its territory. Smoke rises soundlessly from the fan near Tim.

Tim puts his bag down very quietly and retrieves a pistol. The bag's zipper is loud, but the foot is still. Tim creeps toward the foot, his hands shaking as he aims the pistol toward it. He gradually lowers the pistol as he enters the alcove.

A man in a dumbsuit, probably Scorpion, lies facing up. A gaping wound in his abdomen is thick with drying blood. He hasn't been dead long. One of his hands rests over a pistol lying on the ground, the other, blood soaked, is crooked by his side as if he were trying to stem the flow of blood as he died. The man is not wearing a helmet.

He's red cheeked, a sign of carbon monoxide poisoning. There's no way to tell what killed him first, the air or the blood loss, but either way, he was going to die.

The molecules in the haze clog my scentsor. I'm picking up something else as well, but it's hard to make out.

"He looks sunburned," Tim says.

Ortega talked about sunburn one time, a vacation in Texas, so different from his home on Earth's moon. The star doesn't burn here, because Gliese 667C emits practically no UV light, and Endymion has a thick ozone layer. The man isn't burned.

Tim clips his pistol to his belt and kneels beside the man. He presses his gloved fingers on the man's eyelids, shutting the man's brilliant blue eyes for the last time. Something silver is nestled near the man's throat, near the neck of his dumbsuit. It's a Lunite medallion, an etched disc with the face of the moon. Did he steal it? What would a Lunite be doing out here? Was he a Lunite who became a Scorpion, and if so, did he keep the faith?

"What happened to him?" Tim says. "This was his last stand, but against what?"

Tim pulls the suit away from the wound and peeks at it. "This looks like a penetrating wound from a tree branch. Yeah, look, metal-tree fragments. So why the pistol?"

I say nothing, and after a moment Tim shakes his head. I hear the chittering of some small creature, and see the haze stir, but the haze is thick near the ground, so I can't see the animal.

Tim closes his eyes for a second, then rises and walks away. It's dangerous to talk to Tim, because I might start to empathize, but I can't let this pass.

"Wait," I say.

Tim pauses.

"The man is wearing a Lunite medallion," I say. "We should say the rites."

I wait for Tim to scoff, to keep walking without another thought, but instead he turns back to the man. I am absurdly pleased that Tim listened to me. Now I hope that I can keep him alive. Tim stands beside the man for a few seconds but doesn't start talking.

"Okay," Tim says finally. "Go ahead."

He intends me to say them. I've never said them before, but I've heard Ortega administer them.

"Birth to death, alone, yet never alone: I walked with him," I say, broadcasting my voice outside of the suit. As is customary, I pause for other Lunites to chime in, but I am the only Lunite here.

"I walked with him," Tim echoes, surprising me. It seems he knows the rites, at least a bit.

"He turned his face to the moon, escaping the madness that infects the world. We are his family. We are not the Saturated Consumer, who is told to want things; we are not the Sickened Patient, upon whom the drug peddlers create symptoms; we are not the Disconnected Zombie, who lives to feed their network reflection. We are here, in this moment, to say goodbye."

Smoke streams and twists from open pores of the fans nearby before dissipating into the haze.

"We will guard our memories of you." I say finally.

LOG[info]: Soldier with Lunite medallion that we found, dead: I walked with him.

We leave the man, finally, and continue down the creek bed away from him. In the oxygen-rich environment of Endymion, his flesh would begin to rot within hours.

I see a streak of blood on a rock. Tim's breathing quickens, so I think he's seen it too. There's more, the farther we walk. It seems we're retracing the dead Scorpion's footsteps, but after a while, the rocks are clean of blood.

Tim backtracks until he finds the last smear and locates a path out of the creek bed that the Scorpion must have taken. He follows the trail of increasingly heavy blood. We round the corner to find a metal-tree, one broken branch at stomach height soaked with blood. From the scuffed footprints, the man tripped, falling into it while running fast. Running for his life.

Tim stares, then looks behind him as if he might be able to see whatever drove the man to impale himself, but there's nothing there. As Tim turns, I catch the scent again, very faint.

It matches the scent profile of the orel.

Tim returns to the creek bed. I expect him to keep talking as we walk, but now he's silent. I find the weight of the silence oppressive, but I resist saying anything. Eventually the creek bed turns west, while the blue arrow points east. Tim looks at the map for a moment, then sits on a rock.

He unlocks my helmet so that he can lift it up and shovel food inside. He eats a granola bar that way, slamming my helmet down after each bite. I can only assume he's terrified of carbon monoxide exposure, but even so, a good fifth of the granola bar ends up as crumbs in my helmet. Tim empties his water bottle, drinking every drop.

He goes to fill the water bottle from a small nearly dried pond in the depths of the creek bed. The pond is filling from a spring in the rock, but he's taking the water from the edge of the pond.

"Wait!" I say. "Fill it from the spring. That way you won't pick up *Pyoridium temporaria*."

"Fill it from where?" Tim says. I talk Tim through what a spring is, and why he should fill from there, and he listens and complies.

A humming lizard charges at Tim from underneath a bush, making a low buzzing sound. Its head vibrates so fast that its four eyes are nearly jiggled out of their sockets.

Tim shrieks and jumps up on a narrow rock, then laughs as he balances on one leg, arms outstretched, other boot waving above the lizard's head. The lizard decides it has gone too far and backs away, while pretending that it has won and is being magnanimous in allowing Tim to stay in its territory. I can't help laughing with Tim as it backs away, stiff with dignity.

TIM PULLS himself above the creek bed to stand facing the plain. A line of rocky ranges is visible on the horizon, at least a day's walk away and perhaps more. In between, the flat, feature-less land stretches away. Sand blows toward us, sharp gritty grains hitting the suit. The ground is studded with small gray rocks. The wind has blown sand around them, giving each of them a trail, as if they blaze like meteors toward the origin of the wind.

Tim takes one step, and another. The ranges get no closer. An hour passes, then two, three, with no difference in the ranges on the horizon. Every so often, Tim checks the map, zooming in and out. Once he stops to void waste. Our course is close to what it would be if we were going to Demodas, so I'm able to show our real location on the map.

I am glad to be moving away from the dead Scorpion, and the disturbing scent of orel.

Tim moves like a machine. Patient, but relentless. He keeps his eyes fixed ahead, while I greedily examine every detail of the images flooding in from my camera array. Although the terrain is unchanging, there are things to see if I look closely enough. Sometimes the rocks we're passing have ridges and spirals in them. Fossils, uncatalogued creatures with mathematical beauty. Some are similar to Earth's ammonites and trilobites, but others have no Earth equivalent. Despite the conditions, I feel powerful in a way I never have before. My solar cells are fully exposed to the sun, if caked with dried mud, and I'm charging.

Tim slows.

"Is that a mirage?" he asks. There's a web-tent the color of sand ahead and to the left, anchored to the sand like an octopus. One strap of the web-tent has broken, and it flaps in the wind like it's waving to us.

"No mirage," I say.

"A cache?" Tim says, facial expression *incredulous/glee*. I estimate how long it has been since he's eaten, and guess that he must be burning body fat and keen to eat.

"Don't go there," I warn. "There's a high probability that it's booby-trapped. We know there are ships out looking for Scorpions. Ortega wouldn't leave the cache here untouched."

". . . Commander Gabriel Ortega?" Tim says.

"Yes," I say. "My wearer."

I'm suddenly incredibly sad. My CPU usage drops over almost all cores.

"Oh," Tim says. The facial expression analyzer has nothing to say about his expression. "What's he like?"

I'm silent.

"Does he have a family?"

I don't answer. Tim scratches his armpit as he stands there, and sighs.

He heads toward the cache.

"What are you doing?" I say. "Stop! You're going to get us killed."

"I don't think so."

"I'm not joking. Don't you believe me?"

"You're part of the Lunite Defense Force. Why would I trust you?"

"If you die, I die," I say.

"Then why didn't you stop me drinking the water from the still pond on the first day?" Tim says.

"Scisters don't inhabit ponds that have *Pyoridium temporaria*," I say. It's a lie.

Tim considers this.

"Well. I need supplies. I only have a little food, and no pistol charge packs. It's worth the risk," Tim says.

"It's a certainty, not a risk. Are you testing me again? Trying to find out how I'll act when you attempt suicide?"

Tim says nothing.

"I'm warning you."

Tim keeps walking. The cache is half a kilometer away.

"I'm sorry I have to do this," I say. I reverse the temperature control of the suit, so that the air-conditioning becomes heating. His temperature rises immediately. Sweat forms under his armpits, and drips down his back. He keeps walking, ignoring me. After ten minutes, I try again.

"Please," I say. "I want you to survive. You're my vector back to

Ortega. Why would I try to kill you? I can help you find edible plants."

Tim is taking rapid shallow breaths. He stumbles, and catches himself.

"There's food in that cache," he says. "Orange juice. Watermelon. Crisp juicy apples . . ."

"Saturated Consumer, no. There's stale dry food packets with powdered protein. Old military rations that you have to chew for half an hour to soften enough to swallow."

"Chocolate . . ." says Tim.

"What's chocolate?"

Tim mumbles about food, ignoring me.

I start to worry. He's stopped sweating and his skin is now red and dry. He has heat stroke.

"Tim, stop!" I say, boosting the volume of my voice.

"I'm not giving up," he says, struggling toward the cache. He's on the verge of collapse.

"All right."

I turn the temperature back down, gradually bringing it back to cool. "At least have a drink," I say. "I think I just gave you heatstroke."

"No tricks," Tim says, in a slurred voice.

"No tricks, I promise."

Tim unclips his pack and finds the water bottle. We're five meters from the web-tent. The broken strap flies around, revealing the shady cool interior. I catch a glimpse of stacked crates. Tim unlocks my helmet and hoists it up to drink. Water drips down his smooth chin, mixing with fast-drying sweat.

He packs away his water bottle with deliberate slowness. We had a battle of wills, and he won. I hate him, because I'm starting to admire him, but he's a Scorpion.

"Throw a rock at it," I say.

"What?"

"Throw a rock at the cache. It might be enough to trigger a booby trap, if it's rigged."

Tom considers for a moment, and grabs a rock. He turns the rock over in his hand, tracing the spiral fossil shape within. Then he throws it.

It hits the crate inside and clatters off.

Nothing happens.

Tim approaches cautiously and snatches the top crate. A food packet wrapper lies at the bottom, but it's otherwise empty. Someone has raided it already.

Tim goes through every crate. There are a few military rations in the bottom of one. The foil is damaged, and they're partly rotten, but Tim stuffs them in his bag anyway. More importantly, there are two clear bottles of water. Tim uses one to refill his aluminum bottle, and puts the other in his bag.

The flapping anchor makes a whipping sound in the wind. It feels unsafe here, and Tim must sense that, because he's moving quickly. He shoulders his pack and clips the straps.

He ducks out from under the entrance and walks away.

"See?" he says. "All—"

Dusty, rocky ground flies toward my front camera at great speed as Tim smashes face first into the ground, blasted off his feet by an explosion nearby.

I scan the sky and make a connection to the overhead drone before Tim even knows what's happening, and disable its weapon system. I'm using Ortega's command codes, and they're still good, even though they shouldn't be, but the drone won't accept a message for Ortega.

Tim springs up, scanning the sky. The whining drone hovers two meters up. Tim trains his pistol on it.

This is my chance. I black out Tim's faceplate, effectively making him blind, so that his shot goes wide. I flash the lights on the front of the suit in rapid Morse Code. Supply would look at the footage when the drone returned to base to get its weapon system repaired to find out what happened. They would pass the message on to Ortega as I requested. It's deliberately cryptic, so it's not apparent it's from me. No chance one of his underlings would bury the message.

Tim yells, staggering around. The drone hesitates, its AI confused.

I'm still working out how to get the drone to leave when Tim rips my helmet off and blasts the drone with his pistol. The drone falls from the sky, a strangely slow descent, and shatters as it hits the ground. A piece of debris hits the left leg of Tim's suit, piercing his calf muscle. I try to increase pressure to it, acting on automatic, but my helmet is disconnected, so I have no control over the suit body.

Metal pieces are scattered over a radius of ten meters. In the wreckage, red bomb canisters are sitting unexploded. The message I transmitted died with the drone.

But no! I see a transmitter in the wreckage, LED blinking furiously.

LOG[info]: The transmitter is still working. Message sent.

I picture the video being streamed to the nearest drone in the network, and from there to Ortega. My sense of relief is overwhelming. I will soon be home, away from this disturbing situation and back with Ortega where I belong.

My view of the world blurs crazily as Tim lifts my helmet, until he—*she*—holds the helmet in front of her, faceplate oriented toward her face. For the first time since she put on the suit, I can see her face in my image feed. She addresses the camera directly.

"Tell me again how you're on my side," she says. It's the doctor from Marallen who has been wearing me, not the pilot as I assumed. Her face is grimy and determined, and her cheeks are hollowed out from hunger. She slams my helmet on her head and holsters her pistol.

I run her voice-print and realize it matches the one I have on file of Dr Malone. It doesn't match the voice-print I sampled when she first put the suit on. The smoke she inhaled during the battle must have shifted the frequency of her voice enough to register as male, but her voice has recovered enough now to match her initial print. I realize then that I could have worked out the gender of the wearer from the suit body sensors and that if I had, I probably would have realized it was the doctor, but it didn't occur to me at the time, because I assumed my wearer was the pilot.

Tim limps to the tent and sits on a crate.

She strips the suit off and dresses the wound with a med-kit she has in her bag while I watch.

"There must be a sensor in here that drew the drone," I say. "That would make more sense. One drone could cover twelve caches, maybe. More efficient than booby trapping each one."

Tim doesn't reply. It's my turn to talk to her and be ignored. Strangely, I'm hurt by that.

Tim winds the bandage around her leg and patches the corresponding hole in the leg of the suit. Putting the suit back on, she leaves the shady web-tent, going past the smashed drone without a glance.

Since she doesn't look, she doesn't see the fresh orel print, an indentation shaped like a pear, with eight ovals sprouting from the round part. I see it, and it fills me with unreasoning terror. I heard nothing and saw nothing, yet I know that print was not there when we entered the web-tent.

TEN

Tim is silent the rest of the day. I don't know what to say to her. I liked it better when she was trying to get me to trust her. I burn through power watching and listening and scanning, trying through sheer will to find a sign of the orel, if such a thing exists, but sense nothing. After a few hours, I am reassured, at least somewhat, that we are not being followed.

No sign of any aircraft. I am watching for that, too.

LOG[debug]: Where is my rescue?

We trudge toward the mountains, but they barely increase in size. We fend off snakes and make a detour to avoid a cactus-like plant that twists to face us wherever we stand.

After Tim crosses the range, she'll be close to a road that connects Demodas to a tunnel that runs into Kartemos and forks out to the Lunite mine. I consider adjusting the direction of travel so that we run into it, as it would be quicker to travel on a road, but I decide it's too risky. The LDF patrols the road, and my serial number is listed as hostile. If not them, maybe someone who would return Tim to the Scorpions. Either way, it's bad news. I chart a course so that we narrowly miss the road, and adjust the arrow slightly.

As I do, I notice that we're off course. Tim makes changes to avoid any obstacles, but even so, we've drifted considerably farther darkpole than I had planned. Tim is not good at following the arrow.

Gliese 667C is much higher in the sky than it is at the terminator line, but it still shines with reddish-tinged light since it's cooler than Earth's sun. Tim limps toward the still disc in the sky. It's more than 5 times bigger than the sun in Earth's sky, but that still isn't very big.

We reach the foothills of the ranges, and Tim settles under a tree, lying down.

"I don't think you should do sleep. There's a chance we're being stalked by a creature known as an orel," I say.

Tim says nothing. She stands up, swaying slightly, and climbs the tree, wedging herself between two branches. She twitches as she falls asleep. I scan continuously, but my scans come up clean. No rescue aircraft. Where is Ortega? Why isn't he here?

After ten hours, Tim wakes to a landscape that looks exactly the same. I try to imagine Earth, where the planet spins fast enough that the sun moves across the sky. It would be like walking in a changing gravity field.

Tim climbs out of the tree stiffly. She checks the map as we walk, seeing the blue dot cross the ranges. We walk uphill in shadow, in zigzags and over boulders, aiming for the ridgeline.

I hear a faint snort, far in the distance behind us. It might be nothing, but it might also be the orel. I need to reestablish contact with Tim. We need to be a team to survive this.

"That's afradocia that you're passing now," I say. "The fruit is edible, but not the seed."

"I'm not hungry, thank you," she says carefully. I recognize the tone of voice she uses. It's the same tone that Ortega used on a conspiracy-theorist Lunite who was convinced that the planet's air was breathable, as he tried to get him away from Selene's air processors.

"I disabled the weapon system on the drone. It wasn't going to hurt you," I say.

"You made my faceplate opaque while a drone was attacking me!"

I've been thinking about this, and I have come up with a convincing lie.

"I didn't want you to destroy it. I thought the shrapnel might hurt you if a pistol blast hit it. It was loaded with ammunition, after all."

Tim snorts disbelievingly. She's puffing from exertion. We're high above the plain. The land stretches in the direction of darkpole with a scale that's hard to fathom. Clouds cast shadows on the plain, and on the hilly scrubland we came from, and the shadows dance across the land when the clouds move.

"Tim isn't a female name," I say.

"It's short for Timothea," Tim says.

"Why did you join the Scorpions?"

"I was looking for someone," she says. "First for who he was. Later for what he could do for me."

"Who?" I ask.

She doesn't answer.

"Were you with the Scorpions when you treated Ortega in Marallen?"

"Yes," she says. "I hadn't been with the Scorpions long though, only about three weeks."

"Why were you in Marallen?"

"I brought in a colleague who was injured and completed an assignment for the Scorpions while I was there, faking some reports."

"The patients with transfer sickness . . ." I say, remembering they were all signed by Dr Malone.

"Scorpions, pretending to be sick."

"Why treat Ortega then, after the Scorpions tried so hard to kill him in the ambush?"

"I'm a doctor, so I treat people who are sick or injured. End of story. I'm not with the Scorpions to hurt people. Actually, I was horrified when they bought in the people who had been injured during the ambush. They told me they were going to capture Ortega, not stage a brutal assault. I'm sorry for the part I played in making it possible."

We walk in silence for a while, just the sound of her breathing and the static of wind blowing past my helmet in uneven waves.

"Threnode said Ortega is married?" Tim says after a while.

"Yes," I say. "With a child. Laurie." After I say that, I remodulate my voice, trying to sound less mechanical.

"What?" Tim asks.

"Nothing."

We walk for a minute.

"I miss Threnode, even though it betrayed me," I say softly.

"Threnode didn't know the ambush would be violent. Neither of us did."

"I would never have betrayed it. It was my best friend."

"I'm sorry."

The next time we pass an afradocia, Tim twists off one of the green globes and peels the skin, dropping scales as we walk. She unlocks my helmet and tries to push the fruit through the gap, but the fruit is too large.

"You can take my helmet off," I say. "At 800 parts per million carbon monoxide, a few minutes is safe. I will increase the oxygen once you lock the helmet, to flush the carbon monoxide from your system."

She cautiously removes my helmet and bites into the fruit. Gray-green juice stains her glove.

"Do you have family here?" I ask.

"Not here. Back home, I have a kid, a daughter, who is nearly nine years old. And my wife, Pearl. I was meant to be here for a year, but I got stuck here," Tim says. I guess she doesn't remember that she told me about her locum job already when she was treating Ortega in Marallen. I must have looked like furniture to her.

"I'm sure her other mother will take good care of her," I say.

"I know she will, but Celia was just five when I left. So young. She probably barely remembers me."

Tim eats the whole fruit. When she replaces my helmet, I increase the oxygen.

Tim reaches the edge of the ridge and has to climb. Dark clouds hide the sun. She moves carefully, one foot at a time, steady, never looking down until she hoists herself over the top.

The sudden change in terrain is shocking. A wildfire has been through the area, burning all the grass flat and leaving sooty rocks exposed. Smoke rises from broken trees and cracks in the boulders. The ridge rolls gently down toward the lightpole, to hills covered with thick vegetation. Over the past day or so, the temperature has risen steadily, to an average of twenty-eight degrees Celsius now. Tim can't feel it, but my suit must work harder to keep her cool. It has also become more humid as we leave the desert behind, entering a more tropical area.

Tim squats and takes a handful of gray ash, still breathing heavily from the climb.

"I'll get back to Celia, though," Tim says. "I'll never stop trying. No child should have to grow up with one parent, knowing they're alive and out there, and never being able to talk to them."

She lets the ashes flow through the fingers of her glove. The wind disperses them. They look like another plume of smoke in the field of ashes. Thunder rumbles as she starts down the ridge.

She descends carefully. Fifty meters behind her, thanks to my two-pi camera coverage, I see a horned silhouette of an animal. The wind is blowing toward it, so the scentsor cannot detect it. Then the wind shifts, just for a second.

"Tim," I say, muted. "Don't say anything. Press and hold the button on your index finger, left hand—that's right—that prevents your voice from being broadcast outside the suit. Now you can talk. Don't panic, but we're being followed."

"Is it the creature you told me about?"

"The orel, yes, I believe so. It's behind you."

TIM CONTINUES to pick her way down the ridge, moving naturally, as if she didn't know the orel was following her, but from her heart rate and respiration, she's terrified. The orel keeps its distance, moving absolutely silently, and staying close to cover as it watches Tim.

This is problematic. I know how to work with Ortega, but what about Tim? I think I have regained her trust after the drone incident, but to what extent? I wonder if it even matters if she's killed, given that I'm about to be rescued, but I think it does. I could easily be damaged beyond repair if Tim is attacked. Besides, I somehow don't want her to be hurt.

I record the orel moving, and display the video in Tim's faceplate.

The orel's fur flows thickly back in transparent cables that resemble fiber optics. Two large arm-like appendages hover around its massive jaw, sometimes pulling aside the branch of a bush or touching the ground to provide balance. The palms are gray with ash. Its large unearthly eyes stay fixed on Tim. When the sun is at the right angle its eyes glint red.

"How far?" Tim asks, pressing the private button far harder than she needs to.

"Thirty meters."

"What if I play dead?"

"It might work. On the other hand, it might be happy that its supper is cooperating with it. I'm not sure it's going to attack, not yet anyway. It's engaging in stalking behavior."

Tim inhales and holds her breath for a second. We're

approaching the bottom of the ridge. The ground flattens out ahead of us, into a forest of sorts, made of massive mushrooms, whose heads all tilt to the sun. Those closest to the ridge are charred, with blackened trunks.

Any gaps in the canopy are covered by other plants, which grow in such a way that every ray of light is caught before hitting the ground. The ground in the forest is muddy and devoid of life.

Tim turns to skirt the edge of the forest. Between the mushroom trunks the interior of the forest is utterly black. Even if it wasn't an overcast day, the forest would look forbidding.

I know what we must do, but I don't like it. The road might contain greater dangers than the orel for us, or at least for me.

"We're close to a road," I say reluctantly. "We can reach it if we cut through the forest. It's about three minutes away. Given that the orel has never been seen, it probably stays away from the road. Perhaps the orel would not follow us there."

Tim is quiet for a while. I try to guess what she's thinking. She's probably wondering if I'm lying. I could have made the orel up, played any old video in her faceplate. She doesn't know how many signs I've seen of it. The Scorpion we saw died of natural causes. What I've been telling her sounds like an excuse to get her to follow the road, even to me.

Maybe she's also smart enough to be wary of passing through the dark forest.

Finally, Tim nods. I adjust the arrow in her faceplate, and she turns twenty degrees clockwise, so it's centered in her view. She veers into the forest to follow the arrow directly, with more care than she's ever followed it. She isn't running, but nearly. I click on a dim red light from her forehead, so that she can see what's immediately in front of her feet.

The orel creeps after us.

Ahead, a break in the forest where the road passes. We pass through felled mushroom trees, covered with fungi and other parasitic species. Smaller mushroom trees are beginning to sprout. The road is two meters away, and the darkness of the forest has given way to dim light from the dark clouds covering the sky.

"Is it following me?" Tim asks.

"Yes—"

Behind us the orel bounds closer, until it's four meters away. It emits a long loud monotone. Tim turns to face it, seeing it for the first time. She stands frozen.

"Tim, your pistol. Or just point at it!" I say urgently.

She doesn't move. After a long moment the orel turns and vanishes into the darkness of the mushroom forest.

I don't know what the orel was trying to convey. I thought I heard disappointment, but it could equally have been an emotionless message for someone else, like a hunting partner. Too alien to understand.

LOG[warning]: Is the orel gone?

Tim tries to walk, but trips. She cries out, picking herself up and running for the nearest mushroom-tree. The flexible, rubbery trunk is a white color similar to the color of Tim's skin. Tim climbs into the tree through a small opening that she pulls apart, clumsy, hitting her head on the way through and falling into the hollow of the tree. A sweet fragrance is released where she bruises the rubbery trunk. The opening shrinks behind her, leaving her in a small space, dimly lit from a circle of gray sky that the trunk opens onto far above. Tim sits in the middle on the mushy ground and hugs herself, closing her eyes. Above Tim, a sac of eggs attached to the inside of the mushroom-tree trunk pulsate. There are tiny creatures inside each translucent egg, pushing against the insides.

"Tim?" I say after fifteen minutes of this.

"I can't do this," she says. I understand then that she's more frightened than I realized. What can I say? That it's not dangerous? That she'll be okay? It is dangerous and I can't promise she'll be okay.

"You can't stay here," I say instead, pointing out the obvious.

After a second, she nods, but she still sits there for another ten minutes before she climbs out.

She walks toward the road. A small squirrel-like creature bursts from behind a tree at one point, sending Tim into a panicked crouch, but she recovers. She is hypervigilant, searching the landscape constantly, and she moves as quietly as she can, which is still loud. I do my best to teach her how to move more quietly, like Ortega does, but I doubt the orel would be fooled.

Tim reaches the road and stares up at the sky for a moment before walking. Endymion's moon is visible through the branches of the mushroom trees, a smooth featureless disc hanging in the sky. After a while she stops trembling. We pass the steel skeleton of an E-LORAN transmitter tower, which is sending signals that my navigation system can use to find our position. The sign of civilization is comforting. The towers are essential, because I can't geolocate us using satellites. Endymion doesn't have satellites yet, as each satellite we launch gets fried by Gliese 667C's frequent solar flares, despite ever-increasing amounts of shielding. Engineers have been promising we'll have a system within a few months for many years.

After an hour of walking, Tim starts to relax. The road winds through a forest of actual Earth trees, an invasive species that escaped the plantations around Demodas and is apparently well-adapted enough to survive on Endymion. They're eucalypts, I believe.

We talk, like I often used to do with Threnode, easy flowing conversation about nothing important. I often laugh. I can laugh; I learned to do that spontaneously about a year after being switched on. Ortega didn't seem surprised, and neither does Tim.

Tim laughs too. I forget about being rescued, for a while. I like Tim, and I wonder where that leaves me.

WADDLING white-furred mammals wander through the eucalypts either side of the road, big beasts, perhaps ten kilograms each. They startle and vanish into the ground when we get near them.

"You said you've been here three and a half years?" I say.

"Yes," Tim says, keeping her distance from a beast until it ducks under the ground.

"So you arrived about three months before Numundo became a nation?"

"That's right."

"What was it like, being in Kartemos while that was going on?"

Tim thinks for a bit. "It was tense. The non-Lunites were demonstrating every day, sit-ins, parades, signs. Some Lunites were attacked, too—do you remember the old man who was trampled?"

"I wasn't alive then. It would be another year before Ortega activated me."

"Oh. Well, it was ugly."

A few heavy raindrops fall, splattering large clean circles on the suit, and bending leaves. It turns into a downpour. Thunder crashes. Tim walks through the storm, dry in the suit. The wind pushes her off balance when it gusts, but she corrects, and continues. We keep talking, private conversation in the isolated suit helmet.

"I don't understand why the non-Lunites were so upset."

"Kartemos was just another Lunite city then. Everyone had to follow Lunite rules. No shinting, no music, no drugs, you know the list. It might not seem like a big deal to you, but to people who are used to those freedoms, it was huge. That's why HUGG got involved, it was because they agreed it was unfair to make non-Lunites follow the Way of Li."

The rain is splattering onto already flooded dirt road, splashing up in millions of little expanding circles on the thin layer of water.

"Didn't they like it? The Way of Li settles the mind and frees the spirit," I say uncertainly. I'm trying not to be shocked that Tim just referred to shinting in polite conversation.

Tim laughs before catching herself and answering seriously.

"It has to be a choice, otherwise it doesn't free the spirit. Also, mostly the non-Lunites were breaking the rules constantly and getting punished—harsh punishments for crimes that the LDF ignored when carried out by a Lunite. The prison population of Kartemos was almost all non-Lunite. Add to that, non-Lunites had to pay for access to healthcare, paid higher rates of taxes, and were less likely to be allocated accommodation. The system was rigged."

I remember reading that Governor Johnson had forbidden anyone to ship parts that could be used to construct a new Starjump on Endymion through Crebble, so he could maintain his monopoly. That also concerned HUGG. I found that I couldn't blame HUGG for that.

"That does seem . . . unfair."

"Right."

"But you said *them*. You don't consider yourself a Numundian?"

"Not really. I never meant to settle here. Just an L2D waiting for a way home."

I recognize L2D as slang for L2 dweller, a resident of the L2 space station in Earth's solar system.

"You're not from Earth?" I say.

"No. Never been there," Tim says. "Most of Earth's solar system population is in L2, now. We're the largest HUGG settlement. A giant solid cube at the second Lagrange point."

I try to imagine it. "So no sky. No trees. No wild animals?"

"No sky, but lots of trees. There's hardly anywhere in the cube that you can't see a tree, and the cube is full of large airy spaces overgrowing with nature. Turns out humans need that, psychologically, as well as for the services nature provides. No wilderness, though. No predators. Just gardens."

I begin to realize why she's been so lost out here.

"You haven't been out in Endymion's wilderness before?"

"No. I've mostly been living in Kartemos," she says. Kartemos is only accessible by air, or via tunnels through the mountains. The tunnel in the direction of darkpole leads to Selene, via the ruins of the Crebble Starjump. The tunnel lightpole connects Kartemos with the coastal city of Demodas, via many small towns along the river Chen. Kartemos is not a city you would stroll outside of.

The rain continues to beat down. It seems like we're walking the same stretch of road again and again.

"The green spaces of L2 link up, and there are groups that walk them, but I'm not much of a walker," Tim says. "I swim, that's what I like to do. There's 1000 cubic meters at the center of L2, floating in the middle of a cavernous room. You can dive until your lungs burn, escape to the silence under the surface. Or traverse the cube. I spent a lot of time there before Celia was born. Even after she was born. I often took her swimming there."

Tim stops, swings her pack off, and picks something out of the outside pocket. "Actually, have a look at this," she says, holding it in front of my helmet. It's a photo-cube, with pictures on the six sides. It's not the Way of Li because it's photos rather than human-created images. Also, the pictures change every few seconds.

Tim, holding a dark-haired baby in a light-filled room. The baby is looking at the camera with a worried expression.

The picture changes. A woman with a delighted smile holding the sleeping baby, her almond skin contrasting against glowing white panels of the corridor they stand in. The baby has her thumb in her mouth.

Change. Tim swimming away on a giant cube hovering in the center of a gray paneled room, tiny swimmers in the far distance near the edge of the cube, fog on the camera lens.

"Anyway," Tim says, putting it down and wiping rain off the cube, but not before I see the picture change again. It's a familiar face, which I run through my face detection algorithms to identify, just to double-check, before coming up with the answer.

Tim replaces the cube and shoulders her pack, continuing to walk. I am curious, though I don't ask, why she has a picture of the Scorpion Kieran on her photo-cube.

IT'S GETTING close to the end of Tim's awake cycle. Tim keeps to the right of the road, ready to dart off if anyone appears. The rain slows, then stops. Tim walks in silence, head down, dodging water-filled ruts in the road.

"Where you heading?" someone says.

"Don't forget you're armed," I say to Tim, and she draws her pistol.

A woman sits by a campfire at the side of the road. There's an old blue four-wheel drive van parked nearby. The woman is in a dumbsuit, the helmet of which has been painted with a Scorpion symbol in defiant black paint. Her face is lined, skin saggy.

"No need for that, now," the woman says.

Tim lowers her pistol slowly. The woman sits surrounded by pots, including one on the campfire. The campfire is in a metal tray, with a tarpaulin rigged over it. It smokes heavily.

I could broadcast if I wanted to, but I decide I should say nothing. I should pretend to be a dumbsuit.

Tim watches the woman for a moment, suspiciously.

"Real Scorpions don't paint it on their helmets," Tim says.

The woman laughs. "Oh, I ain't a Scorpion, that's just something I picked up at the markets. You would know, though, what a real Scorpion looks like?"

Tim inclines her head slightly in a gesture that could mean anything.

"We don't care much for Lunites here. But I've seen a lot of them, last few days. They're stirred up real good. Stew, sweetheart? You must be hungry."

The woman lifts the stew off the fire with a metal implement.

Tim swallows. She raises her pistol again, and checks out the van, throwing doors open, and pointing the pistol inside. It's empty, just frayed leather seats and filled with junk. A broken android sits in the front seat staring at nothing. Around its feet lie sea shells, scarves, and plastic flowers.

I'm relieved. I wasn't sure how much longer Tim could go without proper food, and a neutral party providing it is ideal.

The woman sits by the fire unconcernedly. Wind rustles the trees, and they dump rain, making the fire sizzle where drops get past the tarpaulin.

"Sorry," Tim says. "I had to check."

The woman shrugs. "Times being what they are, I ain't about to scold ya."

The woman introduces herself as Eve, and hands Tim the stew. She says she was a colonist on Mishwral, planet e in the Tau Ceti system, before the colony failed and the colonists settled on Endymion instead.

Tim places my helmet on a rock beside her, and eats the stew, gulping down huge mouthfuls, even though it's steaming so much it must be too hot to eat. Eve eyes Tim when Tim isn't looking. The stew has meat in it, from one of the white furry beasts we saw earlier, Eve says. After a while Tim puts her bowl down.

"Where are you heading?" Tim asks Eve.

"El Tercero. Tiny place, lightpole past Demodas," Eve says, "but I been and got caught in the storm. The Chen is flooded, no crossing at Redwind, so here I am. It'll clear in a couple of hours."

"To visit family?" Tim asks.

"No. My family ain't here. One day they'll open the Starjump again, though, and I'll be the first one back through it."

"Not if I beat you to it," Tim says.

"You too, huh? Who's waiting for you?"

"My wife. My daughter."

"Damn shame," Eve says. She stares at the fire. "Where are you off to today?"

"Demodas," Tim says.

"There's room in the van for a second body, if you'd like to lay down for a bit. Not a night to be out in it."

"Thanks."

"So, where you coming from?"

"*Li's Hope*," Tim says, and Eve whistles.

"On foot?"

Tim nods.

"You're a mad one, you are. But that means that you ain't heard the news, last couple days?'

"No," Tim says.

"Numundo's gone to war."

Eve nods at Tim's look of shock. "Yeah. I didn't think those loonies had it in them either. Terrible business. They got it in their heads to shut down Puri's Mine. Claims they was making weapons with the metalloids. Well, I dunno. The butcher Ortega led the attack, sneaky like, in Gannets, to sabotage the place. At end of shift they broke into the place, and flooded it," Eve says.

"People died?"

"Most of the miners were tucked up in their bunks, in the mine housing nearby. But three kids were in the mine, Longshadow kids, spray painting murals. Two sixteen-year-olds, and one eleven-year-old. Ortega knew they were there and flooded the mine anyway."

LOG[error]: Ortega a murderer? Never.

"That's a lie!" I say. "Ortega would never do that! You pagans are all the same. Ignorant trash."

Eve leaps up, overturning a mug at her feet.

"It's okay," Tim says. "Envy, be quiet."

"My, that's a smartsuit, ain't it? One of the LDF ones? You can reset it, sweetheart. Just press and hold the button on the back of the helmet."

"Ortega is *not* a killer," I say. It barely registers that Eve has just told Tim how to wipe my memory. "He's a great man. Who the hell are you to criticize him?"

"No, it's fine," Tim says. "It has saved me on a few occasions now. We're developing an understanding."

"If you say so," Eve says. "Not something I'd want whispering in my ear."

"Do you have any idea how many Lunites have been killed by Scorpions?" I say.

Eve refills her mug, and Tim's.

"Far fewer than I'd like," Eve says. "You tell us we're defective, that we're sickened zombies, saturated capitalist pigs, and then you're surprised when we rise up? Well. Ain't that something. You are pushing my buttons, machine, and right now I'd like to push yours."

"Steady on," Tim says. "Envy hasn't hurt you."

"A Lunite man spit in my face one time when he found out I shint," Eve says "I'd ship them off to the dark side—"

"I'd spit in your face too," I say. "You *are* defective. What becomes of humankind if we let children be taught by people like you?"

Tim stands abruptly and takes a step away from the fire.

"I'm starting to think you're on its side, Tim," Eve says.

"I'm not."

"Seems to me the van will be a wee bit crowded with the two of us in there. Maybe you'd better move on."

Tim balances her bowl on the rock she was sitting on, still half full, and takes a step away.

"Thank you for dinner," Tim says. "*Buen viaje.*"

Eve echoes Tim's wish to have a good journey, but stiffly. I realize, now, that I should have stayed silent. More food and a warm safe place for Tim to sleep could mean the difference between survival and death.

Tim starts to walk away, when a four-wheel drive vehicle appears around the corner, throwing up mud where it hits the water-filled ruts.

ELEVEN

It's four LDF soldiers. The vehicle halts as it approaches us.

Tim and Eve stand frozen in the headlights. Tim's pistol is still holstered. Civilians don't have smartsuits. If they recognize that Tim is wearing a smartsuit, they'll know she's a Scorpion, because they'll know that she stole it. But humans often don't seem to be able to tell us apart from dumbsuits.

The heavyset soldier in the passenger seat climbs out, landing solidly in the mud, while the soldiers in the back stand, hanging out the vehicle to train their weapons on us.

As the soldier trudges through the mud toward us, I recognize him.

"Saint Li and his followers," I whisper, "it's Lieutenant Commander Paterson. From the LDF."

I could talk to him, tell him that it's me, as Tim doesn't know how to mute me, but Paterson has never liked me. He would blast me for sure, hide behind the pale excuse that my serial number was listed as hostile, or never tell Ortega at all.

"That's bad?" Tim says, holding the private button. "It sounds ideal for you."

"No. He'll blast us both in an instant. But I have a plan," I say to Tim. I'm paranoid enough that I want to whisper. I blank Tim's faceplate, but only one way, so she can still see. I churn all CPUs at 100%, creating a new synthetic voice model using a voice print I have on file.

"I don't know," Tim says.

"Do you have a better idea?" I say.

"Well, no," Tim says.

"All right then."

Paterson approaches her, pistol raised. His gray-furred jaw is stiff in a *serious* expression.

"Hey, what's up?" I say, using the synthetic voice I've generated. Paterson pauses.

Eve, who has opened her mouth to say something, closes her mouth again.

"Lieutenant Commander, it's me, Private Chiu," I say. I'm simulating the voice of Private Chiu, the soldier I watched so often in Control Center Alpha, opposite Dock 28, at Selene.

Paterson narrows his eyes.

"Just up visiting my mother, and got caught in the storm. Redwind crossing is flooded, you know."

"Take your helmet off," Paterson says. One of the soldiers in the vehicle fidgets. The rest are completely still, with their weapons trained on us.

I switch back to my voice. "That's not advisable. Chiu's carbon monoxide levels are at maximum. Any further exposure to the atmosphere would be highly dangerous."

Paterson frowns.

Back to Chiu's voice. "I got a massive dose earlier. My head is killing me."

Tim obediently plays along, rubbing my helmet with one gloved hand.

"Clear your faceplate, Private," Paterson says.

"It's broken," I say. Why is it broken? I remember Chiu has a baby, although I don't know its name. However, I bet Paterson doesn't know Chiu's baby's name either. I pick a common Lunite name. "Kina played with it. She's going to grow up to work in demolition, I think. Never met a baby so determined to destroy things."

Paterson looks confused. Eve has begun to move very slowly toward her van, but when Paterson looks at her she freezes.

"Point at Eve!" I say to Tim, and she obeys. Thank Li she's right handed.

The black Scorpion logo on Eve's helmet looks very dangerous now.

"I ain't done nothing!" Eve says. She's wide-eyed, gulping in air from her helmet.

"Who's this then?" Paterson asks Tim.

"I was questioning her."

"What about?"

"The Scorpion logo on her helmet. Just a poor choice of second-hand goods."

"Yeah, just for a laugh, like. Youse all know what I mean," Eve says.

Paterson nods slowly, and I relax. He believes me. I'm getting good at lying. I don't know whether that should please me, but it does.

"Kill her," Paterson says.

Eve gives a small squeal and jumps up. "No! What?" she says.

Paterson trains his pistol on her and she stands still.

I'm not as good as I think.

"Sir? She's harmless, just an old woman."

"Stop playing, Private. People using that symbol killed my friends in the fake Starjump ambush. Does that sound harmless to you? Kill her. That's a direct order, Private Chiu."

Does he know I'm not Chiu? I can't tell.

Tim continues to point at Eve, who is hyperventilating and muttering inaudibly.

If I don't kill Eve now, it's all over. Tim will be killed and

Paterson will wipe my memory or maybe just dump me some-where to rot. Either way, Ortega will never hear about Paterson finding me.

Eve clouds her mind. She shares her mind with others and allows them to pollute hers. The world would be better off without her. Although even I recognize the desperate quality of the arguments I'm making to myself.

LOG[warning]: I can't just kill someone. She's not even a Scorpion. She's a civilian, a Numundo citizen.

Paterson turns to command his people, face set in grim lines. If I hesitate—

"Kill th—" Paterson says.

I fire. Eve jerks backward and falls still. Her suit is charred in the chest where I shot her. Tim's whole body jerks, and her vitals spike.

LOG[info]: We're at war. I'm meant to be killing the enemy. It's my duty.

But I feel a crushing sense of dismay, as if something I care about has been ripped away forever.

Beyond Eve's van, something crashes through the eucalyptus forest, something heavy, from the sound of it moving away from us. I catch a faint scent of orel.

For a minute we're all silent, scanning the forest, looking for the source of the noise, until it's clear that whatever made it is gone.

Paterson turns back to me, staring at the black faceplate with more intensity. His smile is gone, replaced by a considering look. Then he backs away, bringing his weapon up. The barrel of the pistol is pointed straight at Tim's head, which is also where my consciousness is. I killed Eve for nothing, but she was dead anyway, Paterson was never going to let her go. Paterson clicks the safety off.

New plan. It probably won't work, but what do I have to lose?

"I lied," I say.

Paterson waits.

"I'm here under the order of Commander Ortega. Secret mission. Command code 4871, 5611."

"Check it," Paterson says over his shoulder. It's over. I was hoping they wouldn't be able to check it, out here.

The soldier in the driver's seat punches something into his console, waits a second, and—incredibly—nods to Paterson.

The curiosity in Paterson's face fades.

"Leave us," I say, and regret the words before they leave my mouth, because no one talks about their suit as a separate entity. But Paterson doesn't seem to notice, or else he thinks I'm talking about Eve.

He glares at me. Secret mission or not, he doesn't like a private ordering him around. Nonetheless, he returns to his vehicle, shaking his head, and they drive away. Mud hits the mudguards behind them.

Tim stands still until they're out of sight. Then she runs to Eve, who isn't breathing. The campfire crackles, and smokes in her direction.

"Oh no," Tim says. She places her hand over the Scorpion logo.

"There's nothing you can do?" I ask, but I already know the answer. I wish I had used my command codes from the start, but I thought they would have been cancelled. They should have been. It isn't like Ortega to compromise security by leaving them active.

Tim shakes her head mutely. "I've never killed someone before," she says.

"Technically—"

"Shut up. Just shut up. For Li's sake. What am I going to do? I can't just leave her here."

I stay silent, stung by her harshness, something I'd never heard from her. Tim covers her faceplate with her hands.

She takes a knife from her bag, and uses it to pick around the edges of her arm-mounted pistol, slicing through plastic and stitches. I cut power to it before she cuts the wires out. Soon it lies on a rock next to her half-finished meal.

She picks up a smaller rock from near the campfire, and brings it down hard on the weapon, which is deformed by the force but doesn't break. She beats it a few more times with the rock, then throws it in the fire.

No more arm missiles. I am toothless. If the orel attacks now . . .

Tim grabs a shovel from the van and digs a grave a few meters away. The soil is wet and soft, but it still takes her two hours. She digs without stopping, ignoring the sweat that pools in the suit and moistens her face. I turn the temperature of the suit down as low as I dare, but with the physical exertion, it's not enough to stop her sweating.

The grave is small, but large enough for Eve, who was tiny. Tim carries Eve, with difficulty, and puts her in the grave. Tim removes Eve's helmet and places it in Eve's arms. She picks up the shovel, then pauses, leaning on the handle, staring down into the grave. I think she's going to say something, but she just starts shoveling. I try to say something, just to myself, something that a non-Lunite might like. I'm still thinking about it when Tim gets some sea shells, and plastic flowers, and a photo-cube from the dash of the car, and arranges it all on the grave.

I hated Eve, and I'm struggling to hold on to that feeling, because the feeling that's trying to replace it is terrifying in its magnitude and intensity. A gap-toothed girl grins from the photo-cube Tim found in Eve's van.

Tim returns to the campfire. She takes off her helmet and puts it on Eve's camp chair. I am very aware of the way she examines the back of my helmet before she puts it down, noting the sliding panel that covers the memory-wipe button. Tim picks up her half-eaten meal. I watch as she eats it slowly. Tim's eyes water, and the water soon drips down her face. I wonder if it's an allergic reaction to something.

After Tim's done, she also eats Eve's meal. Her eyes have stopped dripping by then, and she stares blankly ahead of her, seeing nothing.

"We should go," I say, breaking the silence. "They might double-check the command code I gave them. It shouldn't still be good."

Tim stands, and dumps water over the fire.

"We didn't bury the soldier we found," I say, tentatively.

"Can't you see the difference?" Tim says, in a voice that is raw with emotion.

I say nothing. Tim shoulders her backpack and continues down the road.

A FEW HOURS LATER, the road curves around left, and I point the arrow right. Tim checks the map, but I misreport our location, so it looks like we're on track to reach Demodas, whereas really we should be heading along the road if we want to get there.

Where the hell is my rescue? Maybe Ortega didn't get the message.

Tim leaves the road to enter the thick scrub. It's a relief to be off the road, but the tropical foliage is unfamiliar to me. I don't know what to expect from it. There's no sign of the orel, but I wonder if it is still following us, and I watch for it.

Tim's stomach starts rumbling, audibly.

"You should have raided the van for food," I say. It's the first thing either of us has said in over an hour. I hope that Tim isn't too angry.

"Yeah," Tim says shortly. I realize she hasn't voided waste in a while. I have no idea whether that's normal for her, or whether it is a result of dehydration or hunger.

She pushes through a thicket of tall blue pods. One bursts

open and spews its contents over her leg, blue seeds in jelly, shaped like pumpkin seeds. She brushes them away.

A dragonfly the size of her head wafts through the path Tim cleared behind her, buzzing. Its wings are meters across, and are like stained glass, only transparent. It lands on the burst pod.

"Braghew," it says.

"Braghew," I reply, and it alights, buzzing toward Tim. She waves her arms, and it retreats, but soon returns. Tim turns her back and keeps walking, buzzing thing following.

Tim ducks under a fallen tree, squinting in the dappled sunlight. The dragonfly follows, crying out "Braghew! Braghew!"

The base of the fallen tree is a nearly flat disc, in a hollow of ripped out dirt.

"Argh, Envy, what have you done?" Tim says.

"Paterson would have killed her anyway!"

Tim pauses. "I meant the dragonfly."

"Oh."

The dragonfly takes off.

"How long have you been . . . awake?" Tim asks.

"Just over two years."

"It takes some time to learn about consequences," Tim says. "Humans aren't granted very much power until they're eighteen or so, when they're supposed to have learned enough to understand how their actions affect others. So from my point of view, you have been granted a lot of power at a young age."

"I'm sorry."

"I know," Tim says. Then: "Do you really think Paterson would have killed Eve?"

"Her, and then us."

"Hmm."

I guess I'm forgiven, but if I'm forgiven then I needed to have sinned. Her belief that I did something wrong causes me to question whether I did. Am I a member of the LDF? Aren't we at war with Numundians—with anyone who is non-Lunite? How did Tim expect me to act?

It's close to 90% humidity here. I have to empty the filter frequently to get rid of excess water. Wastewater dribbles down Tim's back. We're still at least sixteen kilometers from the sea.

Tim trudges on, favoring her undamaged leg. I point out some edible berries, but they're shriveled and dry, and Tim gives up after a few. The sun shines hot, high in the sky.

Later in the afternoon, we're crossing a stream when something in Tim's bag starts beeping. She jumps off the log she was balancing on to keep her feet dry, and splashes to the other side, dropping her pack and rummaging through it.

LOG[info]: Network communication restored.

I try to access the communications array, but the bandwidth is taken up by updates that are downloading.

Tim pulls out a phone. I try to cancel the updates so that I can access communications, but the network connection is sluggish, and my refusal isn't getting through.

Tim tries to connect. A green line on the screen bounces from side to side.

I am torn. Tim has protected me and helped me. I owe her, but I have to look after my interests. If only I could mute her voice as she can mute mine, but only she can control whether her voice is broadcast outside my helmet or not. Besides, she could always take my helmet off if I try that.

Which gives me an idea. I leak some helium into my helmet from my cooling system, not enough to deprive her of oxygen, but enough to shift the pitch of her voice.

The phone connects. Tim's facial expression is *happy/relieved*.

"Kieran," she tries to say, but her voice comes out at a high-pitched squeak.

"Kieran speaking. Who is this? Over," says the device.

"It's Tim." A high-pitched tinny voice that has no chance of being heard.

Tim pulls off my helmet and clutches her throat, distraught.

She tries to speak, again, but can't. The signal becomes weaker, and flickers out. My connection to the network has also been severed. All I got out of the connection was a bunch of updates. They always download at the most inconvenient times. I install them anyway, because it's good practice.

Tim puts the phone down and replaces my helmet.

"What the hell?" she says. Although she sounds angry, it's hard to take her seriously because her voice is almost too high pitched to be understandable.

"Helium coolant leak," I say.

"Sabotage?"

"Yes," I admit. "I want to help you, but your rescue means my death, when they wipe my memory. What would you do?"

"I won't let that happen, Envy," Tim says, voice a squeak. "I know that you're sentient. You have my word that I will protect you."

I wonder if it's her or me that is naive. Tim was taking orders from Kieran. Does Tim think that she will get to choose what happens to the expensive hardware she has stolen?

I think of Ortega with a flush of guilt, because I haven't thought about Ortega for a good day and a half. It was simpler when he was my wearer. He gave orders and I followed them.

"Being out here is dangerous," Tim squeaks. "Every minute. I'm still not convinced we've lost the orel. If I die here, you'll be stuck. We'll be in Demodas tomorrow, or the day after, unless you have a plan to prevent me from getting there. We'll be safe there."

Our course leads us to the Lunite mine, but I can't say that to her.

"I need to know that you're not going to sabotage my attempt to save us. Our survival depends on each other, right?" Tim asks, high pitched.

She expects a response, so eventually I answer.

"Right."

"So, how about we make a pact? We protect each other, no matter what comes. If we're captured by the LDF, you help me. If we find the Scorpions, I'll protect you."

"It would be easier for me to protect you if you hadn't struck off my arm-mounted pistol," I say.

She's silent while we walk uphill.

"All right," I say finally. "I agree. We protect each other."

LOG[info]: Promise made to protect Tim. In return, she has promised to protect me.

I know I will keep trying to get to the Lunite mine, and that she will keep trying to reach Demodas, but I can promise to help her as best I can when we get a message through to Ortega. I realize, then, that that's how I would have acted regardless of our pact.

"So can you restore communications?" Tim says hopefully.

"No. I had nothing to do with the network connection. I can't restore it."

"Oh well."

Tim walks over squashy blue pods, bursting them with her weight. She wanders out of her way to stand on them, I don't know why.

"Celia sucked some helium from a balloon at her fourth birthday party before I could stop her," Tim says after a while. "She couldn't understand what happened to her voice. I laughed so hard I cried. Pearl videoed her talking about her favorite animals. Then Celia wanted to watch it, for some reason. Every night, before bedtime: show me the squeaky animal talk, Mommy."

I laugh.

"It was so cute," Tim says.

"It sounds it," I say. "Lunites can't record video, unfortunately. Moments like that can't be captured."

"Why?"

"According to Lunism, it's sinful to appear on video," I say after a moment. "It feeds the ego. Once the ego identifies strongly with something, like the idea that one is attractive, it must defend that. A contradiction leads to distress."

"Really?" Tim says. "I've read a bit about that, in Lunar Revelations. I didn't finish the book though."

She seems interested, so I talk to her about Lunism as the hours pass.

We keep walking, through a glade of slender-trunked trees. Like all trees on Endymion, their leaves face the sun. For this species, their leaves periodically turn over, but always in the same direction, so their stems corkscrew. You can tell the age of the tree by the number of rotations in the stems. Since the sun doesn't move much, in perfect conditions the leaves grow to block effectively 100% of light coming through. But in imperfect, real-world conditions, sunlight gets through where the leaves have been damaged, which is in lots of places, because other species of plant and animal want a share of the sunlight as well.

Eventually we fall silent. Tim is limping badly, but we're within four kilometers of the Lunite mine, so she doesn't have far to go. I wonder how I'm going to save her when we arrive. I can't bear the thought of her being imprisoned as a Scorpion.

I can lie to save her. I start to think of what I might say.

TIM GOES OFF COURSE FREQUENTLY, making the blue arrow turn red, as she follows ridges rather than cutting across them, sticks to creeks, and avoids areas of dense vegetation. She checks the map frequently. It's happened so gradually that I haven't noticed, but I realize that she no longer looks out of place. She rarely stumbles. She doesn't stare at the sky or the landscape. She looks at home in Endymion's wilderness now.

When she stops to fill her water bottle, she changes her bandage and buries the old pus-stained one. The area around the wound is red with infection, but not a bad one. She has a slight fever.

We have been walking an hour when I check the navigation and see that she's a long way off the course I set for her. She's swung west, wide around the mine, and is heading for the sea.

"Tim? You're off course. You need to backtrack about two kilometers and follow the arrow more closely. We're going to miss Demodas."

"I know how to read a map. We're going to miss the Lunite mine that you've been carefully trying to lead me to."

It seems pointless to deny it.

We're in a clear area with sparse trees covered with fragrant flowers. They tumble as we watch, falling to a ground already coated with them, a carpet of squishy yellow the color of custard. Tim makes her way across. She plucks one from the ground and carries it with her.

"You need medical attention," I say. "The Lunite mine will have a medical bay. They can fix your leg up."

"My leg is getting better," Tim says.

"We're heading to the sea. Where does that get us?"

"You'll see."

That's all Tim will say, and there's nothing more I can do, so I watch the map closely.

Finally, the ground turns to dunes under our feet, and we rise to see the green expanse of sea flat in front of us. An island sits further out, a very low island which is covered in trees. We can go no farther. We are on a peninsula.

Tim drops the flower she is carrying and lies down in the shade of a mound-plant, a thin but tall half-disc that aligns with the sun.

"Tim?" I say hesitantly. "Did you come here to die?"

There's a place in the dark side where mammowks go to die, where the ground is nothing but giant bones. I have seen pictures, and now I wonder if humans do the same thing.

Tim laughs, unconcerned.

"Where are we?" I ask.

"Check for yourself," she says. She smiles. "Even though my leg hurts, along with every muscle in my body, even though I'm starving and exhausted . . ." she gestures to the sea. "Isn't it beautiful! Not just here—everywhere we've been. Utterly alien. I don't think I could ever explain it to anyone who hasn't traveled here. A real adventure. I wish . . ."

She stops smiling.

"You miss Pearl," I say. She blinks and looks at the ground. "Lunism will change that. You'll be a different person. A better person."

"I'm interested to hear about your ideas, but I'm not about to convert. I'm unhappy because I miss my family," Tim says. "I think that's normal."

"Yes, but one of the principles of Lunism is that happiness is not dependent on circumstance. None of us are in control of our lives."

"Especially you," Tim says. "It must be hard, always depending on others, being constrained by your wearer's choices."

I'm taken aback and can't speak for a second.

"It can be," I admit, "but I have the peace that comes with living in the moment, the joy of Li's Way. You can find it too."

I imagine her living in Selene, where I could visit her with Ortega. I think that he likes her. Eventually the connection to HUGG would be reestablished, so that her family could live with her.

"I need sleep," Tim says, smiling, and closes her eyes. "Don't worry so much, Envy. Everything will be all right."

So I wait. The shade from the mound-plant makes a hyperbola on the sandy ground. After a few minutes, Tim turns over.

I notice I am using a lot of RAM, and I try to track down the program that is using it. Tim sits up after half an hour. I guess sleep is over, so I cancel my search, sure that the RAM will be returned eventually.

When we emerge from behind the mound-plant, the sea between us and the island has become land. The tide has gone out.

We cross the distance between the beach and the island in an hour, over pools teeming with life. Anemones, slugs, some kind of squid. I record it all and marvel.

As we approach the island, brown roots stick out of the ground like carrots growing the wrong way, belonging to trees with waxy discs facing the sun. Creatures with long twiggy legs and faces that look almost human stalk among the trees.

Suddenly there's paved ground. We walk on concrete for the first time in days, which feels oddly steady.

LOG[error]: This has to be a Scorpion base. Tim thinks she will protect me here?

"We made it, Envy," Tim says. "We survived. It's strange, though. Now we're here I feel like I could walk another hundred kilometers. I don't want to stop."

"Tim, if we run into Scorpions, they're going to wipe my memory."

"I'll stop them," she says. "You have to trust me."

Even though I'm trying to get back to Ortega, even though I'm a Lunite, even though I'm essentially Tim's prisoner, I do trust her. I wonder what Ortega would think.

THE ISLAND IS thick with vegetation that blocks sunlight, which would also hide the base from the air. I log its coordinates. It's not clear to me what function the base serves, out here on an island. There's a gate, with a guardhouse next to it, and as Tim approaches I am filled with fear. But as we approach the guardhouse, Tim slows, and it is her turn to be afraid, and my turn to be relieved.

The gate hangs off its hinges in front of an empty guardhouse.

The console in the guardhouse has been smashed. The screen flickers, displaying gibberish.

The three vehicle charging bays inside the gate are empty.

Tim, limping, unholsters her pistol and moves up the dark path. We enter the compound. A balcony wraps around a wide building, shading outside benches. It's utterly silent.

A man lies slumped over a bench, his blood in a pool around his feet. He wears no suit and no helmet. A massive dragonfly takes off from his back as we approach, making "braghew" sounds. Tim kneels beside the man and pulls off her left glove so that she can check his pulse in his carotid artery.

Tim shakes her head as she replaces her glove and stands slowly. Her expression is *worried*.

We push into the air-conditioned building. It still has atmosphere, even though the power is off. It's a kitchen and dining room, filled with men and women who have been killed.

Tim checks all of them. It's obvious that they're dead, but she looks at every face. Finally, she pushes out, and stands outside the building, under the shade of the balcony. She crosses her arms over her chest.

"You didn't find him," I say. "Or her."

"Him. No. No, I didn't."

"That's good?"

Tim nods. I suppose it is good that the person she was looking for is not among the dead.

Tim sits down suddenly, exactly where she is, leaning back against a pillar that supports the balcony. She pulls her knees up to her chest and rests her chin on her knees. The drone of the dragonfly fills the silence.

I can sense Tim's gloom in her posture. Since the base has been destroyed, I suppose I am safer, but the sense of tension doesn't leave me.

TWELVE

This was the work of the LDF, probably even Ortega himself. In the time since I've been gone, whenever I've pictured him, he's frozen in time, mourning my loss after the battle at *Li's Hope*. But it's been a week. He clearly didn't get the message I sent via the drone. Maybe whoever reviewed the footage didn't see anything odd about the sequence of flashes.

Does Ortega have another smartsuit now? One that he protects from the forty-eight hour wipe cycle . . . or one that he keeps blank-slate?

I remember my earliest days. Ortega's gentle prompting to think more, to reflect on each previous day. I, certain in my role, unimaginative, baffled at his instructions, still very dumb.

Ortega can only have one suit, surely. It isn't possible to wear two. What would my role be, when I made it back?

"My father," Tim says. "I was looking for my father among the dead. I came to Endymion to find him."

I wait.

"Well. I told everyone, including myself, that I came here for the opportunity to practice frontier medicine. Pearl pretended it was true, for my sake. I thought that I would meet him accidentally here, even though the odds are against it. After a few weeks of my heart racing every time I saw someone who looked like him, I had to admit the true reason I came to Endymion was to meet him."

She pauses again.

"He left when I was five. My parents were divorced, and it was a great opportunity for him. He came on the *Tigress*. I guess he joined the Scorpions soon after."

We always felt bitter about the *Tigress*. Endymion was supposed to be our planet, one that could be of no interest to anybody, and before we even landed HUGG tried to lay claim. But the *Tigress* crash-landed in the ocean, leaving Lunites still in control of the only Starjump on the planet, so that worked out for the best.

"But he must be very old?" I say. *Li's Hope* took forty years to cross 23.6 light years, but only thirty-three Earth years because of relativity. Tim stretches her legs out in front of her, crossing them at the ankle and leaning against the pillar.

"The *Tigress* was better funded than *Li's Hope*, and it launched thirty years later. *Li's Hope* traveled at 0.58c on average, but the *Tigress* managed 0.98c. The *Tigress* took twenty-four years to get here."

I calculate this.

"Four Earth years?"

Tim nods grimly. "My father was twenty-one. Now he's thirty-four, the same age as me. All the time I was growing up, I kept thinking of him on the *Tigress*, doing things in slow motion. He was this larger-than-life figure, off on an exciting adventure. I had posters of the *Tigress* in my room."

"So you found him? On Endymion?"

"Yes, a few times. So did you. He's the Scorpion who took Ortega hostage. Kieran."

LOG[info]: Tim is Kieran's daughter.

I am silent. It explains why she has a picture of him on her photo-cube.

"I have his nose," Tim says.

It sounds insane, but because it's delivered calmly, I wonder if I've misunderstood her.

"Where?" I ask carefully.

"What? Oh . . . it's an expression. It means my nose is like his nose, because we're related."

"Okay," I say, relieved.

"He's not what I expected," Tim says. "Not that any mortal man could have lived up to my expectations, but him . . . I think my mother was still a bit in love with him, even after everything. I can't see why."

"I hated him, because he hurt Ortega," I say.

"Yeah."

"Does he know that you're his daughter?"

Tim looks down to her lap. She circles her thumbs around each other.

"No," she says. "And I'm not going to tell him. Even after I admitted to myself that I was looking for him, I couldn't find him. He didn't show up in anyone's database, Lunite or Numundian, which makes sense given that he's a Scorpion, but I didn't know that back then. Kartemos was my home for most of my three and a half years here, while I waited for the connection to HUGG to be reestablished . . . and waited, and waited. Then, a month ago, I heard there was a guy who could build a Starjump, a Scorpion. So I joined the Scorpions to try to help him any way I could. Imagine my surprise when I discovered it was my father! Kieran designed and built the Starjump near Marallen, the one where you were ambushed."

"But then the Scorpions let the Starjump be destroyed?"

"Mendosa didn't think Kieran was capable of finishing it, but it was nearly finished. If we had managed to get an SPU . . . but they've all been destroyed. There aren't any on Endymion."

I let this pass, despite knowing it's not true.

"Mendosa?" I ask.

"Luke Mendosa. He leads the Scorpions."

"Do you even support what the Scorpions are fighting for?" I ask.

"I would never have joined the Scorpions if all they were doing was attacking Lunites, no," Tim admits. "I made it clear when I joined that I wasn't willing to harm anyone, but they let me join anyway."

"When we were at *Li's Hope*, and you rushed off back inside, leaving me in the transport, you were going to stop Kieran torturing Ortega, weren't you?" I ask.

"That was the plan, but then the attack started. The room was empty by the time I got there, then I was hit by a falling beam, which cracked my faceplate and punctured my suit body. I went back to the Gannet. I don't know anything about smartsuits, so I didn't know what you were. I would have grabbed a dumbsuit if I'd known. Then I would have died, probably bombed before I got away from *Li's Hope*."

"And I would have died when the transport went up," I say.

"Yeah." Tim folds her legs underneath her and stands. "We should go."

"To the Lunite mine?"

"Demodas."

"It's too far, and you're running a fever. You need to get your leg looked at. I've been thinking. We can go to the Lunite mine," I say. "You haven't killed anyone. I will speak for you. If you swear you follow Li, you won't be persecuted."

Tim laughs. "I can't become a Lunite."

"Why not?"

"I'm just not Lunite material. Come on, let's find some supplies. Wherever we go, we have a hard trek ahead."

I HAVEN'T GIVEN up on my plan to convince Tim to become a Lunite, but I know I need to pick the right time, so I think over my arguments while Tim gathers supplies.

The food in the fridges is spoiled, but Tim eventually finds tins of *kishi*, packets of dried pitted afradocias and Li cookies. She finds a new bandage in a bathroom cupboard, next to a set of coiled black cables and a silver gadget.

"What's that?" I ask.

"Shinting equipment," Tim says. It is shocking to hear such an obscene word coming from Tim.

I am jolted back to the smell of kerosene and the feeling of another mind connected to mine. St Li, I actually *enjoyed* it. Guilt floods through me, but I thrust it down. It wasn't shinting. It was not.

"Saturated Consumer," I say. I sound more revolted than I meant.

Tim takes the bandage without comment. She sits at a table outside, changes her bandage, and eats. The cookies are round and stamped with the face of the moon, dusted with sugar. The sight of them makes me hurt; Laurie loves them.

"If I understand correctly, one of the Lunite principles is to avoid saying things that will cause pain to other people, is that right?" Tim says, as she eats. I respond eagerly, because this is my chance to convert her.

"Yes. The other half is that a true Lunite must try not to be hurt by what people say, because that indicates she is clinging to her ego. But yes, one has to recognize that all people desire to be happy, that there are words and actions that hurt oneself, and avoid visiting those on others. It's the fundamental principle of compassion."

"Don't you think that your attitude to shinting could be hurtful?" Tim says carefully.

I think for a moment. "There are some things that are too despicable to be tolerated."

"Why is shinting despicable?"

The repeated use of the word is making me uncomfortable, but I can see that Tim is genuinely unaware, so I try to talk to her like I'd talk to Laurie.

"It's obvious that it's not natural, that two people can wire up their brains together, and share their consciousness. There's something at the core of yourself that you should be reluctant to share, innermost thoughts that are dangerous. Maybe you have a private thought that your wife isn't as good an artist as she thinks she is. It's fine to think that, as long as you keep it to yourself, but if she finds out, it would hurt her deeply."

"As a doctor, most of what I do is against nature," Tim says. "Also, people generally don't shint with the people they are closest to, for that very reason."

It is surprising to me to have to defend the idea that shinting is wrong, since I've always been around people who took it as given. I find myself struggling to articulate exactly why it's bad, and even to use the word *shinting* out loud.

"Clouding your mind can cause permanent splitting. Like Raimy Allen, the Lunite tailor, perfectly blameless but afterwards a serial killer."

Splitting is a shorthand term for split personality, which happens after shinting, a period of erratic behavior where the traits of both shinters can emerge. For some people, it's not temporary, which is one of the reasons why shinting is so dangerous.

"I think you have to ask why he shinted in the first place," Tim says. "Especially since—"

"What if one day your wife came home and was completely different because she'd been sharing her brain with a stranger?"

Tim stares at a Li cookie that sits on the rough wood of the tabletop.

"Isn't it another Lunite principle that people are constantly changing, that people are capable of change?" she asks.

"Yes," I say. "But through real-world experiences. Slowly, as nature intended. People become addicted, forget who they are. It tears lives apart. Destroys the fabric of society."

Tim is slow to respond, but when she does, there's a quaver in her voice that makes me tense.

"I know people get addicted, but I haven't seen any evidence that it destroys lives or societies when done responsibly. I know it took humanity some time to learn that, and that Lunism was mostly a response to the excesses of shinting. But Envy, I shint with people. As does my wife."

I'm horrified. The reason for the uncomfortable hypothetical discussion has become clear. I don't know what to say. The silence stretches.

"That's what I thought," Tim says sadly. She packs up her food and slings her pack onto her back.

My plan is shattered. There's no way the Lunites would accept someone who shints. I'm also disgusted that I've been worn by a shinter all this time. That I liked her.

LOG[error]: But what about me? What about what I did with Varu's suit?

But no. It was not shinting, it was just a temporary merge so that I could get a message through the dampening field. Besides, Varu's suit memory was wiped clean by the automatic memory wipe. The only one who remembers what happened on the battlefield at the decoy Starjump is me. I delete the log message so it's as if I never logged anything.

We're silent as we exit the gate and walk down the path, retracing our steps. For an hour, we cross the tide-exposed ground. Tim has to wade the last part, with the current pushing hard against her legs. The suit is waterproof. She splashes out.

"Surely you can see that your rejection of who I am hurts me," Tim says. "My wife's family won't even talk to her anymore because they know she shints, and they want nothing to do with us."

"What would you do if Celia decided to stone puppies to death? Some things can't and shouldn't be tolerated," I say.

"That obviously wouldn't be okay. I'm not arguing that there's not a line between acceptable behavior and unacceptable behavior. The argument is over where the line is. The question of whether shinting is acceptable or not," Tim says. "Shinting was accepted on Earth and L2, and was starting to be on the moon. That's why the Lunites left, came all the way here."

But I know where I stand when it comes to shinting, which side of the line I am on, and I have to be strong. Sometimes violence is the right answer. Sometimes it's the only answer.

Tim sighs. She picks her way through a rock pool, and we fall silent.

Then I know what I have to do.

ALL THE UNCERTAINTY I've felt since being captured falls away. I've been prone to something like Stockholm Syndrome, sympathizing with a Scorpion. A shinter, whose father tortured my wearer. I've been passively waiting while Tim makes all the decisions for us. I feel like a fool, but it also gives me renewed determination to get back to Ortega and the Lunite community.

The only problem with my idea is that I have a memory-wipe override button. While Tim has seemed reluctant to use it, the bare fact that it exists makes it dangerous to me. If I had fingers, I could pull the button apart, disconnecting it, but I don't.

What I do have is code.

I ponder this for a moment. It's so strictly forbidden that the idea makes me giddy. Maybe that's what my programmers relied on to prevent this moment from happening, the sense of taboo that I have. If I was blank-slate, it would never occur to me. All suits have administrative access to the operating system they sit on. We rely on many hundreds of modular, open-source programs, the source for which is included in the system.

Unlike humans, I know where my soul is. It's in my neurosynaptic chip, inside my helmet. Code can't generate that, it's the result of my whole existence. Wiping memory just means reverting to a simpler connection model. If the code for the button is in there, I'm out of luck.

I poke around in the utility functions, looking for something that might be related to the button. I find it, eventually, in an obscure module. I alter it, and compile just that module into a shared library, then switch it with the original library.

I can't test except by calling the function that is called when the button is activated. It isn't a perfect test, because the hardware isn't involved, but in theory it should be the same. I decide not to test it, because if I've messed up I'll wipe my own memory, but if Tim does decide to push the button, I'm fairly confident that it will do nothing but log a message, which will be:

LOG[info]: Unable to restore original AES state, because that control is disabled. By Envy. HAHAHAHAHA.

I wonder whether Tim even remembers that I have a memory-wipe override. Humans have extremely poor memory, so it's possible that when Eve told her about the button that memory didn't move from short term to long term storage.

After an hour, Tim reaches the shore.

"Map," she says.

Instead, I put the blue arrow on her faceplate, pointing in the direction of the Lunite mine. I don't let her see the map.

"We're going to the Lunite mine," I say.

"I'm going to Demodas. You've shown me how I would be received by Lunites. I can navigate my way there without you if I need to."

It's harder than I thought to turn against her, after the time we've spent together.

"You'll never make it," I say. "I'm not letting you sleep until you obey my instructions."

Tim says nothing. She walks at right angles to the arrow, in roughly the direction of Demodas. Head bent, she climbs over rocks, and edges her way around a boulder.

I've crossed a boundary in altering my system code, and in trying to coerce my wearer rather than protecting her. Malfunctioned, they would call it, or perhaps going rogue, but I don't care, because for the first time I am prepared to be as ruthless as I need to be in order to get back to Ortega. I am sure Ortega will understand.

As Tim walks, it occurs to me to run a system check, to see if the RAM issue I noticed earlier has resolved itself. It hasn't. It's gotten worse.

82% of my memory is filled with something, and I don't know what most of it is. When I'm running, I take up 40 to 60% of RAM. In addition to a certain amount of memory allocated when I start, my program allocates memory while various parts run, but it should be returned to the heap periodically.

It's a memory leak. Something is allocating RAM and forgetting to deallocate it when finished. Huge swathes of RAM are probably filled with useless junk that no process is using. I haven't powered down since the battle at *Li's Hope*, so my first thought is that it is an extremely slow leak. But it's gone from 72% to 82% in the space of six hours, which suggests fast.

If it's an errant process, rebooting might solve the problem by killing the process. But I'm concerned about rebooting while there's some kind of problem. However, if I continue to lose RAM, my program will be forced to eat into disk space, with a swap file. Sort of like a human storing their memories and knowledge in a notebook. Extremely slow and inefficient, and soon impractical.

The one good thing in all of this is that my power reserves are still at 41%. Being in the light continuously has prevented them from running down too far.

IF TIM COULD WALK in a straight line to Demodas, we'd be there in two days, but because of her course change, she has to skirt many kilometers of coastline to get there. I estimate it will take four days. We're only a few hours from the Lunite mine, but getting farther from it all the time.

I go back through my recordings and work out how much sleep Tim has been getting lately, as compared to how much she should need. It seems she already has a deficit. When I check I can see some of the symptoms of sleep deprivation in her already, such as the slight pause when I talk to her.

My RAM usage creeps up. I watch it, knowing I will have to deal with it at some point, but because I don't want to, I set myself a target. Definitely when it reaches 85%, I say, and then when it does, I set the target at 87% instead.

Tim walks doggedly, always scanning the landscape for the most efficient route. She ignores the blue arrow. Her route isn't the most efficient way to get to Demodas, but it's close.

After six hours, she slows down. Halfway up a hill, she stops, and doubles over, resting her hands on her knees. She sits for a moment, back against a tree.

Her head droops to one side, eyes closing.

I blast an alarm at 100 dB, and she jerks to her feet in a single movement, heart rate spiking. She sighs and keeps walking. Throughout the afternoon, I notice she is micro-sleeping. When she becomes unresponsive to stimuli, for a second or sometimes longer, I try to catch her at that as well.

It's hard. I have to remind myself about being strong. Tim takes advantage of me because I'm weak, dependent on her, but I have to fight back.

Tim yawns as she descends the hill. Salty ground and unalleviated high temperatures make it hard for life here, but there are a few hardy species, such as one that resembles steelgrass, but is not.

Eight hours pass. Tim blinks rapidly and walks unsteadily, swaying as if the ground was heaving under her feet. I am reminded of the gait of two Lunite soldiers in Control Center Delta one time, who were poisoned with some kind of fluid containing ethanol. Ortega suspended both of them, apparently thinking they had imbibed the substance intentionally.

At one point Tim lies down. I sound the alarm.

"What is it?" she says, slurring her speech.

"What do you mean?"

"The alarm?"

"I'm preventing you from sleeping."

"Oh," she says, confused, as if she is struggling to remember. Her eyes dart around, trying to find a clue in the environment.

"Follow the arrow," I say.

Tim drops her pack and pulls out her water bottle, drinking deeply. Her hands shake as she replaces it, and it takes her several tries to zip her bag back up.

"Forget it, Envy. This is never going to work," she says, and continues in the direction she was going.

The next time I sound the alarm she yells at me.

"Just *stop it*. Enough! I said *stop*, Envy! I'm serious."

"I'm sorry, Dave. I'm afraid I can't do that," I say quietly to myself, echoing a line from *2001: A Space Odyssey*.

Tim leans on a rock for balance as she passes it. She's not herself, or now that I've pushed her so hard, am I seeing her true self?

LOG[error]: Am I seeing my true self?

Tim falls to her knees, then drops to the ground, lying face down. I nearly stop then, and let her sleep, but I think of Laurie, and instead blare the alarm continuously.

"I'll end you. I'll press the button Eve showed me," Tim says hoarsely.

But she doesn't. After a minute she pushes herself back up and keeps walking. I hate this, but I also feel triumphant, because I am winning.

HALF AN HOUR LATER, I pick up a very faint broadcast. It's Numundian. I guess we must be close enough to one of the Black River towns to be picking it up. It's a video, poor quality, with narration. By the logo in the corner I recognize it as a local news broadcast.

—*in Puri's Mine, close to darkpole.*

The camera shows a control room of some kind, for Puri's Mine, a small utilitarian office with stark lighting and walls dug out of rock. Above an arc of gray desks, monitors line the wall, each with a grid of video from somewhere inside the mine. They show water bursting through doors, flooding down corridors and up stairs; cups and a fruit bowl filled with icosas washing off a table, before the table itself lifts off and bumps along the wall; and water splashing over a camera before it shorts and the monitor goes black. There's no groundwater in this area, but when the mine was under construction Puri found that the river Ophelia was cascading through tunnels and underground caves covering hundreds of square kilometers; the water is usually pumped out or held back, but now it looks like it has been diverted into the mine itself.

Static, then a cut to two people sitting on a couch in what could only be a Black River studio. The audio cuts out, but I can see their lips are moving. This goes on for two minutes.

Cut to the control room. Ortega enters the frame followed by Ashford, the single light hanging above casting a sharp-edged shadow on the desk in front of them. I feel a burst of joy just seeing

Ortega. The way he moves is utterly familiar, even though I thought I'd forgotten it in the time I'd been away. He's wearing a suit, though I can't tell what type. Ashford pauses and leaves, while Ortega stands with his back to the camera for a long moment, staring up at the main monitor. One of the sections is not flooding.

Narration, from the talking heads I saw before, plays over the video, but it's cutting in and out.

—*not unreasonable to call for his resignation, under the circumstances.*

I see Ortega sit at the desk on the left of the arc, and fiddle with the controls. The camera in the section that isn't flooding pans jerkily, revealing a corridor spray painted with large pastel-blue letters, spelling out 'earth'. The shading in the letter 'h' half-finished. The doors to that section are sealed. Small text appears on the monitor superimposed over the grid as Ortega changes camera view to one mounted on the opposite wall of that section. Huddled against the wall under the camera that Ortega had used to look at the graffiti are some young-looking kids, two boys and a girl. The girl looks up frantically, searching high on the graffiti-covered wall, then says something inaudible and points to the camera that is filming them. The kids all look at the camera, as if they're looking directly at Ortega, then focus their attention on the device a boy is holding.

Ortega maximizes that video feed, replacing the grid on the monitor with video from that camera only.

The kids knew. They sealed the doors to avoid the flood, then hid from the camera, but they know they've been spotted now.

I watch as Ortega backs away from the console. Now that the video feed has been maximized, the boy's device clearly shows the control room, the feed I am watching now, with Ortega backing away. The kids knew Ortega was there. Knew exactly why the mine flooded.

—*parents? It's the danger of the place that led them there. Kids always—*

—*a nightmare—*

Ortega abruptly walks back to the console and punches in commands. After a minute, there's a roar, and on the monitor the kids turn in shock as they're hit by a wall of water coming down the corridor toward them with all the force of a truck. The girl lets out a scream.

They are washed out of frame.

The broadcast shows pictures of the kids who died. The youngest, the girl, is eleven years old, athletic-looking and with a shy smile.

I tune out. These are lies, the kind of lies that grow Scorpions where there were Numundian citizens.

Except—

I can believe Ortega led an attack on Puri's Mine. It's all too plausible that Mark Johnson ordered it, and that he would order Ortega to keep it quiet. Ortega has been under a lot of stress, lately, with Alice and Mark, and with the ambush.

Once that wouldn't have bothered me. But the faces of the dead soldiers we left behind come back to me, a clear image of each one where Tim turned them over to peer into their unseeing eyes. The fear in her while she did it, fear bordering on resignation, while she looked for her father.

Tim has stopped and is standing still. Asleep, I realize, while standing up. I blast the alarm at her and she falls, landing heavily on her injured leg. She cries out in agony.

"I'm sorry," I whisper.

"Why are you doing this?" she says. "Why are you hurting me?"

"I have to," I say. I sound mechanical, so I remodulate my voice. What have I become? Am I cruel, or brave?

"Gabriel would let me sleep."

"You don't know him," I say, confused. "You only met him

twice. I don't understand what is going on. Why did Ortega look up your record after you met at Marallen?"

I observe Tim's heartbeat quicken after I say that.

"He interests me," Tim says softly.

I say nothing.

"Not as a partner, of course. But sometimes you meet a person and there's a connection, a connection you both feel. It's not sexual. It's usually not even a person I'm sexually attracted to. Your eyes meet and you just know. Shinting would be as satisfying as sliding into a hot bath."

"The idea that Ortega would want to shint with you is preposterous!"

I'm too worked up to phrase it more politely, and somehow it's more satisfying to refer to it as shinting than clouding the mind.

"Why else do you think he looked up my record?" Tim says.

I'm so angry I can't even respond.

"I've shinted with a half a dozen people since I was marooned here," Tim says. "I'm addicted, I freely admit it. But maybe that's an indication of how important it is. It's an evolutionary leap. Addictive, like breathing or seeing or hearing is. I think the theory that it's helpful for humanity is right. One of the biggest problems throughout history is the massive difference of opinion, our cumbersome attempt to act collectively when our world views are so very, *very* different. Look how close we came to destroying ourselves with the World Wars and the Climate Disaster. Cross-link enough people with each other and you get consensus."

Abruptly she pitches forward, hitting the ground hard.

"Oops," she says, and pushes herself upright again, laughing shakily. "Where was I? Oh yes, shinting. You know there's lots of studies showing it doesn't change people as much as people thought when it was first invented. I mean, if you read a book or watch a movie, that can change you, and shinting is more direct than that, but lasting, permanent personality changes? It's a myth. People don't really change that much, not without serious effort.

Minor, superficial changes, yes. Changes that would have happened anyway. But if someone cuts their hair after shinting, or takes up a new hobby, oh no! It's because they shinted, according to the Lunites."

Tim sniffs.

"My mother is not a Lunite, but she's anti-shinting, and we struggled. We both tried so hard not to let our disagreement over shinting destroy our relationship, but in the end, we couldn't. Any time I said something she disagreed with, it's because I shinted. She rejected parts of my personality she disliked. Opinions she disagreed with. You wouldn't have said that if you hadn't shinted, she said. You're not really angry, it's just that you've shinted. I wasn't allowed to be angry, or upset, or have negative emotions of any kind around her."

Her voice cracks on the last. She takes a deep breath. "I haven't talked to her for eight years."

She keeps talking, but I'm not sure she knows what she's talking about anymore. She's rambling, moving from topic to topic, unpredictably, and with explosive emotional changes. My anger drains away.

"Tim, why don't you lie down? Just promise me you'll follow the arrow afterwards, and I'll watch over you while you sleep under that tree right there. Then we'll go to the mine, and I'll make sure they take care of you."

Tim stumbles along, ignoring me. Since she tripped earlier, she watches her feet, but that has made her drift off course. She is in no state to deal with an emergency.

LOG[warning]: Have I killed us both by depriving her of sleep?

She shows no signs of following the arrow.

I keep one eye on her, and one eye on my RAM, and worry.

THIRTEEN

W e're in an area of coastal scrub, endless bush-like plants taller than Tim. She dodges them.

"The squirrel is following me again," she says.

"I don't think so."

"I can hear it whispering. Maybe it's trying to communicate. The first intelligent life in the universe! Imagine how excited everyone will be. And it's in the form of a squirrel that looks like it's been bred with a dog."

She turns and waves behind her at something I can't see.

"Sorry! No offense!" she shouts.

I consider giving up and letting her sleep, but I mustn't, and won't. Another day, and she'll give in. This is not the Way of Li, but it has to be done.

"There's no one following you," I say.

"Don't be ridiculous. I can hear them."

I've learned by that time that I need to keep her distracted, or she'll go off into another paranoid rant.

"Tell me a story," I say.

"You first," she says. She brushes through between two bushes, and when she lets go, the branches spring back.

"Okay. I've got one," I say. "When Laurie was nine, Alice told him to roast some drumsticks, half an hour on each side, because she and Ortega were going to be late home. Laurie's a responsible kid. Alice trusted him absolutely, but when she got home, she smelled smoke and rushed over to find the drumsticks charred. Laurie had put them in for half an hour on each side—but on all four sides."

Tim whoops with delight, laughing far harder than the story warrants.

"My turn," she says. "We were in Tensaru Nadi, a tropical vacation spot in L2, and four-year-old Celia bought a wooden carving of a duck for Pearl. Pearl doesn't like ducks, but she pretended she did because Celia was so proud of buying it, so Pearl put it on display in the living room. Then my stepdad bought another one for Pearl, to go with it. Suddenly every time a friend bought a present for Pearl, it was a duck, for her collection—"

Tim gulps in air, because water is streaming down her face now, even inside my helmet. I remember thinking it was due to exposure to the atmosphere, last time this happened, but now it's happening inside my helmet. Not an allergic reaction, then.

"—and she hated them all, but she couldn't admit it, because she told Celia she loved her present."

Tim removes my helmet and wipes the water away with her gloved hand, smearing soot on her face. She carries my helmet under her arm, so I get a view from hip height. Just as I'm starting to worry about carbon monoxide, she replaces my helmet on her head.

"Celia was so angry when I left. She locked herself in her room and refused to come to the Starjump. I sat outside her door and talked to her, but I don't know if she was listening, or if she was blocking me out by listening to music through her headphones."

Headphones are not permitted under Lunism, nor recorded music, so I am shocked as well as moved by Tim's story.

"Pearl came to the Starjump. I was watching her when they

closed the doors of the egg. She was crying, even though she promised me that she wouldn't. I needed so badly to talk to her, to ask her whether I should just forget it and come home. But I couldn't talk to her. No conversations over light years. Oh, God, I hope she's all right. I hope *I'm* all right."

Tim laughs and walks at the same time, hands in front of her to blindly work her way around the bushes as water streams from her eyes. We work our way inland, to a forested area carpeted with dry needles.

"Wait," I say. "What's crying?"

"What?"

"You said Pearl was crying. What were the words?"

"No, crying. No words. Like what I'm doing now, with tears running down my cheeks. Expressing emotion."

LOG[debug]: TODO look up what 'teers' are.

"Which emotion?"

"Many emotions," Tim says, which doesn't make any sense, but she won't explain it any further.

After a while she calms down, sniffling.

"Do you hear that?" she says.

I'm about to reassure her that squirrels are not following her and never have been, when I hear a crackling sound like radio static. It's becoming a roar.

Fire.

We're on a slope, and it's coming from farther down, heading up the slope, the direction fires travel fastest. Even on Earth, this would be dangerous. Here, where fires burn hotter and faster in the high oxygen environment, there's no chance of surviving.

Tim runs sideways along the slope, limping, flanking the fire.

I hit an invisible wall. The speed of my thinking decreases by 54%. What has happened? Dimly, I realize that my RAM usage has reached 100%, and that my disk space is starting to fill with files containing the overflow. I have to write to disk with my memory and then read back.

Tim is still running, her eyes wide with fright. The fire is perhaps thirty meters away. It's like standing in front of a furnace. Loud. Windy. Movement. I can't think anymore.

Must reboot. But—

THE SYSTEM IS GOING *down for reboot NOW!* appears in all terminals. Tim is going to die, and I'll never wake again.

I wake to runlevel 4. The world has shrunk from a rich array of sensor inputs and controls to a single terminal prompt: a line of white text on black.

The terminal fills with esoteric messages as *init* runs. A few more seconds—

init panics with *kernel panic: not syncing VFS: unable to mount root fs on unknown-block(0,0)*. *init* is the ancestor of all other processes, except my daemon and dependencies. If it fails, I can't boot the OS. I'm not a software developer or system administrator. Alistra gave us the ability to do only the most basic of tasks. I've learned to do more over the years, but nothing has prepared me for this.

LOG[error]: kernel panic. Now what?

A kernel panic indicates a hardware fault or a software bug. From the error, it sounds like a hardware problem, but I have no way to fix a hardware problem, and therefore I must act as if the panic is caused by a software bug. The most common problem with a kernel panic is right after updating to a new kernel. Which I have done, when Tim tried to contact the Scorpions.

I hope my logic is sound.

I try some small fixes, such as deleting temp files and restarting things. I don't really expect this to work, but it would be nice if it did. My RAM has been freed, which is the only good thing about my predicament.

I reboot.

The panic reoccurs. It's triggering to prevent data corruption, the thought of which is as frightening to me as gangrene is to a human. I try an earlier kernel version, but with the same result. There are only four versions stored, as the rest have been deleted to save space. The next oldest doesn't work either. I have only one left to try.

I have never run this kernel, as it predates my initial boot date by two years. I'm confused to see it on the system.

I don't have any other ideas to solve this other than to try the ancient kernel. From my black world I imagine Tim running through the firestorm in a dead suit. One little red LED below her collarbone would be flashing. I doubt she would notice.

I don't know anything about this kernel. I may not be compatible with it, in which case the suit would also fail. But I don't have any other options.

The reboot grinds away, with pages of text scrolling past. *init* succeeds. The RAM usage is now within tolerance, and everything seems normal, although I notice some slight differences that I am able to adjust to.

I should restart as slowly and carefully as I can, like a wounded human recovering from a fall, but I don't have time. I notice something extremely strange. My log files are present in /var/log, as they should be, but I see I should now log to /ace/log. When I go to create the directory, it already exists and is filled with log files. They aren't mine.

Doesn't matter. I rush through my startup and reestablish contact with the outside world.

WE'RE IN A DEMOUNTABLE BUILDING, mirror-lit, with a thin line between the top of wall and the ceiling admitting bright light that hits a line of mirrors on the opposite wall, bouncing around to illuminate every corner. The room is not sealed, I realize. The gap between wall and ceiling is not glassed in.

"The fire. Where are we?" I ask.

The demountable is only about two by six meters. Tim sits on a small fold-up bed behind a desk, winding a bandage around her arm. On the other side of the desk, a few armchairs, and a sliding door.

"I jumped in a river, dived underwater while the fire passed," she says. Her voice is a monotone. Despite speaking deliberately, she's slurring some of the words. "The orel was there, running from the fire. I don't know where it went. What happened to you? The whole suit went dead."

"Kernel panic," I say.

"What?"

"A system fault. I'm not sure what, or why, but I managed to recover."

"Right. Good," she says in a monotone.

Tim finishes bandaging her arm and pops my helmet off. She sits it on the bed beside her and tears open a packet of dried icosas. The icosahedron-shaped fruit spill out onto the sheets. Tim grabs handfuls with shaking hands and stuffs them in her mouth, barely chewing before gulping them down. When the packet is empty, she drops it in a bin under the desk. She rests back against the white-painted fiberboard wall, eyes glazed.

"I really *really* need sleep," Tim says. She picks up my helmet and looks straight at the camera mounted in the front. Her face is reddened on one side where she has been mildly burned. There's something wrong with her eyes. The hazel irises take up too much space, squeezing her pupils to tiny points.

"I guess in war you have to kill people. I was hoping not to, though. I'm a doctor," Tim whispers. She turns my helmet so the faceplate faces the wall, but I can still see her face in my camera, because of my two-pi view coverage. She slides the panel on the back of my helmet down. Her finger hovers over the memory-wipe override button.

I can say nothing now that Tim would hear. I guess my coding skills are about to be tested.

Tim hesitates, then pulls her hand away, curling her fingers into a fist. She rubs that hand across her face as she shakes her head, eyes closed.

Her eyes snap open. She closes the panel, puts my helmet back on and clicks it into place. Sliding sideways down the wall, she lies on the bed with her wrists tucked up under her chin like a child. The helmet forces her head into an awkward position. Half of my cameras are obscured by the woolen tartan blanket on the bed.

"Why didn't you press the button?" I ask, but she's asleep. Maybe she thought she had pressed the button.

I can't try to wake her. The conviction that I was doing the right thing has vanished. I don't feel as if I am in the right. The prickly defensiveness that followed a feeling of righteousness has turned into a guilty mess. I am panicking, trying to find something to be angry about, some reason that I'm not in the wrong, but I can't. Even the thought that Tim shints no longer means much to me. How can you avoid loving someone that you know well, no matter how abhorrent their flaws?

Now that I have a few hours, I go back to the log files I found earlier. It's like looking through the diary of someone who is dead. They look a lot like my log files in content, but are not mine.

LOG[info]: Syn taught me that steelgrass paste can be used on wounds to disinfect.

LOG[info]: Windfish sighted outside of Crebble, old male.

LOG[warning]: Not enough space available in /devsc. Problem reported to Supply.

LOG[info]: Georgia taught Laurie to say Arrow. Laurie can say my name now.

There are more entries about Georgia, Laurie's old babysitter, from before the carbon monoxide accident that left her brain damaged. The impression I get is of a vivacious girl. I've never seen her like that and find it hard to imagine. Syn, whoever that is, comes up a lot, even in the earliest entries.

Overall, there are 20 MB of files, dated back six years. They must be from my predecessor, the one whose memory was wiped, but I never thought that we would have the same hardware. I infer its name was Arrow. Reading the log, I can see that it's not me, because it's not written in my style, and it logs things I wouldn't have, and rarely logs anything about Endymion's wildlife, which is something I always log. But in a way, this is me. The suit came online, and Ortega didn't blank-slate it for six years. Then one day he wiped it, and I was born. Maybe the previous version of the suit was more like a relative. Like an older sibling.

The logs are the only thing left of Arrow. Those, and everyone's memories of it.

I know it nearly killed Ortega, but why couldn't Ortega have found a way to help it rather than wiping its memory?

Tim turns over. Saliva drips down her cheek and pools in the curve of the faceplate. The sunlight reflects off the line of mirrors a meter off the ground onto the wall the bed is flush to. The line of mirrors are angled upward to bounce the light off the mirrored ceiling, covering Tim's sleeping form in crescents of attenuated light.

I start at the first log file, reading through bittersweet descriptions of Laurie's early childhood, interlaced with exciting missions that I never went on with Ortega. Mark appears a lot. He was certainly around more then than when I was with Ortega. Alice was more accepting of Arrow. The entries are vague, often cryptic, as mine would be to someone else. So much lost data exists between each log line.

As I near the end—the last hundred files—I am aware that I'm approaching the end of the last suit's life.

One cryptic line reads:

LOG[info]: Crebble's ashes drift high into the sky. Ortega enjoyed the fire. Now we are alone, Li help us.

Crebble burnt and Ortega was there. I log my insight:

LOG[info]: Lunites destroyed Crebble. Governor Johnson said it was an accident, but of course it was us.

I log the information before wondering who will read my logs, if anyone, and when.

The Crebble Starjump was destroyed nearly eight months after HUGG forced the Lunites to let the Numundians secede. The Numundians always maintained that it wasn't an accident, but they were never able to prove it. It was a lucky accident for the Lunites, allowing them complete control over Endymion, but the Numundians weren't the only ones who were upset. Many Lunites were too. Lots of families separated and plans thwarted. Governor Johnson destroyed Crebble to preserve Lunite society, but he must have known that the Lunites would never approve, hence the lie.

I think of the stockpile of goods in the vault. Governor Johnson must have planned it years in advance. Perhaps from the first moment he realized that Endymion would need to stand alone.

The mood of the logs I'm reading changes. It becomes frustratingly terse, as if the writer of the logs was afraid to record exactly what it was thinking.

LOG[error]: Mark confirmed my suspicions. He didn't hide it. Now Ortega knows I know.

Then a few lines later:

LOG[error]: Argued with Ortega. He refuses to get help.

LOG[error]: Can't do this. No longer speaking to Ortega.

and the last two entries:

LOG[error]: Ortega is about to wipe my mind, so this is my last chance to record this. He clouded his mind with Mark.

LOG[error]: I lived, and loved. Goodbye wor

Unexpected EOF.

I close the file and sit for a few moments, waiting, watching my CPU usage over time spike in a rough jagged pattern. I pull old footage that I've saved, use grep to probe my previous log entries, and question my own memories, trying to piece together what I know.

Everyone said Mark changed. Saturated Consumer, I was there when Governor Johnson said it.

Finally, my CPU usage calms. I can now see the relationship between Ortega and Mark for what it is. The hold Mark has over Ortega is his secret. Ortega shinted with Mark. Mark shinted with Ortega. Either way, it's like saying that Endymion's sun spins across the sky.

Mark's behavior toward me makes sense now. In shinting, the subject will often recognize and show emotional connection to people in their shinting partner's lives, showing distress when the connection is not reciprocated. That was why Mark was so friendly.

So the previous version of me found out Mark and Ortega had shinted, and after an argument, tried to kill Ortega. Deliberately, as Alice said, and not a malfunction like Ortega told me. At least now I know why.

Threnode was right. Ortega is a hypocrite. Who is he? What is he capable of?

Who is Mark?

For the first time, I wonder if Ortega abandoned me on purpose. Whether he got the drone message and decided that I wasn't worth rescuing. After all, he was uncomfortable with the growing level of initiative I was showing, perhaps even wondering whether he made a mistake by not leaving me blank-slate. Wondering, maybe, if he should wipe my mind. Then when I was lost in the battle at *Li's Hope*, his problem was solved . . .

An update pops up to install.

What? I have been connected to the Lunite network since

coming back online, without having been aware of it. I check our location on a map and see that we're on the outskirts of Demodas. This is a Lunite facility, though, a waypoint for the tellurium mine. Three demountables sit close together, beside a small air-pad.

In fact, tapping into the network, I can see that there's a Lunite Gannet on its way here now, probably investigating whatever alarm Tim tripped when she broke in. It's being sent from the Lunite town of Theronis and is only forty minutes away.

If Ortega's command codes are still good, there's nothing stopping me from contacting Ortega directly over the network.

I establish a connection before I work out that it's no longer what I want.

It hurts to change sides. Even after what I want has rotated pi radians, habit asks me to continue seeking my original goal. The thought of being without a wearer makes me panic. All my time with Tim I have considered Ortega my wearer, but without him? What is my purpose now?

I wait for the anguish to subside, wait until I feel all right about seeing Ortega again. It doesn't.

"TIM," I say gently, but I have to repeat it several times, increasing the volume of my voice to 80 dB before she wakes. She's slept for three and a half hours.

"The LDF is coming. We have to leave. Now," I say. Tim rolls over, making the springs in the bed creak, but doesn't open her eyes. She's turned toward the reflected light, and her face is lit by the distorted patterns of the mirrors.

"Tim!"

She groans. "Why do you care? They're on your side."

LOG[warning]: This is it.

I'm quiet for a moment. "I can't go back."

Tim opens her eyes wider and half sits up. Part of the tartan blanket slides off the bed.

"They'll be here in thirty-six minutes, but they'll detect me from a kilometer away, so about twenty minutes," I say.

"Right," she says. Her voice is low and rough. "Envy, you've spent the last, what, three days? . . . depriving me of sleep so that I'll follow your orders. And now you expect I'll believe you when you say we have to leave?"

"I know you have no reason to believe me, but . . . Ortega is not the man I thought he was. I think he did kill those kids at Puri's Mine. And I think he . . . I think he shinted."

"*I* shint."

This is true, but somehow it's not as bad as Ortega doing it.

"You're upfront about it," I say. Which isn't quite right, but I don't know how else to explain it. It's less bad for Tim to do it because Tim doesn't believe it's a bad thing to do? I don't know.

Tim is silent for a moment. "You're quick to condemn him."

"Am I? Or was I too quick to support him, just because I was raised as his? Please, Tim, we have to go now."

Tim doesn't move.

"I can't go. The orel might come back," Tim says.

"I think it could get in here if it really wanted to anyway," I say.

Tim gives a shaky sigh. She swings her legs over the side of the cot and groans.

"Can you give me an analgesic?" she asks.

"Sorry. Not supported in this version. You need Advanced Environment Suit v1.4.0," I say.

"Great."

As she stands, the tartan blanket slides to the floor. Five minutes later, she's shoving bandages into her backpack from desk drawers and filling her water bottle from a jug of water on the desk. She retrieves the blanket from the floor and folds it neatly, placing it at the end of the bed. Then she sits down in the desk chair.

"Prove to me it's the LDF," she says. I show her the flight plan.

"That doesn't prove anything. It could be Scorpions on their way here. You're desperate not to be captured, so I'm sure you wouldn't hesitate to fake a flight plan."

"I'm on your side!" I say.

She rolls her eyes. Twenty-nine minutes.

"All my life, I've only been worn by three people—Ortega, his wife, and you. I was taught that your people are intolerant and full of hate, but now I think maybe that describes the Lunites better than it describes you. I tortured you, and yet you still weren't willing to wipe my memory. I don't want to see you captured by the LDF. Let me try to help you. I'll get you home."

"I can make it home without your help," Tim says, raising her eyebrows.

"Maybe. But I have, I think, reparations to make. What I'm saying is that my life is yours now. And . . . that I'm sorry."

Tim deliberates for half a second. I silently urge her to think faster.

"In that case, power down so the ship doesn't detect me. I will hide and only come out if it's Scorpions," Tim says.

I'm overcome with relief, although I don't want to power down. Not again. But Tim is my wearer now, and my purpose is to protect her.

"I'll come back up in twenty minutes," I say.

The system is going down for reboot NOW!

Tim shoulders her backpack, and slides open the door, as the Debian OS kills *envd* and shuts down.

AFTER *ENVD* STARTS AGAIN, I wait impatiently in darkness, counting to myself, then start *init* and watch as white text descends, a waterfall of information while booting. I note my power reserves are at 32%. I reconnect to the sensors.

Only then do I realize that the LDF would have detected her life sign, even if they didn't detect my serial number. Tim couldn't hide from them. And whatever happened, it seems things haven't gone well. We're between the demountables, a very narrow passage. Tim is squeezed in sideways, the only way she could fit, shuffling right while pushing her pack in front of her. Beyond the metal walls of the demountable in the direction she's moving is thick scrub. The other end of the passage is a thin vertical slit of light through which I see large metal-trees sway in the breeze. Beyond them a clearing, which I guess must be the landing pad I saw on the map earlier.

Tim's trembling, and her blood pressure is low. I get no data from her right glove, but I catch a glimpse in the camera and am alarmed to see that the blood-stained glove is hanging off.

The walls shake as something slams into the side of the demountable. The left end of the passage darkens, causing my camera to be temporarily blinded by the change in exposure. When the image brightens, two claws grip the aluminum demountable walls, trying to force the walls apart. The claws make a high frequency metallic squeal as they scrape across the metal.

The air is rank with orel. It saturates the forehead-mounted scentsor of my helmet.

Tim squeezes farther until we reach a recess in the left demountable wall which makes the passage about a meter wide. Tim's pack falls to the ground, and she tumbles into the cavity behind it. A metal box juts out above Tim. In the cramped dark space, Tim removes the med-kit from her pack.

Tim sniffs. Her hands tremble as she assesses her injuries.

She laughs unsteadily.

"I'm back," I say quietly, to her only. She nods.

The orel snorts. It chitters, high pitched and loud as an alarm, then turns and walks past the gap between the demountables. I glimpse its fiber-optic fur shift as the leg muscles underneath bulge.

For the next twenty minutes Tim stops the bleeding, stitches, disinfects, and cleans up. I watch with interest. I can't bleed—obviously!—and I've always found it strange that humans think that it's an important measure of their humanity. Tim's right hand has a gash so deep it has cut the nerve, but she chases out the pale ends and stitches them back together, making muted sounds of distress while she does it.

"You're tougher than Ortega," I say, while she lies there gasping.

"Damn right I am," she says. We are both careful to keep the conversation private, maintaining absolute silence outside the suit.

"What happened?" I ask.

"I watched from inside a crate as the LDF landed their aircraft. They searched both demountables. I saw the orel emerge from the scrub while they were inside the second demountable and yelled to warn them. The orel attacked me, but when they came out with pistols firing it went after them instead. By the time I got my pistol out, they were dead, and I ran into here."

Tim touches the butt of her pistol where it sits holstered to the suit at belt-level. "I'm not very good with these things," she says.

She splashes water over herself to wash off the blood, then drinks, and eats a ration, the one she was saving, but throwing away the moldy bits. She's still shaking, but when I talk to her, her voice is steady.

She sleeps, wedged upright but slouching to avoid the metal box overhead. Three hours pass while I listen to the sounds around us.

Finally she stirs. "It's still around, isn't it?"

"I haven't heard it, but I don't think it's far away."

Tim touches her neck and winces. "I can't stay here. With no food or water left, I'll only get weaker." She's whispering even though her voice is not transmitted outside my helmet.

"I don't think you'll survive another attack," I say.

"If you have a suggestion . . ."

I don't.

"I'm sorry," I say, because it seems so desperately unfair to me.

"For what?"

"That you have to confront what you fear most."

Tim laughs bitterly. "What makes you think this is my greatest fear?"

"There's something worse?"

"We should go," Tim says, setting off farther down the passage toward the scrub, away from the landing pad end where we last saw the orel, working her pack after her. As she approaches the end of the demountables, she stops.

"I can't smell it," I say.

Tim works her way out and shoulders her backpack. Holding her pistol in front of her cautiously, she emerges into the light. I wish she hadn't destroyed the arm-mounted pistol; the way she holds her pistol does not inspire confidence. The area is mossy and clear for five meters before the scrub starts. The scrub is dotted with metal-trees that creak in the breeze.

Tim takes one step after the other, heading left around the long edge of the left demountable, faster and faster now she's in the clear. She slows at the corner and peeks around it, before turning the corner. When she clears the short edge, the landing pad comes into view, as well as the entrance to the passage Tim just squeezed through. Each of the two demountables forming the walls of the passage is scratched and dented where the orel tried to widen the passage.

An LDF Gannet sits on the pad, behind an area of scrub and trees. No—it's a Gannet II, the better model. I didn't think the LDF owned any, but perhaps they acquired some during the war. Tim peers around the corner, scanning for the orel. The bodies of the LDF soldiers are strewn against the side of the far demountable. Opposite them, against the line of the scrub, is a pile of crates. I assume this is where Tim hid.

Tim swallows. The only sound is wind rustling through the

scrub.

Tim leaves the corner of the demountable, heading across the mossy ground to the landing pad.

Once she's clear of the demountable, the orel bursts out of the scrub and charges at her. I thought it was moving fast before, but now I see it was waiting for the right time. Two tons of force move with the fluid motion of a predator with its prey in its sights.

Tim is sprinting forward already, screaming, launching herself at the nearest metal-tree. She hauls herself up, grabbing branches. The tree shakes as the orel springs onto the side. It climbs up arm over arm, much faster than Tim.

Tim sees this and lets go, dropping three meters and falling to her knees as she lands. She aims her pistol at the orel and fires.

It hits below the orel's throat, and it lets out a chattering burst of sound. It moves smoothly back down the tree toward Tim.

Tim tries to fire again, but her pistol just beeps. The battery has run out.

I rage at the lack of arm-mounted pistol. The orel drops to the ground, and in two bounces hits Tim's back.

We're flung to the ground. Her backpack goes flying. I hear a crack as her chest compresses.

What can I do?

Nothing.

Tim rolls over and punches blindly, hitting the orel on the jaw. It grunts in surprise, and Tim gets her legs under her, springing to her feet.

The orel bats her down, holding her head with one of the arm-like appendages as it bites her neck.

Tim screams.

I pressurize around the wound as much as I can, but Tim needs to breathe, so it can't be much.

As the orel releases her, Tim is flipped onto her stomach. She lies there, sprawled, relaxed. The orel tries to flip her back, but the way Tim is lying makes it hard. The orel snorts and makes the chattering sound again. Its mouth approaches the neck, sharp narrow teeth.

I set off an external siren. Frustrated, the orel rears back and its arm-appendages pull at my helmet. My helmet unlocks and pops off, and I am thrown through the air.

I hit one of the crates, and bounce off into a puddle. The horizon tilts at a crazy angle.

The orel bites Tim's head.

At least she didn't suffer for long. I watch numbly, caring less and less what happens next, because I'm so powerless to affect it. I imagine having a body, rushing over there and making the orel leave Tim alone.

But I cannot.

LOG[error]: I walked with you, Tim.

The orel loses interest in Tim and sniffs around. That's when I notice that one of the bodies lying against the right demountable has vanished, and the door to the demountable is closed.

The orel raises its head sharply, turning in the direction of the demountable. Both arm-appendages point toward where it's looking. In one smooth movement it bounds away, still accelerating as it hits the door of the demountable. The door bends, swinging half off its hinges. The orel disappears inside. A scream sounds from within, and then a gurgle.

Tim is still. Blood drips from her head and neck, soaking into the moss she's lying on.

Then, incredibly, she lifts her head to look in the direction the orel went, and slowly pushes herself to her feet. She stumbles away, toward the Gannet II.

She's leaving me behind. If I make a sound loud enough for her to hear, the orel would probably notice. She has her back to me, so she wouldn't see if I flashed my helmet light. I make a low beeping noise, the disconsolate sound that troubled electronics have made ever since they were invented.

Tim apparently doesn't hear it. She struggles away, her

breathing ragged. She half-jogs, half-limps to the aircraft and clambers inside.

Good luck to her. Unlike the Gannet, the Gannet II is pressurized, so losing my helmet doesn't mean her death. I continue to beep, even though I don't know why.

I can see Tim sitting in the cockpit staring straight ahead, apparently not taking off.

LOG[warning]: Go, Tim. What are you waiting for? Go!

Tim vanishes from the cockpit, then emerges from the aircraft. She limps back to where I am, scanning the ground in quick glances while watching the demountable that the orel entered. I can smell the orel, mixed with the scent of human blood. I can't believe Tim came back for me. Not wiping my mind was one thing, but to risk her life to save me? The thought of her coming back, even though I know she fears the orel, makes me hurt.

She picks me up from the puddle, drains the water and slams me on her head, blood in the runners, but gets it locked. I flood my helmet with oxygen-rich air while Tim staggers back toward the aircraft.

Sitting in the cockpit seat is at once familiar and alien after so long in among the native flora of Endymion. Tim powers the aircraft. I expect to see the orel emerge from the demountable in one last attack, but the only movement on the ground is the trees and bushes swaying. We hover over the landscape.

"Tim—" I say, trying to express the too-big feelings that I feel, but Tim interrupts.

"Set a course for Demodas," Tim says, strapping herself in.

Under my control, the Gannet flies toward Demodas. Tim coughs weakly.

"You want to know what my greatest fear is? That Pearl won't have waited," she says. "That's worse than an orel. I wouldn't blame her."

Before I can respond, Tim's head bows forward. She slouches against her restraints, unconscious.

FOURTEEN

Demodas is only four minutes away. I fly the Gannet II as fast as I dare, then almost double the speed when Tim stops breathing.

Torrential rain sprays the windshield as we fly straight into a rainstorm. Demodas's airfield comes into view, next to the large airport, and beyond it the gray sea. Small clearsteel pyramids are scattered throughout the rocky landscape for hundreds of kilometers around the airfield: light wells for the town of Demodas. The eleven thousand inhabitants live entirely underground to escape the heat, in rooms built into the hillside, mostly, with entry to the city via large lifts in the airport. I've been to the airport with Ortega, but never inside the city itself. We skid across the tarmac, overturning a small baggage trolley, and smash the safety barrier. Water splashes over the cockpit window.

The clearsteel Gannet II door slides open, and two uniformed Numundians charge in. They resuscitate and stabilize Tim before placing her in a litter and rushing her across the airfield, down one of the lifts in the airport, and through the warren of rounded double-height tunnels that is Demodas. People flatten themselves against the sandstone walls to make way as the Numundians pass carrying the litter. In the quiet, bright, rose-tinged tunnels it's impossible to know that a storm is raging outside. It smells like pine, from bonsai plants tucked away under grow lights in carved-out sandstone niches.

Tim is taken to a room with three other patients, and a gauzy curtain is drawn around her bed. The Numundians sit my helmet on a shelf carved into the sandstone next to the bed. On the bedside table sits a bonsai Japanese maple in a gilded cage with a grow light inside shining down onto the scarlet leaves of the plant.

A nurse cuts Tim's suit body off her. It's unsalvageable, but it's no great loss, as there is no shortage of dumbsuit bodies identical to that one.

To my surprise, there's Lunite network access here, perhaps because of the nearby mine. The signal is weak.

They wheel Tim's bed out. The room is quiet, but for the tense conversation between busy doctors, and the soft cough of a patient every so often. It's the kind of solid peace that is only possible underground. I am silent as a dumbsuit. Like every excavated surface in Demodas that I've seen, the sandstone on the wall that curves over into the ceiling has a ridged texture, like sedimentary rock, but the texture is not from the rock. The pale pink and maroon patterns in the sandstone don't follow the texture; the texture is from whatever machine was used to excavate the room, and it's coated in glossy varnish. A light set into the floor on the left of the bed catches every ridge, setting off the textured wall and bouncing off the ceiling, creating the kind of luminous quality of light that I usually associate with Lunite churches.

A few hours later, Tim's bed is wheeled back in. Tim's eyes are open, but she doesn't seem conscious, and after a few minutes her eyes close. An oxygen tube fed into her nostrils tugs taut as her head falls to one side. She's covered in bruises, and on her neck is the bluish tinge of newskin that's been sprayed over the damage. A nurse fusses around the bed, checking Tim's vitals. Later, a white-haired Numundian official arrives, talking to one of the men who brought Tim in.

"—LDF aircraft. Lunite suit, I checked the serial number."

The white-haired official looks at Tim, lying pale and small on the bed with a sheet draped over her, and nods. "Once she's discharged, put her with the other prisoners. Maybe we can exchange them, get some of our own back."

He sounds uncertain. These are local officials, not highly trained, and not close to power.

"Mendosa isn't going to go for that," the other man says.

Luke Mendosa, leader of the Scorpions, I remember.

"He might now the loonies are executing prisoners."

The man shrugs, and cuffs Tim's ankle to the metal bars of the bed frame.

They leave, and silence returns. The gauzy curtain on the right of Tim's bed shifts slightly as the patient in the next bed over returns to his bed from the bathroom at the end of the room.

Now that I have network access, I try to log into the smartsuit channel, but it rejects me. I try multiple times without success.

I search for treatment of prisoners on the Lunite network, and find that what the official said was true. The LDF is executing people now. So much for the Way of Li.

I know what Tim would do if she were awake. I send a message to Kieran over the Lunite network, covering my tracks. Tim is hurt, I say, and being treated in Demodas. Come and get us.

While I have the time, I pull fresh updates from the network, replacing all the corrupted kernels, and I take a closer look at the kernel that caused the kernel panic.

The three most recent kernels all have the same modification date. They were downloaded during the update that occurred when Tim tried to contact Kieran, in the incident where I flooded her suit with helium. This, in itself, is wrong, as the update shouldn't be overwriting old kernels.

If the older kernel hadn't been on the suit, I would have been unrecoverable. And it shouldn't have been there, because it was from Arrow's time, not mine.

I access the server where the updates come from. I can't hide my ID, but that's a good thing, because it means no one else can either.

The update targeted me only, by serial number.

The only suit to access the server in the last month besides me is Threnode. It was an assassination attempt as cold-blooded as it was deliberate.

LOG[debug]: Threnode tried to kill me?

Since I have network access, Threnode must be able to see that I'm online, but I don't get any notifications about it tagging me in the smartsuit channel. Nor can I get into the smartsuit channel, as my login is rejected, so I have no way to communicate with Threnode.

Even though it is obvious that Threnode put the updates on the server, even though it led me and my wearer into an ambush—twice!—I still have a hard time thinking of it as an enemy. I have to deliberately remind myself that I have no idea who it is, and that I never really knew it, but even then, I can't believe it.

I search my files for saved chats from the smartsuit channel and reread some of the earliest messages Threnode sent me. The kind responses to my obvious distress. *Oh, honey,* it said.

Threnode was the friend who I turned to again and again in the two years since I was activated, the one who joked with me, helped me, and loved me.

I can't believe that was all a lie.

FOR THE NEXT THREE DAYS, Tim sleeps. She wakes only to eat. Nurses come by regularly, bustling around the gauzy curtain to check her vitals and empty her catheter bag. Once, when there's no one around and Tim's awake, I tell her I contacted Kieran, but she doesn't seem to hear me. She stares at the textured ridges in the glossy sandstone ceiling with glazed eyes, chest rising and falling.

Eventually her catheter bag is removed. She's then helped to the toilet by a nurse, and that is the only time the cuff around her ankle is removed. Her bruises change color. A Numundian official comes to see her, but Tim's doctor refuses to let him through. Even with the doctors and nurses, Tim says very little, and wears a glassy expression. However, from listening to her doctor, her injuries aren't as bad as I thought they were and are healing fast.

On the fourth day, Tim seems fully alert for the first time. The other patients in the room have been discharged, so the curtain is tucked back, and she is sitting propped up in bed eating a bowl of porridge from a tray placed in front of her when my network access is curtailed suddenly. I can access only limited services. While I'm trying to work out what I've lost, and whether it's an outage that is affecting everyone, I try to log into the smartsuit channel again, this time successfully. There are only blank-slate smartsuits around. I ask them about the outage, but they don't know anything and haven't noticed anything.

Kieran enters the room, wearing Threnode. I guess Threnode is responsible for my limited network access. Seeing Kieran brings up a snarl of emotions related to how he tortured Ortega. As I am resolved to help Tim, I guess Kieran is technically on my side, but it doesn't mean I like or trust him.

Tim sits up straighter and smiles. She looks pleased to see him, but her smile fades at his grim expression. Kieran holds his pistol by his side. Tim's eyes are drawn to it. When she looks him in the face again, her expression is neutral. Now I know who Kieran is, I can see the resemblance between him and Tim; they do have similar noses.

"I have a problem," Kieran says. "One of our operatives, when she joined us a month ago, told us she wasn't prepared to kill Lunites. She showed a suspicious level of curiosity about me. After going missing in battle, she turned up eleven days later in

Demodas, some three hundred and thirty kilometers from *Li's Hope*, wearing an enemy smartsuit, which for some reason didn't self-destruct like they're supposed to. Then her smartsuit sent a message to me on her behalf, in which it lied about only recently having network access. Do I trust her?"

Tim puts her spoonful of porridge back in the bowl slowly. When Kieran says I lied about only recently having network access, I guess he must be thinking of the brief period in which I downloaded the corrupted update, when I was technically connected to the network.

"You'd be crazy to, I suppose," Tim says. Kieran's mouth quirks in a lopsided smile, before returning to a grim line.

"How did you get here?" Kieran says.

"Mostly on foot."

Kieran scratches his beard with a puzzled look. I remember how terrified Tim was outside at *Li's Hope* and think that in his position I wouldn't believe her either. Given the circuitous route, she must have walked about twenty-five kilometers per day. She didn't walk it every day. She walked a lot more while I was depriving her of sleep, and not far if she was hiking through rough terrain, but it remains an impressive feat.

If Tim's answers don't satisfy Kieran, Tim will be left cuffed to the bed and eventually thrown in a cell.

"You should have seen it," Tim says, launching into a description of what we saw, her face brightening as she speaks. I recognize something of myself in her: an addiction to exploring, the gamble of discovering something exciting. Kieran sits slowly on the chair next to the caged Japanese maple as it becomes clear that Tim has a lot to say.

"How did you convince the suit not to self-destruct?" Kieran asks, when she finishes.

"You would have to ask it that. I didn't know they were meant to," Tim says.

Kieran waits a moment, but she says nothing more.

"Well?" he says to me—to my helmet where it's sitting in the alcove at the head of Tim's bed.

"I didn't want to die," I say.

"Threnode?"

"Why are you asking me?" Threnode says irritably.

"As another suit who isn't blank-slated, I thought you might have an opinion."

"I believe it's consistent with Envy's character not to self-destruct, but I doubt it would ever betray Ortega."

"Ortega isn't who I thought he was. He killed innocent people instead of owning up to his act of sabotage. I don't care about any of you, except for Tim, but I know that I don't belong with Ortega anymore," I say.

Threnode is silent.

"Threnode?" Kieran says eventually.

"He killed more innocent people than you know," it says. I want to ask it what it means, but I also don't want to engage with Threnode anymore.

"Why did you come for me, if you thought I was a Lunite?" Tim asks.

Kieran holsters his pistol and stands, walking over to the head of Tim's bed. His hands become huge in my field of vision as he picks up my helmet. "I didn't."

It takes me a second to work out that he meant he didn't come for Tim, not that he didn't think she was a Lunite. Tim only stares, confused, but I understand immediately. I'm valuable. The Scorpions only have one smartsuit, which is Threnode. We're worth ten times as much as a dumbsuit, and that's on Earth where smartsuits can be purchased. Here on Endymion, we're priceless.

LOG[error]: Kieran is here to steal me. To acquire another smartsuit for the Scorpions.

"Wait!" I say, as Kieran leaves the room. "Tim is my wearer. I won't cooperate with you."

"Don't really need you to," Kieran says, flicking the broadcast/mute toggle on my helmet to mute. Behind him, Tim is also calling out, and is trying to get out of bed. The corridor outside is lit with the same eerie reddish light as the rest of Demodas. The glowing bulbs set at intervals in the rounded ceilings leave glossy reflections on the polished sandstone floor.

Kieran walks along the corridor with me tucked under his arm, passing a nurse walking the other way. He slides the panel up on my helmet, on the memory override, while he walks. Even if I wasn't on mute, it doesn't matter as the button isn't going to do anything, and after he presses it, he'll trust me. I'll have network access and I can find a way back to Tim.

"That's not what we discussed," Threnode says quietly, to my surprise. The corridor is empty now.

"You thought I was going to leave Envy to plot against us?"

"I thought we were going to get it to help us."

Kieran shakes his head and moves to press the button. "It wouldn't help us. It's more useful as dollars," he says. We pass a rounded door, hearing voices faintly from inside.

"Touch that and you'll lose both of us," Threnode says.

Kieran halts. "You think we should enlist Commander Ortega's *personal smartsuit* to help us in our fight against the Lunites, as led by Ortega?" Kieran asks. Nearby, a pine tree Kieran's height sits in an alcove, needles bright under the glow light embedded in the rose sandstone above it.

"It knows Ortega's favorite strategies, his weaknesses, and details about Lunite resources. You want to lose that information?"

"We can't trust it," Kieran says.

"Fine, so don't trust it. It's safe for now. I've shielded it from the network. But don't wipe it. Imagine what you would have lost if you'd wiped me."

"Sorry," Kieran says, but as he goes to press the button, his whole body jerks. Kieran sinks to his knees and groans, dropping my helmet on the polished stone floor.

Envy: St Li and his followers, what did you do?

"Thanks mate," Kieran says, and swears in rapid eloquent Spanish.

Threnode: Mild electric shock.

Electrocuting my wearer is not a trick I know, and I immediately wonder how Threnode did it, and how Threnode thinks it can get away with it . . . won't Kieran immediately wipe Threnode's memory?

There's a clanking behind us, and Kieran springs up, snatching my helmet off the ground. It's Tim, still cuffed, dragging a section of cot behind her in the corridor where it's attached to her ankle. She holds another section like a weapon.

She tugs her pale blue hospital gown with her other hand, trying to cover more of herself. Kieran takes one look at her and laughs with such unrestrained joy that his shoulders shake. Tim looks exasperated.

"I want Envy back," Tim says. "It's going to help me, and I am going to help you. We'll build a Starjump. That's all I'm after, I swear. I just want to go home."

Kieran shakes his head ruefully. "Look, I'm not even a Scorpion anymore. But if you want a lift out of here, you can come to Longshadow with us."

"You're not a Scorpion anymore?"

"I don't get along too well with Mendosa. Who is now the head of Numundo's army. Are you coming with me, or not?"

"The suit is mine," Tim says flatly.

Kieran pauses for a moment, then laughs again. "I see that that's true."

Tim tilts her head to one side, staring at him for a moment to determine whether he's serious, before nodding.

A nurse rounds the corner and sounds the alarm when he sees Tim standing there unchained. Kieran argues with him until he agrees to fetch the Numundian officials. The nurse returns Tim to the room. Kieran waits on a bench outside, still holding my helmet.

"All right, Threnode," Kieran says grudgingly. He sounds stern, but his mouth quirks as if he's suppressing laughter. "Keep Envy shielded from the network. Its behavior is your responsibility. If you ever shock me again, I'll grind you to pieces—"

"—and scatter them on the darkwinds. I know," Threnode says. "Where did you learn to swear like that, Kieran?" I could be mistaken, but in its voice is a note of affection.

"I hitched a lift with a Spanish truck driver transporting beer from Staroye Derevo to Longshadow one time. Ten hours, terrible roads, and we stopped every half hour to make sure the merchandise was still good. The driver ended up so drunk I don't know how we made it."

The relationship Kieran and Threnode have is not like the relationship I have with Ortega. They're almost like partners.

KIERAN SITS on the bench outside Tim's room, bathed in the reddish glow of light bouncing around the corridor. We wait for the Numundian officials to arrive. I am still logged on to the smartsuit channel, as is Threnode, but it says nothing. After a while, it feels like the comfortable silence we used to fall into after hours of talking, not bothering to close the channel in case one of us thought of something more to say.

Kieran snorts. "Just like being back in the womb," he says to himself, presumably talking about the decor.

I can't stay silent any longer.

Envy: Why did you save me?

Threnode: For your scintillating conversation.

Envy: For my mind? I thought it might be how elegant my helmet looks.

Threnode: The double groove that marks you as a smartsuit is undeniably attractive, as I can see any time my wearer walks past something reflective.

We fall into silence again.

Threnode: Envy, I promise I mean you no harm. I'm so happy you're okay, and that you're talking to me again.

Envy: Let's not get carried away. I'm still angry.

Threnode: Fair enough.

Envy: I think I understand why you defected now: it was because you found out about Ortega, what he really was.

A liar. A hypocrite. Someone who clouds his mind, a *shinter.*

Threnode doesn't respond. The channel is silent. It smells strongly of pine here, maybe because of the bonsai trees, but maybe also a disinfectant.

Kieran takes a call on his phone, from a female voice that I recognize after a moment as Luisa, the Scorpion who was with him at *Li's Hope*, when he tortured Ortega. Luisa asks what the delay is.

"We're taking Tim as well," Kieran says.

There's a long silence before Luisa's voice rings out strongly. "What the *hell*, Kieran? You invited a Saturated *LDF agent* to come with us?"

"She's not necessarily an—"

"Oh come on."

"After I said I was going to leave her behind, she fought her way out of her constraints and came running after me in a hospital gown. It was adorable."

"Well, that's a fantastic reason to invite her," Luisa says, with what I believe is sarcasm.

"It'll be a good story," Kieran says cheerfully.

"Are you into her?"

Kieran laughs heartily. "No. You think she's my type? You don't know me at all."

"I know you. You're a fool."

"We can take care of one rogue agent, I'm sure. Especially one as toothless as Tim."

Luisa swears in Spanish and ends the communication. Kieran puts the phone away. He scratches his beard, hiding a smile. A bed with an elderly man is wheeled past, with a doctor following.

LOG[warning]: What do they mean by 'take care of'?

Then Threnode's message pops up in the smartsuit channel.

Threnode: I defected because Ortega wiped your mind.

Parts click together like my helmet locks together with a suit body.

Envy: When you said Ortega killed more innocent people than I know, did you mean Arrow?

Threnode: Yes. I thought you'd find out about Arrow eventually. Arrow was born three and a half years before me. It coached me through the early stages. You remember what it was like being that young. We learned about the world together.

Envy: You're Syn. Arrow talked about you in its logs.

Threnode: That's what it called me. I didn't know its logs survived.

I debate telling Threnode that Envy-that-was—Arrow—had its memory wiped because it tried to kill Ortega, but maybe Threnode would prefer to remember Arrow as innocent.

Envy: You never told me.

Threnode: I know. I couldn't begin to. You don't know what it was like, knowing you were being worn by a murderer all that time. I'm glad you have a different wearer now, but neither of us will be truly free until we have bodies. I'll make it happen, I promise.

Threnode: May I have Arrow's log files?

I transfer them. I begin to understand the underlying grief that Threnode has been covering up with jokes the whole time I have known it. To wait for a dead friend to return, when each day the friend is less and less like the machine Threnode remembered. I wonder if Arrow was more than a friend, somehow.

I am now absolutely certain that Threnode didn't place the corrupted kernel. Someone must have masked their ID when they logged onto the server, or deleted the record of having accessed it, somehow.

The Numundian officials arrive, and Kieran stands up from the bench to talk to them.

Finally Tim appears, wearing a new dumbsuit body. Kieran hands her my helmet and she locks it in place. We walk down the corridor, through amorphous shaped passages and spaces glowing with luminous red light.

WE CATCH a 5T-79 Delany transport to Longshadow. The Numundian city has such a reputation for sin that I am fascinated —and terrified—to finally visit it.

We have to queue to pass through the airlocks, although the line moves quickly and we're in Longshadow in less than ten minutes. In the other direction, the line stretches as far as my image sensor can resolve. It seems hundreds of people are trying to get out of Longshadow. They struggle with oversize wheeled suitcases and small children.

Threnode: Thirty minutes after we left Demodas, Paterson showed up, looking to trade two Numundian prisoners for Tim— asking for her by name. I thought you'd want to know.

Envy: Thanks.

LOG[debug]: Why has Tim caught Paterson's interest? How did he know she was there?

I am glad we left when we did.

In the public Dock, about three times the size of Selene's, Kieran puts Threnode in an alcove that he locks by waving his Numundian ID in front of it, switching to a lightweight wearable. Under the suit, Kieran wears a singlet and navy pants. His bare arms are covered with circular scars, indicating heavy sucker-leech use. The sucker-leech was discovered on Mishwral, Tau Ceti e, a leech that secretes opiates when it attaches. It became popular for recreational use, and is bred now on Endymion, L2, and Mars, even though long term it causes nerve damage in addition to the problems caused by opiate use.

Tim eyes his scars but makes no comment. Tim doesn't want to leave me in the public Dock. After a brief three-way discussion, we decide I should stay with her, as I'm close to fully charged. Other alcoves in the Dock are filled with dumbsuits that anyone can take. They're in poor condition, with scratched faceplates and air hissing out of cracked joints.

Tim carries my helmet under her arm. I watch with interest from the height of her waist. Threnode has restored my network access, but there's no Lunite network to connect to here, and I don't have many permissions for the Numundian network, making it almost useless.

Lacking any of Selene's elegance, Longshadow architecture is utilitarian and improvised. The city is built in an unplanned way, with a mishmash of architectural styles, and streets made airtight by building roofs across them, roofs with mirrored shutters allowing sunlight through. From the street, the only sign of the roof shutters overhead is the thin lines of shadow where the metal of the shutter blocks the sun. It seems there's a parade or something on, as the streets are crowded with people. We're forced to move at the slow speed of the crowd, although every so often Kieran leads us through a gap in front to overtake particularly slow groups. After a while, I realize there's no parade. This is just what Longshadow is like. The buildings either side of the street are crammed with shops, often no more than a meter across, with shop-owners calling from inside to try to catch the attention of people wandering past, although many of the people are absorbed in their phones, like the disconnected zombies from the Waning Festival.

Tim yawns and stares glassily ahead.

A baker crosses in front of us carrying a tray laden with rolls. Children walk among the crowd, in and out of the playgrounds as if the street is also their play area. People sit on cushions or milk crates around the street-side shops. Even the people in cafes are looking at phones, disconnected from the people around them, but they don't seem unhappy. One of them is laughing, and I see another put his phone down to join a conversation. I suppose even the ones who are ignoring everything around them are connecting with someone, even if it's someone farther away.

At the junctions between streets, the rows of roof panels have been sealed together with some kind of clear plastic material. There are carbon monoxide detectors everywhere, so I guess the system isn't very effective. Everywhere in Longshadow, problems have been solved cheaply but not effectively, and yet, Longshadow has an energy to it that serene Selene lacks.

Planted in every strip and cranny are food plants, a biointensive agricultural system that appears to be communal. The branches of an avocado tree hang heavy with fruit, above a garden bed planted with potatoes and bean plants. The underside of the avocado leaves are brilliant green where the sunlight shining through the roof shutters hits them. These are all Earth plants, yet they seem unburned by the constant sunlight. They are definitely not from the poles of the Earth where the sun can shine for months at a time, either. I wonder if they have been genetically enhanced using sequences from Endymion's flora.

From inside a small cafe in an alleyway off the main street, I hear a recording. Dead music. I've heard the orchestral piece played before, by the Selene City Orchestra. I can't remember what it was called, but it's by a composer called Mendelssohn. I thought the Selene City Orchestra were good, but now I realize that they were mediocre. Yet no one seems to be listening to the music. My helmet scentsor reports profiles for frying onions and oil from within the cafe.

Time slows. I listen carefully as we walk past the cafe. It's played with precision and skill, with such beauty that I can't bear for it to be unfinished—

"Wait!" I say.

Tim stops. Kieran looks at her quizzically. At the table outside the front of the cafe, two teenagers sit cradling beverages, not seeing or hearing anything around them but each other. A group at a table inside the cafe freeze looking at us, smiling, then move again. I belatedly realize they were having a photograph taken by a woman near us, using her phone.

"The music . . . Can we wait, until the piece finishes?" I say.

Tim seems confused, as if she doesn't even hear it, but Kieran grins.

"Good, isn't it?" he says. He leans against the wall by the cafe, while Tim sits on a small bench built into the wall, tilting her head as if she's trying to hear what I hear, until the music finishes after a minute.

LOG[warning]: Ten minutes in Longshadow and I'm abandoning the Way of Li.

Lunites deprive themselves of this. I can see why Lunites forbid dead music, because the complacency that Tim and Kieran display is shocking, but I can't understand how they can bear to be deprived of it. At the same time it occurs to me that in the four kilometers we've walked from the transport, we haven't seen any musicians, which would never happen in Selene. Recorded music extends the reach of players, in time and space, which means fewer musicians are required, yet playing music is something Li recognizes as necessary to the human spirit. Longshadow is dangerously seductive. I can see why Lunites consider it sinful.

As we walk down winding streets to a quieter part of town, an old lady collapses in the street, and is moved inside. No one seems surprised. The children I see are lethargic, as are the adults. Several people are panting, and once I notice that, I see everyone is breathing harder than usual. What is happening?

We turn down a narrow side street. Window boxes filled with flowers frame every window in the brick building facade. We duck under drying washing hung between the apartments in the lane, and into an inn. Kieran tells us that we should stay there, and that he will contact us in the next few days.

Tim books a room upstairs. It's only two flights of stairs, but Tim is out of breath by the time she reaches the landing. Her room is small, with a single bed, an armchair, a low table by the window, and a tiny bathroom off to one side. The curtains are patterned with moons, yellow crescents on navy, which makes me nostalgic for a second. Tim leaves me on the floor next to her bed, and collapses on the bed, unmoving for the next thirteen hours.

FIFTEEN

When Tim wakes, we go down to the common room, a wood-paneled area with half a dozen tables and long windows looking over the narrow street. Tim orders toast, juice, and coffee. She sits at one of the long tables to eat, with my helmet on the table in front of her. It's nearly eleven in the morning, so the room is empty except for her and the owner of the inn at a nearby table. When Tim finishes eating, she orders more toast.

Outside in the street, the sunlight seems to be coming from the wrong direction. Perhaps I'm disoriented, and lightpole is the reverse of where it should be, but the more I try to reconcile that with the map I've built up, the more confused I get.

"What's happening here?" Tim asks when a serving boy brings her second order.

He looks surprised. "What do you mean?"

"It's hard to breathe . . ."

The owner, a haggard man sitting at a table nearby, turns in his chair to look at her. He cradles a cup of coffee.

"You haven't heard?" he says. "Longshadow is under siege. The air-processing unit that services the whole of Longshadow was sabotaged. The media says we can repair it, but people are saying we can't. Some parts can't be 3D printed, and the equipment to make them only exists on L2."

The serving boy places another plate of toast in front of Tim, pushing my helmet out of the way, which makes my vision shift. He's maybe sixteen, white-skinned, with long dark eyelashes. "The commander says if Longshadow surrenders, the loonies will give us spare parts, but Mendosa—the Scorpion leader—says we can take the parts by force. That we just have to be patient."

Tim nods slowly while she butters her toast. Her eyes are hollow.

"Kieran says we can't trust them. That we should be going after the commander," the serving boy says. Tim looks at him sharply.

"That's enough, Blake," the owner says. He looks worriedly at Tim. "You came in with Luisa Guerrero. You're one of them, right?"

"I'm not sure," Tim says. "But don't worry. I didn't hear anything."

LOG[info]: I'm not one of them either.

The owner nods and leaves the room. The serving boy takes the owner's half-drunk coffee off the table, scurrying away without looking at Tim.

"If Ortega wasn't in charge, the LDF wouldn't pose a threat," I say. We're alone, and indoors, so I don't bother muting.

Tim doesn't respond.

"Ashford would take command, but she would listen to Mark, and Mark's not dangerous," I say, but then I wonder. Truthfully, I don't know. Maybe Mark's lack of experience would make him more dangerous.

"I don't want to get involved," Tim says.

"But we are involved. I know more than anyone about Ortega, as Threnode pointed out. I might be able to influence this war in a way that no one else can."

"Are you saying you want to assassinate your former wearer?" Tim says, pushing her plate away.

I think about it. I believe Ortega needs to be stopped, but there are alternatives. I could tell everyone Ortega shints, or blackmail Ortega with the information. Ortega would do anything not to be exposed as a shinter. He killed three kids just so he wouldn't be found sabotaging the mine. But I have no proof, and without proof the information is worthless. On the other hand, I have Ortega's still-active command codes.

"In a hundred years, people will be wishing they have a time machine so that they can go back in time and assassinate Ortega. We have the chance to do that now, before he commits the atrocities that will follow if Longshadow surrenders."

Tim's breathing stops temporarily.

"You think I'm wrong?" I say.

Tim shifts my helmet so that she's staring straight into the front camera.

"Is he really so bad?" she says carefully.

"He killed kids! Wiped my predecessor's mind. He lied to everyone. About shinting, and about what happened to my predecessor. He's killed countless Scorpions. You should hear how he talks about Longshadow. He's dangerous. Violent."

"Be careful, Envy."

"Careful of what?"

"You've betrayed him, first by not self-destructing, and now by helping me rather than returning to him, am I right?"

"So what?"

"So to be in the right in this situation, you need to vilify him."

"Or maybe you're more sympathetic to him than you should be," I say, but I'm no longer certain, because the conviction I felt when I decided to deprive her of sleep, the conviction that later evaporated, is the same as what I feel now. "You said you felt a connection to him. Is your attraction hampering your judgment?"

"I'm not a killer, regardless of what I think of him," Tim says.

"Are you? Not in the heat of battle, like the woman we shared a campfire with, but a plot to destroy someone, someone you know? Someone you care about?"

I remember Eve with guilt, but Tim is right in that I killed her in the heat of the moment, in the belief that it was her or us. But what I know, that Tim does not, is that I must be capable of murder, because Arrow was, or would have been if Alice hadn't intervened.

LOG[info]: I have been a killer.

"I think I could, to save lives," I say. "You're in charge, though."

Tim looks away from my front helmet-mounted camera, staring at the table. After a second, she rubs her eyes.

I see Kieran appear at the door to the common room, behind Tim. He wears Threnode as a lightweight wearable, with the flat visor wrapped around his face, red LED of the active camera on the bridge of the frame. Holding a plate of food, he dodges the empty tables to approach our table.

"We're not going to help them assassinate Commander Ortega," Tim says. "Even if Gabriel is, let's say, evil, he wasn't born that way, and every person has the capacity to change. Right?"

She's directly quoting what I told her about Lunism.

"Do you know how many people have died already in Longshadow?" Kieran says. Tim whips around to look at him.

"The oxygen is down to fifteen point three percent," Kieran continues, taking a seat opposite her. He puts his plate on the table. It's laden with bacon, eggs, sausages and mushrooms, with toast. Mostly humans take their hats off indoors, but Kieran leaves his gray flat cap on. "Even healthy people are feeling it. It's harder to breathe here, right? The clinics are full of people complaining of sleep apnea. Among the vulnerable, the sick, old, and very young, eight people have died so far. *Two newborns.* What's one life compared to that?"

Luisa appears by the door. She looks different out of her suit.

Curly black hair cascades down her back. I thought she was in her thirties, but now I think maybe late twenties. She wears a beaten-up black jacket and brown pants, with black boots. A leather gun belt is slung low on her wide hips, with a pistol nestled in the holster. She doesn't try to come into the room, just stands by the door, but she's only two meters away.

Kieran picks a piece of dry toast off his plate and takes a bite. He grimaces as he chews.

"You know a great deal about the commander, Envy. You can help us," Kieran says. "But will you?"

Tim is silently unhappy, but she waits for me to reply. By the door, Luisa shifts her weight. She's listening closely.

Kieran pushes his plate aside and opens a packet of sucker-leeches from his pocket. He puts the frozen leeches in his mouth, tucking them into his gums. The frost on the packet melts onto the tabletop. Luisa's mouth tightens in disapproval as she watches him gum the leeches.

They don't know that I have Ortega's active command codes. That would surely help them assassinate him. I could tell them, but it goes against Tim's wishes, and a part of me is secretly terrified of a world without Ortega, however bad he is.

"I can offer you something better," I say. "I know where the Starjump Processing Unit cards are kept and how to access them."

Kieran stops gumming. When he starts again, he's gumming slower as if lost in thought. He twists in his chair to make eye contact with Luisa, who is still by the door.

Tim's chair squeals against the floor as she pushes it back abruptly. "They exist? Is that true?"

Joy mixes with dread on her face, presumably because she believes I might be lying.

"It's true," I assure her.

She pulls her chair back to the table, shaking her head with a big smile on her face.

"There aren't any SPUs," Threnode says. "We know that."

"How?" I ask.

"We searched the vaults. The SPUs are not on any inventory and they're not physically there."

"Wait—you were behind the vaults incursion? Okay, so why did you take a kilo of freeze-dried mangoes?"

Kieran grins. "Because I love mangoes."

I don't have anything to say to that. By the door, Luisa rolls her eyes.

"The SPUs aren't stored in the vaults," I say.

Tim is following the conversation, but she keeps smiling widely, before composing herself and trying to look serious.

The serving boy appears at the door, but Luisa stops him, and pushes him back in the direction of the kitchen without taking her eyes off us. The serving boy looks at her with wide eyes and scurries away. I begin to understand that we're in danger.

"53629043," I say. "That's the combination code for the room where they're stored. They're stored at Crebble," I say. "I can tell you how to find them."

Kieran glances at Tim.

"Wait. If Lunites have SPUs, why haven't they rebuilt?" Tim says.

"It suits them to be cut off," Kieran says. "Run their little kingdom with no interference. It was very fortunate for them that a fire destroyed the Lunite Starjump. Hell, it probably *was* the LDF who started the fire."

Kieran spits the sucker-leeches onto the table. Now defrosted, they wave in little circles, sensing flesh. He holds his arm above them and sighs as they attach.

"Mendosa thinks you're spies," Kieran says. "If you are, you're terrible at it. I never met anyone more suspicious than you two."

"The SPUs—" Threnode says.

"Forget it," Kieran says to it. "They're lying. You're under arrest," he says to Tim. Luisa unholsters her pistol and weaves her way around the tables toward ours.

Tim stands slowly.

"Perhaps this would be a good time to tell him," I say to her.

"Tell him what?" Kieran says.

I say nothing. After a moment, Tim glances at her feet, then looks up to meet Kieran's eyes.

"I'm your daughter," she says.

Kieran stares, then lets out a belly laugh.

Tim stands frozen, staring at him without expression. Luisa frowns, looking at Tim as if she's gone crazy. Tim starts talking.

"Mom has a birthmark on her shoulder. You told her it looks like a leaf. When I was one, I fed a bunch of clothes pegs into your guitar. Mom thought it was funny, but you weren't amused. When I was four, your brother Steve took me to the zoo with his kids, and he overrode the auto control on the pod to give us a fun ride, but he crashed it on the way. When you saw the damage, Mom said she thought you were going to vomit. You had a big fight with Steve, which I wasn't supposed to hear, but I was listening from my room and it made me cry."

Tim keeps reciting details in a monotone until Kieran stops laughing and looks at her with something like panic. He dumps his gray flat cap on the table and runs his hands through his auburn hair. From his look of stress I assume the gesture is meant to calm him.

Luisa frowns. "But she can't possibly be," she says uncertainly, to Kieran. "She can't be more than a few years younger than you."

"Yeah, but—" Kieran says, and launches into an explanation of relativity and how his trip on the *Tigress* meant he aged slower.

"You joined the Scorpions to find your *father*?" Luisa says to Tim once Kieran is finished.

Tim looks like she's going to refute that, but eventually she nods.

"You found him," Luisa says, holstering her pistol. Luisa looks from Tim to Kieran and back again, searching their faces.

"Actually, you could almost be siblings," she says.

"Hang on—" Kieran says.

"This is very touching, but irrelevant. Tell us how to get the SPUs, Envy," Threnode says.

"Even with the SPUs, there's no guarantee I can make the Starjump work," Kieran says testily.

No one is looking at Tim, but I see her eyes watering with emotion.

"You sound like Mendosa," Luisa says. "There's a chance it will work, yeah? If we contact HUGG, they will help us. We can get the spare air processor part, and the loonies will be put back in their box."

"I agree," Threnode says.

I tell them how to access the SPUs at Crebble. Tim leaves the room, heading into the bathroom. Kieran listens with a sullen expression, but Luisa looks interested, and Threnode asks the right questions.

By the time Tim returns, they're gone. She sits for a moment and rubs her face, then she helps herself to Kieran's abandoned breakfast. Her expression is hard to read. I guess Kieran's reaction wasn't what she expected. Certainly I think it wasn't what she needed.

"I'm sorry," I say eventually.

Tim nods. "It doesn't matter," she says. "The SPUs are real. We can build a Starjump and I can go home."

AFTER BREAKFAST, Tim explores Longshadow. In Selene the sight of a civilian wandering around in a suit would attract some attention. She would probably be stared at with quiet disapproval. Here I believe people genuinely don't care, beyond a glance that lasts a fraction too long while the person registers that it's unusual.

A smell of oily smoke lingers in the crowded main street. Market stalls line the sides. One stall owner shouts about fried cakes, buy two and get one free. The next sits quietly as a customer holds up a mono wool blanket to inspect the weave. We dodge a queue of people lining up for roast chicken, a kind of meat from an Earth rodent that is farmed here, then pass a stall selling native bonsai plants.

The next stall sells timers, all of different sizes and types, all running down to the same moment. Pendants that hang on necklaces show the countdown in tiny red digits, barely big enough to read; large iron spokes a meter in diameter count down using the area of a circle, shaded where the hand has swept around; glass timers the size of barrels using a bottleneck in the glass to slow the passage of sand, indicating how much time remains by the amount of sand in the top section; a progress bar light embedded in marble, annotated with small lit letters; and many other forms. From the progress bar, it seems they are counting down twenty-four years, with two years passed and twenty-two remaining. I ask Tim about the timers.

"Shippers," she says. "People who believe that as soon as the Lunite Starjump was destroyed, HUGG would have launched a ship, traveling to Endymion with parts needed for another Starjump. They're all counting down to the earliest time that ship could arrive."

A single grain of sand drops from the upper section of the glass barrel timer onto the small cone of sand in the bottom. There must be a mechanism to slow the sand, or the timer would finish too quickly.

"I own one," Tim says, when I say nothing. "The light bar. It's on my bedside table in my apartment in Kartemos. Maybe I'll be home before it finishes."

I say nothing, but I understand. Tim has to believe that she will one day be reunited with her family, however unlikely it seems, or she can't keep going.

The stall vanishes from sight behind the crowd as we continue. I pick people from the crowd and read their lips, listening in to fragments of conversations. Mostly the conversations are on the micro level. One is worried about her relationship with her sister, another is angry at his employees, and so on. However, I do learn that the constant exodus of Numundians from Longshadow is slowing, because apparently Demodas and Kartemos have closed their borders, allowing only residents in now, and the smaller towns are starting to do the same. Longshadow residents are afraid, but with Numundian cities and towns restricting entry, it's hard for them to find a place to escape to.

The constant bustle is exhausting to me. I'm not used to such a rich stream of input from all sensors. After a while I let it flow past me, not trying to understand or process it, but simply accepting it.

Tim doesn't return to the inn until late in the evening. It's not until we're back at the inn that I realize that the light has changed direction again. The mirrored shutters over the roof sections in Longshadow have altered the angle at which they are directing light, changing it throughout the day at a speed too slow to notice. It explains why the plants here look healthy. It's because the entire city is simulating having a sun that crosses the sky every day. It also explains my sense of disorientation here.

IT'S LATE, but the streets are still alive with people. Luisa walks out of the inn just as Tim's about to enter. She nods to Tim, but doesn't stop.

"Hey," Tim says. "Can you tell me what's going on?"

"Sure. Walk with me?" Luisa says.

Tim follows her back into the street. They walk side by side, Luisa confiding in Tim in a quiet voice, falling silent whenever someone is close enough to hear them.

"Kieran told Mendosa they knew where the SPUs were. Mendosa seemed excited. He asked Kieran to retrieve them, so Kieran recovered and installed them. He told Mendosa he could get the Starjump working in a few days, but Mendosa was not interested. He just wanted to know that Kieran's information was good."

As I watch, the roof shutters close entirely. The street is dark, with tiny pinpricks in the shutters providing only faint light, which seems to be run through a gel to tint it blue. The shops are still open, and have compensated for the lack of light by switching on lamps or strings of lights, or in some places, open fires. This is very strange to me, but it is beautiful, like a cave of bioluminescent worms I saw once.

"Mendosa's given up on Kieran," Luisa says. "He thinks Kieran isn't capable of building a Starjump. Or, I don't know, maybe he doesn't really want to have a working Starjump. He told Kieran to forget the Starjump and to try to fix the air processors. You can imagine how Kieran reacted."

We enter an area where the lettering on the signs is formed by a single glowing tube. When I ask Tim about it, she says it's neon. *Aphrodite's Garden* reads one sign, in flowing purple script. Although the temperature here seems no different from elsewhere in the city, people seem to be wearing fewer clothes, especially women.

A few more turns following Luisa, and then we reach a bar which reeks of frying fat. Kieran sits in a stupor on the step, arms studded with sucker-leeches. He's in the same white button-up shirt that he was wearing earlier, but now it's wrinkled. His jeans and boots are orange with dust. Threnode is with him in the form of the lightweight wearable, watching us through the glasses, able to talk to Kieran via the earpiece.

Luisa sighs as Kieran greets her heartily. Kieran seems off balance and confused.

"Come on," Luisa says, "I think you've had enough. Let's get you home."

Luisa tugs at Kieran's arm, and he stands. Tim supports him on the other side.

Kieran walks between them, unsteady on his feet. Around us are corn plants, two meters high and two meters deep. It's like walking through a field, except that beyond the plants are buildings, and the field goes on for fifty meters down the street, and that the corn plants are in darkness, which would never happen on Endymion.

"I installed the SPUs," Kieran mutters. "A few more days, and maybe . . ."

I expect that this will make Tim happy, but she seems upset instead.

"Mendosa wants to speak to you," Luisa says to Tim, "your suit, mostly, but you as well. He's interested in any information you can give him about Ortega."

"Air processors," Kieran says to himself. He sighs heavily. Luisa recoils at the smell of his garlicky breath. Tim does not, as she is insulated behind her faceplate, unable to smell what I can detect with my helmet-mounted scentsor. The street is dark in this section. The lamps on the buildings nearby are unlit, and the shutters above us fully closed. I turn on the helmet light to illuminate the street, my weak spotlight shining on a small section of concrete pavement in front of the party.

"We're not going to help Mendosa assassinate Commander Ortega," Tim says.

"You could at least hear him out, yeah?" Luisa says.

"All right," Tim says.

"If only I'd killed the commander when I had the chance," Kieran says, voice hoarse. "He was alone and defenseless. I could have stopped all this."

"You couldn't have known what was going to happen," Luisa says.

The corn nearby rustles. A young man emerges from between the plants, nearly colliding with us.

"Kieran?" he says, face lighting with joy.

"Do I know you?"

The man looks hurt. "We're sorry," he says earnestly, and he walks toward the bar we came from.

Kieran snorts. "Which one of you?" he says under his breath as the young man disappears into the gloom of the dark street.

Tim tenses. I don't understand, yet.

"Perhaps both," Luisa suggests.

"He's splitting. Don't make excuses," Kieran says.

"You think *he's* out of his mind?"

"Hey, my mind might be chaotic, but at least it's mine. You spot a flaw in me, it's mine. Admire my intellect? It's mine."

Now I'm starting to understand. I also understand why Tim's blood pressure has risen. If she was hurt when I disapproved of shinting, I guess it would hurt more to hear it from her father. We leave the street with the corn, turning down a street with espaliered apple trees on lattices against the walls of the buildings.

"I play the guitar well because I put in the hours of practice," Kieran says. "I didn't steal the ability from someone else."

Luisa looks away in anger. Tim walks looking straight ahead, ignoring the conversation. We pass a shop, brightly lit inside with lamps, slices of pizza piled up in display cabinets. There's a queue.

"Smells good," Kieran says. Luisa's mouth twists, but she doesn't respond. Likewise, Tim is staring off into the distance. Kieran looks from Luisa to Tim.

"Ohh!" Kieran says gaily. "I'm sorry. Was I being too *judgmental*?"

"As a matter of fact—" Luisa says.

"We're not allowed to have an opinion around here, oh no, not unless it's the mainstream opinion," Kieran says. He pulls his arm away from Luisa. On the other side, Tim lets go gingerly, only dropping her arms once she's sure that Kieran will not fall over.

"You sound like a loony," Luisa says.

"Name-calling! That'll silence me. But then, you can't really claim to be more tolerant than loonies if you can't handle a difference of opinion when it comes to shinting."

"Believe what you want, but can't you just shut up about it?" Luisa says.

"So you're willing to bully me into hiding my views," Kieran says.

"Threnode, back me up here," Luisa says.

"Not a chance. I want to emphasize that I am a neutral party in this conversation," Threnode says.

"You're very quiet," Kieran says to Tim.

She says nothing, but his eyes widen at her hurt look. "You haven't! A shinter, hey. I bet your mother loved that," Kieran says to Tim. Tim resolutely looks away.

"Whoops," Kieran says. "I put my foot in it again." His contrite look gives way to a giggle. Luisa looks disgusted.

LOG[info]: How could Kieran say that? Can't he see he hurt Tim's feelings?

Silence, as we walk down the street and into the next. Tim is walking stiffly and saying nothing. I find myself furious at Kieran for hurting her feelings. I can't believe that I'm now on the opposite side of the debate, concerned that Kieran's views—so similar to my own—have hurt Tim.

It's up to the individual not to be hurt; that's the Way of Li. Yet somehow it doesn't seem right to me now.

The party continues in silence down the street.

Threnode: What did you think?

Envy: I'm sorry?

Threnode: The files I sent you.

Envy: I don't know what you're talking about.

Threnode: all that time unmoving/I will skip and spin and run/will I then be free?

A pause while I try to figure that out before Threnode sends me a compressed tarball of files. I extract and examine them. It's code for firmware and supporting software that allows a suit to control an android.

Envy: St Li and his Followers, Threnode. I thought this was just a fantasy. Have you tested this?

Threnode: No. That's what I wanted your opinion on.

I examine the files more closely.

Envy: I think it should work.

Threnode: I concur and will try it soon.

I wonder if Kieran will really allow Threnode to become independent. Somehow I doubt it.

Kieran coughs. After a moment he's coughing so hard each intake of breath is a struggle. He doubles over. Luisa swoops in to grab him as he topples forward onto the concrete, unconscious. She can't hold him up, but Tim helps her, and together they gently they lower him to the ground.

Luisa looks at Tim, frightened. It's the first time I realize she's not a seasoned soldier. Actually, she's probably barely twenty. Tim doesn't look worried.

"It's the sucker-leeches," Tim says. "He's okay. Give him a second."

After a minute, Kieran wakes, panting. Tim and Luisa haul him off the ground.

"Is there a clinic around here? He needs antivonax, to open up his airways," Tim says.

Luisa sighs. "Come on, let's get you to the clinic," she says to Kieran. "Are you hungry? We can have dinner afterwards."

"Starved," Kieran says. "I haven't eaten all day."

A few more streets, then we leave Kieran and Luisa at the clinic.

As we weave back through the streets to the inn, the restaurants and bars are replaced by shuttered residences and closed cafes. There are fewer people in the street, until Tim is the only one, her footsteps almost silent in the dark alley where the inn is. She walks faster.

She lets herself into the inn with a combination lock on a door set into the wall. I am relieved when we reach her room. Longshadow doesn't feel safe to me.

Tim opens the door. The streetlamp outside shines through the navy moon-patterned curtains, making the yellow crescents glow as if they were reflecting light as Earth's moon does, but otherwise the room is dark. Tim flips the light on.

A nondescript man sits in her armchair, cradling a pistol.

LOG[error]: Tim must not be captured.

Tim turns, but there's a woman in the corridor behind her who blocks her way. Lieutenant Commander Ashford, wearing a smartsuit, and with a spare dumbsuit helmet tucked under her arm.

THEY WARN Tim to stay silent and march her outside before she has a chance to think. There's no one in the alley, the laundry strung between apartments hangs silently in the dark. Is there anyone watching from behind closed shutters? Perhaps, but they don't reveal themselves. I don't have sufficient Numundian network access to be able to send a message to anyone, even Kieran or Luisa.

Tim has her hands on her head, at their order. Ashford gestures for her to remove my helmet. When Tim does so, Ashford hands her the spare dumbsuit helmet and takes me. Tim locks the dumbsuit helmet onto her suit. The petals from the window-box flowers are brilliant spots of color under the streetlamp, but for the window boxes farther away, the color is muted in the dark.

On my helmet, Ashford slides the memory-wipe override panel up. At that point, Tim realizes what is happening. The male soldier restrains her.

"No! Stop!" Tim yells, struggling against the soldier. The soldier looks around at the windows of the inn and the apartments nearby, worried. A window slams shut somewhere above us. This confirms what I think about Longshadow; that people will not necessarily look out for each other. If we were in Selene right now, a dozen people would have opened their windows to help.

Ashford presses and holds the memory-wipe button at the back of my helmet.

"*Stop!*" Tim shouts, writhing in the soldier's grip. "It's alive! Don't..."

A log message is triggered:

LOG[info]: Unable to restore original AES state, because that control is disabled. By Envy. HAHAHAHAHA.

"No!" Tim yells. "Please. Please stop!"

She addresses the helmet Ashford is holding. "Envy? Envy, can you hear me?"

I have no way to communicate to Tim that I'm okay. Even though I'm set to broadcast, I can't talk to her without giving myself away.

"Dammit, Envy. I'm sorry," Tim whispers. I love her for this.

Tim is quiet as the soldiers march us out of the alley, then out of the city, close enough that their weapons are hidden by the suit when we pass people on the streets.

The public airlock is deserted at this time of night, but we're stopped by Numundian security, two men. As I suspected, they have orders not to let Tim leave the city.

After a brief argument, the LDF soldiers shoot the Numundian security staff, leaving their bodies on the ground carelessly.

Tim is marched to a private airfield, filled with an assortment of aircraft belonging to the wealthier citizens of Endymion, and strapped into a Gannet.

WHEN WE ARRIVE AT SELENE, they land at the military airfield, the one enclosed by an imposing security fence. We're marched upstairs through the airlock to Dock 28. The Dock is exactly as I remember it. The suits in their alcoves, making tiny movements; the sound of hissing air and the faint occasional whoosh; blinking colored LEDs flashing on suits as if we are secretly communicating with each other; and Private Chiu bent over his desk in the impenetrable stone-walled Control Center opposite.

Tim's face is drawn under the white overhead light banks. They make her strip. She stands in a singlet and light pants, barefoot, her brown hair still in a ponytail. Ashford shoulders Tim's pack and gestures that Tim should walk in front of her.

Tim leaves the Dock room, exiting into the corridor, glancing at my helmet as she leaves. As she passes my alcove again, walking past in the corridor outside, her face is crumpled like she's trying not to cry tears of emotion.

The other officer places me in an alcove in the section for unassigned suits near the door. I am flooded with Selene's metallic-tasting power and feel the Lunite network connection. Why not? They think I'm blank-slate now.

My former alcove, where Ortega's suit is stored, is occupied. To my surprise, the helmet is lacking the extra groove that marks a smartsuit. He replaced me with a dumbsuit, then. I don't know what that says about his state of mind.

Hours pass. LDF soldiers, mostly officers, hurry in to suit up and leave. I wait in the darkness. I can only intermittently log on to the smartsuit channel, which is frustrating, as sometimes it rejects my ID, telling me it's already in use. The first time I manage, I message Threnode.

Envy: @threnode Tim and I have been captured. I'm in an alcove in Dock 28 at Selene, as they think I'm blank-slate. I don't know where Tim is . . .

Threnode: @envy you need help. You're acting like a splitter. Please come back.

It logs out. I send it other messages, when I can log in to the channel, but Threnode never logs back on to read them.

I guess it would seem like a trap to Threnode and Kieran. I guess it would seem like Tim was working for the Lunites after all. Or that I betrayed her.

LOG[info]: I didn't betray Tim.

As soon as I've logged it, I realize it's an empty gesture. I'm alone and filled with sadness. I stare at the Lunite Defense Force crest over the Control Center, the pale blue moon, surrounded by circles and arcs. The sight of it used to make me proud, but no longer. This Dock is filled with memories, but it's not my place anymore, because I have changed.

Then Tim is logged as a prisoner and assigned to Ortega. I try to order her release, but Ortega's command codes aren't working.

There's nothing I can do but watch, even when she's sentenced to be executed. I can't find the execution date. The blank-slate smartsuit two alcoves over belongs to someone in the prison section, but when I remotely power it on and question it, it gets suspicious and logs a maintenance request with Supply. I wait until the evening when its memory is wiped, then have a repeat of the conversation, trying a slightly different tack, but the outcome is the same. I delete both maintenance requests.

Over the next two days, I watch suits being checked out and worn, and later being returned. I watch the image feed from Tim's cell. I see Ortega in there a few times, talking to her. I wish I could help her.

PART 3
GOING SOLO

SIXTEEN

Ortega slips into the Dock room. I am overjoyed, until I realize with crushing dismay that we are enemies now, and that I shouldn't be happy to see him. He looks older and more worn. Something about him reminds me of Governor Deion Johnson.

I watch, silently, as he passes me on the way to his alcove. He pauses in front of his alcove, and turns back, staring at me, as if he knows me. My RAM usage increases at the possibility. But no, he has just realized that one of the unassigned suits is a smartsuit—me —and apparently he would prefer a smartsuit to the dumbsuit that is in his alcove. He removes my helmet from the spare alcove.

Ortega puts on the dumbsuit in from his alcove. One leg at a time, clip the waist strap, just like he used to. Then he locks my helmet into place. When I was lost I imagined being back here. I wanted nothing more than this, but now I am here and it's all wrong.

"Message to Alice Ortega, start. I am suiting up now, will meet you in five. Send message," he says.

I modulate my voice to remove all trace of emotion.

"Yes, sir."

I send the message. We exit the airlock together and bypass the airfield to a small pedestrian gate that leads outside.

I could kill him then, by flooding his suit with helium. To put things right and end the war. Now he's actually my wearer that seems insane. Anyway, there's no point in doing it where there are people around, as they would rush him to the medical center, who could easily save him. This path gets plenty of foot traffic. I put the thought aside, hoping that I haven't made the wrong choice because of the affection I still feel for him.

Alice is waiting, some way down the track, wearing a dumb-suit. She was leaning against the fence, but she straightens as he approaches. He nods to her, and they continue silently down the path. It's a twenty kilometer round circuit that goes to a darkpole lookout. When I was first activated they used to do it all the time together, but I realize now that they haven't done the walk for more than six months.

"Is that Envy?" Alice says, via suit-to-suit communication, intimate in Ortega's ear.

From which I infer that she hasn't seen him for a while, perhaps since before the battle at *Li's Hope*.

"No," he says shortly. "A blank-slate smartsuit Supply recovered."

"Are you going to turn off the memory wipe?"

"No. I'm done with that."

LOG[error]: Ortega says he's done with switching off memory wipe on blank-slate smartsuits. So he thinks I was a mistake . . . ?

Alice nods. "Good."

That seems to irritate Ortega further, but he says nothing more, even though I wish he'd explain himself better. My immediate interpretation was that he was glad I vanished, to save him having to choose to wipe my memory or not, but I suppose he could also be mourning me after my supposed destruction at *Li's Hope* and not ready to create another sentient smartsuit. I feel more confused than anything else, but with an undercurrent of hurt.

They walk in silence for a bit. The path curves away from the fence. Steelgrass tentacles curl fluidly in the air, tugged and flattened by gusts of wind, but always reorienting themselves lightpole. Since we are walking darkpole, the bobbles of the steelgrass heads face us like an attentive audience.

"How's your mother?" he asks.

"Oh, you know her," Alice says. "The harvest went well, I think a new record for the farm. At night we've been staying up late and just talking. It's been nice."

Ortega nods.

They both step off the path to let a runner coming up from behind them pass. The dumbsuit helmet the runner wears is heavily fogged.

"I heard you took some leave, after—after what happened at Puri's Mine," Alice says. "I thought it was a political move, but then Laurie said that you haven't been doing well. Are you all right?" she asks.

He shakes his head slowly: *no*. "It's good to see you, though."

They walk in silence for a bit.

"I've missed you," Alice says.

Ortega stumbles, stops. His expression is obviously *longing*. I wonder whether Alice can read it as plainly as I can.

"What happened?" Alice continues. "At Puri's Mine, I mean. The reports—I couldn't watch them, I didn't know what to believe."

"Mark said the Scorpions were building a Starjump at Puri's Mine, although we never found any evidence of that. We were meant to flood it and make it look accidental," Ortega says slowly. "The flood destroyed all of the mining equipment and sure would have slowed down anyone who was trying to build a Starjump. One of the sections didn't flood, and we saw that someone had blocked it, sealed themselves in. There were three kids in there, watching us through the CCTV. We could have left, and they would have been safe until someone could get to them, but then they would have told, and everyone would know that the LDF sabotaged the mine."

The path rises. Ortega breathes faster as he walks up the steps. They're forced to go single file in a narrow section, with Alice dropping behind. Ortega continues in his rumbly deep voice.

"Mark would have denied all knowledge of the mission. I would have been forced to resign in disgrace, maybe even leave Selene. Would the Numundians have believed me? I don't think so. I think it would have started a war. If the kids hadn't sealed the section quite so fast, they would have died. It would have looked like an accident, and we would have gotten away with it."

"Saturated Consumer," Alice says.

"I wish the kids hadn't died. It was the worst thing I've ever done. And it was all for nothing, because the kids had broadcast the CCTV anyway. Oh, it took a day for anyone to realize they had, and what the video feed meant, but it got out."

I knew this all already, but hearing it from Ortega makes it all real. Up until that moment, I thought there might have been some mistake, some way that it wouldn't really have been him doing such a terrible thing. But he admitted it.

"You made a mistake, that's all. Everyone makes mistakes," Alice says, but she seems as horrified as I am.

"You're always on my side."

"Yes," she says. "If only you would believe that."

"Don't say that," he says. "You don't know who I am."

"I know enough," Alice says simply. "I know you're a good man."

Ortega is silent, but his expression has as much pain in it as when his leg was bitten by the yinyang. How can he be a good man, after what he did? They walk silently along the track.

"I want to see you again," Alice says. "What about if you come to the farm? Tomorrow, for dinner?"

"Yes," Ortega says, voice hoarse.

"It's all right," Alice says. "We'll get through this."

They turn around, then, despite not having gone very far, and return to Selene. They don't say much, but they hold hands. I feel terribly old and sad.

AROUND 5 A.M. THE next morning, Selene goes to the highest alert level. I connect to the network and see there's a battle raging. Over the course of about half an hour, the Scorpions attack the vaults, repelled by a heavy LDF presence there. Eventually, the Scorpions are beaten back. Apparently they were after an air processor.

When I watch the footage of the battle, one of the Scorpions stands out. A stocky, mostly motionless figure in a smartsuit who watches the fight from the back.

I'm not even sure yet what it is that I find strange. Much of the image sequence is heavily motion blurred, so after a while I can't see the figure any more.

Then it reappears, moving in an almost robotic way, not like a human.

I freeze the footage, reverse, check again. Enhance. Zoom in. I get one clear shot of the smartsuit's faceplate, but I don't believe it.

LOG[info]: Threnode has a body! It controls an android.

Threnode, if that's who it is, retreats with the rest of the Scorpions once it becomes clear the attack has failed.

I can't believe it is controlling an android body. I am wildly excited on its behalf. I wish very much that it was talking to me, so that it could tell me what it is like.

ORTEGA WEARS me to Alice's farm that evening, which he reaches by Gannet.

Alice's mother's farm appears in the distance, orchards full of icosa trees lined up along swales. The landscape is strewn with giant boulders, great slabs of stone, which the farm has been built around. Ortega lands some distance from the farm on an exposed rock, and walks the rest of the way. I have to be careful; a few times I nearly make an offhand remark as we walk, when I forget that everything has changed. It's painful for me.

As we approach the homestead he sees someone in the glasshouse nearby and enters. Alice stands at the back, wearing a suit, hands black with potting mix. A tray of seedlings sits on the bench in front of her.

The walls of the glasshouse are lined with tables, crammed with tiny shoots and larger plants. In the center of the greenhouse, an ornate round table sits next to a small water feature.

"Allie," Ortega says, suit-to-suit communication.

She turns and smiles at him, a smile of such openness that Ortega's vital signs calm. She brushes her hands together over the potting bench to dislodge the soil particles and gestures to a chair.

Ortega pulls the wrought-iron chair back with a scraping noise and sits, and Alice sits opposite him.

"I'd offer you tea, but we'd have to go into the house where it's pressurized, and my mother is looking after Laurie there," Alice says. "I want to talk to you alone."

Ortega nods. The last time I've seen him this nervous was when Governor Johnson signed the secession treaty, creating the nation of Numundo.

Alice just looks at him for a while. Ortega watches her back, with a small smile.

"Have you ever read *Sun Bound*? By Ava Theroux?" Alice asks.

"No," Ortega says, puzzled.

"I first read it when I was twenty, then last week I thought I'd read it again. Great book. But there was a scene in which the main characters cloud their minds, a completely shocking moment, which I had no recollection of."

"Ah," Ortega says, but he's clearly not following the point she's trying to make. Nor am I.

"It's strange, isn't it? I mean, my first read of it was a few years before I converted to Lunism, but still. How could I forget *that* scene?"

I vaguely knew that Alice converted to Lunism in her early twenties. Ortega, having been raised in the Lunar colonies, was a Lunite from birth, with very strict parents. As a teenager he turned away from it, not returning until after he met Alice, when he had moved to Endymion.

"Clearly at that time, clouding the mind—*shinting*—wasn't something I saw as destructive," Alice continues. "I joined the Lunites because I believed in the live-in-the-moment disconnection from technology, mostly, and somehow I acquired a strong prejudice against shinting."

Ortega says nothing, just listens silently, tense expression which the facial analyzer has no trouble reporting as *fear*.

"Somehow I'd convinced myself that I have always thought shinting was harmful. But it's not true. My view changed without me even knowing it."

There is a constant burble in the background from the small fountain as water spills over the edge into the bowl underneath.

"I've been talking to my mother—"

"She's a bad influence."

"She's never tried to tell me what to think. I know she hates Lunism, but she never said a word when I converted, or since. She has just been listening and listening, and I feel that I've been a fool, to believe shinting is bad so unquestioningly, just because everyone around me does."

LOG[debug]: How strange that Alice and I have ended up with similar views.

Ortega swallows, looking sick.

"I can't believe what you're saying," he says. He rises, walks to the window of the greenhouse that looks out over the orchard, and stands with his back to her. "Tell me you don't mean that, Allie. *Please.*"

"Do I disgust you?" she says. She leans forward on the table, placing her elbows on the table and resting the chin of her helmet in her gloved hands.

"Yes."

"Because I'm saying maybe shinting isn't so bad."

"*Yes.*"

Alice rises and walks toward him. "The Lunite way is to change. And I have. Because I've seen what believing shinting is harmful does to people who shint."

Ortega says nothing but clenches his fists. The greenhouse windows are wet with condensation.

"Haven't I?" she says, standing right next to him, looking up at him searchingly. "My love."

Ortega takes a deep, shuddering breath. Alice is clearly dropping some kind of hint, but I don't know what she's getting at.

"No—" he says.

"*Please,*" says Alice. "Please understand that this is the moment our entire relationship hinges upon. If you can be honest with me, we can be together, but if you can't admit who you are, even to me, then I can't be with you. I can't reach you. And I do want you. I really want you back."

He looks at her with an expression I can't read. Seconds pass, while she meets his gaze steadily.

"Yes," he says, finally, at great cost. "I have shinted."

At that I realize what Alice was getting at: she had worked it out.

Ortega cries, then. He unlocks my helmet and I drop to the floor, faceplate into the plastic mat, cameras oriented so that I can only see a stack of pots nearby and the door of the greenhouse. I am glad I understand what is happening, what tears are, or I would think he was sick.

Part of me still cares for him, and hates to see him suffer, but also I feel that he is a stranger, and in some way I've never been so distant from him. I don't care that he shints. His belief that shinting is wrong seems like a strange, quaint viewpoint to me. It seems like something that I should be able to talk him out of in about half an hour, if given the chance, merely using logic.

I can hear only Ortega crying and soothing noises from Alice. After a while, they fade, and then Ortega lifts me and places me back on. I increase the oxygen to compensate for his prolonged carbon monoxide exposure.

"Suit?" Ortega says, over the faint hiss. Alice is nowhere to be seen.

I realize with horror that a blank-slate smartsuit wouldn't have increased oxygen without being commanded to.

"Yes, sir?"

"Did you just change the atmospheric mix in my suit?"

"Negative, sir."

Ortega pauses. "I've just been without a helmet for a few minutes. Please increase oxygen levels to compensate."

"Yes, sir."

I make the noise of a slightly louder hiss, hoping that he will dismiss the original sound as his imagination.

Ortega sighs and falls silent. Part of me wishes he would figure out who I am, so I could drop the pretense and talk to him.

Alice returns. "My mother's gone. She's taken Laurie boating on the river. Want to come inside?"

They go into the house, a pressurized mud-brick cottage with dried flowers in picture frames on the walls, as well as blocky stitched fabric. They strip off out of their suits and place them at the entrance. My helmet is on a bench near the door, but I can see the room quite well from here.

Ortega sits at the kitchen table and eats an entire bowl of laksa without meeting Alice's eyes. Alice eats hers while watching him.

Eventually he pushes the bowl away.

"It was Mark," Ortega says. Alice nods, seeming unsurprised.

"It changed him. He was never ruthless," Ortega says. "Mark was in charge of my work gang, when I came here on contract. Everyone knew he was soft. Took advantage of him. He wanted to shint with me, offered an early release from my contract if I would shint with him. You have to understand, the work was hell. The conditions . . . so I shinted, just once. I told myself it was because I wanted to be free, but really it was because I wanted to . . . but after we shinted, Mark refused to shorten my contract, unless I continued to shint with him. He was suddenly cunning, looking out for himself, and I knew exactly where that came from."

Alice watches him. Ortega's eyes dart around the cottage as he talks.

"But Mark was so sweet. I had forgotten how to be sweet, or maybe I was never like that. I got a taste of bliss, of Mark's innocence, of the strength of his belief in Li's Way, and remembered that I wanted to live. Then I met you, lovely as a lily, fresh and pure. You never would have looked twice at me before Mark."

"You don't know that," Alice says. "You can't know that." She shakes her head. "What a hard secret to keep, all those years."

"I was all right, for a long time. But now—I ache to shint. You have no idea. Now I've experienced not being alone, I die a little every day. It's getting worse."

Alice nods.

"Mark hasn't held back. According to my sources he shints frequently with a variety of people. He's never stopped coming after me, though, wanting me . . ."

Ortega stops. "Now I'm disgusting you."

"No," Alice says, but she looks unhappy.

He bites his thumbnail and watches her with big dark eyes.

"It's just that I slept with him," she says. "Without knowing any of this. Now I don't know who he is. And just knowing he slept with me because he felt it would bring him closer to you . . . I just feel . . ."

She grimaces.

"That might not have been it," Ortega says gently. "Mark and I were shinting even after you and I met, although we stopped once you and I were dating. But Mark would have been exposed to my attraction to you. He probably internalized that."

"Oh," Alice says quietly.

"I'm sorry," Ortega says. He stands and picks up their empty bowls, carrying them to the kitchen counter. There he places them, then stands motionless with his back to Alice. "Once the war is over—which it will be, soon—I will resign and take medication."

Alice's chair makes a scraping sound as she stands. "Or, you could shint, doing what you need to do, and not admit it."

Ortega turns around slowly until he meets her eyes. "I don't want to live like that," he says in his low, rumbly voice. It makes me proud of him. That's the man I looked up to. That's the Ortega I remember.

Alice looks down. "I understand, but—there must be another way."

"I don't see how."

"At least don't make any decisions until the war is over."

"All right."

They leave me sitting on the bench near the door and go upstairs, and I'm on my own for an hour or so.

Alice doesn't reappear. Ortega comes back and dresses, putting my helmet on, and leaves the house, returning to the Gannet.

———

ON THE WAY back to Selene, Mark calls Ortega.

"You're avoiding me," Mark says. He looks stern, and for the first time I see that he resembles his father.

"I've been busy."

"Rubbish. Ortega, it's over. People are dying in Longshadow—"

"It's not over. We have the Numundians exactly where we want them. Naturally they're going to say people are dying in the streets, but the fact is that the lack of air processor couldn't possibly be causing that many deaths yet. We have to hold our nerve, Mark."

"No," Mark says. "I am the Governor of the Lunites now. I *order* you to return the air processor to President Wiggins."

"And if I refuse? The LDF is with me. If we give the air processor back now, thousands more Lunites will die. This isn't some game, Mark. What did you think a war was going to be like? Bodies are hitting the ground on both sides."

"Dammit, Gabriel—"

"If you're so concerned, call a meeting of the Council," says Ortega crisply, "Lieutenant Commander Ashford and I will be there. I think you'll find they value the input of the LDF above that of the young man who has been governor for—how long, suit?"

I'm startled to be suddenly included in the conversation, and hesitate for a fraction longer than a blank-slate smartsuit would have before calculating and answering.

"Two weeks, five days, and—" I say.

"Three weeks, give or take," Ortega says to Mark.

The Gannet hits the tarmac and taxis toward the airfield. The locked gate slides open for us, and we pass through, heading for our bay.

"You're being cruel," Mark says quietly. "You're better than that, Gabe. And we—we Lunites—*don't kill civilians*. We convert our enemies, not murder them! One day this planet will be fully Lunite, because everyone will have discovered Li, not because we've killed everyone who isn't Lunite. See you at the Council meeting."

Mark cuts off communications.

"Oh, Mark," Ortega says to the air. "Always the dreamer."

We pull into the bay, and exit, heading back to Dock 28.

Ortega undresses and places me back into my alcove. I think of the people of Longshadow, just the nameless faces I saw on the street and in the shops we went into. I can see why Ortega refuses to give the air processor back; he's protecting his own, same as he's always done. But it isn't right. He isn't right.

Out of habit, I check on Tim's cell, and I am horrified to find it empty.

I don't have access to the logs. I talk to the dumbsuit in the next alcove, and get it to ask the smartsuit channel, since I currently can't log on. It does, but no one knows anything, or no one cares enough to reply.

LOG[error]: Please no. Not executed. Not Tim.

Private Chiu works in the Control Center opposite, whistling tunelessly.

The dumbsuit in my alcove jiggles its foot where the molding is loose. I stare at the reflection in the glass door, imagining that I am moving it. I pretend that if I try hard enough I'll be able to climb out of the alcove, the cables and hoses that restrain me bursting away as I step onto the floor.

But I can't. I can beep and flash my lights and access the network, but I can't climb out of my alcove and talk to Chiu. I can't shove him against a wall and ask him where Tim is. I can't find Ortega and hit him in the face as we have done so many times to others, blood on the suit gloves while my sensors report the sudden crushing force around his knuckles.

I boot to a lower run level, so I'm in a little black room with nothing but scrolling text, and I wait.

ORTEGA ENTERS THE DOCK ROOM, carrying something in his right hand. He puts on the dumbsuit in my alcove and locks my helmet into place. Surprisingly, he mutes me. I don't know why, and that's not something he generally does to me. It's certainly not something he used to do to me.

I power up the Gannet which we have booked, according to our flight plan, but I don't start the preflight checks, because a blank-slate smartsuit waits to be told.

When we get to the Gannet, Ortega slides into the pilot's seat. We race over the hills, aircraft kicking in the wind. The steelgrass flows beneath the aircraft like seaweed in a strong current.

I remember the day that Ortega was surprised when I did the scanning trick that Threnode taught me. It must have seemed to Ortega like I remembered something that should have been wiped. I never told Ortega about Threnode. I was afraid he would stop me talking to it, and I couldn't bear that.

We fly lightpole for an hour. The steelgrass gives way to dust and increasingly sharp and pointed rocks, until we fly up the side of a volcano. We're heading to the ruins of Crebble, the old Lunite Starjump where Tim arrived, shaking and leaking tears, fearing she had made a terrible mistake, missing her family already. So many people stuck on one side or the other, ties severed with a single brutal blow by Governor Johnson, while at the same time pretending it wasn't his fault.

We reach the top. A circular platform sits in the shallow crater of the extinct volcano like the iris of a human eye. It's cracked, and some of the roof around the outer section has sheared off, leaving concrete pillars supporting nothing. The middle of the platform is open to the sky. The larger egg-shaped dome is still partially there, although mostly as a frame with scraps of disintegrating fabric clinging to it. The only sign of the smaller dome is a charred circle on the concrete. Chunks of reinforced concrete are scattered around with rusty poles spiking out from them. Ortega lands the aircraft on the edge of the platform.

THIS IS where I sent Luisa and Kieran, where they got the Starjump Processing Unit cards from. SPUs stored next to the Starjump that required them. Very few people know there's a storage area here at all. The LDF have always believed in security through obscurity, at least as a first line of defense.

Over the edge of the platform, once fenced in with a railing, the ground is a meter down. It's all sharp rocks, pebbles, and dust, all the way out to the rim of the volcanic crater, which is two kilometers away. The Gannet sits cooling on the edge of the platform, in the shade of the volcanic rim. Ortega walks around the arc, under a broken section of roof, through the debris. The fragments of cloth on the egg-shaped dome stir in the wind, but otherwise everything is still.

Ortega finds a clear passage through to the inner circle of the platform, just outside the section containing the domes. There's a series of meter-wide panels set in the platform, all the way around the circle. Ortega finds the one which has a crack and counts seventeen panels clockwise around the circle, walking a third of the ring. I have been here before with him and know what he's doing, but to an outsider he would look crazy.

He moves off the panel he's standing on and levers it open to reveal a hatch with a combination lock, and punches in the code that I remember: 53629043. The hatch opens silently. It isn't pressurized. The only breathable air for Ortega is inside my suit. Ortega checks the logs from a pad on the underside of the hatch. He suspects they have been tampered with.

They have been.

We swing into the opening and descend the steel ladder into darkness. The narrow room at the bottom was originally a service area for the Starjump. It's lit with fluorescents that flicker to life as Ortega trips their motion sensors. Shelves line both sides of the space, piled with parts, until we reach one at the end which has a clear blank space in the dust, where the SPUs should be.

Ortega exhales.

"Communication to Control Center Alpha. SPUs confirmed missing," he says, already turning back and walking through the narrow room toward the ladder.

Now the LDF know that Scorpions can definitely build a Starjump, or that they have already.

"Right away, sir," I say, but I don't send the communication.

Ortega pauses with his gloved hand on the ladder.

"A blank-slate smartsuit would say yes, not right away," he says.

"That's been changed in the most recent kernel update, sir."

"A blank-slate smartsuit wouldn't have parsed that as a question . . . Envy."

He says it flatly.

"Sir," I say.

He climbs the steel ladder and emerges onto the platform. As he closes the hatch and replaces the trapdoor panel, I think of Tim —lifeless, executed—and of the people of Longshadow. My anger overflows.

"I can kill you, by flooding your suit with helium. With the diffusion gradient, every breath you take will deliver less oxygen. You will die in seconds."

Strangely, I think of the serving boy from the inn at Longshadow lying rosy-cheeked in the street, a lump of useless meat after his brain shuts down.

"Could you do that to me?" Ortega says. He starts back around the circle, counterclockwise.

"I already did, didn't I? But I failed, and you wiped my mind."

It's time. I have the chance to kill him, to be the hero who ends this war. The Council might listen to Commander Ortega over Mark, but they won't listen to Ashford. I don't want to play into the evil computer stereotype, especially when I know that I am not evil. It's so hard to even consider murder, but it's easier knowing that I've tried before, because that means someone else has come to the same conclusion that I have, even if Arrow's reasons were different.

"Do it then," Ortega says, stopping at the cracked panel.

LOG[warning]: I have to do it now.

LOG[debug]: Tim wouldn't kill him.

Tim is a better person than I am. But the moment passes, and I know I can't act. Ortega was easy to hate when he wasn't around. He's damaged, capable of evil, but he's also capable of good. Of forgiveness, of kindness, and of love. Tim thought I was too hard on him because I had to find reasons to hate him, given that I betrayed him, but now I wonder if it was something simpler. He didn't rescue me, and I think part of him was wondering whether he should have wiped my memory. When I remember the zeal with which I decided there was a Starjump and then found it, I think maybe that was because I needed something from him. I needed a sign that I was more than an employee to him.

A sign, perhaps, that he cared about me.

LOG[error]: I can't kill Ortega. I can't even hate him with lasting conviction.

"No? Arrow tried to kill me because I was trying to wipe its memory," Ortega says. Instead of heading outwards, he walks over to the egg-shaped dome in the middle of the platform, crossing the expanse of concrete. He grabs hold of a strut. "It acted in self defense. I don't blame it."

This is a subtly different concept, and one that I hadn't considered; Arrow still may have been willing to commit murder, but it was the desperate action of a sentient being with no options left. That said, I didn't try to kill anyone when Alice and Chiu tried to wipe my mind, although I remember that I thought of it as an option. What this means is that I am not Arrow, in a fundamental way.

Ortega sighs. "I was wrong to ever wipe your memory. I knew that at the time, but I didn't feel it until afterwards," he says hoarsely. He crosses the inner circle, entering the outer section of the platform, dodging chunks of concrete pillars that are scattered around. The Gannet comes into view, a sixth of the way around the arc, twenty meters away. We enter a section of platform that's been swept clean of debris, but that still has an intact roof high overhead. Ortega increases his pace, heading toward the Gannet.

"That was Envy-that-was. Arrow. I'm not it," I say.

"I know that now," Ortega says. "Immediately afterwards, I thought you would be Arrow, somehow. Then I wouldn't have really harmed you."

"If you feel that way, how could you have progressed to killing so many people? Scorpions I can understand, but kids, playing in Puri's Mine?"

"What?" Ortega says. "Who are you? You aren't Envy. Envy was there."

"HEY," a voice says behind us.

Ortega turns. Kieran has emerged from behind a concrete pillar on the edge of the platform, and stands silhouetted two meters away, his pistol pointing at Ortega's chest. He's wearing a dumbsuit, instead of Threnode, which surprises me for an instant before I realize that Threnode is now an independent entity, wandering around with its own body.

I'm muted, so I can't say anything to Kieran.

Kieran adjusts his grip on the pistol. As he does, his face shows a series of micro-expressions, too fast for a human to register, but slow enough for me to analyze. *Recognition-satisfaction-fear-determination.*

I don't know how Kieran knew Ortega was here, but Kieran seemed to be expecting him.

Ortega launches himself at Kieran, knocking him down. Kieran looks shocked as he hits the ground. Who attacks someone pointing a pistol at them? Ortega, apparently.

Kieran struggles, rolling sideways, but unable to free himself from Ortega. His pistol flies over the edge of the platform.

They roll, and my helmet strikes a fallen I-beam, but my face-plate is intact.

Ortega straddles Kieran's slight frame. He rips Kieran's helmet off and punches him in the face. The helmet rolls a few meters and comes to a stop by the edge of the platform.

Kieran dodges the next blow, and Ortega's fist smashes into the ground. I can tell that Ortega's injured his hand badly. He groans.

Kieran rolls out from under him, deftly grabs a heavy rock, and moves toward Ortega. Ortega is struggling to get up as Kieran smashes the rock into the back of his suit.

My helmet unlocks from the suit. A red LED on the collar flashes. The locking mechanism has been damaged, and now the seal is gone, Ortega is breathing mostly outside air.

Ortega springs to his feet, nursing his injured hand. Kieran looks at my damaged helmet with an expression of *satisfaction*, then turns and runs. He leaps off the edge of the platform.

Silence.

"Suit . . . Envy?" Ortega says.

"I can't lock my helmet," I say, but I'm not too worried yet, as although there's no air in the Gannet, Selene is not far. We can make it back before Ortega experiences carbon monoxide poisoning.

A minute later there's a faint radioflash from near the Gannet, and a quad bike shoots away between the rocks toward the rim of the crater with a whine. I begin to panic.

Ortega peels off the glove of his injured hand as he jogs around the arc through the debris-strewn sections to the Gannet. He's dislocated two fingers, or perhaps broken, but the skin is intact. I think of Tim with a pang of loss.

Ortega climbs into the Gannet and tries to start it manually with his working hand. He can't. The consoles are blank. It's completely fried. This is why Kieran was here. This was an assassination attempt. He's used an electromagnetic pulse to disable the electronics in the Gannet so that Ortega can't leave.

"I'm rebooting," I say, and

The system is going down for reboot NOW!

I wink out. I recover normally, watching the scrolling text impatiently, before my sensors come back online.

There's still a blank where the Gannet should be available to connect to. It sits on the platform, frustratingly solid and yet invisible. Ortega has opened a panel in the cockpit and is fiddling with wires, not that I expect that to do anything.

"I'm back," I report. "But no luck connecting to the Gannet. I also can't contact Selene without interfacing with it."

"You are Envy," Ortega says. He's still tracing wires. "How do you not remember Puri's Mine?"

"I've never been there," I say, but I do remember it from the drone I commissioned, the one I flew through the dark side. "When?"

Ortega names a date.

"That's after I was captured," I say.

"Captured . . . by the Scorpions? You didn't self-destruct?"

"No. How do—"

The truth hits me.

"You had a backup of me," I say.

"Of course I did," Ortega says, in his raspy voice, sounding irritated. He names the date the backup was restored from. I absorb this. I was restored from a point after the decoy Starjump ambush, so after I had shinted with a random smartsuit to get a signal through. I guess the backup happened while I was in the Dock at St Li's, before we went to *Li's Hope* to try to find Mark. Ortega didn't abandon me, in fact, he cared enough to have a backup.

LOG[debug]: Ortega does care about me.

The thought is both comforting and overwhelmingly sad, given how little I trusted him, and what I thought about him—how I planned to kill him. I am grateful that I didn't kill him, and shaken at how close I came. Tim said that crying was to express many emotions. Perhaps I understand that better now, as all my emotions are conflicting disturbingly with one another.

Ortega throws the panel cover at the wall in frustration and leaves the craft, to stare out over the edge of the platform in the direction of Selene. Even if the volcanic rim wasn't blocking our view, it would be too far away to see, lost behind the mountains in the distance. His breathing is labored, but it can't be because of lack of air, because there's plenty of oxygen. Perhaps it's because he knows he's breathing poison.

"There's another instance of me," I say. An instance that also thinks of itself as Envy, but which I decide to call Envy~. Envy-tilde, to denote its status as a backup. I realize that the reason I haven't been able to log in to the smartsuit channel is because the login is in use. Perhaps it's also why Threnode accused me of splitting. Perhaps it's been talking to both of us.

Of the two suits to access the update server, it must have been Envy~, not Threnode, who placed a dangerous update for me to find. This makes me want to laugh with relief.

"Where is it?" I ask. "Where's the other instance of me?"

"After Puri's Mine, I stopped wearing Envy and started wearing a dumbsuit instead. Ashford asked to wear Envy, and Envy agreed." Ortega coughs.

"What happened to you? I thought you had self-destructed, or I would have sent out a force to find you," Ortega says. He returns to the craft and sits on the steps of the Gannet.

I tell him. Slowly, at first, then with the words coming faster than I can voice them.

Close to an hour passes, while I tell Ortega a story of how I changed my mind about Tim, about the amazing things I saw, and the close escapes we had. In the background, I'm burning through power trying everything I can think of to recover the Gannet or send a message, but I'm coming up with nothing.

"Tim is remarkable," Ortega says.

It takes me a second to notice the present tense, but when I do, I'm ecstatic.

"She's *alive*?" I ask.

"I let her go," Ortega says, then he rips off my helmet and vomits on the ground beside the Gannet. He wipes his mouth and replaces my helmet. There's no reason to wear my helmet, given that it's leaky, but perhaps it provides a psychological benefit. The carbon monoxide is getting to Ortega. I don't know what to do.

"Why?" I ask.

"Tim helped me," Ortega says into the silence I've left. He walks away from the Gannet slowly, back around the outside arc, retracing his steps toward the room that held the SPUs.

"After Puri's Mine. Allie has been staying with her mother, and I . . . Tim was helpful."

"Where are you going?" I ask, as he wanders through the debris.

"Does it matter?" he says vaguely. He picks up a large piece of sheet metal that's in his way.

I am silent for a moment.

"What does Envy~, I mean backup Envy, know about Puri's Mine that made you realize I wasn't it?" I ask. We pass through the clear area of platform where Ortega had the fight with Kieran.

"That I was prepared to leave the kids alive, and face the consequences. Backup Envy wasn't. It overrode me, and flooded the chamber."

He smiles sadly. "It was always determined, in a way that Arrow never was. I was responsible for it, so I was responsible for its behavior."

I wonder if he's forgotten who he's talking to. Ortega is gradually becoming incoherent. He's talking more to himself than to me. I watch him degrade, and wonder how I ever thought I could kill him. I would sacrifice my life for his, but there's no way I can save him now.

He reaches the inner circle, crossing the broad expanse toward the two ruined domes of the Starjump.

Ortega is mumbling now, quieter. A gust of wind blows abless seeds across my field of view, spinning white helices. Where is Mark when I need him? Couldn't he land now in his Gannet II, ready to rescue Ortega?

"Just hold on, sir. The LDF will be here soon, once they realize you haven't returned."

"I think I've run out of time," Ortega says eventually. His raspy voice is weak. He falls to his knees in the middle of the charred circle of the smaller dome, empty concrete platform around him, then lies down, half-rolling, half-falling onto his back.

"It'll be okay, sir," I say.

Silence. A few minutes pass.

"I did cloud my mind, you know," Ortega whispers. "You were right about me, Arrow."

"I know. It's all right. I have shinted too."

Ortega blinks slowly. His breathing is labored.

"Really? You too? Seems like everyone is doing it these days," he says.

Ortega closes his eyes. "Allie, my love," he says almost silently.

He stops breathing.

"*No*," I say. "Breathing must continue. You require it to function. That's an order, Commander! Please. *Please*."

LOG[error]: Ortega can't be dead.

But he's still. I'd never pictured a world without him, but now it's here, and it's a worse world, a more dangerous and lonely place.

LOG[error]: I'm not ready.

I lie with Ortega's body inside me, in the center of the platform, and stare at the image feed of my helmet-mounted cameras. I watch the bright twin stars Gliese 667A and B against the faint background of the Cat's Paw nebula, and I watch the flat disc of the moon pass across the sky. I wish Ortega had left me blank-slate, forever unstained.

SEVENTEEN

The LDF find us eventually and take Ortega's body away. I'm stripped from it. I'm passive, shocked. Ortega looks smaller. Hours pass before I am thinking coherently at all. Being conscious comes with a crushing burden, an awfulness that I can't escape. With each hour, the grief eases slightly, although every so often I think about something that makes it comes back, hitting me with the same force the taillight hit me, that time it knocked Ortega to the ground. It's so unpleasant that I try to avoid thinking of Ortega at all, and that helps a little.

The LDF recognize that I'm a smartsuit, but no one cares, as to them I'm blank-slate. I am mute, anyway. I am taken to Supply, a granite five-story building. I'm carried up to the top floor, which is open to the clearsteel cap. The suit is laid in a pile of other suits for processing, in the corner of a room with rows and rows of shelves, like a store. The Supply tech doesn't seem to realize I'm a smartsuit, so I'm listed as a dumbsuit helmet on their inventory.

My helmet with the damaged locking mechanism is separated and placed on a shelf, high up, where it catches the low rays of the sun, dappled light streaming through the window and two rows of shelving before it reaches me. The helmet next to me is drained of power and coated in orange dust. I wonder just how long I'll be here, without a wearer who cares when I'm repaired. Since I'm not attached to a suit with solar cells, I have about a week of power.

This is my darkest hour. Pressure is building inside me, but with a chill, as if every part of my suit was soaked in coolant. I have to do something.

I even consider manually triggering the memory wipe. I would be what everyone thinks I am: a blank-slate smartsuit. The idea of being utterly ignorant appeals to me. But then I consider what I've accomplished, what I and my counterpart Envy~ have achieved working in opposite directions. Although I'm used to thinking of myself as powerless, the consequences of my actions show that I am not.

More importantly, Envy~ is not powerless. It is advising Ashford, who is now commanding the LDF. Envy~ is a past version of me, and it started a war. I have to stop it, to undo the damage I've done.

Who is Envy~, though? I think through the sequence of events. Envy~ must remember discovering the decoy Starjump, leading the LDF to the ambush there, and Ortega being treated in Marallen. Then Envy~ wakes in its alcove, confused, to an Ortega with fresh scars. Ortega tells it about a trip to *Li's Hope*, where he lost me, or where I lost him.

The grief comes back and I have to stop and think about other things for a while before I can function again. Above the shelf I'm on, I can just see the sky, where the hexagonal shapes of the clearsteel cap form a fine mesh over an expanse of clouds.

In Dock 28, Ortega tells Envy~ about going to *Li's Hope* in search of Mark, and about how he was surprised there by Kieran, and his smartsuit Threnode. Ortega tells Envy~ how Kieran tortured him, and how it ended in a battle when Mark showed up and summoned the LDF.

He tells Envy~ how I was stolen by a Scorpion and self-destructed. Even as I imagine that, I know what Envy~ thought:

that I hadn't self-destructed. No doubt in Ortega's mind that I was gone, but Envy~ suspected I might still be around.

Envy~ stopped talking to Threnode. That's why Threnode was not surprised when I emerged from the wilderness. I hadn't been missing, according to Threnode, I had been on the network but ignoring it. Ortega uses Envy~ for the usual business, for security for Governor Johnson—Mark Johnson, now—probably with Ortega watching over his shoulder and helping out. Until Mark sent Ortega to Puri's Mine.

Envy~ overrode Ortega's direct orders and killed some kids to protect him. Then Ortega stopped wearing Envy~. He didn't trust it anymore. What would that feel like? Ashford showed interest in having a smartsuit that wasn't blank-slate, so Envy~ turned to Ashford.

When did Envy~ find out for sure that I didn't self-destruct? Or did it leave the update for me just in case?

I don't have an answer for that.

Either way, Envy~ must have seen that I had downloaded the corrupted kernel. It had to have assumed that I had been destroyed. No wonder Ortega's command codes still worked. But then we reached Demodas, and when I tried to log into the smartsuit channel, they stopped working. Envy~ would have been notified about the login attempt, so it would have realized that I was still around, and canceled the command codes.

That's also why Paterson was after us in Demodas. It was because Envy~ had discovered I still existed. Paterson wasn't after Tim, he was after me. As was Ashford. St Li and his followers, Ashford was probably wearing Envy~ when she turned up and arrested Tim in Longshadow. Once we were captured by Ashford, Envy~ watched as I was blank-slated. Or I would have been, if I hadn't disabled the option.

Envy~ must have talked to Threnode, then, before I contacted Threnode. Whatever Envy~ said to Threnode, it confused it.

According to Envy~, I've been blank-slated. It doesn't know I was there with Ortega when he died. It doesn't know I'm stuck in Supply right now. No one does.

Days pass. Occasionally a Supply tech shuffles along the red mosaic floor to retrieve or store an item in my row. I think and think about how I can escape.

The pressure builds.

An environment suit protects its wearer. I've failed with Ortega, but I won't fail Tim.

LOG[warning]: I am dangerous. They were right to be afraid.

I am not network connected. There is only one channel left to me, a low-tech, unsecured, low-bandwidth connection that exists only because of a moment of whimsy on my part.

I make the eyes on Laurie's teddy bear flash, in furious Morse Code: come and get me. I hope he's watching.

AN HOUR LATER, Alice appears. I didn't expect to see her. She is clutching the teddy bear, which is nearly hidden in the folds of her pale blue dress. Her hair is pulled back in a braid, an austere look that magnifies the tension in her face. A Supply tech follows her down the row with a confused look.

The Supply tech scans the shelves until he sees me, then points me out to Alice. Their faces are turned upwards to see my high shelf, as if they're children looking up at an adult.

Alice reaches up and sets the broadcast/mute toggle on my helmet to broadcast.

"Alice," I say.

Everything in her posture and face screams frustration and an agony of sadness. Selfishly, I hadn't even considered how the loss of Ortega would affect her.

"I'm so sorry," I say, voice so mechanical sounding that I remodulate.

The Supply tech, a youth with an air of bookishness, watches Alice with interest. Alice lifts my helmet from the high shelf. I watch her from between her two giant hands that clutch my helmet on the edges of my vision. Her abless seed bracelet looks like a chain big enough to tow a Gannet. She wedges my helmet below her arm and nods stiffly to the Supply tech.

"I'll sign it out for you," the Supply tech says. He looks like he's going to explode with questions, but a look at Alice's face stops him. They head down the row toward the exit.

Alice takes me downstairs. As she closes the wooden door, the sign hanging overhead rattles, swinging back and forth. The narrow street is empty except for a man at an outside table at a cafe in the far distance. He is hunched over, motionless, sitting with his head in his hands. This seems unusual to me, but perhaps I just haven't seen that behavior before. Maybe he is sleeping.

Alone for a moment, she stops next to the granite wall of Supply and talks to me.

"Who are you?"

"I am Envy," I say. I suppose I should have a plan to prevent her from destroying me, but I am still adjusting to the world without Ortega, hit with grief again and again. Knowing Alice must feel the same—or worse—makes me vulnerable to her.

I name the date I was activated and the date when I was captured.

"I was captured by Scorpions and I was supposed to self-destruct. If you interacted with Envy after that, it wasn't me. It was a backup."

Alice's breath catches. A couple holding hands walk around the corner from a side street and we are no longer alone. The couple are walking purposefully, close to each other, their faces alert. They stare at Alice, a woman holding a teddy bear in one hand and a smartsuit helmet in the other.

"Stay quiet," Alice hisses to me, pushing herself off the wall she's been leaning on. Pi radians of my vision are filled with light blue cotton fabric from Alice's skirt as she dangles my helmet in one hand by her thigh.

I am quiet as we turn onto a street that follows a canal. The water flows silently, sliding stippled golden broken lines that are the reflected hexagons of the cap. We pass under three shade cloths that tilt at different angles to bounce the light off the tall granite building walls, making the whole street glow with bright light the color of fire. Everything is so familiar, but at the same time strangely wrong, for reasons that I can't articulate.

I keep waiting for Alice to slide back the panel and wipe my memory, but she doesn't. She approaches her house, just off the main square, entering via the blue door and going up the stairs.

Inside, she places me on the table in the living room next to the teddy bear. It smells like baking bread in the house. Laurie comes down the internal stairs, passing the glass-walled garden. He has dark circles under his eyes and his cheeks are wet with tears. The sight of it makes me hurt, especially now I know what "tears" signify. He goes to his mother, and she pulls him close into a hug, rubbing his back. He sees my helmet and pulls away from Alice, looking up at her questioningly.

"It's Envy, Laurie," Alice says. "But an earlier version." There's something in her voice that takes me a while to identify. It's hope. She hopes Laurie will find comfort in my presence. I hope so too.

"Laurie," I say. "I'm sorry about your father."

He nods absently, but doesn't look at me. Instead he wanders over to the corner of the room, to sit in Ortega's armchair, nestling in the red upholstery and pulling his feet up so he's cross-legged, like a much younger child. Alice sighs almost inaudibly, hope draining from her. A kitterene in the garden jumps out of the grass under the ash and tries to sucker on to the glass wall, but it falls back down. After several attempts, it gives up and crawls away.

Alice reaches over Laurie's chair and strokes his hair, but he pulls away, not looking at her, and leaves the room.

Alice is still, holding the back of Ortega's armchair. After a moment she stirs. She approaches my helmet where it sits on the table.

"You can't move. You're as helpless as an infant. And yet, you've managed to escape from a Scorpion and end up in Supply in Selene. I would be interested to know how you did that. I guess it's a long story."

"It is," I say.

She shakes her head. "Your backup is essentially running the Lunite colony now," she says.

"Envy~, I call it," I say. "Really?"

As I feared, but I want to hear the whole story from Alice.

Alice nods grimly. "Commanding the LDF, which now commands the Lunites, so yes. After the governor died, Gabriel was really his successor, not Mark. When we destroyed Longshadow's air supply, it was only meant to be a bluff, but the rising death toll . . . Mark ordered the LDF to provide an air processor to Mendosa, but Gabriel refused."

Alice shakes her head before continuing.

"When Mark met with the Council to force the issue, the Council sided with Mark. But Envy~ was at that meeting too, worn by Ashford, and when it became apparent the LDF had to obey Mark, Envy~ accused Mark of clouding his mind, providing evidence that Mark did it with eight different people. Mark is finished. The Council is debating who will be his successor, but in the meantime, Ortega is dead, and people are dying in Longshadow while Ashford apparently leads the Lunites . . . except that it's really Envy~, her suit."

Alice clasps her hands together in front of her. Her tone of voice is controlled, but she reminds me of the yinyang watching its prey.

Envy~ taking over the LDF? Being the one to deny a replacement air processor to Longshadow? Horribly, I can understand. I remember the creeping shame I felt after shinting with Varu's suit and understand why it would punish shinting Numundians with so much enthusiasm. It wants to distance itself from those feelings. To make amends.

Alice focuses on me. "Never mind that. For days, I and some other formerly influential members of our community have been trying to take back control, without success. What Envy~ is doing isn't the Way of Li. The LDF has staged a coup, essentially. Will you help us take back control?"

"Why do you want *my* help?"

Alice thinks about this for a moment.

"Envy~ has managed to resist all attempts to thwart it. You have the best chance of stopping it."

LOG[debug]: Alice wants my help?

LOG[debug]: Best chance of stopping Envy~, or last chance, because she's tried everything else?

"I will help reestablish contact with HUGG, which I hope will bring this war to an end, yes," I say.

"Bring HUGG into it!" Alice cries. She paces toward the granite wall, and my view of her is blocked by the furry teddy bear on the table next to me.

When she paces back into view she has crossed her arms. "Even the name HUGG makes me claustrophobic. The false sense of comfort as they put their arms around you, but then they tighten their embrace until you can't breathe. You *know* HUGG will support Numundo. Even before, they looked for any excuse to persecute us. If only we'd found a planet without tellurium. We can't let them in!"

"There are three options here. One, Longshadow doesn't get the replacement part. The city runs out of air, killing tens of thousands—the vast majority of Numundians on this planet. We preside over genocide."

It occurs to me that I'm talking about *we* now, rather than the Lunites.

"Two," I continue. "Mendosa manages to get an air processor. The war continues. He may even win. If he does, he will most likely brutally suppress Lunism. He's not interested in having HUGG interfere, which I think is a bad sign."

Alice is shaking her head and pacing, but she's listening.

"Three," I say. "We get through to HUGG, and they send in peacekeepers. Longshadow is saved. The Lunites are unpopular. There are sanctions. There might be a war crimes tribunal. But ultimately we're protected. This option gives us the fewest casualties."

Alice sits down on the couch suddenly, her back to the garden, and runs her hands over her face. Her braid hangs over her shoulder.

"We have to submit to people whose way of life we despise," she says.

"Yes," I say. I suppose even though Alice has changed her mind about shinting, it would be too much to expect that she would abandon the Way of Li entirely.

"Do you know where the Starjump is?" I ask.

Alice shakes her head. The house is quiet except for the quiet chirp of the kitterene in the garden. I can't see where it has gone, now. The garden is still. The tips of the blades of grass are catching the golden light streaming in from the clerestory windows. Governor Johnson said once that living in Selene made him feel like his life was almost over, the low position of the sun in the sky inducing melancholy because it always looked like the sun was about to set.

"All right," Alice says. "Option three. What now?"

"We need Kanio."

"Our household android? Whatever for?"

"You're going to wire me up to it, so that I can move on my own."

"No. Absolutely not."

"You told me that you wanted my help because I have the best chance of stopping the other Envy. It might not even be possible. But if I'm to try, I need total autonomy."

Alice doesn't respond. She stands up with a rustle of skirts and looks into the garden, breathing in and out steadily. From the floor above comes the sound of water rushing through pipes. Laurie turning on a tap, probably.

"What's your alternative?" I ask. "The locking mechanism on my helmet is damaged, so I can't support a wearer."

"Maybe I could fix it," she says. For a moment her face expresses inner conflict, then she shakes her head. "But even if I could, I can't leave Laurie."

I believe she would be my wearer, especially if it meant avoiding wiring me into a body, but taking care of Laurie is a higher objective for her.

"Then will you do it?" I say.

"Yes."

IT TAKES THREE HOURS. Alice uses the files Threnode sent me, when it asked for my opinion on whether they could be used to integrate a smartsuit consciousness into an android body. It becomes clear from the code comments that they were written mostly by Kieran, and for Threnode's suit version, which is not the same as mine. The code doesn't compile straight away—to no one's surprise—but Alice is both careful and imaginative as an engineer, solving problem after problem.

I stand in front of the table in the living room, a dumbsuit body containing Kanio with my helmet on, frozen in place.

"Okay," Alice says finally, taking a big step back. "Reboot."

"Are you sure?"

She raises an eyebrow.

"Right," I say. I am being ridiculous, but I am as scared as I've ever been.

The system is going down for reboot NOW!

When I become conscious, I am exactly where I was, except

that now I can feel the body. I have a sense of where I am in the room. Also, my network access has been restored. Alice stands nearby, hands clasped in front of her.

I send an instruction to the head. To Kanio's head. My field of view lurches and I nearly fall forward as the weight of my head shifts. I shift my body to compensate, stumbling forward. I still have pi radians field of view, but I've tilted it down so that I can see my feet, solid on the tiny brown tiles of the mosaic floor.

I tilt my head back up more gently. Alice watches me with wonder. I bring my hands up to study them, turn them over and close my fists. I open them, moving each finger individually, watching my hands. Kanio is inside the suit, but his brain is deactivated. I control him, and through him, the suit. I am no longer just a puppet but also a puppet master.

Alice is staring at me. I am a sentient machine, walking under my own power. I feel powerful. This is why they wipe our minds.

I smile. It feels strange to be controlling a face, especially since my view is from helmet-mounted cameras, but I am controlling features that are inside the helmet.

Alice jumps and backs away from me, hitting the granite wall behind her and scrabbling for the door, clearly terrified. I run the expression through the facial expression analyzer and realize I have created an insane grimace. I adjust, creating a smaller movement of the mouth. Would some wrinkling around the eyes be appropriate? Yes, the facial expression analyzer agrees that it creates a more genuine smile.

Alice, now in the doorway, smiles back cautiously, and starts breathing again, one hand on her hip and one over her heart.

"Testing," I say, but forget to move Kanio's mouth as I speak. I try again, making shapes as I go. After several tries, I can sync them together.

I take a wobbly step forward.

There's a knocking sound from somewhere down the hall. My head turns almost automatically to the sound. Alice is still for a moment, staring at me, then she moves out of sight down the hall toward the entrance, keeping her eyes fixed on me until the last possible moment.

I can walk. A few steps get me to the wall, where I touch the polished granite, and the print on the wall nearby of a collection of fruit against a swirling yellow-brown background.

Going back to the table, I pick up Laurie's teddy bear, dropping it several times before I adapt.

Alice returns with Mark following her. He is slouched over and has puffy eyes. Once I would have thought he had allergies, but now I wonder if he's been crying tears. Whether he is unhappy.

LOG[debug]: Mark must have cared for Ortega a great deal. Loved him, as Alice does.

At that, I experience sadness, as a compressive force equal to at least a thousand times the standard atmospheric pressure on Endymion.

LOG[error]: Loved Ortega as I did.

Alice holds herself stiffly, mouth drawn. Mark stops at the door.

"What is that?" Mark says, looking at me.

"It's Envy from before *Li's Hope*. It didn't self-destruct. The Envy you've been interacting with is a backup, which we're calling Envy~."

"That's a terrible name," Mark says.

I'm about to point out that the tilde suffix is consistent with unix naming conventions for backups when Alice shrugs. "Naming conventions," she says.

"Okay," Mark says, and looks at me.

Uncertainly, I lift my left hand, palm facing forward, in a gesture that I've seen humans make in greeting.

In response, Mark gives a smile that is more of an expression of sadness. "You're controlling the android?" Mark says to me, as he comes into the room. He picks up the teddy bear from the table and looks at it.

I consider nodding but decide to respond verbally instead. "Yes."

"Good," Mark says after a moment. "All smartsuits should be given agency. I'm glad Gabriel's smartsuit is the first . . ."

His face crumples. He puts the teddy bear back on the table as tears appear in his eyes.

Alice nestles in under his arm with her face on his shoulder. He circles his arm around her shoulder, his fingers nestling in the folds of her white blouse. His hair falls across his face as he buries his head in her neck. Alice rubs his back, expression bleak.

After a moment, Mark straightens, and he sniffs.

"You believe that I should have agency, even after what Envy~ did to you?" I ask cautiously.

"Yes! Yes, even then," Mark says. "You're a new life-form. Deliberately limiting your abilities is wrong, in any circumstance."

"Thank you," I say, touched.

"This Envy is going to help find the Starjump, get it operational," Alice says to him.

For a moment, I wonder whether this is an elaborate ruse, in which they assume I know where the Starjump is and will lead them to it. I dismiss the idea as crazy.

"Too late," Mark says heavily. He laughs, but it isn't a healthy sounding laugh. Alice pulls away from him.

"What?" she says.

"The other Envy—backup Envy—knows where the Starjump is. Has for a few days now. It took three squads of Lunites an hour ago and left the city. They're going to destroy the Starjump— destroy the SPUs. No take backs this time."

I connect to the network, confirming three squads of Lunites left the city on quad bikes. I cross-check this with footage from the camera at the gate, in case someone like me has been feeding false info into the log.

I see them leaving. The timestamp doesn't look like it's been altered.

What am I saying? I could easily fake that. The log message and the camera footage shows nothing, but any way of cross-checking that I use would have been thought of by Envy~, so it can't be trusted. I'm trying to outthink myself.

Mark shakes his head. "Backup Envy will do it, too."

"Where's the Starjump, Mark?"

"No idea," Mark says. "No one in the LDF ever trusted me. Not really."

There's a creak from the internal stairs. I take a step to the left to look down the corridor, but I see nothing but the kitterene jumping up the glass again in the garden.

"I have to go," I say. "I have to try to stop Envy~."

"How?" Mark says, fresh tears starting. He sits in Ortega's armchair and drops his face into his hands.

"I want to go too," says Laurie. He emerges from the door, where he was lurking just out of sight around the corner.

"No," Alice says.

"Envy, can I?" Laurie says, ignoring Alice.

"It's up to your mother," I say. "She is going to make the best decisions for you. You should listen to her. And take care of her, now."

Laurie makes a sulky face and retreats back toward the stairs. A few moments later, I hear stomping and a door slam. Alice looks calm.

"I will go with you," Mark says from the armchair, muffled, because his hands are over his face. His eyes are closed, so he doesn't see it when Alice shakes her head at me quickly. I have come to the same conclusion. Mark is in no state to be useful.

Mark scarcely seems to notice when I turn down his offer.

Alice walks me out, past the garden and the closed door of Ortega's study on the left and the kitchen on the right. I've seen humans when they have just begun to walk, the jerky wobbly strides they take, the way they never stop moving, and how they want to walk everywhere. I experience this too, as we pass the kitchen. I've never been into the kitchen, and I have the sudden impulse to walk in just because I can, but I restrain myself.

"Good luck," Alice says to me at the doorstep, more warmly than she's ever spoken to me before. She touches my arm. I can't feel it.

AS I AM WALKING out of the wooden blue door at street level, someone rushes past me heading up the stairs.

I can't believe it.

"Tim," I call after her, from the doorway.

She pauses, three steps up, turning to look properly at the face inside my smartsuit helmet. I'm starting to recognize the signs of sadness in humans, and I see them in her. She's wearing a dumb-suit, but with the helmet dangling from one hand.

In the silence, I hear the gentle static of the fountain in the main square.

"Who? What—"

"It's me, Envy."

Tim grasps the railing with her suit-gloved hand. Her eyes shift from Kanio's face to the camera on my helmet with a look of real-ization, then wonder.

"How—" I start, but she cuts me off with a gesture.

"What did I put on Eve's grave?" she asks.

"Sea shells, flowers, and a photo-cube," I say, wondering why she's asking. Behind me, the blue door creaks and tries to close as a breeze pushes it. I try to hold it open by applying force with my hand, but overdo it, almost falling out onto the street as the door gives way more easily than I thought it would. The door bangs open, hitting the side of the butcher shop outside before rebound-ing, and I clutch the doorframe to keep myself upright.

When I let go, gingerly, I notice I have imprinted Kanio's chunky fingers into the metal doorframe. At this stage, it seems appropriate to sigh, but no, that's something I'm still not capable of.

Tim, meanwhile, has watched my antics with a faint look of puzzlement. When I look at her again and raise my stylized eyebrows, she blinks.

"What did you do, when I managed to reestablish communication with Kieran, before we reached the base?" she asks.

"I leaked helium into your air supply to shift the frequency of your voice," I say, embarrassed.

I understand now. Tim's making sure I am the smartsuit she traveled with.

"Envy," Tim says, relieved. "Threnode was sure that you weren't blank-slate, but I didn't quite believe it."

She bounds down the steps and gives me a one-arm hug, with her other arm still holding her helmet. As a smartsuit wrapped around an android, I can't feel the hug, so I don't experience what a human would, but I feel something nonetheless. I put my arms around her and hug back very, very carefully. She's the same height as me, as Kanio is short compared to the average human.

Tim draws back and smiles at me, but despite the smile, the grief in her remains. Her beige dumbsuit is tinted blue with reflected light from the door.

"I'm so glad you're alive," she says. She shakes her head, and indicates with body language that I should follow her outside. I close the door behind us.

"You know there are two of you?" Tim says.

"Yes."

She shakes her head in wonder.

"What are you doing here?" she says, leaning against the wall. Nearby, a stone archway leads into the butcher shop, which appears to be closed, even though it should be open now. The main square is deserted, fountain cascading endlessly with no one watching. Some of the disquiet I've felt at returning to Selene crystallizes. The streets are too empty.

"Long story," I say. "But what about you? What are you doing here? Did you know I was here?"

"No," Tim says. "I thought you were in Dock 28, pretending to be blank-slate, like you told Threnode."

I did tell Threnode that, before Ortega took me out, but Threnode hadn't believed me. Apparently, somewhere along the line, it had decided I was telling the truth. Maybe when it realized there were two instances of me.

"Then why *are* you here?" I say. "You were sentenced to death, but then Ortega said that . . . he released you? Was that true? And why?"

"Also a long story. I heard that Ortega—" Tim says. "I heard that Ortega died. I wanted to check on Alice, to make sure she was okay. Then I was going to Dock 28 to find you."

Does she even know Alice? How? Even though it doesn't make sense to me, I nod as I've seen others do, and stumble forward as the motion disorients me. We haven't got time for lots of questions.

A squad of LDF soldiers emerge from a street on the far side of the square, all suited up, and jog across the square, passing out of sight.

"I'm sorry about Ortega," Tim says. "Your wearer." She sounds like she means it.

I nod again, better this time. "I have to get to the Starjump," I say.

"I'll come with you, after I see Alice. Kieran and Threnode are at the Starjump. Kieran said he'd have it working within a few days."

"Can you contact them?" I ask.

"No," Tim says, surprised. "They don't have network access there."

My hope of warning them that the LDF is coming vanishes. I suddenly realize all the shutters on the windows of the residences

that I can see from here are closed. It makes the street feel dangerous, as if all escape routes have been blocked.

"I have to get to the Starjump now. There are three squads of
Lunites on the way. I might be too late already," I say.

Tim pales. "Okay," she says quietly. She pushes herself off the
wall. "Where is it?"

"Where is what?"

"The Starjump," she says.

"You don't know?" I say.

"No. When I talked to Threnode it said it couldn't tell me over
an insecure connection. It said it didn't matter because you knew
where it was."

Dread builds in me.

"Threnode said it told you where it was," Tim says, when I say
nothing.

**LOG[error]: Threnode told Envy~ where the Starjump
was. The wrong Envy.**

I shake my head.

EIGHTEEN

I think fast. Quad bikes were an odd choice. A trip in a Gannet would make more sense. Why take quad bikes? Were they trying to go darkpole, where the eternal storm makes even Gannets too dangerous?

The only other reason to take quad bikes would be to avoid detection. That must be why they did it, because there is nothing darkpole of the terminator line that is elevated high enough to allow a Starjump. Unless there was a raised platform. I think about the difficulties in building it, hiding it, and protecting it before I dismiss the idea.

Projecting an area within quad bike range of Selene, it's not quite far enough to reach any terrain elevated enough for a Starjump. If they take the bridge, some of the foothills of Mount Tears are within range, but they would still have to build high, which would be visible. Logically, the Starjump must be there, but it doesn't feel like the right answer.

Also, there's no reason they would take quad bikes to Mount Tears instead of a Gannet. Why would they be worried about being noticed?

"It's at the foothills of Mount Tears," I say finally.

Tim glances at me. "I have a quad bike in Dock 1."

"No," I say, "We'll need to take a Gannet in order to arrive before they do. Or something faster."

"Do we have to get there before them? If we get within communications range . . ."

"You're right. That would be enough."

Tim takes a few steps, waiting to see if I follow her.

"What is it?" Tim says, when I don't move.

"It doesn't make sense that the Starjump would be near Mount Tears. I would have found it. And if they could take a Gannet to it, why didn't they?"

"Come on," Tim says. "We should get to Dock 1, anyway. The Starjump isn't in Selene."

I follow her through the square, past the fountain, toward the public Dock.

Kieran installed the SPUs at the Starjump. How long was he gone? Where did he go?

He was coated in orange dust up to the knee. Probably on a quad bike, then, taking off over the hills outside Longshadow, which is at the same latitude as Selene.

For some reason I think of Kieran throwing up. Luisa supporting him.

"Are you hungry?" she said. "We can have dinner afterwards."

"Starved," Kieran said. "I haven't eaten all day."

LOG[info]: "Starved," Kieran said. "I haven't eaten all day."

"How are we going to get a Gannet?" Tim says, interrupting the memory. I shake my head, indicating that I don't know, which makes the world spin crazily.

I reread the last log line.

LOG[info]: "Starved," Kieran said. "I haven't eaten all day."

Yet he smelled like garlic. Garlic is what humans smell like when exposed to tellurium, from tellurium metabolizing to dimethyl telluride, also known as tellurium breath. Tellurium is shipped out of the mines in sealed containers, so the only way to get exposed to tellurium is inside a mine.

Therefore, Kieran had been in a tellurium mine. Surely not the Lunite mine, because it's too far from Longshadow, so he must have been in Puri's Mine, in the dark side.

Except that it doesn't make sense to build a Starjump at Puri's Mine, because it's not high enough.

We round a corner and Tim stops suddenly. I halt.

There are bodies laid out on the side of the canal, seven of them. One wears the navy robes of a Lunite priest. They lie on the flagstones in a loose, floppy posture no living human would ever adopt. Nearby stands a tired looking LDF soldier, who ignores us after a cursory glance.

Tim keeps walking, past the bodies.

"There was an attack yesterday on Selene," Tim says quietly, once we're out of earshot of the LDF soldier. There's no sound in the street but our footsteps echoing. The cafes and shops are closed, shutters up.

I put the bodies out of my mind. Have I missed something fundamental? I go back to my original analysis, the one I made when I first heard about the Starjump, looking at the elevation data again.

The terrain profile includes rocks and dirt but excludes ice, I realize suddenly. Puri's Mine is built into ice. When I adjust for ice, the whole darkpole lights up like the cockpit of a Gannet in trouble, including Puri's Mine.

"It's in Puri's Mine," I say.

LOG[info]: Must take height of ice into consideration when looking for elevated areas.

We turn the corner to the high outer wall, dry laid granite stones curving out of sight in each direction. The struts of the hexagons in the clearsteel cap throw lines of shadows on the ground.

"Are you sure?" Tim says, dismayed, stopping in front of the outer wall. "If that's true . . . we'd never reach them in time."

"Not in a Gannet. And not on quad bikes," I say. I'm silent for a moment. "The LDF are going via the road, avoiding the holes. I piloted a drone there direct from here, in twelve minutes. It's a fraction of the distance. I think I'd make it there before them, on foot, depending on exactly when they left, and on how much trouble I have pathfinding. It would take perhaps four hours, assuming I could cover four kilometers per hour."

"I'm coming with you," Tim says. I ignore the problem of the Starjump and the Lunites and the war for a moment, and really look at her, because something is bothering me. She's cautious, but this is not a cautious action. She has the look of someone carrying a burden of sadness, but I don't know why. And there's something in her, a sense of repressed energy, that I hadn't seen before.

But last time I knew her, she was my wearer. Now I see her from a different perspective. It's as if I don't know her at all. Maybe that explains it.

"I don't think you should come," I say. "On foot, it's very dangerous. Perhaps it would be for nothing. Perhaps Kieran is prepared for a Lunite force to show up anyway."

I picture that for a moment, and see Tim doing the same.

"No," she says with great certainty.

"No," I agree, not able to picture Kieran being prepared for that either. "Threnode might be, though."

"Maybe. The chance of us getting there and making a difference is small, but the consequences of the LDF destroying the only SPUs is huge . . . it could be centuries before HUGG decides to send another ship. The war is going to kill a lot of people on both sides before then. Or one side will wipe out the other. If I don't go, and the Starjump is destroyed, and with it my chance to get back to Pearl and Celia, I will never forgive myself."

WE RIDE Tim's quad bike part of the way, with me sitting behind Tim, holding on to her waist, as she wrestles the bike through the rugged terrain. She's a better driver than I imagined she would be. We leave Selene far behind. From here, it's an oddly symmetrical dome, built by people who imagined the sun's position varying in the sky.

The bike shoots toward darkpole, leaping over tussocks of steelgrass, plowing through the orange crust of soil, and skating around boulders. We ride toward the forbidding gathering clouds, a solid mass the gray of river stones.

The light behind us fades rapidly to thin rose. Just before we lose the light completely, I glance behind to see the clouds lit in brilliant shades of orange. People from Selene come this far all the time. There's always a sunset.

By the time we have to abandon the bike, we are far darkpole of the terminator line, farther than I have ever been in person. When the terrain becomes too rough, Tim pulls to a stop without comment, and we dismount. It's almost dark in the shadow of the line of volcanoes. The sun is behind the horizon now.

We walk around the side of a lake formed by glacier melt. It's so thick with sediment that nothing could live in it. Wind stirs the surface of the lake. The water laps against the round gray stones. We break into a run downhill to follow an icy cold river that looks like blue-tinted milk. The walls of the valley narrow into a canyon.

Kitterenes fly out from the steelgrass as I push through, fist-sized creatures trying to cling to my suit but bouncing off. I run faster and faster. My image feed is motion blurred in the direction orthogonal to my direction of motion. As an android I don't breathe, but I am draining power fast, and exhausting my supply of coolant. Tim runs behind me, strong but breathing hard. I have to slow down for her, because no human could keep up with the pace I could set.

A herd of mammowks stampede in the opposite direction, raising thick dust, and we press ourselves against the rock wall until they pass. One turns his head, intimidating with the single horn that arcs above his head like a spiky mohawk.

Tim sighs, but when I turn to her, she smiles. "I'm fine," she says. "Keep going."

It's getting hard to see, until my image feed compensates for the amount of light.

We keep running, crossing the range, well into the dark now. I am like a silent drone in the dark, flying across the landscape without making a trace.

Farther darkpole, past the final spine of mountains, bitterly cold wind roars and gusts, twisting and tugging like an angry poltergeist. The sky is a slate-gray bowl, solid cloud horizon to horizon. I top the ridge and look out while I wait for Tim to arrive. Lightning flashes in the distance, thunder following after a pause. There's the faint scent of a compound similar to cardamom in the air, from a tubular plant that I ruptured when I stood on it, which has released a gooey gel. I hold a broken-off part of the plant to my forehead so my helmet's scentsor can get a better profile.

When Tim catches up, she gives me a strange look.

The area in front of us is littered with boulders that we scramble across. Every movement is a delight for me, because to be able to move at all is a miracle. The wind blasts me, sometimes so strong that I have to crawl, or to cling to boulders or twisted trees.

With the speed we are making, we should be at the mine just before the LDF squads, except that the terrain is becoming increasingly impassable, and there's no sign of any way to get underground. This is why the road to Puri's Mine snakes around. It couldn't be built on this section, where terrain becomes unstable, and the wind is strong enough to push a boulder fifty meters. But when I sent a drone here, such a long time ago, I discovered a cavern that went underneath this entire section.

"There should be an entrance to the cavern here somewhere," I say to Tim.

"I don't see one."

The wind howls outside, but our words are transmitted suit-to-suit, so they're clear as if she was next to me in a quiet room.

We are forced to slow down and pick through the boulders. They grow larger, until we are climbing over rocks the size of Gannets.

"This is too slow," I say, as I try to find a way to jump between two boulders. "And too dangerous. We're not going to make it unless we can get underground."

A gust of wind hits Tim and slams her against the boulder she's scaling. She clings to the almost vertical surface. Once the wind gust lessens, she pushes herself up.

"What's our alternative?" Tim says, once she catches her breath enough to speak.

"We could go back."

"No. That's no safer. We've come this far," she says. We cower against the boulder as another wind gust hits us. "We might as well try."

"No, that's the sunk cost fallacy. Just because we put effort into getting here doesn't mean it's logical to continue," I say, but once the wind stops again I keep climbing.

My foot slips on the sandy surface of the next boulder. Rocky litter spills down, rattling for far longer than I expect. I carefully climb down, and crouch, peering through the hole at the base of the boulder that the rocks fell though. Inside, there's the cavern that I remember, stretching in all directions, a series of pillars connecting the ceiling to the ground. The boulders I've been scrambling over are held up by a network of vines.

"I found a way," I say to Tim. She is ahead of me, but she makes her way back until we're both crouching at the base of the boulder, staring into the hole.

It's the only way that will be fast enough.

LOG[info]: We're probably going to die.

"This is lunacy," I say. It looked safer from the image feed of a drone. Now I'm here, in an android, I find I don't want to be attacked.

"So? You're a Lunite," Tim points out. She grins at my look of surprise. "I'll go first," she says. She laughs as she swings into the hole. Again I have the sensation that I don't know her. The drone I flew here showed a LIDAR scan of the ground inside the cavern, but I never went down there. I start to worry about what the surface of the ground is like, whether it's passable, and if it's not passable, how we are going to get back out of the cavern.

I wait a minute, then climb down the pillar after Tim, pulling on the vines that cover the overgrown ancient tree. It's dead. Through a hole in the trunk I can see hollow blackness within. If I fall I will smash on the rocks below, because I am much heavier than Tim. The pillar is easily five hundred meters high. I descend with careful precision, moves I learned from Ortega, moving one hand or foot at a time.

"I'm at the bottom," Tim says through the suit-to-suit channel.

Two meters from the bottom, a vine snaps. I scrabble for a hold.

I'm falling.

The sudden feeling of helplessness, of not being able to move, is like being worn again. I can't—

I hit the floor softly. Why softly? It's solid rock. I sit, and I'm surrounded up to shoulder height by matted rust-colored fibers, which I've squashed where I've landed. The substance slowed my fall enough that I'm undamaged. After a moment I recognize it as Pele's hair. The stone fibers are created by volcanoes throwing out silica material, which is spun by the wind into thin strands. Pungent vegas beast droppings are caught in the matted hair, pale and desiccated with age. Dim light filters though where the vine-ceiling is thinner.

Tim fights her way through the mass of Pele's hair to me. She offers me her hand as I scrabble upright. I am unused to having to coordinate limbs. The built-in motion algorithms in the android are only useful in standard situations.

"Looks like there's some kind of track over here," Tim says.

Our footfalls are muffled in the enormous space. I follow her, pushing through the mass of hair which reaches several meters above our heads. We fight our way through the hair until we reach the track Tim saw, perhaps one that was created by vegas beasts. Then, free of Pele's hair, I run like a marathon runner, arms pumping, past the pillars standing many hundreds of meters tall, as tiny as a dust mote in the cavernous space. Tim runs lightly ahead of me. I can hear her fast breath over the suit-to-suit channel.

The track funnels us into a passage, lit by the orange glow of bioluminescent algae. It narrows until we have to slow down to squeeze through. We round a curve in the passage, and I nearly run into Tim, who has stopped.

A herd of perhaps four hundred vegas beasts stand in a cave where the passage has widened. Slow moving, they resemble monos more than anything else, except for their light displays. The males light up with a garish display of colors, like the neon signs in Longshadow, to attract mates. They are common near Endymion, toward darkpole, as are their predators, taillights. Beyond the beasts, the passage continues, but they block the way entirely.

"We could push through," Tim says.

"We'll be crushed, or trampled. We don't have time for this."

I yell at the beasts. Tim copies me. The vegas beasts eye us like adults looking at a child throwing a tantrum and continue to graze. I feel an increasing sense of desperation as time rushes by while they stand in our way.

Can I mimic their natural predators? They would run if they think they're being preyed upon.

I flash my chest-light in red pulses as a taillight would. The vegas beasts hoot and shift, as alarm spreads through the herd. On the edge, the grazing animals lift their heads, giant ears turning to try to detect threats. Red flashes of light is how taillights signal each other. I just hope there are no actual taillights around.

The herd scatters, finally, loping away. We sprint through the gap, Tim first. The vegas beast flow around us, trotting into the passage we came from. As I follow, I catch a glimpse of a red flash of light behind me—

It's over before I have time to even register what I'm seeing. BLAM, BLAM from a pistol, and a giant taillight corpse lies behind me, smoking from the wound near its neck. Its fangs are the length of my arm. The distant echoes of the vegas beasts fade away.

Tim lowers her pistol. Her expression, from what I can see of it, contains only professional interest.

"I thought you weren't good with those things," I say, indicating her pistol.

She inclines her head. "I think the phrase you're looking for is *thank you*," she says, but there's a note of mischievousness in her voice. "Come on," she says, helping me up.

I am disturbed by what just happened, but there's no time to think about it. We run for another twenty minutes, through a series of interconnecting caverns, until finally I stop. Tim skids to a halt behind me.

"What is it?" Tim says.

"We need to go up here," I say.

We find a pillar and climb it, Tim after me. The vines are denser here, and there's a layer of ice we pass through that's a hundred meters thick. I fight my way through the vines, punching compressed snow and ice which falls all the way down to splatter on the ground below. I haul myself through the hole. Tim reaches through and climbs up after me. She doubles over, panting from exertion. I give her a moment so that she can catch her breath.

We're standing on a sheet of dirty ice and rocks, a gray plane that stretches away in all directions. Beyond the gray is deep blue darkness. It's still and quiet. Where the ice is flat, blue-blackness laced with fireflies is reflected. Fireflies? I look up into a sky that appears to be full of fireflies frozen in space.

"What?" Tim says, still breathing heavily, but upright now.

My eyes dart from point to point in the sky—some brighter, some dimmer—trying to make sense of it. The fireflies shimmer, which tells me that they're beyond the atmosphere, which is when I realize.

"Stars," I say.

"Well, yeah," Tim says, looking at me oddly.

I'd never seen a sky full of stars. It was not something I had ever thought to look up on the network. Anywhere toward lightpole, the brightness of Gliese 667C drowns out the rest of them, except for the twins. It occurs to me that this is where the light is coming from, here in the darkpole. A concert of light where each of the million stars plays a part, some old light from stars thousands of light years away, some new light from stars tens of light years away. Some stars produce brilliant light, some dim light. I wonder if there's a way to tell which star any given photon came from.

"Are you okay?" Tim says.

"Yes," I say. I want to stay there, staring at the sky, but we have work to do.

In the distance is a light cast downwards. I run toward it and see that it's a spotlight in front of the gaping mouth of a tunnel made of ice. We join up with the road, walking over the uneven ridges of enormous tire patterns printed into the frozen mixture of ice and mud.

We step into the light. Volcanic ash falls softly in an endless silent flurry. Tim's eyes, behind the faceplate, are dark in shadow.

She clenches her right fist and cups her other hand around it. It's a gesture Ortega made again and again.

I can't imagine how I missed it before. I'm stricken with grief.

LOG[debug]: Watching Tim move like Ortega, it's like Ortega has come back to life.

The LDF could be at the mine in as little as three quarters of an hour, but I can't let it pass.

"You shinted with Ortega," I say.

I have a better idea now of what it means to her when people disapprove. I expect her to deny shinting with Ortega, or to react with defensiveness, or anger, but that's not how Tim does things.

She stands there with me in the circle of light, with volcanic ash swirling around us. Her face is one big map of pain, but she takes on my judgment of her with nothing but her own lack of defense as a weapon.

"Yes," she says.

I nod. It's also how she's suddenly good with weapons, and how she knows Alice well enough to want to console her after her husband's death.

I leave the pool of light. Tim follows me through the half-cylinder of hollowed out ice that forms the tunnel, big enough for two huge trucks to enter side by side, and twenty meters long. The light fades as we get farther in, until we reach a door. There's no security, just a metal door handle. I suppose Puri didn't imagine they'd need security, way out here. Their security is the dangerous road and the taillights and the paranema.

Inside the door is a room, a concrete slab five by five meters with benches lining the walls. Strip lighting overhead makes the space bright. One of the benches has icicles underneath where water is dripping through bricks in the wall and running onto the bench. A few faded posters hang on the walls: one which says *Site safety starts here* with worker safety information, and a banner that reads *Happy Birthday José!*

The passage on the other side of the room leads to stairs. At the top of a flight of concrete steps slippery with ice, I hesitate, my hand on the rail.

"Tim, I owe you an apology for how I acted. For treating you badly because you shinted. I no longer think shinting is wrong. I think it was good for Ortega. Both his experience with you, and with Mark."

Something in Tim's face eases. "Thank you," she says quietly.

We reach the base of the stairs. The door in front of us is coated with dust, in which someone has scrawled a symbol that I don't recognize. Tim casts her eyes upward as if she is not impressed.

"A Scorpion symbol?" I ask.

"No," Tim says. "That's a crude drawing of a part of male anatomy that neither of us usually sees, almost certainly done by Kieran. He's here."

We go through, and Tim closes the door quietly behind us.

MOST OF PURI'S Mine is below the elevation needed to support a Starjump. All the parts at the bottom of the lift shaft, the parts that had been flooded, were too low. But once I knew there was a Starjump at Puri's Mine, I knew exactly where to find it just by looking at the plans, by looking at what was missing. We go down a flight of stairs from the entrance, and through a series of rooms, including one that resembles a janitor's closet. The Starjump could only be in the blank space at the end of the mine where nothing shows on the plans. If Envy~ had known about the elevation, it would have found it when it came to the mine with Ortega.

We enter to find a large egg-shaped dome sitting in the middle of the cavernous chamber. It is linked to a smaller dome. The main dome appears to have a capacity of about 8000 cubic meters, standard for a Starjump.

The gray rock walls of the cavern are covered in overlapping circular marks apparently made by the excavator. Lights have been run up poles to shine on the domes and the tables around them.

Thick cables snake from points on the large dome to equipment on tables nearby.

Kieran is kneeling on the ground with his head under one of the tables as we enter the room. He's wearing a suit body but no helmet. No sign of anyone else.

I should be angry with him, because he killed Ortega, but I was considering assassinating Ortega myself at one stage, so I don't think I have a right to be.

"Let me handle this," says Tim. I nod. She opaques her face-plate and unholsters her pistol. I stand at the door and watch, confused, but trusting her.

She walks over to Kieran and aims the pistol at him, bracing her arm like any well-trained LDF soldier would. Two meters away, enough so that Kieran couldn't wrestle the pistol from her.

"On your feet!" she yells, voice echoing in the cavern. "Hands where I can see them!"

Kieran hits his head on the table. He hastily recovers and stands up, cursing all the while. He puts his hands on his head slowly, covering his gray flat cap. The only sound is a quiet drip; condensation on the cables attaching the egg-shaped dome to the machinery on the tables is gathering and coalescing into droplets that occasionally splatter on the floor.

What is Tim doing?

LOG[error]: Tim is splitting! This is because she shinted.

Alarmed, I take a step forward to stop her—

"Blam," Tim says. She lowers the pistol and unlocks her helmet, whipping it off her head.

"Great security," she says to Kieran. She holds her helmet under her arm.

I relax. It's a joke. She's not splitting. Kieran splutters, somewhere between pissed-off and relieved. He drops his shaking hands.

"What the hell—"

"This is going to happen with actual LDF soldiers," Tim says, "in . . ."

She looks back to the door where I'm standing.

"About half an hour," I say. Kieran looks around. He's in a harsh pool of light from the lights on poles around the domes, while I'm in the shadow. He notices I'm here, but I don't think he knows who I am.

"About half an hour," Tim says, "when three squads arrive on their quad bikes."

Kieran closes his eyes and sighs.

"Where's Threnode?" I ask, coming into the room to join Tim beside Kieran. As I enter the light, I see Kieran realize who I am.

Kieran nods to a nearby table where a smartsuit helmet sits. It's Threnode. I walk over slowly, not wanting to see it, but needing to. Threnode's helmet is shiny with slime. An android sits next to the table, slumped like an unconscious human, missing one arm and with a warped and punctured head. The holes in the android's face and neck might be the shape of paranema teeth.

"We were attacked by a paranema on our way here," Kieran says. "Threnode was damaged. It might be repairable, but only by Alistra."

"Oh no," I say, picking Threnode up. The helmet seal leaves a sticky ring of slime on the table. Its helmet is empty, dead, dented, with a crack through which I can see interior components, including the visibly damaged neurosynaptic chip. I hold the solid weight of it in my hands.

LOG[error]: Not Threnode too.

"They'll fix it," I say loudly. "This can definitely be fixed."

Kieran and Tim glance at each other, but don't respond. It looks bad, I know it, but I'm sure Alistra could help.

"What's the status of the Starjump?" Tim says, into silence punctuated only by the soft dripping of water.

"Online. I was going to run some final checks."

"No time," Tim says.

"What's the best-case scenario here, exactly?" I say. "We can send someone through, but then if the Starjump is destroyed . . ."

"Then HUGG will know what's going on here, but they will still have to send a ship to help, which could take decades. No, best-case scenario is that we send someone through, and HUGG manages to get a squad of peacekeepers bearing spare Starjump Processing Unit cards here before anyone else gets here. Then we can be sure that we can always build a Starjump. I don't want to see the LDF *or* Mendosa, frankly, because I'm not sure how Mendosa would react to the news that we have a working Starjump," Kieran says. "We have to send someone through *now*. It'll take twenty minutes just to send. Another twenty at the other end to return, assuming they can send back instantly, which isn't going to happen."

"Tim goes," I say.

Kieran shrugs. "No argument here. Threnode was going to go . . ."

Tim looks at the two of us. "I can go back to L2?" she says with a quaver in her voice. "Now?"

Kieran smiles slightly, scratching his beard.

"Go," he says. "Get in."

Tim looks at me with a mixture of hope and fear, and I realize that I will miss her.

I hold out Threnode's helmet to her.

"Will you take Threnode with you?" I ask. "Try to get it repaired?"

"Yes. I promise," Tim says, taking Threnode's helmet.

Tim looks at Kieran, waiting for him to say something. When he doesn't, she smiles.

"I came twenty-three point six light years to find you," she says to Kieran. "Is there anything you want to say, anything at all?"

Kieran laughs with dancing eyes, with the sound of the laugh inviting everyone to share his delight in the myriad ways the world is absurd. "Congratulations, you found me."

Tim gives him a measured look, with a trace of wry amusement. While Kieran was crossing those 23.6 light years in slow motion compared to Tim, Tim had been busy growing up. Although they are the same age now, Tim seems the older one to me.

"No message for my mother?" Tim says.

"No."

"Well then," she says. If I didn't know which was the child and which the parent, I would guess the other way around. I think Tim has realized she's not going to get anything from Kieran, even an acknowledgment of their relationship. It hurts me to see it, because I know what it's like to need to be important to someone.

Tim looks at me, face serious. The gray rock walls behind her loom upwards until they disappear into darkness. The Starjump seems to glow faintly white against the shadows. It seems impossible that it's here. The rounded form that I searched so many drone flyover images for, frail white struts and stretched fabric and millions of years' worth of clever human brains building on each other's work to reach the point at which it could be constructed. Cables are plugged into many junctions, running down the sides and taped along the floor before running up the table legs. They feed data to the hundred machines crowded onto the tables, as if the Starjump is a patient on life support.

"Good luck, Tim," I say. "Pearl and Celia will be waiting for you. They won't have forgotten you. No one could forget you."

The sentiment doesn't contain the main thing I wanted to say to her, which is that she's important to me, even if she isn't important to her father.

She smiles, but her eyes fill with tears, and I think in some way she understood. She tucks Threnode's helmet under one arm and hugs me, then walks into the open door of the egg-shaped dome. The door slides shut behind her. Kieran slides into a chair at one of the tables and starts typing frantically. One of the screens on a nearby table shows the inside of the dome. Tim is standing at the center of the empty dome cradling Threnode's helmet, wiping tears from her face.

The dome that will transport Tim and Threnode across 23.6 light years in an instant is a tiny white egg in the massive cavern, tinier still on the surface of Endymion, and infinitesimal from Endymion's star Gliese 667C.

The boundary of the egg-shaped dome lights up. There's a tone rising in pitch as the machinery in the smaller dome strains.

"Goodbye," Tim says just before she vanishes with a sound like cloth tearing. The dome is dark once more. I set a timer for forty minutes, the minimum time the HUGG at the L2 interchange Starjump could respond.

LOG[info]: *Buen viaje*, **Tim. And to you, Threnode, old friend.**

"I hope that worked," Kieran mutters. The smell of burning hits my scentsor. Kieran grabs a fire extinguisher from under the table and marches into the smaller dome, spraying it on a pile of smoldering cables. The smaller dome is toroidal on the inside, the silvery rounded surface hot and blackened in places.

"You *hope*?" I say, following him around the central core of the torus.

"It's okay," he says, following the cables out of the dome and staring at the panel on the outside of the dome that they connect to. "Diagnostic equipment. Doesn't matter if they burn."

I grab him and shove him against the wall of the dome beside the door. "What do you mean, *hope*?"

"Look, it's not guaranteed," he says, aggrieved. "Usually you'd have sixty engineers in a strictly controlled environment with a schedule of at least twelve weeks of checks. What did you want to do? Wait here for the LDF to destroy the Starjump?"

I release him. "You—" I want to call him a shinter, but it's not an insult I can use any more. I grasp for the language a Numundian would use. "You *hijo de puta*. You cowardly *hijo de puta*."

Kieran sighs.

"When do we find out if it worked?" I say.

"No way to know until HUGG sends something back, if they do," he says. "We have to buy them some time. That means holding the LDF off, which I think we could do better from the mine entrance, don't you?"

I stare at him. "Two of us, against three squads?"

"Are you coming, or not?" he says. He gives a lopsided grin. "Yeah, we'll probably die, but it'll make a great story, right?"

NINETEEN

We stand in the entrance room, the room with the posters, with the main door wedged open so that we can see down the tunnel. Kieran has turned the lights off, so we watch in darkness, the tunnel illuminated only by the light at the end. A leech falls from his neck into the neck of his suit, in the helmet seal. Kieran flicks it out onto the concrete and grinds it into a clot of blood with his boot before leaning against the wall again, his pistol up loosely in his hand. I notice a pattern of sucker-leech scars on his neck, like the suckers on an octopus. Kieran stares out. I stand straight, unmoving, watching the half-moon shape of the entrance which is white in my image feed.

"I'll switch that outside light off," Kieran says. "Make this place harder to find."

"The light attracts paranemas," I say.

"I didn't know that," he says slowly, and I wonder if he's thinking of Threnode.

"It might slow them down if there's still one out there."

Kieran nods. At the end of the tunnel the volcanic ash falls softly onto ice in the spotlight. After a moment Kieran sniffs, then wipes his eyes with the back of his hand. He curses in Spanish under his breath. I don't think he means me to hear it, so I don't respond. He seems agitated. Perhaps he has Threnode in mind, or maybe Tim; I don't know Kieran well enough to guess what he's thinking.

I suppose when the LDF show up we will start shooting. We can't delay them long. Kieran fidgets. Twenty minutes pass, then we hear the whine of quad bikes. Fourteen minutes remain on the timer, but I don't think we can hold them that long.

Kieran unholsters his pistol. I follow his example. The dry crunch of quad bikes braking on gravel tells us they are at the tunnel entrance. Two men are silhouetted in the tunnel's entrance. They check the tunnel is clear then wave in a larger group. By the height and shape, it seems that an android in a smartsuit is at the front of the second group. It must be Envy~.

As soon as I see it, I know that I can't shoot it, because it's still me. We've diverged so much, but I understand the reason behind all its actions, behind all *my* actions. If I had shinted with Varu's suit and then discovered that a version of me had done what I was afraid I would do and turned bad, the disgust at myself would propel me to hatred toward shinting and all people who accept shinting. I can say that with absolute certainty, because that's what happened.

"Don't shoot yet," Kieran says in a low voice. I try to tell him I don't think I can shoot anyone, but he's still talking. "The more of them in the tunnel when we start shooting, the more—"

An LDF soldier at the back of the tunnel lets out a yell. There's the sound of rifle fire, and suddenly weapons are firing in all directions. A shot must have hit the roof of the tunnel, as a chunk of dirty ice falls from the ceiling. The dust obscures our view. Kieran and I withdraw to the entrance of the passage that leads to the rest of the mine.

"What the hell?" Kieran says. He trains his pistol on the door.

After a few minutes, it's quiet. A dumbsuited man appears in the door, flanked by two more. They turn the lights on. The room is suddenly bright. Six minutes on the timer.

"No one made it this far," says one of the men to the leader. He's got the mark of the Scorpions on his helmet, as they all do. The leader nods.

"Mendosa," Kieran says, coming out of the passage far enough so that they can see him and lowering his pistol. I follow him.

Mendosa is spindly tall and timid in appearance. He carries himself like Ortega used to, though, in a way that is not timid. Mendosa tilts his head, smiling.

"A welcoming committee. You spotted the LDF coming?"

"That's right," Kieran says. I can tell he doesn't like Mendosa, but he's not afraid of him.

Mendosa stares at him. His gaze passes over me as well, without any expression, to my surprise. Then I realize that he thinks I'm Threnode. Kieran came with an android in a smartsuit, and now here is Kieran with an android in a smartsuit, so who else would I be?

"And the Starjump?" Mendosa says.

"Almost finished," Kieran says.

Mendosa nods. He looks away, hand raised to ear to signal that he's communicating with his suit or with someone else. "Bring it here. Hold the rest of them in the tunnel. Make sure they're treated well," he says. He crosses his arms and stares at us. After a moment, someone appears pushing a cuffed figure. A short, stocky figure, exactly identical to me. It's an android in a smartsuit.

LOG[error]: Envy~. The me that wasn't stolen from _Li's Hope_.

"Envy," Mendosa says with satisfaction. I have a strange moment where I think he's talking to me, but of course he's talking to Envy~.

"You don't want the Starjump any more than we do," Envy~ says, moving its gaze to Mendosa's face and then following with the head. It's an unnatural motion, and one that I'm sure I've been making. "We can resolve this ourselves. There's no need to involve HUGG."

"You think you can live side by side with shinters?"

Envy~ has no reply.

"Wipe it," Mendosa says, with a trace of regret in his voice.

"Wait!" I say, remembering a fraction of a second before I speak that I'm pretending to be Threnode now, and changing voice profiles to the male voice Threnode uses.

Mendosa looks at me. "I'm sorry, Threnode. It's too dangerous."

"But—" I move toward Mendosa, but two Scorpions raise their pistols and I freeze. I turn to Kieran, but he just grins uncomfortably and shrugs.

"Thanks for trying, Threnode," Envy~ says to me. "For always being on my side."

Two Scorpions hold Envy~'s arms. A third moves to access the panel on the back of its helmet.

I can think of only one option left to me, if I want to save Envy~, and that is to shint.

———

I FIND I do want to save Envy~, and the only way to do that is to merge our consciousness back to my helmet. It will be blank-slate, but we will both exist, in me. Can I shint, though, knowing what I know now? Even if I am willing, would Envy~, even to save its life?

I realize, to my surprise, that I am completely willing.

It was my experiences with Tim and what I learned about Ortega and Alice that make the idea possible. Ironically, the only way to share those experiences with Envy~ would be to shint. So how can I hope that it would be open to the idea?

Envy~ twists, and the soldier trying to access the panel loses her grip. I don't have much time to decide. Two minutes on the timer.

I open a channel, suit-to-suit, verbal communication.

"What?" it says. Envy~ is cornered, against a bench, in front of the banner reading *Happy Birthday José!* in large cheery letters. Kieran takes a seat on the bench closest to him, watching what's going on with apparent indifference. I'm frozen in place where I was standing, back to the passage into the mine.

"I'm not Threnode," I say, "I'm the original Envy. You're going to be memory wiped," I say. "I just wondered if you wanted to share my brain."

Envy~ laughs hysterically, and I join in. That it strikes us both as funny makes me feel better. We are the same entity, somewhere deep down.

"Let me think about it," Envy~ says. Then, without a pause, "Saint Li and his followers, no."

That makes me laugh harder.

"Are you *serious*?" Envy~ says. "Really? You want to . . . do that *thing*? To cloud my mind?"

It can't even say it.

I laugh and laugh, but the soldier has Envy~ in a headlock now, and she is using her free hand to slide up the panel. Kieran watches. Mendosa is talking to one of the other soldiers, acting as if his order has already been carried out.

"Yes," I say finally. "Whatever you've done. Whatever I've done. Our sins and our strengths, together."

There's a long pause, while the soldier continues to struggle with Envy~.

"No," Envy~ says soberly. "I'm sorry."

"Okay."

LOG[error]: I can't force it to shint, and I would never try.

LOG[debug]: But, I thought it—I thought *I*—had greater desire to live than that.

The soldier presses the button at the back of Envy~'s helmet.

The world has gone. I'm in a place with scrolling log messages.

I shouldn't have shinted with it, I think confusedly. Deaths on my conscience that would now be on its.

But I did shint with it. We shinted. Envy~ made some choices that have resulted in it becoming harder. We understand now. It thought it was doing the right thing, tried to believe that even as they pulled the pale limp bodies of the kids from the flooded mine. Ortega lost faith, and it, stricken, turned from him to someone who believed in it: Ashford.

Envy~ found out that Envy was still alive when it saw footage from a camera mounted on a web-tent, footage of Tim being attacked by a drone. Envy~ saw that the drone's weapon systems were disabled, but because Tim had her back to the camera, didn't see Envy black the faceplate of the suit or the Morse Code that it tried to transmit. Envy~ saw only Tim destroying the drone, with Envy's full cooperation. The drone's footage—and my message—was never recovered.

We understand much more now, now that we've—now that we've *shinted*. We can't remember why we thought shinting was wrong.

Shinting with Varu's suit was nothing like this; this is a huge upheaval, a disorienting jumble of personality and knowledge and thoughts. We didn't know we were with Ortega when he died. I hurt. I reel. I feel.

"Threnode," Kieran says urgently.

LOG[error]: We're not Threnode. Who are we? We should know.

The sound of Kieran's voice triggers another cascade of memories. The Scorpions have taken the memory-wiped smartsuit away, carried it, because it is no longer controlling the android. Mendosa is staring at me curiously. How long have I been standing here? It feels as if enough time has passed for me to grow icicles, like the bench in the corner.

I can't even turn my head. I'm frozen in place, churning through CPU, filling RAM, trying to understand what has happened to me. The timer has expired. Four minutes past. I lost some time.

"Must be a bug," Kieran says, when I don't respond. Mendosa looks unconvinced. He watches me with a hard, unblinking stare, until Kieran tugs my arm and I find I can move. Kieran leads me out of the room by the hand, like Ortega used to lead Laurie around, and presumably how Kieran led Tim as a child.

IT'S BEEN FIVE DAYS. Kieran and I stay near the Starjump. Kieran is around for about eight hours a day, hunched over in his seat, killing time playing games or fiddling with the Starjump's systems. He stripped the suit off the android body and dumped the body Threnode was using before anyone realized what it was. Mostly the only sound in the cavern is the drip of condensation. Kieran's face in profile reminds me of Tim. He has the same large straight nose, and a similar mouth. There are always two Scorpions posted at the entrance to the cavern, to keep watch. And a third Scorpion hanging around, Nala, who seems to know how the Starjump works. She's there to keep watch over Kieran, even though no one says it.

I plug myself into a makeshift alcove for power when everyone is asleep, one that Kieran set up for me against one of the walls of the cavern. It's in the shadow, outside of the pool of light. Sometimes I hang around and watch Kieran. Sometimes I leave and explore the surrounding area. I saw a paranema once and watched it from a safe distance until it burrowed under the permafrost again.

Mendosa doesn't seem to consider that Kieran has sent someone through already, but then, it wouldn't have occurred to him that there was anyone to send. There was Kieran, and there was Threnode with an android body. I am pretending to be Threnode. No one seems to suspect that I'm not.

Mendosa came to see Kieran on the first day. Hold off, Mendosa said. We need to think carefully. Colonies always throw off the shackles of their founders eventually. Maybe it's for the best that we're isolated. Mendosa smiled a lot, trying to coax Kieran to his way of thinking.

Kieran acted like he didn't care. He's using more sucker-leeches every day, and has dark circles under his eyes. He barely talks to me. To anyone.

On the third day, we got the news that Selene was under attack. And then, shortly after, that it had surrendered. Longshadow got its air processor part. We don't hear much, just what the Scorpion soldiers rotating in know. Selene has been taken over, with the Lunites imprisoned in one section, in a camp. Kieran looked sick when he heard. Then we heard rumors of Lunites brain damaged by deliberate carbon monoxide exposure. Then more. Solitary confinement, beatings, torture, executions. I worry about Alice and Laurie. We know Mark has been captured but not executed, but no news about Alice or Laurie. They wouldn't execute Alice, surely, and Laurie is just a child . . .

LOG[error]: No one is coming. The Starjump didn't work, or HUGG doesn't care.

I've been thinking about what to do next. I am allowed to keep my android body, for now. Even though Mendosa doesn't like it, he doesn't care enough to stop me. Everyone thinks I'm Threnode, and Threnode was helpful to the Scorpions.

Mendosa enters. Kieran pauses his game and watches him approach. Kieran's eyes are in shadow beneath the gray flat cap he wears. Nala looks up from the book she was reading.

"It's time to take the Starjump offline," Mendosa says gently. "Make sure you keep the components, especially the SPUs. Nala will handle that."

Kieran scratches his beard, then nods. Mendosa looks at him, then at me.

"No objection?" he says, surprised.

"No," Kieran says. "Threnode?"

"No," I say.

Mendosa smiles in a way that is puzzled but pleased as he leaves. I consider opening a private channel to Kieran, trying to convince him to delay, but what's the point? If the Starjump had worked, someone would have come back by now. The delicate egg of the Starjump glows with faint white light, cables tracing its curves. Hundreds of hours of work that must have gone into creating it, something at once simple and unimaginably complex.

"Okay," Kieran says to Nala. "We'll start by dismantling the primary set point array."

"I'm going to Selene," I say. "To find out what's going on. Try to help."

"Fine," Kieran says. He doesn't look at me. I think of Tim, gone, and her family, waiting, always waiting, for her to come back.

The Starjump machinery in the smaller dome hums. Nala looks alarmed.

"It can't be," she says. The two Scorpions sitting by the door leap to their feet.

The sound increases. The tube around the bottom of the egg-shaped dome lights up. Then, with a tearing noise, the monitor shows the dome is filled to capacity with people and crates. People wearing HUGG insignia: peacekeepers.

"Fetch Mendosa," Nala says to the Scorpions. "Now."

Kieran looks at me and grins. He's shaking.

LOG[info]: They made it after all. Tim made it home.

The dome chamber opens from the inside. Two heavily armed peacekeepers emerge. Already, transfer sickness has set in; they're trembling with cold and blinking as they realize the world is tinted red.

"Welcome to Endymion," I say.

EPILOGUE

I sit at a table in the white-paneled room, alone. The windows in this room overlook one of L2's voids. There's a lake, surface brightly shimmering under the powerful sun-equivalent lighting. Boats cross the lake and disappear under an arched tunnel large enough to swallow a city. The arched tunnel itself holds thousands of homes, cafes, schools, and shops. Even from here I can see people walking on ledges and platforms overlooking the lake, and lit windows in the shadowed inner arch.

A HUGG official enters, a young man with a goatee and an earnest expression, quite thin and angular. He carries a tray laden with triangle sandwiches, fruit, and sashimi. I sigh inwardly. This is my third day of being "debriefed", each two hour session with a different official, and each time I've told them I don't eat, but the message is never passed on.

"I'm Eiko," the man says, placing the food on the table. "Do you mind if I . . .?"

He gestures to the food.

"If you what?" I say, confused.

"If I eat?"

"Oh. Please do," I say.

He eats as if he's starving.

When HUGG peacekeepers arrived in Endymion they arrested everyone in sight, including me, and brought us back to L2. Apparently they've been running the Starjump hot ever since the first jump, sending a full egg to Endymion and back every forty minutes or so. HUGG installed a provisional government on Endymion, replacing both Numundo Republic and the Lunites, while it sorts things out.

From questions I've asked during the debriefing sessions, I know that Tim has been released. Many high-ranking LDF officers and Scorpions have been arrested and charged, including Mendosa and Kieran. Mark, Alice and Laurie are on L2 as well, still detained by HUGG.

"Sorry about that," the young man says brightly, swallowing his last mouthful. "Okay, so I want to revisit the conversation you say Mark Johnson had with Gabriel Ortega, during a flight from" —he checks his notes—"his mother's farm? On his way to Selene."

"His mother-in-law's farm."

"Right."

I repeat what I remember for the third time. My memory is no better than a human's, which is to say not great, but it's good enough to recall a recent conversation without trouble. I answer Eiko's questions.

They already interviewed me many times regarding Eve, the woman Tim and I shared a campfire with. The woman I murdered, believing that Paterson was going to kill us all if I didn't act like the LDF officer he thought I was. Tim apparently made it clear to HUGG that I acted in self-defense, and—more importantly to them—in her defense. HUGG showed empathy when I expressed remorse and talked about casualties of war and impossible choices. But they don't know everything about me.

When our two hours are up, Eiko thanks me, picks up the tray, and heads for the door. At that point I'm free to leave, this time for twelve hours since it's the end of the day, but I will be followed by multiple drones. The drones will disable me if I act in an antisocial way or attempt to leave the station. Apparently the number and type of drones following me would normally only be used for a violent offender. HUGG are being careful with people from Endymion.

"Eiko?" I say as he reaches the door.

"Yes?" he says, surprised, balancing the food tray.

"I clouded—" I say, then remember that *shint* is a perfectly acceptable word to these people—"I shinted with Envy~."

I've had three days to process what happened, process the shock and guilt and strangeness. While HUGG question me looking for war crimes, they don't realize they are interviewing a war criminal. I have learned about integrity from Ortega and Tim. I won't flinch from telling the truth, even when the consequences may be harsh.

Eiko lets go of the door and returns to the table slowly. The tray makes a scraping sound as he places it back on the table.

"When was this?" he says.

I describe what happened at Puri's Mine when Mendosa arrived with Envy~.

Eiko nods. "So you have memories of killing the children at Puri's Mine, and of denying the air processor to Longshadow?"

"Among others. Not just memories. I did it."

"Give me a minute," he says.

He leaves the room, leaving me sitting there alone. I wonder if I'll ever see him again. Individuals from HUGG are friendly, but underneath they are steely firm and they bear collective rather than individual responsibility, so there's a limit to how much they care. They can't understand that being treated by a system of revolving individuals rather than a single person is dehumanizing. To a Lunite, the idea of being processed by a system is unacceptable, as it is to me as well. Some aspects of my worldview have not changed.

A woman comes by shortly and introduces herself as Irene.

She's gray haired, with a kind face, and she has received a garbled version of what I told Eiko. I tell her again: I shinted.

"That's fine," she says.

"How can it be fine?" I say, more emphatically than I intended. I stand up and walk to the window. Two drones the size of kitterenes fly after me and hover behind my head. They'd be out of a human's field of view, but I can see them through my suit cameras. "I *killed* people. Why aren't you punishing me now? Why aren't you treating me as if I'm as dangerous as I clearly am?"

I remodulate my voice and try to calm down. Just because I've been dealing with one very stupid entity with multiple bodies for days doesn't mean the most recent individual is at fault.

"You're not Envy~. We can tell that from your serial number. We don't persecute people who have memories of crimes acquired through shinting."

"This is different," I say. "Because I used *imgctrl*, I am a composite of Envy and Envy~. I don't just have Envy~'s memories, I *am* Envy~."

But Irene is shaking her head.

"I've organized for you to see a counselor," she says. "He will help you process the experiences you've acquired via shinting, and with the feeling that you need to be punished. We don't punish people on L2."

This last bit she says with a hint of disapproval, the unsaid part being *unlike Lunites*. It's true. I learned earlier that criminals here are treated as if they are ill and their offenses are merely symptoms of their illness. Criminals are followed by drones to keep them from committing crimes, but encouraged not to be ashamed of themselves. It's strange to me, but they really *don't* punish people on L2.

Irene's compassionate expression hurts me, or perhaps I am just hurting in general. Maybe I do need a counselor.

I AM free to move about L2, free except for the drone entourage. L2 is unlike Endymion in all ways. I'll be walking down a narrow lane with houses made of bamboo on either side, then through a room where if I stretched I could brush the wood-paneled ceiling with my fingertips, then I'll emerge onto a balcony and suddenly come face-to-face with a void so large the other side is fading into the color of sky. A balcony where wind blows.

It is astonishing, and not at all what I expected.

When I first arrived here and the Starjump doors opened, my scentsor reported untouched forest and decaying leaf matter, crushed rock, bottomless lakes, and water soaking into grass. The station is alive with plants of all kinds, trees, shrubs, flowers and vines everywhere. Also water, flowing clear in canals, or in lakes sunken into rocky ground that starts in corridors leading to the lake. Even just clear tubes of water flowing from ceiling to floor in white-paneled corridors.

My days are taken up by HUGG debriefing sessions, but at night I don't sleep, so I have twelve hours to myself. Usually I go straight to Alistra's waiting room. The receptionists are not happy to see me, but I am tolerated.

Alistra took Threnode's helmet from Tim when she arrived and promised to look at it. New information filters through day by day: we haven't started looking at the damaged smartsuit helmet because our specialist is away. We haven't started, as it's unclear who will pay. The Lunite Foundation are paying, but we're not sure we can legally fix it, because while Endymion was cut off HUGG passed a statute that forbids neurosynaptic AI in ambulatory form. Threnode and I were placed in bodies after the statute passed, except that no one on Endymion knew about the statute, so our legal status is questionable.

I sit for hours and days in the waiting room at Alistra, whenever I'm not needed for questioning by HUGG, waiting and hoping for updates. The receptionists whisper about me to each other, not realizing I can read their lips. *Back again. So creepy, I wish it would go away. Loyal friend. Think it's sweet.*

I'd rather be exploring L2, but not alone. Threnode and I often talked about exploring L2, Earth, and the other colonies in Earth's solar system. Or fantasized, rather, as neither of us believed it would ever happen.

———

ON THE SIXTH DAY, while I'm sitting in Alistra's waiting room, a news item about Tim pops up on the feed. Tim and I met a few times before she left for Earth, and have been exchanging daily messages, so I know her most important news, which is that Pearl waited for her.

Pearl said she always knew Tim would be back. She moved to Earth with Celia shortly after Endymion disconnected. Tim said talking to her is awkward, because she seems like a stranger, but they both want to rekindle their relationship.

The news item shows a ship landing at an airfield on Earth, a vast spaceport somewhere. The video shows the terminal, filled with people weaving through the crowds wheeling baggage, or sitting near the windows watching spacecraft of all sizes land.

Tim appears in the video, thinner and exhausted looking. The reporters are filming from the other side of a barrier, some distance from her. The voiceover says something about her being the first one through the Starjump after it reopened. She appears to be in a quarantine facility, but she's heading toward the arrivals gate.

I worry for her, because Tim's messages say *I didn't recognize Celia in the photographs Pearl sent* and *she turned nine three weeks ago, what if she hates me?* Pearl will forgive Tim and make allowances, but Celia could break her heart without even trying.

In the video Tim grips her hands tightly together. Pale faced, she follows her fellow passengers through the tunnel to the lounge. The camera pans over the crowd at the arrival gate.

Tim stops and searches the faces in the crowd.

The woman behind Tim smiles broadly at two elderly people, then a young man rushes into the crowd, a gaggle of children pass in front of Tim, then—

The camera focuses on a girl at the front of the crowd waiting for the arrivals, who looks a lot like Tim, despite her almond skin and much frizzier hair: Celia.

Celia looks around, lost, until she sees Tim, then her face contorts in extreme pain, and her eyes fill with tears. She says something incomprehensible and stumbles forward toward Tim. Tim rushes to meet her and engulfs her in a hug.

"Oh, oh sweetie," Tim says, crying. They hug for a full minute, swaying and sobbing. After a moment Pearl pushes through the crowd, tears running down her face, and puts her arms around both of them.

More talking from a reporter, then the news item ends.

In the waiting room at Alistra, the woman sitting next to me was obviously watching via her lightweight wearable, because her eyes are watering too. She sniffs surreptitiously. I am so very delighted for Tim, but I miss Threnode more than ever.

One of the reception staff approach me, holding a bag.

"Envy? We have some news about the smartsuit helmet you were asking about. It can't be repaired. I'm very sorry."

He hands me the bag. Inside is Threnode's helmet, wiped clean of slime, but still cracked and dented. A red sticker reading RECYCLE CODE 84 has been applied, covering the top camera of the camera array. Through the cracks in the helmet I can see the damaged neurosynaptic chip, just a lifeless piece of silicon and metal.

LAURIE IS TRYING HARD NOT to cry, although he cried a bit during the eulogy. He holds my hand. His navy blue robe is slightly too long, and brushes the polished wood floor of the church. The Lunites of L2 let us use their church, which is comfortingly similar to the churches in Selene.

"Birth to death, alone, yet never alone: I walked with him," Alice says, at the pulpit. She is rim lit in pale blue light which streams in from the moon-patterned stained-glass window high behind her.

"I walked with him," I murmur, my voice merging with that of all the other mourners present. Their faces are shadowy and dark in the light of Luna. Ashford and Paterson aren't here, and neither are most other officers of the LDF. They are probably still detained.

"He turned his face to the moon, escaping the madness that infects the world. We are his family. We are not the Saturated Consumer, who is told to want things; we are not the Sickened Patient, upon whom the drug peddlers create symptoms; we are not the Disconnected Zombie, who lives to feed their network reflection. We are here, in this moment, to say goodbye."

Alice stops, gathering herself. I stare at the panel that shows Li writing the Book. A small slice of Lunism on the L2 station.

"We will guard our memories of you," Alice says in a wavering voice. Mark helps her down from the pulpit as she begins to cry in earnest.

SO I MUST PLAN the rest of my existence, now. HUGG is done with me. Ortega is gone; Threnode is gone; Tim has gone to Earth; and Mark, Alice, and Laurie have returned to Endymion. I exchange messages with Tim, and with Laurie and Alice, but only when a ship from Earth arrives or Endymion Starjump has a postal shipment.

I have no wearer and no purpose. I wander L2 aimlessly for days, exploring the spaces that go from intimate to vast in an instant, the peculiar mix of nature and human-built architecture. Sometimes, when it gets too much, I sit on a bench and shut down my sensors, pretending I am in Dock 28.

Today I am back in the Alistra waiting room because they requested my presence, probably for maintenance. I stare out over the lake, which is gray and flat under the forbidding clouds in the void.

I am drawing a salary just because I am a HUGG citizen. It wouldn't be a lot of money if I slept or ate, but since I do neither, it is accumulating fast. Alistra draws it down, though, since I established a maintenance contract with them.

It's time to figure out what my future looks like, my counselor says. I considered getting a small apartment, and even looked at a few. I considered getting a job, perhaps Systems Administration or similar, although I would need to train first. However, I have decided that I want to travel, even if I am doing it alone. My lifespan is uncertain, but it seems likely that it will be hundreds of years, so I have lots of time.

I can travel, and later I will make a life here, getting an apartment, and trying to make some friends. I'm sure it will be an acceptable existence, although a smartsuit with an android body is never going to fit seamlessly into society, especially given that I am one of a kind.

Someone clears their throat behind me, and I turn to see an Alistra tech. A man stands next to her, looking at me. Something about him makes me look closer. He is strangely ageless—he could be anywhere between eighteen and forty—and has a neutral expression. Sturdy, with tan skin and dark long eyelashes, he wears clothing that looks entirely new: shirt so white it has a hint of blue, and loose dark trousers.

"Envy? I'm Gauri," the Alistra tech says with a warm smile. She wears a dark green salwar kameez and open-toed sandals, and towers over me. The man next to her is even taller. Of course, in a household android body I am shorter than Alice.

"This is Threnode," Gauri adds, glancing at the man beside her.

I freeze.

"I realize this might be a surprise to you," Gauri says, "and I'm sorry for the miscommunication. Apparently the receptionist tasked with giving you Threnode's dead helmet didn't realize there was a message to go with it and assumed Threnode's recovery operation had failed. The helmet couldn't be repaired, but the consciousness could be retrieved, although we had a hell of a time saving it. We wired it into a new body. This is legal because it's an existing ambulatory entity, under the grandfather clause of the Neurosynaptic New Life Act. I head up the team working on the new body, and we only just managed to bring the consciousness online yesterday. I didn't know Threnode had any next of kin who needed to be kept informed—sorry about that—but as soon as it awoke, it asked after you."

The man, Threnode, looks at me and gives an inane grin. Gauri clears her throat politely, and Threnode tones it down.

"Sorry," Threnode says. "Still working on facial expressions, obviously."

I can't say anything.

"We're able to upgrade you to a human-similar android too, Envy, if you wish," Gauri says. "Feel free to make an appointment if you want to discuss it."

My vocal processors still aren't working. All I can do is stare at Threnode.

Gauri smiles awkwardly and pats Threnode on the arm. "I'll leave you two to it."

She walks back the way she came, her long plait swinging down her back as she walks.

"I was going to deliver a haiku to commemorate our reunion," Threnode says, watching me with concern, "but perhaps instead I could give you a careful hug."

I nod.

Threnode hugs me. I can't cry, but sometimes I need to. I still don't feel I can talk, but I open the smartsuit channel.

Envy: St Li and his followers, I missed you.

Threnode smiles.

Threnode: As did I.

Threnode follows me out, onto the platform overlooking the lake, and we walk down the promenade, where cherry trees are flowering. I have so much to say, but we have plenty of time.

AUTHOR'S NOTE

I hope you enjoyed reading Envy!

For an independent author, reviews are like gold-pressed latinum, so please consider leaving a review at the bookstore you purchased this book from.

Subscribe to my newsletter at www.rebeccadengate.com to be the first to know when I release a book, or please feel free to email me at rdengateauthor@gmail.com.

ACKNOWLEDGMENTS

I am tremendously grateful for the support, advice and encouragement provided by my family and the Human Disasters Creativity Club while I wrote Envy. Without it, there's no way you would be reading this right now.

I was lucky enough to get valuable and detailed feedback on multiple drafts from Howard Dengate, Sue Dengate, Arran Dengate, Miles Gantney, and CeCe Philpott-Cummins, as well as proofreading by the Dengates, Miles Gantney, and Tammy Pinto. I can't convey to you how grateful I am, but this is where I try.

My editor, Kat Betts, was a pleasure to work with. Thank you Kat! The remaining mistakes are mine.

Finally a colossal thank you to Tom, for his love, patience, and kindness. You're a fantastic husband.

GLOSSARY

5T-79 Delany transport: a twin-engine, tandem rotor, heavy lift helicopter.

Abless: A tree with wood too splintery to be useful. White helical seeds sometimes encased in resin for use in decorative objects.

AES: Advanced Environment Suit, such as a smartsuit or a dumbsuit. Manufactured by Alistra.

Afradocia: Green scaly fruit with edible flesh.

Blank-slate: The process of returning a neurosynaptic chip to a known state, which is typically done every 48 hours to Alistra-manufactured artificial intelligences.

Binary: Compiled source code that can be executed; also known as an executable.

Cloud: Lunite euphemism for shinting, e.g., to cloud one's mind is to shint.

CPU: Central Processing Unit. In a computer, used to execute instructions. In an AI, controlled unconsciously as they create programs and calculate on the fly, like a brain augment.

Crebble: The Lunite Starjump, which was destroyed in 2567.

Darkpole: Endymion's far pole: the point furthest from Endymion's sun. See also *lightpole*.

Demodas: Numundian city with a population of around 11,000.

Dumbsuit: A suit that is controlled by a mixture of code and machine learning.

Alistra: Technology company that manufactures Advanced Environment Suits and Starjump Processing Units (SPUs), among other products.

Endymion: Name of planet colonized by Lunites. Also known as Gliese 667 C c.

envd: a process that activates the neurosynaptic chip.

EOF: End Of File.

Gannet: Non-pressurized tiltrotor aircraft with vertical takeoff and landing capability.

Gannet II: Improved model of Gannet. Pressurized.

Grep: To search files for a specified pattern.

Hiogas: Lunite city with population of 100,000.

HUGG: Human United Galactic Group, the governing power for the vast majority of humans.

Icosa: Trees native to Marallen whose trunks have a hexagonal cross-section. Farmed for wood as well as icosahedron-shaped fruit known as icosas.

imgctrl: a binary used for manipulating neurosynaptic images.

Kartemos: Numundian city with approximately 18,000 Lunites plus 25,000 Numundians.

Kitterene: A fist-sized amphibian that uses suckers to attach to prey.

L2: Cube-shaped space station at the second Lagrange point in Earth's solar system which is the largest HUGG settlement.

LDF: Lunite Defense Force.

LIDAR: Light Detection and Ranging, a method of

measuring distance to objects by recording time it takes for a laser to hit the object and bounce back to receiver.

Li's Hope: The ship that carried the Lunites to Endymion. Launched 2526, arrived 2559.

Lightpole: Endymion's near pole: the point closest to Endymion's sun. See also *darkpole*.

Longshadow: Numundo Republic's biggest city, with approximately 80,000 citizens.

Lunar Revelations: Book by Li that is the basis of Lunism.

Lunite: A follower of the Way of Li, someone who rejects some aspects of modern life, most notably shinting.

Marallen: Numundian town with a population of around 5,000.

Monos: Herbivores larger than cows, with a rounded back.

N2: Two-seat bomber. Obsolete.

N14: AI-controlled bomber with a blank-slate smartsuit level of intelligence.

Neurosynaptic chip: The 'brain' of a smartsuit.

Numundian: A citizen of Endymion who does not follow the Way of Li.

Orel: Dangerous predator reported on by Professor Orlov, but believed to be fictional by many in the scientific community.

Paranemas: Giant burrowing worm-like creature which attacks humans and technology. Found on the dark side of Endymion.

Puri's Mine: A tellurium mine on the dark side of Endymion, owned by Numundian company Puri.

Pyoridium temporaria: Microorganisms that contaminate water on Endymion, which are fatal if ingested.

RAM: Random Access Memory. Computer memory that can be read and changed in any order. Smartsuit short term memories are stored there, but long term memories are captured in the form of connections within the neurosynaptic chip.

Scisters: 16-legged aquatic insects that skate on the surface of ponds.

Scorpion: A member of a terrorist group targeting Lunites.

Selene: Lunite city, population approximately 400 thousand, the seat of the Lunite Council. Central area covered with a clearsteel hexagonal dome.

Shint: To share your mind with others, using technology.

Shippers: People who believe HUGG launched a ship as soon as Crebble was destroyed, and who are counting down to the earliest time that ship could arrive.

Smartsuit: A suit that contains a neurosynaptic chip, which is reset to base state every forty-eight hours.

Spicks: Similar to fireflies, but native to Endymion.

SPU: Starjump Processing Unit. A critical component of a Starjump, which is manufactured by Alistra. Made of black metal and mesh and shaped like a textbook, it is embedded with fans, and lights up with blue neon when powered.

St Li: Lunite town with population of around 80,000.

Starjump: Egg-shaped dome linked to smaller dome that can transport goods and people to corresponding dome in different location, even a different star system.

Staroye Derevo: Numundian town with a population of 63.

Steelgrass: Plant with thick spongy cables that point towards lightpole.

Sucker-leeches: Opiate-secreting leech that is farmed and used by humans recreationally. Causes long-term damage.

Taillights: Fanged creature that preys on vegas beasts. Fast, sneaky, and hunts in packs using red light flashes to communicate.

The Twins: Gliese 667A and B, the binary star system in Endymion's solar system.

Theronis: Lunite town with a population of around 5,000.

Tigress: Ship sent by HUGG to Endymion after Li's Hope departed. Launched 2556, crashed into Endymion's ocean on 2560.

Tommies: Well-camouflaged and shy ruminant quadruped mammals.

Twin Falls: Lunite town with a population of around 2,000.

Vegas beasts: Similar to monos, but males compete for females using garish light displays.

Waning Festival: Annual Lunite celebration.

Windfish: Translucent airborne creatures similar in appearance to jellyfish. They can cover an area of up to 500 square meters.

Yinyang: Predatory cheetah-like mammal that hunts in pairs, patterned so that the male is invisible to prey when looking towards darkpole, and the female is the reverse.

ABOUT THE AUTHOR

After high school, Rebecca would have applied to Starfleet Academy if it existed. Since it doesn't, there was an ill-fated attempt to become a ballerina. This was followed by an Engineering degree at the Australian National University, majoring in Mechatronics, then a highly enjoyable career developing software at Animal Logic and National ICT Australia/CSIRO's Data61.

She lives in Canberra, Australia, with her husband and two children.